# THE ISLAND

*Jean Matheson*

# THE
# ISLAND

COLLINS
ST JAMES'S PLACE, LONDON
1952

PRINTED IN GREAT BRITAIN
COLLINS CLEAR-TYPE PRESS : LONDON AND GLASGOW

*To*
*Alex and Geneviève*

# Chapter One

CONVERSATION, UNLIKE books, is not all a matter of words. It is a sort of code. A few essential words, then a glance, or a shrug, or a tailing into silence; and the ellipsis is filled by intuition or telepathy, or mental adroitness in catching an allusion. To talk with someone who lacks this commonplace telepathy is a laborious process, every idea has to be mapped out with hideous completeness and at the end, as likely as not, complete misunderstanding results.

People who suffer from such mental stiffness (though it is their friends who suffer—not themselves) have a greed for facts. Concrete facts, they like to call them. They find concrete facts useful for crushing vague arguments. " A crushing retort . . ."

" Medicine," they say, " is such a useful profession. More useful than law or architecture, or electrical engineering. I know you don't want to be a lawyer or an architect, or an electrical engineer, I am only pointing out that a doctor can save lives. And has an assured income, if he is prepared to work."

You may have vague ideas of something—well, more creative . . . well, something more . . . well, you thought perhaps you might just . . . or if your mother doesn't like the idea you might take Arts, and then see what openings . .

None of this makes sense.

" Can't you say what you mean quite plainly, dear. Do you mean, be a journalist, like that Mr. Smith who kicked a tin can all down the street, swearing? Well, what do you mean? I only want to know what you would like to do with your life."

You kick your feet foolishly and are told not to do this, with reasons for its inadvisability. You promise not to do it and also not to be a journalist and kick tin cans, swearing.

Even when the question of medicine is settled, conversation on this level continues, year after year.

" Where are you going now, dear? "

7

"Back."

"Where do you mean by back?"

"Back to the vicinity of the College buildings."

"What a funny way to put it. Why have you a class at this hour?"

"I haven't got a class. I didn't say I was going into the College, only near it."

"Where *are* you going, Alec? I wish you wouldn't be so woolly, dear, you can surely give a plain answer to a plain question."

"I'm going back to the drug store opposite the East Gate."

"Why, what have you left there?"

"Nothing, Mother!"

"Then . . . ?"

"I'm meeting a friend."

"Well, you do love to make a mystery! Why couldn't you say at once you were going to meet Bertie? Though it would be nicer to ask him here, I should think."

The revelation that you are not going to meet Bertie, that you are going to meet a girl, that you do not know what sort of people the girl's parents are, do not know if her father is a professional man and have not told the girl your own circumstances nor explained that your mother, a widow, is making great sacrifices to put you through college, that in spite of all this lack of openness you do not think the girl thinks your intentions are any more serious than you think they are—all this leads to an atmosphere of pain and reproach on one hand, guilt and exasperation on the other; and ends in floods of lies, such as "No, I don't care if I never see her again, she means nothing to me, I assure you!" and "Very well, dear, I am only too pleased to have you make nice friendships with nice girls, I have no desire to pry into your private life, you know. I never ask for confidences, I only want you to enjoy yourself."

As for you, at this period you do not realise, or only suspect in sudden gloomy flashes, the speciousness of all this farrago. You remind yourself that your mother's sacrifices, though they are waved like red rags before your eyes, are real enough, and that the love that prompts them is tender and genuine. Your life is moulded by a process of gentle, obtuse coercion.

You find yourself at thirty-eight successful, respected, with an assured satisfactory income; less confided-in than the family doctor but more glamorous; you are a specialist.

8

At that point in your career your mother, the source of the gentle coercion, dies.

The large black-and-brown animal that emerged from the doorway was a dog; beyond that fact any surmise at his ancestry could be nothing but hypothesis. Alec, who had rescued the amorphous creature from a pet-shop window sixteen years ago, had named him simply and, he thought, wittily, Dog.

Dog walked with stiff, elderly dignity to the news-stand at the corner. The vendor folded the morning papers and held them out. Dog paused for a few seconds, all his reactions being slow nowadays, then accepted them and returned to the building. The elevator boy took him up.

Alec had always been the only human being whose existence had, for Dog, any reality. Other people were footsteps in the street, noises in the air, fingers holding out a biscuit—the irrelevant phantasmagoria that made a background for Dog's life and Alec's. Now he stalked past as Betty opened the door and waited for Alec to notice him.

" Ts ! " said Betty. " That dog, he'll trip me up one day. Before my feet—carrying the tray. Dangerous for a girl, never knowing."

Alec turned from the window.

" Thanks," he said absently.

Betty shrugged, laid the dishes on the breakfast table and departed with the empty tray. " Takes two to make a pair," she said as she shut the door.

Dog stood drooping beside the table with the papers in his mouth, staring milkily at nothing.

" Let's have them, Dog," said Alec.

His voice changed when he spoke to Dog, lost its impersonal courtesy and became warm and kind.

" Thinks more of that dog than he does of his own mother," Betty used to repeat when she met her boy-friend. That was two boy-friends ago when Mrs. MacArdal was alive. Nowadays she said, " Thinks more of that old dog than he does of me. Some day I'll just walk out, then someone else can come and clean up after it ! " Betty was not unkind, but it is very wounding to the self-esteem to be treated as non-existent, and that was how Dog treated her.

" Let's have them," Alec coaxed, giving the papers a gentle tug.

Dog sighed and allowed Alec to take them.

9

Mrs. MacArdal, never forgetting their Scottish origin, had always had tea for breakfast. Alec continued this. His movements as he poured out his tea were not clumsy, but were without the economy that practice brings. He remembered, having poured out his first cup, to add hot water to the teapot, but forgot to replace the teapot lid. He leaned his paper against the open pot, focusing on a review of a new musical hit while steam from the teapot darkened the other side of the paper.

He had no idea what he was reading. His eyes flicked across the words, dark grey eyes set in a pale, rather long face, a face whose expression in repose was a gentle, almost apologetic sneer. It was a face Velasquez might have painted.

Alec's eyes were reading the reviewer's witticisms. His mind was saying, Back to the Clinic. Operations this afternoon : remove an inferior turbinate, repair a septum and the polypi. Then more clinic. Then home. Then back to the clinic to-morrow. Day after day, over and over.

He did not notice that his eyes and his brain were not co-ordinated, or that he contrived to eat without noticing what he put into his mouth. Only when he heard a distant commotion from Betty did his attention focus, his head lift from its automatism.

" Same again ! " Betty exclaimed, throwing open the door and waving a pair of maroon-striped pyjamas. " Just when I was going to put these in the laundry box in your room and not looking where I put my feet, it's too much, Dr. Alec, it's too much, no consideration, all over the bedroom carpet ! Think more of that dog than . . ." She burst into sobs.

" Sick again ? "

" Sick plus ! " Betty waved a foot in the air, displaying the damage, sniffing tears into Alec's pyjamas.

" I'll take him to the vet," said Alec with a shiver of apprehension. " I'm sorry, Betty, it's too bad."

" Sorry don't clean the carpet," said Betty angrily, but departing on the promise Alec had made.

Dog lay on his side ignoring the scene. Even when Alec fondled his head he only gave a few flaps with his tail. But a little later, when Alec, departing from custom, invited him out for a walk, he scrambled to his feet with the same pricked ears and waving tail as when he was a puppy ; only his legs stalked woodenly instead of springing up and down with indiarubber bounds.

The veterinary surgery was a hollow white cube, gleaming with asepsis, as functional as Alec's own in the clinic. The young vet himself struck Alec as faintly formidable in his starched linen, head nodding gravely as he listened to a recital of the old dog's infirmities ; a bit pompous in his specialised knowledge. This was how people felt when they brought their adenoidal children to Alec's clinic, a defensive irritation at the confidence of the expert.

Dog submitted to the examination with stoicism. Against the gleaming white his coat looked dusty and rough, his drooping head seemed stupid. Alec knew that Dog was refusing to admit the vet's reality. Only Alec and Dog were real, not this white-overalled young man prodding at his stomach and loins ; therefore the pain Dog experienced when the prodding fingers dug deeply was unreal, too, not worth acknowledging with a whimper. Dog flicked his tongue over a dry nose and waited.

" Sick all over the carpet, all over the place," Alec repeated. " And messing. He's a clean dog." He was talking against the abstraction of the expert.

" He's a clean dog," he insisted. " This only began, let me see, seven or eight months ago. Naturally, I thought at first he was pining for mother."

This had been Betty's theory. Alec had known perfectly that Dog's indifference to Mrs. MacArdal was no sham, and that his mother had resented it. But he felt a nervous compulsion to talk, to offer an excuse for his inaction.

The vet muttered condolences on the doctor's recent loss. No one could fill the gap left by a mother, especially by one so prominent as Mrs. MacArdal had been in the district.

" Yes," Alec agreed, " he seemed all right at first, but now—even milk pudding he just throws up."

" He's an old dog." The vet straightened up from his examination, hands on hips.

" That's so."

" Look at his eyes."

Alec was already looking into Dog's eyes, for they were turned towards him with a patient request. Let's go home now and have a rest, said Dog's eyes. This has lasted long enough. Opaque and milky, they could still focus the blurred shape of Alec's face.

"Pretty nearly blind," said the vet. "All but. Deaf, too. Rheumatic. Kidneys all to pieces."

Alec said nothing.

"Sixteen, you said?"

"That's so," Alec admitted. There was a discomfort in his chest.

"I can't treat him," said the vet. "He's earned his rest."

Alec swallowed and stared at Dog. The young man's voice had a perfunctory kindness in it.

"Couldn't you try——"

"He's got no future," said the vet. "He's finished. He's got no future."

"What do you suggest?" Alec pushed words into the silence.

"Put him to sleep."

Alec paused again. Dog made a small pool on the aseptic terrazzo floor, sighed and lay down across Alec's feet.

"I—don't like the idea," said Alec in a voice he tried to keep normal. "Lethal chamber—chloroform——"

"Barbarous stuff, chloroform," the vet agreed. "I never use it myself. Intravenous injection's the thing. It's quite painless. Wait and see it for yourself if you like."

The silence now was wide open and dry like a desert.

"What do you use?" Alec sounded horribly conversational.

The vet opened a glass cabinet, took out a box of ampoules and handed it to Alec, produced a syringe and a selection of long needles.

"I use this stuff myself," said Alec. "In an atomiser, for surface anaesthesia. Useful stuff." He was talking to fill in the hollow of dismay that spread in his chest while he watched the vet fill the syringe. It was unlike him to chatter in this way.

"We'll have him on the table and I'll just run it straight into his heart," said the vet. "Up, old fella!"

Dog ignored the non-existent voice, but grunted as Alec lifted him on to the table. His claws slipped on its shiny enamel and he looked at Alec, offended but patient.

"Is he ever aggressive?" asked the vet. "I'd better muzzle him anyway——"

"No!" Alec was suddenly vehement. "No, he won't bite you. I'll hold him. He won't bite."

He doesn't think you exist, you fool, he added in his mind as he caressed Dog's ears. A fetid tongue lapped over his chin and a fetid breath surged into his nostrils. He held Dog by the shoulders.

"I'll shoot it straight into his heart," the vet promised, his fingers groping over scapula and ribs.

Alec wanted to ask for time. Time to look, to think, to talk to the old dog whose patience was being insulted by this ignominious speed. But he said nothing. He felt Dog wince as the needle stabbed. His hand went on caressing the long ears. He watched the vet pull back the piston, just a millimetre back; a cloud of red tinged the clear fluid in the barrel; the needle had found its target. Then the piston pushed down, pushing the narcotic into the dog's heart.

Dog was aware of Alec's hand fumbling in the long hair of his neck, pulling his ears in a familiar caress. Nothing else was real. Then that reality swam into mist, his head fell against Alec's arm, he collapsed sideways on the white table.

"I got to pump some more in," said the vet, "but he's unconscious now."

"Dog!" said Alec.

There was no responsive twitch.

The vet disconnected the syringe, leaving the needle sticking in Dog's fur while he refilled the barrel. The needle pulsed regularly, embedded in the living heart; a scarlet drop fell from its head.

Another ten cubic centimetres of sleep; then another; then the needle ceased its throbbing.

"That's that," said the vet, but he applied a stethoscope to the dusty black fur just to be sure. He nodded. "That's that," he said again. It had been a neat demonstration. He looked at Alec, confident.

There was a pause. Then:

"That's that," said Alec in the same robust voice. He lifted Dog's head from his hand where it lay. The corpse on the table was as decrepit, as rumpled as an old door-mat. "Well, thank you. I'd better get along. Got patients waiting for me!"

He hailed a taxi and got in, and in the padded privacy cleared his throat, moving his shoulders uneasily. He was still, it seemed, looking down at the dusty corpse, and he heard his own voice, hollow and hearty. Well, that's that. Well, I'll get along. Got patients waiting.

He kept feeling the weight of Dog's head as it fell against his arm. If he could have just one more hour of Dog's company—just one hour to clear away the ignominy of that final scene. . . .

13

The taxi paused at the lights. The longer the better, Alec thought. I'm not ready for the clinic, I hate the place. I detest it.

The revelation slipped into his consciousness through a door that grief had opened, and he accepted it without surprise. He had loathed the clinic for years; now, listlessly, he acknowledged the fact.

## Chapter Two

NURSE WAS watching Dr. MacArdal with mingled anxiety and impatience. She knew the signs. He was trancing again.

She would have liked to give him a shake and a few rough, gay words of advice to jolt him out of his dream; but you couldn't do that with Dr. MacArdal. The others would chaff and spar with her, meet her on her own ground, but he had an aloofness that enclosed him like a bell-glass, and a humility that, oddly, made you respect him.

He sat there as still and stylised as a figure on a Polish ikon. He was unhappy, you could feel it like a chilly mist, but there was nothing you could do about it. He did not want sympathy or the comfort of ordinary human contact. He was enclosed in his bell-glass, unapproachable.

She stirred and coughed, rustling her dress. She lifted the steriliser lid, looked at the instruments simmering in it, and let the lid drop with a clack.

Alec's mind was a blank through which an occasional idea wavered and vanished.

I'm nearly forty. Here I am in the clinic, back at the routine. Dog died six days ago, nearly a week. Yes, that's that. An old rumpled rug.

He heard Nurse's uniform rustle, her impatience touched him somewhere but it was like touching an anaesthetised area. It only reminded him again of the clinic, the shining playground where he and his two colleagues tossed patients to each other, juggling with them like conjurers playing with coloured skittles. I'm going to refer you to my colleague Dr. Harker who specialises in ear work. It seems to me that your trouble originates in the mediastinum,

I'm handing you over to my friend Dr. Weir, the chest man, you know . . . It was quite honest, quite clean juggling. They were each good enough in their line, and if the case fell outside their scope there were other specialists, friends, jugglers who caught and whirled skittles with skill and efficiency. Very friendly and very profitable.

The clack of the steriliser lid jolted him. Here he was, sitting knee to knee with the patient he ought to be examining; each sat in a functional white chair, each motionless; and Nurse was fidgeting because he was dawdling and she had a date. He must concentrate.

"Open, please," he said, and muffled the request with a cough as he realised that it was a nose he was examining, not a throat. He fiddled with the reflector on his brow and stared severely into the nostril that was distended by a retractor.

He must have kept her sitting immobile for about five minutes, poor creature, while he pretended to examine that antrum. He could sense her agony, the agony of muscles and ligaments forced into unnatural immobility, torso tilted forward, head back, eyes wandering over the shiny enamel of the ceiling or focusing on the mystic round reflector tied to the doctor's brow, then wavering again to the window where a bluebottle buzzed behind the screen of white net. She must be conscious of the ache of each separate muscle, she must feel like a flayed anatomical figure, and he was still keeping her in cramped agony.

"Right," he said, releasing the retractor and handing it to Nurse. "Now, Miss Elwood, you say you've tried pretty well everything there is to try, h'm?"

"Yes, Doctor," said the patient, rubbing her spine and moving her head from side to side.

"Well, I'm going to set you on a new tack. I want you to try leaving your nose alone. No drops, no douches, no inhalations, no sprays, nothing. Not even eucalyptus or lavender on your handkerchief. Nothing, you understand? And come back and see me in six weeks' time."

"Yes, Doctor."

He dropped his white coat in the laundry bin and washed his hands. He heard Nurse fix the appointment and show Miss Elwood out; he heard her whisk instruments out of the steriliser. He listened again to the echo of his own voice : Just leave it alone, you understand. And come back and see me in six weeks' time. Six weeks' time. Six weeks. . . .

"Good God!" he whispered, and glanced over his shoulder in case Nurse had overheard the distress in his voice. But Nurse had polished and put away the last of the instruments. She emerged from the dressing-room in mufti, seductive and vital ; off to her date with the boy she referred to as Heart-throb.

"Have a nice evening," Alec said.

Now he was alone in the aseptic, angular whiteness of the surgery. He pulled aside the window screen and looked down to the bottom of a ravine where a dusty river of human beings purled and eddied.

He was alone now. He could face his thoughts. He turned from the window. He had put off this reckoning since his mother's death, always promising himself to face it but always pushing it a little way ahead. To-night, when I have more time. Or to-morrow afternoon when I'm alone. But this was the time at last, the time to face his own life with candour and, if possible, with courage.

It was difficult to begin. He took a few steps across the terrazzo floor and found himself looking into the instrument cabinet. Funny, how dingy his Volkmann's spoon always looked. Other instruments gleamed with brilliant highlights, but a Volkmann's spoon always looked as if it had emerged from some pre-Lister instrument case.

He shrugged away from the instruments and tried again. I must face the facts now, not go on like an automaton till I'm too old to want to change. I must think.

How do you start thinking?

"Mother's dead," he said aloud.

When she died he had felt, for one second, a bursting ecstasy of freedom ; that was swept out of existence by grief that hollowed his will. He had gone on day after day at the clinic, conscientious and humane—except when he had those fits of blankness, of what seemed like suspended animation.

He sat down in his white swivel-chair, alone in the hollow cube. He cleared his throat.

She's gone, he thought, and my old Dog, too. Time I pulled myself together. I've got out of the habit of initiative ; it was easier always to yield in the end, and I got into a habit of yielding. Now I don't know what to do with freedom.

I should have fought harder against her. Now, it's too late to

16

keep on arguing with her in my mind. If I had fought against her for my own way it would have been victory. But now I can do what I like and I'm empty.

He shivered; he had reached a truth that frightened him. It was from inertia that he continued his work. He recognised a creeping weakness that melted his nerves and made his most trivial action, sometimes, an effort of will that tired him. Even to get up in the morning . . . to face a day filled with bustling, cheerful people busy making money. What was the good of all that activity!

He rose guiltily from his chair as the door opened and a cleaner pushed in.

"That's all right," he said, seeing her hesitate. "Come on in, I'm just going."

That's how it is now, he thought. I wait for something to give me a push from behind. A mechanical toy with the spring broken.

He hesitated again on the brink of the street. He could not go home yet, he must fill in time, have a meal, achieve some mental discovery or decision before he faced the empty apartment, the empty hour when he used to take Dog for a walk in the park.

Now he stood on the sidewalk like a post sticking out of the river with water dividing and reuniting round its inertia. He was visualising himself in the park with Dog; he called, and waited, and Dog stalked towards him with eyes groping for his face; eyes with the pupils obscured by a bluish fog.

Someone jolted him impatiently and he returned to the problem of where to go next. Again it was chance that pushed him. Two girls brushed past, talking into each other's faces with the intensity of seventeen years.

"You go to the Park," insisted the pale girl in scarlet. "That's the place. . . ."

To her the Park might be the name of a cinema, a laundry, an employment agency or a night club. Alec accepted the advice, literally.

Twilight was entering its blue period. Trees with cobalt trunks reared up into a sky of turquoise, red flowers had become black, the grass had no colour at all. Without Dog, Alec felt the park vast and mysterious, its personality pressed against him. He wandered along the paths he had never taken before, or not for years, not since Dog was in his prime and bounded ahead leading the way; since then the park landscape had changed at the whim of a new curator.

The trees were leafless still; you could see every small twig. Alec stopped to look from a gnarled and lichenous trunk upward to where the branches separated into a tracery of twigs against the deepening sky, tangling the moon in their fronds. Every twig was still for the first second, then they all moved, like seaweed moving as a slow wave passes to swell and break far away.

Alec turned up his collar. The trees and the deep sky were beautiful, and he was too sad to bear beauty without pain. Once he had groped after beauty, hardly knowing where to look but searching vaguely—like Dog's blind eyes searching for his face. But it had all been too vague and weak.

"I hear you mean to go in for medicine?" the headmaster had said. "You'll have to improve your physics, MacArdal."

For a while he had struggled feebly and negatively, but in the end he had succumbed. Medicine was a bearable proposition and his mother was full of ideals and sacrifices. And he had no sensible alternative to offer. . . .

He turned up his collar and made for an empty bench. The tall lamp above it gave an air of warmth that was false. He sat in a pool of light and ignored the cringing of his skin. He was here to think. He thrust his hands into his pockets and shrank into himself for warmth, stirring his brain, trying to fish for a beginning of thought. Here he was, ready to begin, and his brain was as empty as a hollow shell.

Yet not quite empty. There was one idea always there, lying hidden at the bottom like a toad in the mud of a pond. Once, as a schoolboy, he had stirred the mud, but it had settled again. It was a long time since he had given the toad intelligent scrutiny.

Now his fingers closed round it; it lay in his palm, cold and inert; the idea of death.

For him the mechanics were quite simple. A phial of morphine tablets and a syringe. It would be as easy as it had been for Dog; perhaps rather slower, but an assurance of rest, a release from the need to think. Saturday afternoon would be the time, when Betty left at two and did not return till Monday morning.

He felt a satisfaction in having at least faced that idea, though it thickened the twilight within him. There was the door of escape; he only had to push it open.

Now he turned to look at what life could offer. There was the clinic.

18

At the thought of the clinic such a curtain of sick ennui swept over him that he almost cried out. I won't go on with it, he promised himself. I won't go on with it no matter what I do.

He recovered a little, stirred on his park bench and pressed his arms to his sides to conserve his dwindling store of warmth. He was unaware of passers-by; his will was only now recovering the power of action after years of automatism. He had made a decision, even if a negative one, and if no prospect opened before him there was always the last refuge. He took a deep breath and turned his cramped yet feebly stirring mind to more positive action.

It gave him a shock of dismay when a stranger sat on the bench beside him.

The plump, pink stranger settled himself comfortably against the seat and crossed one knee over the other. His biscuit-coloured clothes imitated opulence; he studied the toe of his cherry-red shoe with satisfaction and glanced at Alec as if inviting admiration. Alec kept his eyes fixed on the tree opposite.

" Pretty cold," said the stranger, rubbing his hands and blowing rather theatrically through wet, red lips.

Alec agreed.

" Mind if I sit here ? "

" Not at all," Alec lied.

" Thought you might be waiting for somebody."

Alec wondered if he should get up and go. But he remained, partly for fear of hurting the stranger, partly because he had found this seat first and partly from inertia.

" Care for a look at the paper ? "

" No, thanks," said Alec, but the paper was thrust at him and he accepted it.

" To be honest," said the stranger, " I knew damn well you weren't waiting for somebody." He looked challengingly at Alec, who did not move. " I'm by way of being a student of human nature and I been watching you. Yes, sir, I been watching. You didn't know it, but I was studying you. No, I said, he's not waiting for a friend. I could tell that."

The student of human nature paused for congratulation, but Alec stared ahead.

" Now don't get me wrong," said the student. " I know what you're thinking. You're thinking I'm a Salvation Army Annie, a Paul Pry. Not me, I'm no Holy Hallelujah, I'm a man's man.

Maybe I got my own gospel; I don't mind admitting that much. Tell you in one word: Pals. That's my gospel—Pals! Maybe that's just the gospel this tired old world needs, son, guys to act like Pals!"

"H'm," said Alec, austerely opening the paper and screening himself from further study.

"Yes, I can see you're hiding," said the stranger with a roguish chuckle. "I'm just going to ignore that. I got a thick hide, I can ignore plenty when it's a question of a helping hand. I been studying your face, and I can see farther than most through a brick wall!" He chuckled again, an imitation of a childish giggle, a sort of *hik-kik* that he seemed to consider disarming.

The breeze blew the paper against Alec's face; he shook it out.

"I said, it's not money," the stranger went on, unabashed. "Not with these clothes. Pardon me being personal. Might be woman-trouble? . . . I don't know . . . Might be, might not. All I can say, and I say it from a rich experience of life, all I can say is, this guy's at a turning point."

"What guy are you talking about?" Alec demanded, becoming nettled.

"Why, just you," said the stranger softly, winningly.

Alec snorted.

"Now don't get me wrong, brother," cooed the fat man. "I'm not curious."

"Good," said Alec.

The stranger was encouraged.

"No," he said, "I'm not curious, every man to his own business, that's my slogan. I don't know you, you don't know me. We're just, you might say, ships that pass in the night, you and me. I just thought I'd maybe give you a hail in the passing, hik-kik!"

Alec folded up the paper with an air of finality. This was getting beyond his endurance.

"Well, thanks for the loan of your paper," he said, thrusting it dismissively at the intruder. But it was thrust back with a wave of generosity.

"Well, brother, that's how we stand, you and me. The old ear's there to be used. What's the trouble? Care to pour it out?"

"You mean this kindly," said Alec, "but—no."

"Don't bottle yourself up," the stranger urged. "Never mind me, just a passing stranger, a friend you'll likely never see again, an open ear, hik-kik! . . . Don't bottle up; why, the psychiatric clinics are filled with guys that wouldn't be there if they hadn't bottled up!—in one way if not in another—my sense of humour, hik! . . . As a matter of fact I visit in one great mental institution, just part of my gospel of pals, dropping a seed, and I could tell you things about bottling up the emotions. Well, for example, there's a guy, was a school teacher, matter of fact, now he's a patient in . . . why yes, I can see you're impatient, let's skip it—we're talking about you. You just go ahead and unburden——"

"You're quite mistaken," said Alec angrily. " We're not talking about me and we aren't going to."

The stranger paused patiently. Two sparrows swerved screaming past them and fluttered on the path, two dust-coloured atomies vibrating and shrieking with fury in a battle that had outlasted daylight. They left the ground again and vanished into the branches. The student of human nature, distracted for a second, returned to his subject.

"Well, I won't press you," he said sadly. "I don't press for confidences, brother. Only thought I might help, son. You'd be surprised the number of times I've been able to drop the right word into a wound, I can tell it's nothing to do with money, you're not the type to get into that sort of jam—I can tell these things—why, only the other day I saw a youngster, he'd be younger than you, say in his thirties, now I'd put you at a guess, maybe forty, maybe a bit more, we won't go into that. Same look of a profession like you, maybe a doctor, maybe a lawyer. . . ."

Alec saw a way of ridding himself of this incubus.

" Look," he said, " give me a hundred dollars quick. Come on, pay up quick!"

The benevolent stranger paused, a flush mounting in his heavy pig's cheeks. There was no goodwill in his eye, now; he blinked with indignant malice. Alec edged towards him on the seat and he fidgeted away.

" A hundred dollars!" Alec hissed again.

The stranger recoiled, stood up and backed away, then turned and sped out of sight.

Alec leaned back, victorious. The bench was his. But he felt ashamed and angry, and was surprised at his absurd behaviour. Why had he not simply walked away from the impertinent pig-faced inquisitor? Perhaps because he had felt a need to exercise his will as a change from taking the way of least resistance. He smiled a little, remembering his absurd demand.

But the cold was chilling his spine. He tucked the paper under his arm and walked briskly towards the streets and restaurants.

# Chapter Three

ALL ALEC'S friends were uneasy about him. He had always been a bit odd; quiet you know. You never knew what he was thinking. And whoever heard of a doctor without a car! There was no sense to it. Every doctor kept at least one car. But Alec wouldn't see the strain it put on his friends, keeping up his prestige, turning it into a joke. Bertie Newnham had tried repeatedly to argue some sense into him, about the car and about other things, too, but he would say, absurdly, that it was cheaper and less trouble to use taxis when his legs collapsed under him. The Scots in him, maybe! No, honestly though, old Alec wasn't stingy; but he certainly was stubborn.

Bertie Newnham was not a doctor, he was a lawyer; but he prescribed confidently for Alec's increasing quietness.

"What you need, Alec," he would say with real earnestness, "is to get around. You old clam! Come on, we're old friends, Alec—let me give you a bit of advice. What you need is taking out of yourself."

"Sounds a nasty operation," Alec would reply. "Like flaying alive, or that nice trick the Vikings used, the Red Eagle . . ."

Then he described the opened ribs, the lungs and heart exposed and flapping to death in the wind. He made it sound horrible.

"Something like that you mean, Bertie?" he would ask. "I don't really want my insides exposed."

Bertie Newnham used to feel hurt; but affection always overcame pique; he always returned to the attack.

Alec edged cautiously into the restaurant, his eyes alert for Bertie or any of the other friends whose hygienic sociability he had proscribed. He saw no one he knew, but he chose a table near the service doors and behind a large Doric column. For additional disguise he spread the stranger's paper before him; somehow he

22

had retained possession of it. He smiled grimly at the memory of his victory over that intrusion. Now that he thought of it, the student of human nature seemed to represent all that was crass and intrusive in Bertie—who, but for an underlying honesty and affection, would be an intolerable creature, too.

Probably, Alec reflected, the stranger was a confidence trickster, even a blackmailer trying to worm out a discreditable story. Or more likely he was merely one of those ghouls who gloat and batten on misery. The female ghouls flock like bats round difficult child-births and deathbeds, munching over details of other abnormal deliveries, births of monsters, fearful deaths they have had the good fortune to witness, hoping for the worst. Males of the species are less common. Failures and bankruptcies and other financial mis-fortunes are their territory ; and suicides. Alec had, after all, been weighing the idea of suicide, and that vulture must have been attracted by the smell of death.

But I put him to flight, Alec reflected as the waiter set a plate before him. I made him flap off in a hurry.

He folded the paper and leaned it against the cruet, preparing for a leisurely meal where he could resume his train of thought. He did not mean to read the news ; the paper was mere protection against intrusion. People are less likely to disturb someone who is engrossed in a paper.

But intrusion persisted. There was a face looking at him from the paper. A bad photograph probably, but you had to look at it. It was of an oldish man in a tweed jacket and a dark tie ; with a square, blunt face and eyes that looked at you with a sort of dangerous candour.

The directness of the gaze reminded Alec oddly of his own boy-hood. There was no veil of reserve over that gaze ; nor had it the pseudo-frankness of some astute business men he could think of.

Once, Alec remembered, I wanted to explore the tributaries of the Amazon. Once I was sure I should visit the Mountains of the Moon when I grew up. Once . . . I was alive. Once I thought I should become a writer. I was alive to other people's ideas. Things were mysterious and interesting. I could be generous then with a gush of eagerness, not with tired acquiescence, and friendship was a living experience, not a habit, not the banal good-fellowship of to-day.

Why am I so different, and need this defeat last for ever ? I'm focusing wrongly; as if I had a bad squint, as if I looked inwards and missed reality or got a distorted vision of it. I must get out of this—this sickness, I must escape somewhere where I can look at things straight like this old guy in the paper.

He stared again at the paper, at the photograph. Not an unusual face, really, just the face of a healthy old man. A bore, probably, if you met him. You could never judge by a newspaper photograph; it was Alec's imagination that read so much into it.

No, it was not imagination. The look of candour was there all right.

Alec read the caption.

" Clan Chief visits New York," he read. " The MacArdal wants tenant for Medieval Castle in Romantic Hebrides."

Alec ordered a brandy with his coffee. He must not let himself be absurd and juvenile. Eccentric millionaires could indulge whims like this; he could not allow himself such foolishness. What rational man wants a Medieval Stronghold in the twentieth century ?

But " The MacArdal." Rather a coincidence. The sort of coincidence a superstitious savage would take as an omen. Alec was too civilised to believe anything at all that could not be explained by science.

He waved for the waiter and asked for all the evening papers. When they came he scanned each one carefully, then went through them more carefully still. Not a word about the MacArdal. He picked up the now rather battered paper the stranger had given him and discovered the reason : it was two days old.

Alec felt a surge of indignation against the pig-faced man in the park whose generosity had not even extended to a fresh newspaper. Then he laughed at himself. The discovery had upset him strangely. Had he seriously thought of this broken-down castle ? Yes, apparently he had. Perhaps he still did, if it was not too late. . . .

But now all the reasonable and cautious side of his nature revolted. He tried the effect of a sober rebuke. Come off it and get your feet on solid ground. It's silly romanticism. Don't be a crazy coot ! The rebuke took on the accent of Bertie Newnham and obstinacy stiffened.

It was no good trying to argue. The sight of that clear-eyed old face in the out-of-date paper had touched a switch in his brain or in his will ; and his will was ticking over like a machine ready for action. Or in action already.

He stood up. I'm through with the clinic, anyway, he decided. It's this or the hypodermic.

The thought of the hypodermic had no reality.

The paper had given the name of the old man's hotel. Alec could at least go there and make inquiries. He took a taxi.

The Wells-Wagstaff Hotel, when they reached it, was just like any other middle-sized hotel with an imposing name. Alec approached the desk.

" Sir Hector MacArdal ? " he asked the clerk.

" I don't think he's in," said the reception clerk, a man who disliked humanity. But when he looked in the pigeonhole his hopes were dashed. " He is in," he admitted. " Does he expect you, sir ? "

" No, but tell him I'm here," said Alec.

" What name ? " the clerk asked discouragingly.

" MacArdal."

" I'm asking for your name, not his."

" MacArdal," said Alec.

" Oh, one of the clan," said the clerk drearily, winning the trick after all. " One minute, please. Hallo, Sir Hector ? Sir Hector, there's a gentleman here asking to see you. Gives the name of MacArdal. No, Sir Hector, just MacArdal, seems to think you'll know him . . . Yes, Sir Hector . . . Exact words, yes, sir. He says," the clerk turned to Alec, " that he'll do what he likes and to hell with you. You understand, I'm quoting his words, no offence." He picked up a pen as offensively as possible and turned a page of a ledger.

Alec drew a hand over his chin.

" He must be thinking of the wrong MacArdal," he said. " Tell him I'm Alexander MacArdal, Doctor MacArdal. He doesn't know me."

" Sorry, sir." The clerk spoke as if his mind were on other matters ; he did not raise his eyes. " Sir Hector isn't a person to presume with or pester."

Alec flushed with annoyance. Either a tantrum or a tip, he felt, would change the clerk's attitude. In fact, he was wrong. The clerk was merely glad of a chance to slight a medical man. His own doctor had done no good at all to his peptic ulcer, merely prescribing a strict régime ; whereas Mr. Cobold the Healer had only to lay his hand on the spot for ten minutes every Sunday afternoon and he could smoke as much as he liked.

Alec turned away from the desk. Too late for a row and he refused to oil the palm of a man he disliked on sight.

The lounge, where the desk stood, was interestingly horrible. Its walls were spattered with orange plaster and dabbled with gilt. Ground glass seagulls flew across a mirror, a nude green nymph did a bubble dance, her bubble being an electric light. The furniture was made of cubes of orange tapestry, the carpet had a green ground criss-crossed by orange and lemon searchlights. Alec trod across the searchlights, sat down in an orange cube, pushed back his hat and wondered what to do next. If this had been a film he would have noticed which room number the clerk had rung. It was not a film.

His eyes turned towards the elevator. He wondered if it would do to go over and just say, " Sir Hector MacArdal " and simply soar up. But what if the boy didn't know Sir Hector's number ? His hand fondled his chin. He would look absurd if . . .

He ought to have kicked up a dust with that clerk. He glanced again at the desk and prickled with irritation. The clerk was joined by a woman whose eyes were as glassy as his own and they were both watching him.

Just as Alec was stirring up his indignation to the pitch of creating a scene there was a metallic crash, the lift doors opened and Sir Hector MacArdal, unmistakably like his photograph, hurried out.

" Has he gone ? " Sir Hector demanded. " Where is he ; where did he go ? "

Heads bobbed up out of orange cubes, clerks replied simultaneously, the attention of the entire hotel focused on the old man. Even the well-fed manager was approaching with unhurried speed.

" Here I am," said Alec, intercepting Sir Hector.

Sir Hector stopped short, his right hand offering itself doubtfully.

" No, you don't know me," said Alec, embarrassed by the interest they were evoking and speaking with more force than was natural. " Perhaps I could explain myself somewhere a little less thickly populated ? "

" There's a writing-room . . ." Sir Hector led the way to it.

" It's about what I read in the papers. The castle."

" Oh, yes ? Sit down, won't you."

" I'm afraid you're disappointed I'm not someone else." Alec was a little chilled by Sir Hector's flat voice.

" Yes, I thought you were my nephew, Dochy. Can't blame

you for that." The old man relaxed in a friendly smile, cast off the ghost of the absent nephew and gave his attention to Alec for the first time. " You giving your name as MacArdal made me expect him. We'll have a drink and you'll tell me what you want to see me about." He pressed a bell and sat down. " Now," he invited.

" You want to—let this castle ? "

Sir Hector nodded.

" You a prospective tenant ? " he asked.

" Well," said Alec cautiously, " perhaps you'd tell me about it, first."

" Certainly." Sir Hector lifted his lip in a grimace that showed his long teeth in a sort of petrified snarl ; evidently it was a symptom of mental activity. " The castle of Fionn," he said, relaxing the grimace, " is on the island of Fionn. The two go together, so to speak. You get the steamer from Oban ; or if you're lucky Torquil MacVean might be in with his motor-boat for the mail and the groceries, and he'd take you, too." He paused to order their drinks and to accept a cigarette.

" Is it a large castle ? "

" Pretty small as castles go," said Sir Hector. " Of course, a large castle is a handicap these days. Think of heating them. Great barns of places, all draughts and frozen pipes. No, no, Fionn is a nice compact little place, good thick walls, plenty of peat to be had for good fires. And then it has plumbing. The plumbing was all modernised by Aeneas MacArdal in the early eighteenth century— before the '45 of course. He regretted it when it came to paying the bills. Still it was just as well he got it done, after all."

" How many rooms are there ? "

" Oh, plenty of rooms, any amount of rooms. You got a big family ? Could sleep twenty or thirty if need be."

" Oh, I don't require all that," said Alec hurriedly. " I'm alone as a matter of fact."

" History professor or something ? "

" A nose and throat specialist. I want to get away from people for a bit," Alec explained, seeing Sir Hector's puzzlement.

" I see. Well, I dare say Fionn would suit you ; there's a good library and plenty of pictures and bric-a-brac if you're interested in Art. Aeneas brought stuff back from Holland and France, some of it very good. He was there, you know, after the '45 ; and when he came back he was able to set up for himself in the smuggling trade—the only one in the family with any business ability; at least till my nephew Dochy appeared; he's next in succession. And unfortunately Aeneas died before he could pile up much of a fortune. Well, now, what else can I tell you. There's the drawing-room and the library and of course Aunt Jane's parlour, I use it as a sort of living-room and I dare say you'd find that the best plan; a warm, pleasant little room, you know, to live and eat and laze in. Then there's shooting and fishing. And scenery—if it's peace and beauty you want, well, you've got white sands, long Atlantic rollers and the greenest turf in the Hebrides. And the air, well, nobody knows what air is till they've been to Fionn, it's so transparent it —sparkles. No rats on Fionn, no doctors, either. We don't need them. You won't do any business there," he chuckled, " you'll be out of your element."

Alec laughed.

" And there's a mountain, in miniature of course, an extinct volcano really, with a lochan in the crater."

" And the rent ? "

" Six hundred dollars a month."

Alec's silence was shocked. The old brigand, he thought. He sits there with his look of boyish innocence and asks for six hundred dollars a month.

" I'd rather buy it," he said.

Sir Hector's face resumed its unmalicious snarl and he scratched his cheek.

" Trouble is," he said, " the entail. Could give you a longish lease if you like. Or if there's anything in the art line you fancy, we could come to an arrangement. Matter of fact, I sold a portrait to come here. Sold it to an American and he put the money in a bank over here for me. Dochy won't like it, but—well, what does he think I live on, hey ? And keep the place going ? "

" But it's a stiff rent you're asking," Alec protested.

" Castle, shooting, fishing, whole island nine miles round, and a mountain and a lochan and haunted caves, and rubies and amethysts to be picked up on the sands——"

" I seem to have read about it," said Alec. " In the Arabian Nights."

" Well, of course," said Sir Hector imperturbably, " you don't expect rubies the size of pigeons' eggs on Fionn, but you won't

28

run into the unpleasant predicaments poor old Sinbad got involved in."

" You guarantee freedom from predicaments," Alec smiled. " I still think the rent is a predicament in itself."

" The money I pay out living in this hotel is a predicament, my boy."

" Well, look," said Alec. " My apartment will be empty if I do take this Arabian Nights island. We might do a deal if you'd like to take it on."

" Describe your apartment."

" Come and see it," Alec invited.

" Let's go there now," said Sir Hector. " I like a stroll before bedtime."

" But it's "—Alec looked at his watch—" it's half-past twelve, now."

" Too late for you ? "

" Not if it isn't too late for you."

They walked through the empty streets of night, their feet beating importantly against the silence. Everything was significant ; the wide spaciousness of the streets and squares, the policeman sharing their solitude, the car that wavered too joyfully homeward, the other car that sped past with grim purpose ; and the tramp who profited by their mood of adventure and blessed them with eloquent sincerity.

Alec looked at the deserted streets with a feeling of bidding them farewell already. I'll finish the week at the clinic, he was thinking. I'll arrange for Dobson to take over my cases. Must see Bertie, I suppose ; that means arguments ; but I'll get it all cut and dried and legal.

" You'll miss the winter, going now," said Sir Hector.

By the time Alec got to bed exhilaration had changed into a meaningless, mechanical mental activity. Scraps of conversation repeated themselves over and over in his ears.

" I'll keep Betty on," Sir Hector said. " I'll keep Betty on. I'll keep Betty on." It was like a record when the needle had jammed. And if he jerked the needle over it got stuck at the next phrase.

That old man had no problems—except financial ones, and they were solved for the time being. He must be walking back now through the empty streets, his feet going plonk, plonk, plonk through the silence that was scarcely touched by the occasional swish of a passing car or the shuffle of the solitary scarecrows who creep about the city at night.

"To-morrow," Alec said, " I'll see my friend Bertie Newnham, who looks after my affairs. We'll get it all cut and dried. You'll like Bertie."

" Like to meet him," said Sir Hector ; then his candid charm was suddenly broken by the petrified snarl that exposed his teeth. " Might get him to draw up my will."

Like to meet him. Might get him to draw up my will. It went on and on until he gave the needle another jerk and the sterile activity continued on a different motif. No, you don't know me, but if we could find some place less densely populated . . . Don't bottle up, hik-kik, in one sense if not in another, hik . . . Well, that's that, got patients waiting for me. Well, that's that. A dusty old dog collapsing on a table.

Grief was like an interior bleeding that he could not check. He knew it to be out of proportion to its cause ; other people lost their mother, had their dog destroyed, without this incessant secret bleeding. . . .

I've got to get away or I'll go mad.

"You'll miss the winter going now. You'll be there for the primroses."

It was like a promise of new life, and he dared not let himself believe it.

# Chapter Four

"COME RIGHT in, Dr. MacArdal," said Miss Winnick with the subdued geniality that was a colourless photograph of her employer's. "Mr. Newnham said he didn't wish you to be kept waiting. I'll just let him know. One minute, please!"

Alec sat down and waited.

"Come right in, Doctor," said Miss Winnick again, fifteen minutes later. "Mr. Newnham wishes you to be shown in right now!"

"Well, Alec!" Bertie heaved his large, billowy body out of the swivel chair to greet his friend. "You look fine, I must say! Good to see you, old scout. Missed you at the Dinner."

Alec accepted a cigarette, wondering indifferently which fraternity had been eating a Dinner.

"And how's things, eh?"

"Fine, Bertie, thanks," said Alec. "You look pretty good yourself, got a touch of sun I see."

Bertie launched into an account of his compulsory holiday. Blood pressure; threatened gall-bladder; literal agony with sagging ligaments; nobody knew.

"Which ligaments?" asked Alec.

"It's the transverse arch, Alec," Bertie explained, taking off his right shoe. "This one, see." He waggled his toes. "Shouldn't be that hollow there, Alec, see what I mean? That transverse arch is down, due to the ligaments sagging. Why, gee, it's like having toothache at the root of every toe—up here, at the metatarsals. Toothache in every bone. And you know what feet are, Alec."

"Yes," Alec agreed, doubtfully.

"Got nothing else to stand on but your feet!"

"Luckily you sit a good deal, Bertie. If it had been——"

Bertie was looking hurt and he stopped. He ought not to

31

indulge his love of teasing Bertie; it was a furtive revenge, and slightly despicable.

"You may think so," said Bertie with simple dignity, "but nobody knows the number of times I have to stand on my feet, Alec. They'd know it all right if *they* had my feet. . . ."

"Poor old Bertie," Alec sympathised.

"The other one's not so bad." Bertie removed his other shoe and they both watched his toes waggling in their purple nylons. "See?"

"You need a pad," Alec suggested. "Or to reduce a bit."

"Not on your life, Alec! Massage, remedial exercises and re-education. That's what I'm having. What's a pad? Why a pad, Alec, 'snothing but a crutch! You see I do this—see this pencil. Roll it . . . pick it up with my toes. That's re-education."

"Interesting," said Alec. "I've seen a monkey do that pretty neatly."

"Luckily my toes are supple. Look. Nothing wrong with these joints!"

"Very clever, Bertie. Wonderful toes."

When they had exhausted the subject of Bertie's fallen arches, Alec broached the subject of his holiday.

"I'm going to Europe," he said. "I'm borrowing an island for a few months and lending the apartment in exchange. I want you to pay Betty her wages and generally see things in order, Bertie, while I'm away."

Bertie listened with his air of worried but sympathetic understanding. This air always meant that the plan—whatever it was—would be opposed. Alec waited for the onslaught to begin.

"You know, Alec," said Bertie with great earnestness, "one thing I always admire about you is, you've got imagination. You're original. You get ideas. How many of the boys would have the initiative to think up an idea like that? An island? Precious few! It's a fine idea, Alec, it's got vision, that's what I like about it— vision. Only—matter of timing. Say when you're sixty, sixty-five, that's the time. Not yet——"

"I'll need some money, too," said Alec, disregarding this.

"Look, Alec, be sensible. Let's think this over for a bit before we plunge. You haven't signed anything yet; that's good: let's give the whole thing a few months to simmer and see how it looks in the light of cold reason. Look, Alec——"

Alec's resolution chilled and hardened under Bertie's douches of cold reason. In sardonic silence he heard Bertie's appeals to realism, to sanity, to practical business sense.

"Tantamount to professional suicide," Bertie pointed out.

Alec smiled. Bertie loved his clichés.

"Now, look, Alecky," Bertie appealed. "You and me, we're old friends since schooldays. Take it from me, old scout, this is one of those whims we're all liable to get round about forty-five. I get them myself. Why, what wouldn't I give right now to be lying in the sun on the beach at Honolulu—but I don't go. Know why?"

"Chained by habit," Alec suggested.

"No, Alec."

"Madge wouldn't let you," Alec tried again.

"Because I know I'd regret it," said Bertie gently and forgivingly. "Because I know I'd lose my self-respect if I gave in to a whim."

"You can't know that till you try, Bertie," said Alec. "You never have given in to a whim. Do you all the good in the world. Still, I know it's hard for you with Madge and the kids, but I can do it and I know I'd regret it forever if I miss this chance. How's Madge, by the way?"

"Oh, fine, fine. Madge is just fine. You know, Alec," Bertie said in an innocent, hurt voice, "there's maybe something in what you say, at that. Once I was the centre of the picture with Madge; if I got an idea she sometimes said it was a good idea. I'm not the centre of the picture now. Why, gee, I'm not even the flyspot on the glass!"

"Of course not, Bertie," said Alec, rallying to the disappointment in his friend's voice. "You're too important to be in the pretty picture, you're what the whole shoot depends on—you're the nail in the wall, the picture would drop if you weren't there and Madge knows it."

"Think so?" Bertie accepted the consolation with no show of enthusiasm. "Suppose so, maybe. Still I don't know that a nail in the wall gets a whale of a lot of attention, Alec. But coming back to you. Now look, Alec. You know I'm not a religious customer, but just the same I've got my own views."

"You remind me of a guy in the park:" said Alec.

Bertie ignored the guy in the park: he was used to Alec's red herrings.

" No," he said, " I'm not ashamed to, well, stand shoulder to shoulder with, well you know, with one who has gone before. You remember how your mother and me always saw eye to eye when you got one of your whims, Alec ? "

" I remember," Alec admitted. " Just like Madge and the kids when you get one."

" Think of her now," Bertie persisted.

" Mind's made up, Bertie."

" Alecky," Bertie vibrated with emotion and looked more than ever like the man in the park, " she and I have turned you back many a time in the past. Come on, be reasonable—for her sake ! "

" No, Bertie," said Alec.

" Alec ! "

" No," said Alec. " Just to change the subject, Bertie, why don't you put on your shoes ? "

Bertie, whose toes had been taking a sinuously active part in his pleading, showed that he was hurt. He stooped over his stomach, grunting slightly, and replaced his shoes in silence. Then, impassively, he got down to business. Alec had won.

As he stood up to go, Alec said, " Bertie, you're a good friend. I want you to meet Sir Hector and maybe have him round a bit. You'll like him and so will Madge."

Bertie, still dignified in defeat, inclined his head.

" You'll both come round to me for a drink one night and meet him before I go."

Bertie massaged Alec's shoulder. It was, as a matter of fact, his first defeat. Hitherto he and Mrs. MacArdal had been an irresistible combination. Now he felt a shamefaced guilt both towards the dead and towards Alec.

" Well, I did my best," he sighed, visualising Mrs. MacArdal's expression of pained reproach. He felt a new respect for his friend ; that laconic silence had been pretty effective. " Why don't you put on your shoes, Bertie ? " Pretty cool when you think of it.

" Well, Alecky, you licked me," he chuckled. " And I'm a year older than you. You've got a nerve ! " He had forgotten his pique. " Sure, Madge and I'll be delighted to welcome this Sir Hector of yours."

They went to the door together, Bertie's arm round Alec's shoulder.

34

"By the way," Alec added the news as he saw escape at hand, "Dog's dead."

"That so?" Bertie had caught a glimpse of his next client through the waiting-room door and his thoughts had left Alec's affairs. His hand added a last affectionate pressure to the massage treatment. "Poor old Dog," he said absently. "Well, that certainly does leave a gap. Well——"

"Well——" said Alec.

The elevator gates opened for him and clanged to again. He dropped down to street level.

That was that over. And he had finished with the clinic. Here was actual freedom at last.

He looked at freedom. It resembled nothing but a huge hollow vacuum of time with nothing to fill it.

Alec stopped short. Well, he told himself quickly, there's plenty to do, plenty to do. What, for example? Why, see about a berth, get a sailing date, and so on, and begin putting things together, and all that. And find some time to do a bit of reading again. Hadn't read Hakluyt since school.

But what he found himself doing was frenziedly turning up a number in the telephone directory. Wells-Wagstaff. . . .

"Hallo," he said, "is Sir Hector MacArdal there . . . Why, hallo, Sir Hector, this is——"

"Well, my boy," crackled the earpiece, "nice to hear your voice. Come out and have lunch with me."

Sir Hector's company had a restorative effect on Alec. His simplicity resolved the tangled conflicts in Alec's mind to plain terms, and that by his presence only, for their conversation was mostly impersonal; tips on each side of the Atlantic; dustbowls, how to grow a groundnut, and the rules of baseball provided good topics. Methods of communication, human, animal and inter-planetary, gave them both occasion for lively speculation. Alec was never sure how serious Sir Hector might be; he looked, always, eagerly interested and sometimes vehement over utter absurdities, and when Alec himself built up an edifice of sheer speculation, Sir Hector would sometimes, with an air of good faith, pick out a flaw that was trivial in comparison with the premise from which the flight of fancy took off.

His views on human beings seemed to Alec bizarre and entertaining. He evidently felt a protective tenderness for the reception clerk Alec disliked so heartily, and the clerk swelled like a pouter pigeon when Sir Hector spoke to him, delighted and fussy and solemn. He liked Bertie and, more surprisingly, liked Madge Newnham too. He listened to Bertie's clichés with an apparent respect that was as irreverent as Alec's mockery, and would quirk an eyebrow at Madge with a look that said, "Listen to the clever boy!" So that Madge found herself in a conspiracy to tease her husband in a style that was quite without spite, that in fact made Bertie the centre of attention and both flustered and flattered him. They invited him to stay with them until Alec left.

"No, thanks," he said. "Very kind of you but I'd rather come in the evenings; I'd start cuffing that son of yours if I saw too much of him."

"Do him all the good in the world," Bertie growled.

Madge took it like a lamb.

He refused to go to Alec, either; he would transfer from the hotel when he had seen Alec safely on board, he said, but not before then. Alec suspected he meant to discipline Betty when he took over and felt it wiser not to start the process while her supposed master was in residence.

"By the way," he said, "what do I do for domestic help in your castle?"

"You go to the hotel and ask Mrs. MacLennan for Maura," said Sir Hector. "And make no bones about it. Say, 'I've come for Maura.' Or better still I'll write, and you can let them know what day you're arriving. Then Maura will be there when you start."

"Is Maura Mrs. MacLennan's daughter?"

"No, no, no, Mrs. MacLennan is a very respectable Presbyterian, my dear boy."

"Isn't Maura respectable?"

"Well, she is in a way, poor girl, but not in Mrs. MacLennan's class of respectability. And she's a Catholic."

On one of Sir Hector's daily walking marathons they went to the Park. The sun shone with the sparkling coolness of early spring.

"Look," said Alec, "let's go and sit on that park bench under the trees."

"Tired?"

"No, but let's sit for a minute."

They sat together on the seat where Alec had conducted his

experiment in thinking. The birds were busy with preliminary flirtations and quarrels, quivering their wings, seizing a desirable straw or twig to entice the affection of a rival's wife, shrieking with rage at the discovery of an interloper on their territory.

"Ferocious creatures, birds," said Sir Hector. "Our Nanny used to have a poem:

> ' Birds in their little nests agree,
> And 'tis a shameful sight
> When children of one family
> Fall out to chide and fight.'

"We used to try to introduce some natural history into her fat head but it was no use. She was a great pacifist and we got no peace to fight as long as she was watching. Luckily, she was a great one for her afternoon nap."

"Were there many of you?"

"Two brothers and two sisters. My brother and his wife were both murdered in Malaya. Dochy was at school in Edinburgh at the time. Nice out," he said, looking up at the trees where buds were swelling in glossy red or brown capsules. "Makes you feel alive, weather like this. It's a great thing, my boy, to do what you want to do while you're young enough to enjoy it. That's why I'm having this holiday before I'm old. Suppose I hang on shivering in Fionn Castle till I'm eighty or eighty-five, what good will it do me then if Dochy dies and leaves me all his money? No use to me then!"

Alec was puzzled.

"I thought," he said, "Dochy was your nephew?"

"So he is. But only twenty-five years younger than me, and he's a business man, a company director and all that. I've been a soldier. Dochy's a prudent, clever chap, a man of substance. Life's no good to a chap like that, Alec. They get blood pressure and duodenal ulcers and die off at sixty."

Alec felt a wind of amused exhilaration blow in his face. It was true: life was more than prudence and position. His two suitcases were packed; soon he would stride along the top of a heathery cliff with a wind from the Atlantic blowing spray into his face; with a castle, a haunted cave and a lochan with a Thing in it all waiting to be explored.

"Let's get on," he suggested.

"Right!" said Sir Hector.

# Chapter Five

BETTY WAS delighted to stay on and work for a titled chieftain. She went about her work during the last week with an air of high responsibility, like a priestess. Her eyes were fixed on the day when he would be in her care, and Alec felt at times as if in her eyes he had already gone.

Bertie Newnham, on the other hand, made a last tremendous effort to dissuade him from going. He organised shock troops among their friends whose tactics ranged from boisterous roasting to buttonhole man-to-man attacks. He himself tried one more pious appeal.

" What would she have said, Alecky ? " he asked. " Just put that question to yourself. What would she have said ? "

" She'd have been on your side while she lived, Bertie," Alec admitted, "but don't you think she'll have a less mundane view now ? By the way, when are you going to stop calling me Alecky ? "

All the same Bertie's appeal had its effect. Alec tried to exorcise the reproachful face that haunted him by clinging to his grief for Dog, a grief uncomplicated by remorse or resentment. Yet he still found himself arguing with her in the small hours when sleep evaded him.

In the end the day of departure arrived with a sudden pounce. He found himself, incredibly, in his cabin with Sir Hector and a selection of parting gifts from Bertie and the others, filling the last trickling moments with trivialities.

" I've a notion that Dochy crossed over a fortnight ago," said Sir Hector. " He didn't bother me after all. He may call on you, Alec. Now, if he does come bothering you about some scheme or other, just tell him it's no affair of yours. And if you have him to stay in the castle at all, see and give him grilled kippers for breakfast. He likes them. Or did when he was a boy, if I'm not mixing him with someone else. He's a good enough chap, Dochy, don't let it put you against him that I can't stand him—— Well, I'd better get off or I'll be crossing with you."

" I wish you were," said Alec.

" I'm glad I'm not," said the other, revealing his yellow teeth in a grin. " I'm going to enjoy myself in your blue-tiled bathroom."

" Let me know what you hatch in the airing-cupboard," said Alec.

The ship, like a neatly-organised floating island, drove a white furrow across the ocean. Like an egg pregnant with new life and crawled over by ants holding fancy-dress parties—all metaphors were mixed and absurd, but none absurd enough to describe the fact of the great ship crossing the Atlantic. The passengers shortened the focus of their lives, struck up friendships and antipathies that changed character so rapidly as to dazzle; every now and then they would stare at the dark element that heaved and coiled and hissed beneath them, fearfully, as if they rode on a dragon that waited to swallow them and their cockleshell. Then they would return quickly to games or flirtations or food and the boat would be enormous and solid again.

At last another continent broke the sleek monotony of the sea.

Glasgow greeted them with a thick, cold sunshine that smelt of chemicals. It was the second of April.

A gust of wind blew Alec along Jamaica Street; he felt dust grate between his teeth. His two suitcases—he was pleased with himself for having so little—were already at the station, he had breakfasted and was filling-in time till the train for Oban was due to leave. He wandered aimlessly. The street was an ugly one, but he looked affectionately at the mud-coloured buildings, mud-coloured scavenging birds, men in mud-coloured coats and black hats hurrying about on important business. He had turned his back on important business. He was like a boy on the first day of his holiday.

The island was going to present him with great spaces of leisure in which to discover his own potentialities. He had been good at drawing at school; perhaps he would take it up again; there was nothing absurd in starting late since Gauguin had set the example. Or he might write. He ought to provide himself with materials before he left Glasgow.

He looked round him more consciously now, seeing the trams

that hurtled past him, yellow, white, scarlet, blue or green monsters with glass bellies filled with pale, human faces. He was looking for a shop where he could buy artists' materials. Occasionally a flash of colour caught his eye ; the gaudy trams, baskets of geraniums and marigolds hanging from street lights, a girl rushing out from a close-mouth with a flying petunia coat ; the colours flared against the prevailing drab of Glasgow.

Glasgow, he decided, judging by the shop windows, spent a good deal of cash on drugs. Cheap dress shops flourished too, and shops selling women's working overalls, ironmongery and bathroom fitments, books and rubber goods ; but he did not see the shop he wanted. Perhaps he should ask.

The people he looked at seemed unlikely to know a good shop for artists' requirements. They were mostly girls with knobbly features and elaborate hairstyles ; or older women who had given up the pursuit of glamour and who displayed the same features minus the layer of cheerful paint. There were few men. The drab overcoats and black hats were hanging on office pegs and would remain there until eleven, when all Glasgow rushes out to drink coffee. Alec, not knowing this, continued to look hopefully for an intelligent man who would know what an artist's colourman was.

Now he did see a man ahead of him, wearing a drab coat and carrying a suitcase, but instead of the black hat his head was wrapped in a snowy turban. He was walking spiritlessly; he set his case down for a moment and put a hand against his back before he picked it up and trudged on. Now he had paused again and was leaning against a window to rest.

Alec passed him, glancing at the fine-drawn face, the colour of pale coffee, against a background of handkerchiefs arranged in rosettes. The next window he came to displayed a palette and an arabesque of brushes and colours and a lay figure seated in the pose of Rodin's thinker. He went in.

The young man in the shop greeted his vague request with enthusiasm.

" A sor'a general ou'fi' you mean," he said, replacing every T with a quick hiccup. " You can't do be'er than this wee ou'door ske'ching se' in a handsome walnu' case, pale'e and brushes ; Windsor'n New'on oils, all comple'e, see, canvas 'n stre'cher in the lid. Lovely bi' o' work tha' is. Aye, wa'er colours, too. Here's the thing, eh ? You'll need some Wha'man paper, too. Pencils, eh ? 6B down to H. Rubbers, too, eh ? Tha's right, it's be'er to ge' everything, it's ro'en to find you're away without something you migh' need. Be prepared, eh ? "

Alec emerged with a large parcel and the walnut-cased box of oils, his wallet lighter and his throat practising the glottal stop of Glasgow. He walked right into the Indian who was again struggling along with his case.

"Sorry," said Alec, " wasn't looking where I was going ! "

The Indian, rammed by a parcel of Whatman paper and other oddments, raised meek eyes towards the assailant ; and at the apology smiled feebly and made a tiny bow.

Alec walked on two steps. Then he turned. The Indian had dropped his eyes to the pavement ; the sickly smile was still there as if he had forgotten to change his expression. There was an aloof loneliness about him.

"You look all washed up," said Alec. " Had any breakfast ? "

"No, sir."

There was no reason why he should fraternise with an under-nourished pedlar. It was enough to give him half a crown and walk on. He was not conscious of loneliness; he had, for a time at least, thrown off the reproaches of the one who had, in Bertie's phrase, gone before, life lay before him like a beautiful blank sheet of Whatman paper.

Nothing warned Alec that he was about to spill a bottle of Indian ink over the fair whiteness.

"Let's go and get ourselves some coffee," he said. " Take my paintbox and give me your case. This is all a lot of new paint-ing stuff I've taken the notion to invest in. Done any sketching yourself?"

"No, sir," said the Indian.

"Neither have I, not since we got it at school. Probably make a whale of a mess."

Alec chatted on pointlessly till he saw a tea-room and shouldered his way through its swing door, his Indian following. It was the same unthinking kindness that had prompted him to rescue a bundle of black-and-brown fur from the pet-shop window. On that occasion his mother had warned him bitterly.

"Alec," she had said, " it's easy to have a soft heart when it's other people who have to pay for it. Oh, I don't mean money. Who do you suppose has had to clean up no less than three pools

41

while you were out? You might have thought before you bought the creature. No, you never think, that's what I say, dear."

On this occasion, too, Alec failed to think.

While Alec tasted his coffee and Kirpu stared into his, Sir Hector's American was the subject of several conversations on the Island of Fionn.

Mrs. MacLennan of the Hotel was full of foreboding.

" I wouldn't say a word against your uncle, Mr. Dochy," she said. " I like and I respect him. But this latest cantrip of his is plain criminal folly ! "

" Cantrip ? " Dochy's voice held the word in delicate forceps.

" Cantrip and worse," said Mrs. MacLennan. " Have a bit scone with your bacon after fishing all night. Forbye depriving me of Maura and the summer looming ahead. If it was you, but this American that nobody ever heard tell of ! And turns his back on his own nephew ! "

" I keep hoping he'll get over it. And we're not going to punish the American for Uncle Hector's eccentricity, are we ? "

" A creeping usurper ! "

" Nonsense. He'll be an ordinary decent chap, plump, clean shaven, smelling of soap, like any other American in fact. I'm pretty sure you'll like him."

" I'll take him as I find him ! " Mrs. MacLennan uttered this threat with an expression so grim that Dochy chuckled.

" I'll go and pay my respects at the castle to-morrow," he said as he stood up.

Mrs. MacLennan stretched her mouth till the corners tucked into a groove on either side ; this grimace was by no means a smile, and Mrs. MacLennan was in no smiling mood ; it indicated a Sibylline foreknowledge that no good would come of letting Americans loose in Fionn, especially when the rightful heir was cold-shouldered at every turn. If anyone should be in the castle it ought to be Mr. Dochy.

She piled the débris of his breakfast on a tray and took it to the kitchen where Maura Rafferty was peeling potatoes.

" Do plenty, Maura," she said. " Do what'll tide me over for three days, anyway."

" I will," said Maura.

Old Mrs. Kilbride gave her husband a glare.

"What do you mean," she shouted, "telling me they're like human beings? I suppose I don't need you to tell me Americans are human beings, I'm asking what they're like?"

Captain Kilbride was imperturbable behind a barrier of deafness. His wife's angry shouts reached him like the roar of a sucking dove.

"I didn't say they were human beings," he remarked, "I said they were very like human beings. Far and away more like human beings than the thing they call the Old Man of the Woods, nothing but a great miserable monkey. But the Americans are clever. They go about whiles with a bunch of feathers stuck in a leather band round their heads, and they smoke pipes. They carry their infants in a sort of a——"

Mrs. Kilbride lost patience. She went to the stuffy, immaculate parlour and stared out at the equally immaculate front garden, her wrinkles working like those of a concertina as she chewed her resentment. And what did she see in the garden? Nothing to comfort her. A great crow, black and untidy as a tinker, straddling about on their grass.

"Ssht! Come on, get off! Broof!"

She threw up the window and shouted at the trespasser.

The crow hunched its shoulders and crouched, eyeing her insolently before it flew off. A bad bird, carrying ill-luck and worse in its bald beak.

To add to her irritation the captain had followed her.

"A crow," she answered his question. "I was chasing a big crow. A crow, I said!"

He would drive her demented with his deafness, and half of it was cantankerosity. He heard when he liked. If he went soon she would grieve, of course, in a dutiful way, but she would get some peace for her declining years.

"Shut the window," said her husband.

"I'm letting some air in."

"It's away. Shut the window."

"I know it's away. I'm letting some air in!"

"You've let the air in," said Captain Kilbride, "now shut the window and keep it from getting out again."

Equably, he watched her obey and fling out of the room. She was old and stupid. That flouncy temper that had been quite

43

attractive in a young girl was nasty in an old woman. But she
wouldn't last much longer.

Captain Kilbride returned to the kitchen where the fire blazed
and where his wife cast a haunted look at him; she suspected, he
knew, that he was just following her round out of wickedness.
He sat down in his chair and mused on the tranquillity that would
be his when she was tucked up in the graveyard. And she would
get some rest to herself, the poor creature; she needed it.

Nell Patrick was suckling her baby and drinking strong tea.
She knew what Americans looked like; the question was what
variety of American this would be. Not Edward G. Robinson, she
hoped. Someone more like Gregory Peck or young Dr. Kildare;
or Humphrey Bogart or George Raft with their handsome, slab-like
faces, impassive and wicked. She longed for his arrival; it would
be even better than a cinema on the island.

"Hallo, Danny," she said dreamily.

"Hallo," said Danny Rafferty. "I'm early for the school so I
just looked in."

"That's right," said Nell. "Och, it's hardly worth your while
going, I'm sure."

"I'll be finished with school on the thirtieth of June," said Danny
with zest.

Nell was an anaemic girl, dispirited in her dress and her house-
keeping but gaudy in her dreams; she was in the throes of a dream
now, and scarcely saw Danny and her two-year-old sparring and
chuckling together. This was the great renunciation scene; the
American's face was tragic, though there was no change in
expression, for he was the marble slab type. She herself was
speaking in the breathless voice of anguish, with her back to him so
that the audience could see both their faces, greatly enlarged.

"Yeah, I mean it, honey," she was saying. "We gotta stop.
I gotta husband an' kids. It's been great while it lasted, but—gee,
honey, don't make it hard for me, I gotta heart an' it's pretty near
breaking at that——"

Her voice broke, she half-turned towards him and suddenly
they were in each other's arms, stealing one last, searing kiss. . . .

"So," said Danny, entertaining wee Pad Patrick, "the porter
says, Well, says he, the train before's behind and the train behind
the train before's behind before besides!"

44

His last words had to squeeze through the laughter that bubbled in his throat.

Pad Patrick went into contortions of glee.

"Befind before befides!" he chortled. "Befind be——"

Nell looked round, wakened by their laughter. The baby was asleep, her mouth rosy and dribbling with milk; her head lolled drunkenly as Nell buttoned her bodice.

"What did you say, Danny?" she asked.

"This," said Danny, "was one of them hustling Americans, and says he to the porter, Porter, why is my train late? Well, it's like this, says the porter, the train before's behind, and the train behind the train before"—he paused to conquer his mirth—"'s behind before besides!"

Pad wallowed on the rug, waving his fat legs in ecstasy. "Before befind befides!" he repeated, loving the jingle that his idol laughed at.

Nell smiled vaguely. "You're an awful one, Danny!" she murmured. "He'll be on the train now, likely. Is your mother at the castle?"

"She went first to Mrs. MacLennan at the Hotel to give her a start off. He won't be there till evening."

"She's a lucky one, getting to work for him," Nell sighed. "Are you for off, Danny? Look in and tell me what he's like, will you?"

"I will so," said Danny, surprised. "If I see him at all. Cheerio, then, Nell. Cheerio, Pad—ye can't come along the road and you with no trousers on you!"

"Cheerio," Nell murmured, striving to recapture the dream.

# Chapter Six

ALEC AND his Indian had discovered little about each other except that for both of them this was their first visit to Europe.

"How interesting," said Kirpu, clasping his fine hands round the white cup to warm them.

Alec watched him with a faint smile. "How interesting," Kirpu had said in a tone of devastating ennui. The poor creature was wrapped up in his homesickness and Alec's attempt to cheer him was in the same crass category as the intrusion of the fat philanthropist in Central Park; only the Indian was too courteous, or not yet sufficiently goaded to snub him as he deserved.

"I'm butting in on you," Alec said with amused contrition. "I'll just pay this and leave you to finish——"

"No, no, please!"

Kirpu was on his feet too now, begging him to sit down. "I am a clod and a dolt to show so little gratitude," he lamented, "and all the time I am overcome by your kindnesses. I show no more feeling than—than a, a lump of clay! My brother studied at Oxford University, he would have known how to behave gracefully, but I am a mere untutored savage!" His eyes gleamed with tears, he wrung his hands.

"Well, let's sit down," said Alec. "I just thought maybe I was intruding——"

"You are my friend," said Kirpu.

"Drink up your coffee, then." Alec was aware of the waitresses' interest in this performance; luckily they were the only clients. "Not that it's much good."

"No, it is filthy stuff," Kirpu agreed. "But for me it has the delicious flavour of your kindness."

"Glad you like it." Alec felt helpless before this.

"On the ship," said Kirpu, whose tongue had been loosened, "I said to them, I have a sore back. But I received no sympathy,

46

only chaff and insults. They told me, You do not need a doctor, you shall not report any sore back. You are not so bad as you think you are. But how do they know this? I," said Kirpu, leaning earnestly forward, " think that I am worse—much worse than I think I am!"

He swallowed the dregs of his greyish coffee and used his middle finger to catch a tear from the corner of each eye. A gold ring glittered on his finger. The tears formed a little mound of salt water into which he gazed sadly. He sniffed, and shook the moisture from his fingers, bored with the contemplation of tears.

" It is perhaps the flu," he said. " I shall probably infect you, too, then your reward for kindness will be sickness. What beastly luck ! "

" I'll cross that bridge when I come to it," said Alec.

" What a brilliant metaphor ! "

" Trite," said Alec.

" I find it highly poetic," Kirpu assured him. " I must remember it : I will cross the bridge when I come to it."

" Were you at Oxford, too ? "

" No, no, it was my brilliant and charming brother. He gave me this ring. He won a scholarship, you see. As for me, I was a mere chuprasi ; but to have a brother at Oxford, and in addition to be the chuprasi of Smith Bahadur, was in itself a liberal education. Smith Bahadur was a man of outstanding ability."

" What does it involve to be a chuprasi ? " Alec asked.

" It is to be a sort of confidential secretary," said Kirpu carelessly. " On board ship I was a mere nothing, a cook, but my work was, as it were, my ticket of admission to the wonders of the West. Travel broadens the mind."

" I believe it does," said Alec.

" Then you agree with Smith Bahadur. Though your mind, I can see, is already pretty broad, and travel will make it extremely broad indeed. My mind is not worth bothering about really. It is a worthless thing."

" Oh, don't underrate yourself."

" I will try not to," Kirpu said, " but alas, I am unpromising material to work on ! "

" Did this Smith Bahadur ever say so ? "

" Smith Bahadur ? Never ! Kirpu, my dear fellow, he would say, where should I be without you ? You alone know where to find my spectacles—and other services," Kirpu continued in his own

47

voice, " too numerous and insignificant to mention. But not too insignificant for Smith Bahadur to appreciate, for he was a gentleman to the fingertips and gave praise where praise was due. In fact, the person he most reminded me of was yourself."

Kirpu joined innocently in Alec's laugh. His eyes now had a nervous glitter ; he no longer drooped, he was tense with the effort to entertain his host. He racked his brains for conversational gambits he had picked up from Smith and from his clever brother.

" Do you make a long stay in Glasgow ? " he asked presently.

" Not long. In fact, I leave in—" Alec consulted his watch— " in forty minutes from now."

Grief and bewilderment quivered across Kirpu's face.

" Leave ? " he echoed. " Am I to lose you, sir, so soon ? But perhaps you require a secretary, a cook, a—a devoted servant whose entire soul is—is——"

" Well," said Alec, " I hardly need a secretary, thanks, but maybe——"

It had been his intention to fish out a pound note and add his good wishes and farewells to it ; but he was having his hand kissed, he was receiving vows of fealty. It seemed he had acquired—he was not sure what. A butler, a cook, an Ariel, a heart that throbbed henceforth with a pure devotion.

" O.K.," he said, withdrawing his hand. " Let's take a taxi to the station and get your ticket."

In the train Kirpu's devotion was tireless. He was all eagerness to know if Alec preferred the window shut, open or half-way ; the door to the corridor shut, open or half-way ; his feet on the floor or on the seat opposite, the blinds down or up. Alec settled down with a paper and tried to stifle Kirpu's solicitude with a *Picture Post*.

Kirpu held the magazine before him, reading with a good imitation of intelligent absorption an article on the survival of the Maypole Ritual. Every now and then his eyes looked over the top of the page to assure himself that Alec was still there and was in no need of any small attention. Assorted scraps of information tucked themselves into the filing system of his memory. His patron chose a smoking compartment, but so far had not smoked. He travelled third class, which had given Kirpu a shock of disappointment ; Alec must be a Socialist. And a good thing too, for only a Socialist would fraternise so easily with an unknown Indian. Or, wait !

48

Were there any Socialists in New York? Surely not! Republicans and Democrats, those were the parties there. And, of course, Communists, those traitors to their country who fraternised with negroes and indulged in black magic practices so that witch hunts were organised against them. Alec was escaping, probably, from a particularly ferocious witch-hunt. A Communist, therefore, and furthermore a Communist who did not mind whether he sat with his back to the engine or facing it.

Alec turned his *Scotsman* inside out and Kirpu, like a child rebuked for inattention, hurriedly fixed his eyes on a photograph of the Maypole. Morris dancers, he noted, wear coloured ribbons round their bowlers. How bizarre and exotic the West was, quite unlike the sober East!

Kirpu leaned back, forgetting his magazine, his mind wandering among familiar everyday scenes. He was standing in the centre of his own village listening to its voice, a voice made up of human chatter, the buzzing of flies, the yelp of some dog, the pat-pat-pat of the hooves of a sacred bull that swiped a yam off Meena's fruit stall. How sick Meena looked! But there was nothing she could do about it. Over in the shade old Gappa was shaving a customer. They squatted in the white dust, silent and absorbed among the busy figures. How many people there were! Everybody he knew was there, even his mother and his sister shrinking modestly against the wall. Their shadows followed them round, rippling over the uneven dust and refuse of the street; everyone followed by a meek, subservient shadow. No, not everyone . . . There was his brother Sepu standing in the bright sunshine, looking all round him, smiling and waving and bowing to everyone in a kind of dance of self-approval . . . His mopping and mowing had a horrible nakedness without any shadow. His body had colour and charm, but cast no shadow. Now the sunlight had become opaque, a white darkness in which everything vanished except Sepu with his smiles and silly, conceited gestures. How exasperating his conceit was! Anyone but Sepu would know better than to dance and simper in the sunlight with his . . . with his throat . . . with a cord. . . . Or was it Kirpu himself who danced and beckoned there in the sunlight?

Alec lowered his paper. Kirpu seemed to be in an uneasy doze, uttering small choked sounds in his throat. Alec leaned forward and gripped his arm.

" Steady ! " he said.

Kirpu jerked and sat erect, staring, swallowing down the memory of a dream. He stretched his mouth in the shape of a smile, picked up his magazine and turned to an article on rehousing for Manchester's slum-dwellers.

They were passing through a gorge clothed in silver birches and primroses. Sunlight slanted through the trees on to the young grass where bluebells were still in green bud, but here and there unfolding a single blue floret. Bracken was still clenched in tight rusty curls. The train roared and clattered through the gorge, but its voice opened to a contented purr as they left the high banks and swept along the side of a loch.

Alec touched Kirpu's knee with the *Scotsman* and the Indian looked obediently at the pair of swans that flew alongside them with creamy outstretched necks and white, beating wings. It seemed to them both that they had known each other for years.

" The boat for Fionn ? " repeated the porter. " Would that be the steamer, do you mean ? "

" I suppose so," said Alec.

" Ach," the porter smiled slyly, " she's gone this three-quarters of an hour if it's the steamer."

" Then we'll have to stay overnight."

" So you will. Indeed, you'll have to wait till Thursday if it's the steamer."

" Is there any other way of going ? "

The porter fumbled through the tickets he held, then tried the sky for inspiration, then gave it up.

" There's motor-boats for hire," he said, " but they don't start till June. It's not likely there'll be one fit to run. Yes, yes, there's only one other way of doing it."

" Hire a plane ? " Alec suggested.

" Where would you land a plane on Fionn ? " The porter was offended by such ignorance. " Where would you get a plane, let alone land it ? Unless, maybe," he became thoughtful, seeing less absurdity in the idea, " you could get a seaplane from Stranraer ? Yes, that might be a possibility ? "

Obviously he had something up his sleeve but meant to extract the last drop of satisfaction from watching the suspense of his victim.

"Otherwise," said Alec, "what?"

"Otherwise," said the porter, producing his ace, "if you're the Doctor Alec MacArdal that Sir Hector wrote about, there's Torquil MacVean hanging about waiting for you with his motor-boat."

Torquil MacVean was indeed hanging about; he had looped an arm over the station railings and relaxed like a puppet with slackened strings; a long, dark, blue-eyed man in fisherman's clothes.

"Well, well, is it you," he said, limping forward as Alec approached. "And welcome to you," he added politely, shaking hands and casting an inquiring look at Kirpu.

"This is my Indian assistant," said Alec, whose ideas as to Kirpu's role were nebulous.

Torquil and Kirpu shook hands, too.

"Is this all your luggage?" Torquil looked down at Alec's two cases. "We'll manage one each then."

He led the way to the harbour where a trim little motor-boat awaited them.

Kirpu's face paled in horror when he saw the vessel he was to sail in. The sea was a horrible element, but to be so near it, so close to its lapping embraces as he would be in that walnut shell, filled him with revulsion.

"I cannot come," he quavered.

"Why not?" Alec asked.

"It is too—and I am not——" Kirpu backed away, closing his eyes and passing his fingers over his brow. "I am ill," he announced with dignity.

"You'll feel better when we get there," said Alec. "Come on."

Kirpu backed again.

"I cannot come," he repeated. "Perhaps to-morrow——"

"Well, I'm going now." Alec's voice was still kind but it held an ultimatum. He stepped into the swaying boat.

Kirpu stood with averted face. The very thought of the sea had turned his skin to a sallow grey.

"Coming?" Alec invited. Then, when there was no reply, he tucked a pound into the strap of Kirpu's case and heaved it back on to the jetty.

"Good-bye, Kirpu," he said. "Good luck."

Kirpu did not speak. Torquil loosed the mooring and pushed off. The engine wakened and began to sputter.

Kirpu stood beside his case, staring landward. He saw a wooded hill crowned by a round tower. From the corner of his eye he saw Alec sit down, Torquil push off. Then he heard the engine. He turned. Already the water was widening between them, soon they would curve out of sight among all those hills that closed in the horizon. A flood of despair broke from his lips, he danced on the flagstones, beseeching them to return for him and they, understanding his gestures if not his language, curved round and bumped gently back.

In silence Kirpu accepted Torquil's help to descend into the boat; then he yielded himself up to wretchedness.

By late afternoon they were still chugging through a sea of opal and pearl. Islands floated past them; the blunt black head and neck of a seal bobbed out of the water, surveyed them glassily, sneezed and submerged. Torquil MacVean rustled in a paper bag and produced apples and sugar buns which he shared with Alec; then they each drank from Alec's flask. Kirpu lay with closed eyes, groaning occasionally, and twice he jerked up to vomit over the side of the boat.

Now they were sailing through the heart of a ruby. The islands they passed lay like rags of blue velvet on the rose-red water. It was cold now; Kirpu shivered uncontrollably and Torquil threw an oilskin over him. Alec cringed inside his clothes. Torquil alone sat unmoved at the tiller, steering them through the ruby and into a twilight of lapping, liquid blue.

Alec breathed the cold blue air, living with great contentment in the present moment.

" And here we are, then," said Torquil, hauling the boat into shallow water. " I'll carry ye; you don't want to get your trousers wet and I've got boots on."

It would have been tactless to protest that Torquil was lame; his bearing ignored the disability. In the Highlander's arms Alec splashed across the last three yards of water that separated him from Fionn.

The dark mass that reared against the sky almost from the water's edge was the castle; what caught Alec's eye in it was the wavering light in one low window.

His hand was almost too cold to hold the suitcase. Torquil took one of his and Kirpu's too.

"Come on," said Alec, "you'll feel all right as soon as you're inside." He took the Indian by the arm and led him stumbling and shivering in Torquil's wake to the door of the castle, which opened wide as they approached. The opening door, giving on deeper darkness within, had a momentarily gruesome effect. Alec's grip on Kirpu roughened; he dragged him forward quickly to contradict his own impulse to quail. Then a woman's voice spoke.

"Am I not daft," she said, "opening the door in the dark as if you would know the way in. Wait now till I fetch the candle, will you."

They were inside. Alec shut the door to keep out the cold. Now he could see nothing but a rectangle of peacock blue where a window looked out to the sky and sea. His feet stamped on stone flags, one foot higher than the other, for the stones were uneven. His nostrils inhaled a cold smell of stone.

In a very few seconds Maura returned with a candle streaming its flame over her shoulder.

"Welcome," she said kindly. "Would you like to go up to your room, Doctor, or will you come through to the kitchen for a bit of a warm?"

"Kitchen," said Alec, thankfully.

"Och, you're frozen cold, poor souls. The kitchen's the only fire that's drawing, the chimneys are cold and the fire in the parlour's as stubborn as the devil's ass. Did you mind the paraffin, Torquil? We'll get some light so."

In the kitchen a great fire blazed in the range. They all gathered round it, Maura set the candle on the table and drew in a chair for Alec and then disappeared.

Here he was. But he had no idea what his new home was like, not even the kitchen he was sitting in, for in the candle and firelight the shadows leapt and fidgeted and sidled, confusing the eye. There was a table, and the chair he sat in, and the fire that warmed his outstretched palms and his face. It was enough for the moment.

Kirpu sat down in a chair by the table with his head drooping. Torquil looked in, said good-night and departed.

The warmth was having a hypnotic effect on Alec. He saw and heard in a dream, uncritical of details but with perceptions all the deeper because the alert surface of his mind was dulled. Time lost

53

its meaning, he experienced with a strange simultaneity all that had happened since he stepped ashore. The voices and movements in the firelit kitchen blended with the feel of uneven flagstones in the hall, Maura's face lit by a candle flame, the door opening horribly on darkness.

Most of all he still saw that first glimpse of Maura. Her chestnut hair was heavy and soft; she wore a faded wrap-round overall, her body was ripe and gentle and the candle cast warm lights and warmer shadows over her. Her face was calm; she might, with that tranquil face and body, have sat as model for an antique Greek sculptor; only her colouring was warm and alive, the sculptor's model painted by Rembrandt.

"There," said Maura, entering the kitchen with a bright lamp. "Now you can see yourselves. I've left one in the hall and one in your bedroom. Where will I put him?" She motioned to Kirpu. "There's rooms upstairs but none of them aired excepting your own. It was only you I was expecting. Maybe I better put him in one of the rooms off the kitchen, he'll get the good of the fire so. Would you like to look and see would it do for him?"

Alec rose and followed her. There were several doors in the corridor outside the kitchen. Maura opened the nearest and revealed a small room with an iron bed, yellow wardrobe and chest of drawers and two yellow chairs. A small drab mat lay on the floor beside the bed and another in front of the chest of drawers, and the window was small and high and set in a deep thickness of wall.

"They're all the same," said Maura. "This one's nearest the kitchen so it's the warmest."

It did not feel warm; it was dank and musty.

"Better open the door and window and let some air through," Alec suggested.

"I will," said Maura, "and I'll hang the blankets on the kitchen pulley and give them a toast. Did he come with you from America?"

"No," said Alec. "He comes from India."

"A Hindoo," said Maura. "I thought it, the poor creature. Likely he'll feel better for a night's rest. Will you take ham and eggs for your supper? And Mrs. MacLennan of the Hotel sent some of her scones and bannocks, and I'll make a good pot of tea."

"That sounds pretty good," said Alec. "And very nice of Mrs. MacLennan. I'll have to call and thank her. I'd like some hot

54

water for a wash, and maybe you'd show me my own room, Maura."

"I will," said Maura, and led the way up a coiling stone staircase to a room where a fire crackled smokily. "It's the chimney," she said resignedly. "You'll feel the smoke a bit, but better be warm and kippered than freeze with the cold. I'll just get your hot water up."

The room was ghostly with smoke. Mahogany furniture gleamed purple behind veils of it ; specks of black floated down to the yellow silk of the counterpane and hangings and the white marble of the washstand. Alec jerked the window open and the smell and sound of the sea rushed in from the darkness.

"Here you are," said Maura, splashing hot water into the basin. "And I'll give the fire a good dose of this. It's a great inconvenience to be out of oil."

She poured a libation from the oil can over the sulky fire and it roared like a bull and flared out at her. She stood by calmly, not intimidated, and the wild beast shrank back and snarled obediently up the chimney.

"I'll have your supper ready inside fifteen minutes," she said.

"That'll be fine, Maura," said Alec.


## Chapter Seven

THE POOR thing, thought Maura. Drooping over the table there like a rag of a wet dishclout.

She stirred the fire and set a big iron frying pan on it and laid two rashers of ham in the pan.

"Ye'll feel better with food in you," she said, speaking loud in case he did not understand English.

Kirpu raised his head from his arms. Maura was standing with a red-striped cloth waiting to lay it over the table. He drew his arms from the table and watched her set out the china and butter and cheese. Each arm felt heavy and separate from him ; he lifted them like objects that had no connection with his body. The bright lamplight pressed against his eyeballs and made them feel too big for their sockets. He passed his tongue over his lips.

"Poor fellow," said Maura. "Will I pour you a cup of tea before I put the eggs in? To be going on with?"

Kirpu nodded.

"There you are. It's a great comfort, a cup of tea. I've known myself what it is to be homesick, and I had no chance of seeing home again."

"I also," said Kirpu. "I can never return home." His eyes hung on her sadly, accepting her pity.

"Is that so now," said Maura. "Drink your tea then, you'll find it a great comfort, like religion, while I fry the eggs. Were you with him long, then? On the boat, was it, you met?"

Kirpu's brain sketched a decorative version of his encounter with Dr. MacArdal, but he was too listless to work it out. To-morrow he would give her a really vivacious account of it; but to-night he shook his head and felt the inside of his teeth with his tongue. Here he was, eating unclean food with unwashed hands.

"It does not matter," he whispered. "I reject all superstition. I am too enlightened to care."

"Eh?" Maura could not hear what he was muttering away to himself. "I put a hot-water bottle in your bed with the pillow on top," she said. "And when these blankets up there have had a good warm you can make it up. The sheets are up there, too. Away and take your hat and coat off," she suggested. "Coat, anyway." She was not sure if they kept their hats on indoors; turbans you called them.

Obediently he rose and went into the room she showed him. He looked at the bed, the pine furniture, the small window, and knew that if he had been less miserable he would have glowed with satisfaction. There was a calendar over the bed, a picture of a small house smothered in flowers; the picture was called "East West Home's Best."

Kirpu stood rapt before the picture. It was magically beautiful; the healing power of beauty calmed him. And it was symbolic. He had a headache but he had found a home, a haven. All those flowers had meanings, no doubt. They were flowers of varieties unknown to this earth, clambering over the house and towering over its thatched roof.

Flowers of the spirit, thought Kirpu. They will blossom here. I shall reject the life behind me, all blasted and barren, but here I shall find redemption ; here in my East West Home. How beautiful that is.

He heard voices in the kitchen and hurried in to wait on Alec, just in time, for Maura would have laid a plate laden with food on the table if he had not forestalled her and seized it himself. He proceeded with dignity round Alec's back and set it respectfully before him, then he stood behind the chair and watched him eat.

"Well," said Maura a little huffily, "if you'll manage now by your two selves, I'm for off."

Kirpu's odd little bow mollified her. She still disliked the way he had snatched the plate from her but he was a poor sad soul who knew no better ; it wasn't disrespect, you could see that by the way he bowed with a little soft movement of the hands.

"We'll be all right, thanks," said Dr. MacArdal. "I didn't realise you wouldn't be sleeping here. When do you come in the morning ? "

"Well, I have to get Danny his breakfast first. When will you be wanting yours ? "

Alec laid down his fork and knife.

"Is Danny your husband ? "

"He is not, he's my son, just turned fifteen," said Maura. "That's what he is, and he has to go to the school till the end of this term, fifteen or no fifteen."

"What does he learn ? "

"Algebra and Shakespeare," said Maura, "and mends her Acme wringer, and if you ask me there's more wringer and such than school learning, and maybe just as well . . . Still, I could manage in at eight or thereabouts and have your meal ready half an hour later. Would that do ? "

"Yes, eight-thirty is as good a time for breakfast as any."

"So it is," Maura agreed, and on this note of harmony she left.

It was a lovely still night outside, but darker than Maura liked. The air was damp and soft and smelt of seaweed, and the waves splashed and rustled. Maura had left the castle hugging a little glow of delight in her breast.

It was a dangerous feeling, and she rebuked it, but with no effect. She had once experienced this small, exciting glow before, and look what shame it had led to ! A small spark can kindle a big fire, she told herself. Men are the devil and all. She shook her head gravely as she hurried along to the cottage. She had learnt her lesson, the deceiving rascals would never get round her again.

Not, she admitted, that he had shown any sign of wanting to get round her. He was the perfect gentleman, with an Indian servant and all. Probably spent most of his life in India, that would account for his pallor and his air of seriousness. That was what India did to white folks, either made them as red as a red pepper and a temper to match, the nasty pigs, or else they came back quiet and soulful because of the things they had seen, all those mummies and suttees and zombies and things that Danny told her about and she wished he wouldn't. It was too dark besides to be thinking of such things !

Maura ran the last little way and let herself in in a hurry, crowding out the thought of white-eyed zombies.

" Are ye in ? " she cried as she clattered at the latch. " Are ye finding a bite to eat ? Did ye get fish ? Is the kettle——"

" I'm at it, can't you see," said Danny. " Did you bring a bite of something back with you ? "

" I did not ! " Maura threw off her dark coat and poured herself a cup of tea. " How would I, and them just new arrived ? "

" Is there more than one, then ? "

" There's himself and his Hindoo waiter," said Maura nonchalantly. " Pass here the cheese will you." She was gratified at the impression she had made.

" Hindoo, did ye say ? " Danny recovered the power of chewing and dealt with the scone and cheese in his mouth. " You mean a real Hindoo or what ? "

" What other kind would there be ? "

" They might be dressed-up play actors," said Danny.

" You and your Othello ! I don't know what takes them to try on that outlandish stuff ; it's sheer obscenery ! "

" It is not obscenery," said Danny in the hurrying voice of one who wastes no time on old arguments. " Does he wear a turban, then ? "

" He does," said Maura. " He's got dark, sinister, flashing eyes, and——" Invention failed her ; Danny always beat her there. She returned to truth. " His hands are as fine as a woman's," she said. " He's got a sad look on his face, the poor soul, he'll never see his own land again."

" Why won't he ? "

" Because he said so."

" But why won't he, Mammy ? Maybe he's done something. Assassinated a Rajah or one of those. Maybe he's a Thug, Mam. A mad killer on the run ! "

" Hold your tongue," said Maura placidly. " That's a nice thing to wish on your mother and me working there ! "

" I never made him one. Ritual murders, that's what they are, servants of Kali. Or Shiva or Vishnu or one of those. I better look it up next time I get into Sir Hector's library. They do it with a cord, Mam, like this, they come creeping up——"

" Sit down, will you, and hold your tongue."

" Behind——"

" Will you stop that, then, I'm not frightened. I'm not even interested in your nonsense ! "

" But let me show you, Mammy. Be taking your tea and pretend you don't know I'm here."

" I will not ! Come away from——"

" But don't turn round, be sitting quiet at the table——"

" Come away from dodging behind me, will you ! "

" Och, Mam ! "

" And put down that cord, shame on you ! "

" There's no cord."

" What's that you have in your hands ? "

" I was just pretending I had a cord in my hands the way the Thug would be creeping up with it in his hand, like this—never a sound till—pft !—you can't make a cry, your windpipe's throttled, your face goes black, you're dead ! "

" I am not. Shame on you trying to frighten me with your play acting. Was there no fish at all ? "

" I sold them to Mrs. MacLennan. I thought you'd bring something back for sure. You're better at the hotel, Mam. I say you're better at the Hotel. He must be a miser."

" He's not a miser."

" He is so. What's he like, Mammy ? "

Maura looked into her empty cup, smiling.

" He's a wee dried-up miser," said Danny.

" Will you stop provoking me ! "

" What's he like ? Is he a Hindoo, too ? "

" Is he a——! " Maura was enraged. " I told you he brought this one back with him from wherever it is ; he's white himself, very quiet and polite and he speaks with that twang they get in those queer-like places." Her voice softened. " He's thin," she said. " Pale and quiet. Those hot countries are no good for white men ; drains their vitality."

" It's the leeches, Mam. They stick on you as you hack your way through the jungle swamps, they suck your blood, and the ticks burrow under your toenails. I wonder did he ever see an anaconda or a crocodile. Ask him, Mam. Will you ask him ? "

" I will not."

" Go on, Mam ! Ask him ! Will you ? Mammy, does he need maybe an odd job man to mend the wringer and sort the clocks and dig for worms ? "

" There's no wringer. Still, I might ask him does he need odd help. It's——" She choked noisily like the victim of an inexpert thug. " Och, Danny ! " she protested furiously, " My hair ! "

Danny loosened his bear's hug. Her face did not match her angry voice ; she was smiling, and the hand she raised to smooth her hair changed its plan and gave a good tug at his own brown mop.

" We'll need to get some of this off before you're fit to be seen," she said. " You're like nothing but a hairy baboon."

" I'll get the scissors, then."

" You'll do no such thing at half-past eleven at night. Go to your bed this minute."

" But baboons are——" Danny began didactically, but Maura interrupted the natural history lesson.

" First thing in the morning I'll do it, when there's daylight. And when the school comes out you can wash your face and comb your hair and come up to the castle."

" I'd better just stop school now. I'm fifteen, and——"

" You will not."

" Och, Mam ! I could, it's legal ! "

" I told Miss Bradshaw you'd stay to the end of the term."

" But that's two months ! Life's passing me by and me doing nothing but quadrilateral equations ! "

" She says you ought by rights to be going on to the High School."

" Miss Bradshaw's nothing but a silly old maid that——"

Maura gave Danny a sharp smack on the ear and he stopped. Not because the blow had hurt him ; he topped his mother by an inch, being five-foot three, and his head was a good deal harder than his mother's hand. But he had a sober respect and liking for Miss

Bradshaw, in spite of her notions, and when he did refer to her spinsterhood in these terms he entirely approved of the punishment that followed.

"That hurt you more than it hurt me," he said mechanically. "I set lines, there might be some fish in the morning. Good-night, Mam." And like a good son he kissed her before he tumbled into bed.

## Chapter Eight

ALEC AWAKENED early. He lay for a while with the soft, monotonous yet uneven rhythm of the waves lulling him towards sleep, wondering what time it was. Then he realised that he had not wound his watch.

He fumbled on the table beside his bed and found it, an expensive flat gold watch with its hands pointing to two minutes past five. The room was full of pale, oyster-coloured light, the furniture had an air of being still asleep but the walls were lively with birds of paradise and roses and pomegranates, against which profusion a variety of watercolours, photographs, heads of children done in red chalk and prints of Highlanders in native costume and warlike attitudes competed for attention.

Alec, sitting up in bed to wind his watch, looked round at the room he had slept in. On a Pembroke table, along with a few books and an inlaid box, was a complicated mechanism, part clock, part barometer. The barometer might be useful but the clock was manifestly a liar; it could not be ten minutes to one. Now his own watch was ticking stupidly, but there was nothing in the sound of the day to help him. No rumble of traffic, no footsteps, no street cries, no chimes, nothing but the rustle of the sea. He tried to guess. Did it feel like six o'clock? Half-past seven? It was no use.

Maura had put a large stone hot-water bottle in his bed last night. He groped for it and his foot came in contact with a clammy slab. Warmth was seeping away from him, and no amount of wriggling would recover the lost snugness.

Suddenly and without decision he was standing at the side of his bed hurrying into his clothes, going over to the window to look out at the pearly sky and sea, and watch the water actually lapping the castle wall beneath him. He leaned out of the window scooping in lungfuls of beautiful cold air, and his eyes seized the shape of a gull as it swooped past him, an arabesque of spread wings with a solid smoothness about its head and the yellow beak dabbed with scarlet. The shape and colour, white and pale grey and yellow, caught his heart as if he saw something exotic.

Farther round he could see a strip of sand with a figure running down it; a boy with gulls wheeling round him, calling their despairing Kee! kee! kee!

Now the boy was throwing stones into the water with a sideways flip that sent them skipping over and under the surface. Alec watched for a minute, then finished dressing and went to find some clock in the castle that would tell him the time.

There was a fine grandfather clock on the landing outside his room, but it was dumb. He explored all the doors that led from the landings. The other bedrooms, small like his own, were all furnished in the taste of a hundred and fifty or more years ago, with half-testers, Recamier day-beds, lyre-back chairs, small elegant mirrors and satin damasks carefully darned at weakened spots. The door farthest from and opposite his own opened on a small drawing-room that Sir Walter Scott might have sat in ; with a French carpet of green, silver and rose, walls of satin stripes hung, like the bed-rooms, with paintings, silhouettes, fans, framed wreaths of seaweeds and immortelles and flower prints. There was a vigorous portrait of a middle-aged man in tartan trews with a gun and a collie, and a still older one of a thin youth with a lace collar and an impudent expression. This, Alec discovered from the inscription, was Aeneas the Jacobite and smuggler, painted by some unknown Dutchman.

The room pleased Alec, even its stuffiness that smelt of dusty rose leaves and orris root. He lifted the lid of a spinet and touched a note ; it uttered a thin, small, nasal sound. In front of the marble fireplace stood a stuffed peacock with outspread tail, mangy but still gorgeous ; and on the mantelpiece were Chelsea figures, vases of bulrushes and a clock in pink Sèvres, silent.

Alec left the brocade and gilt of the drawing-room and mounted higher. The rooms here were small and primitive with stone walls and severe furniture that he guessed to be of a much earlier period than the elegancies below ; here, too, were clocks, all silent.

Now he descended the spiral stairs right down to the hall, the widest space in the whole house, with uneven flagstones, long dark table and chairs and tapestries with strange-looking figures of men and women, deer, wolves, unicorns, leopards and birds. One leopard had had his face darned with colours that did not quite match the original; one eye was different from the other.

There were doors here, too, but Alec ignored them and chose the one that opened on the outer air, noticing with a twinge of guilt that he had not locked it nor pushed home the great bolts.

The castle stood almost in the water, held out on a spoon of rock. He walked along the handle with water lapping among the curtains of brown bladder-wrack on either side. Now his feet crunched on shingle as he hurried towards the boy.

"Hallo," said Danny, who was watching his approach with frank interest.

"Hallo," said Alec.

Danny picked up another stone and sent it skeetering.

"I've got a line laid here," he said, wading deeper into the water.

Alec was turning up his trousers; his shoes stood on the shingle with his socks tucked into them.

"I'll say it's cold," he observed. "What's your name?"

"Danny Rafferty. My mother works to you."

The water was so cold it bit into the bone. Alec kept lifting his feet out one by one to ease the ache of the cold. How white his ankles were beside Danny's!

"Is the Hindoo coming out, too?" Danny asked.

"Shouldn't think so," said Alec.

He was used to the water now and paddled up and down, pushing against the water so that it ruffled like silk against his knees.

"That's my house over yonder," said Danny, pointing to a cottage that seemed to grow out of the cliffside. "My mother's not up yet." As he looked, a curl of smoke puffed from the chimney. "That'll be her now," he said.

"Where are the rest of the houses?" Alec asked. "Where is the Hotel?"

"Round the other side of the castle, beyond the cliff," said Danny. "Wait till I get the fish and I'll show you, eh?"

"Go ahead."

Danny had caught six dabs. He cleaned them at once with a

63

careless speed, throwing the guts to the gulls that swerved and screamed round him.

" The sun's up," he said.

Alec was gorging his eyes as if they were savage, starved animals, gulping great raw mouthfuls of beauty. The sky had opened into a wide blue arch over the green and white of the sea. Danny's skin was the colour of terra cotta, his hair like string, his eyes slaty; and his joints moved with the easy, supple plunges of a puppy, not with the control of a man. He had tied the dead fish together; one of them was still flapping indignantly.

" Are ye coming ? " he asked.

Alec looked now at the boy's face, its broad brow narrowing to a rather long and pointed chin, the mouth wavy and humorous.

" Right, Danny," he said belatedly. " Let's go."

He put on his socks and shoes and they wound up the cliff track past the castle.

" My mother and I was thinking," said Danny, " you might be needing a man about the place likely."

" Do you think so ? " Alec was vague. " What for ? "

" There's things you might need a man for. The like of the boat, for instance. It's a disgrace keeping a boat in the back scullery. And to give a lick of paint to any odd place. Or to climb ladders; you can't drive a woman up ladders, or . . . there's another thing. Mrs. MacLennan of the Hotel, she'll tell you her grandfather was wrong in the insides for years. It was me that put things right, and it wasn't just the mouse nest, it was the whole balance. I put the whole thing in good working order, she'll tell you herself, after it being years disjaskit."

" Good for you."

" Women are no good with clocks."

" I believe you; every clock in the castle is stopped, and I let my own watch run down."

" Then," said Danny invitingly, " is it on ? "

Alec suddenly woke to the realities of the situation. " Oh, I couldn't let you touch Sir Hector's clocks," he said. " I'll try and get one or two going myself, when once I find out the time. Sir Hector's clocks—well, they're in my care, Danny."

" They were in my care while Sir Hector was there," said Danny frostily.

" Is that so ? "

64

" It is.'

" You mean you—looked after them ? "

" Every Saturday morning regular. How would Sir Hector have known the time if his clocks was never wound ? "

" I see. And how much did Sir Hector pay you for this ? "

" It was an arrangement, you see," Danny explained. " Then I got taking out the boat when I needed it, or an odd book in the library. Mrs. MacLennan of the Hotel will tell you."

Alec looked at the boy's serious face and remembered the quick skill of the fish gutting. He had seen surgeons operate with less delicacy.

" It's on," he said.

Danny gave a spring on his toes.

" My mother," he said, " wanted me to have them all ready for you coming, but I knew better. I thought if you found them all run down you'd see the point in having someone regular. I'd better come back with you and do them, it's an awful want not knowing the time of day ! "

Another student of human nature, Alec reflected irritably. But a more likeable one, though he had got the better of him.

" Do you happen to know the time just now ? " he asked.

" I do so." Danny pulled out a watch the size and shape of a half orange. " Sir Hector gave me this," he said. " It's just ten minutes to six."

" Ten minutes to six ? It must be later than that."

" It is not. The sun was just up when you came out."

" Is that so . . . It must have been my watch stopping that wakened me." Alec put his watch forward one minute.

Now they stood on the highest point of the rise and looked down on the village of Fionn.

" Yon's the Hotel," said Danny. " Yon white building with black round the door and windows. That's the Protestant manse just before it."

It was a mere scatter of small houses, stone-built and sometimes whitewashed. A dozen or so white hens, Leghorns and Wyandottes, pecked sedately among the pebbles and grass of the roadside.

" That's the school," Danny went on, " and that's Miss Bradshaw's house beside it. She's the teacher."

They started to walk down into the village, past the Hotel that somehow, Alec felt, was awarded a capital letter in the minds of those who spoke of it, a distinction not bestowed on the castle. Mrs. MacLennan must be a formidable character. Now they passed a small garden so neat that it seemed to have newly received a trim and shave and haircut from the barber.

" Captain Kilbride's," said Danny. " Coming to look through the school windows ? This is the way up."

They looked at a small assortment of desks, a blackboard, a map of Scotland and one of Central Europe. Looking at Danny's face Alec sensed the impatient claustrophobia of his days spent in that room smelling of chalk and varnish.

" Do you like your teacher ? " he asked.

" Yes," said Danny indifferently. Then he added with liveliness, " Look—there she comes ! "

She, Alec saw, was the steamer. They watched her nose her way over the horizon and approach with slow dignity.

" Torquil's got the flag up," said Danny. " Who's going, I wonder."

A rather tattered flag flapped from a mast set in the grass near one of the cottages.

" She used to get into the harbour," Danny explained, " but it's silted up now. Torquil takes passengers out and back ; they can see his flag—they know there's somebody for Oban."

They were strolling down to the harbour now. Torquil was there with his air of deep abstraction, and gave no sign of seeing them till they were beside him ; then he said a grave good-morning.

" Who's going ? " Danny asked.

" The old priest and the minister," said Torquil. " We'll be left without religious guidance if the boat sinks."

" If they both go," said Danny.

" If they both go," Torquil agreed blandly.

" Father Kelly's coming, anyway."

Alec looked along the road and saw a fat black beetle hurrying along on its hind legs. The steamer's siren gave a blast of greeting and the beetle waved to let them know he heard ; he hurried his queer, mincing run.

" Come on, Father ! " Danny shouted, " you'll beat the minister yet ! "

As he spoke the manse door had opened. The minister, a sandy-haired young man who had scarcely left boyhood behind, emerged and hurried down the path, pausing to remonstrate, it

66

seemed, with a woman who hurried after him. Alec watched the pair with interest. The woman was wearing a woollen suit of shapeless cut and the colour of dried mustard. She clutched and shook the young man's arm, talking vehemently, trotting to keep up with his stride. Her son walked with his chin tucked in, embarrassed. Twice he stopped to reason with her and loose her fingers from his sleeve, and she responded with dramatic arguments, pointing to the door, pressing her heart or clasping her hands beseechingly. They could not hear a word, but her whole body was expressive, like that of a skilful film actor, and indeed Alec had the impression of watching a film.

"Good-morning, good-morning!" shouted Father Kelly, interrupting them as they watched the drama. "I'm fair gasping for air like an old broken-winded cuddy. Hey, Danny, put my bag in the boat. You'll be Dr. MacArdal."

He shook hands with Alec; his hands felt soft and fat and were very white, in contrast to his face which was coarse-pored and veined with purple. Whiskers sprouted from his ears and nostrils and the bulbous tip of his nose, but his head when he pushed back his hat to mop it with a ragged handkerchief was bald.

"And have ye had a good crossing? That's fine, that's fine. And you'll have met Captain Kilbride here that has crossed the Atlantic in a sailing vessel more times than he has fingers and toes, eh?"

Alec shook hands with the austere old man who had joined the spectators, and with others whom Father Kelly introduced. They all feigned polite interest in the introductions—or perhaps the interest was genuine, but the real focus of attention was the erratic approach of the minister and his mother. Other figures drifted towards the harbour with seeming casualness, but secret appetite for a stimulating scene.

The steamer hooted again. Torquil looked inquiringly at the minister, who had stopped again.

"Books, indeed!" his mother was exclaiming in a rapid gabble that was now audible to them all. "Books from Oban as if there wasn't plenty in the manse already collecting dust, let alone that Book that should be books enough for you! Come back to your duty, John Forsyth——"

The young man was red but obstinate. They could not hear his reply.

"And what about me?" the woman's voice took up in a high pitch. "What about me wanting to visit Oban? Many's the time I would like a wee change from the kitchen sink, from cooking and cleaning and mending and scouring and scrubbing, working my fingers to the very bone for an ungrateful son—you would never think to ask me to Oban with you—oh, no, John," she shook her head and smiled venomously, "Oh, no, I won't come on an invitation like that, thank you, oh, no—— You ask what I do want? I want you to return to the path of rectitude, John Forsyth, to return to the mother that bore you in sorrow and pain and has had little but sorrow and pain ever since!"

Now they stood beside the group at the harbour, the minister uneasily conscious of the audience, his mother's glowing eyes never straying from his face. The siren hooted again.

"Are ye coming, Mr. Forsyth?" Torquil asked, looking out to sea as if detached from the scene.

"No, he's not," Mrs. Forsyth answered at once without glancing away from her son's face.

"Ye'd better come in then, Father Kelly."

The priest, with Torquil's help, stepped gingerly in and collapsed on a seat; the boat bobbed wildly and settled.

"You'll sink her yet!" said old Captain Kilbride with a sardonic twinkle that was answered by a boastful wag of the head from the priest.

"Now, Mother," said Mr. Forsyth in sudden determination, "let me go." He shook off her arm.

"I'm warning you, John——" She clutched again at him but he wrenched his arm free and ran down the steps, leaping in as the boat pushed off.

Mrs. Forsyth went to the edge of the harbour wall and looked at the boat, then down at the water. Alec was near her; he watched her face, unwillingly fascinated.

She was a woman difficult to describe; perhaps in her fifties, of average build and features, with hair that lay in dull flaps round her head and was drawn into a coil on top. Her skin was pale and glistening and a patch of red lay on each cheek like a postage stamp. She was not ugly, not at least in actual form and features, but her hair, her shapeless mustard-brown suit, her personality that thrust itself before the group of men like something misshapen, gave an effect of deliberately chosen ugliness.

Her burning eyes looked at the boat, then down at the water. A peculiar half-smile sat on her lips. She distended her nostrils with a quick intake of breath, then, with the air of a ballerina, she stepped over the edge and fell with a splash into the water.

Alec, who was nearest, rushed down the steps as she rose to the surface gasping. He managed to catch her hand but she clutched him round the neck, he found himself staring into her hot pupils, his free hand scrabbled for something to hold but after a few seconds of resistance to the force of gravity he lost balance and plunged in too.

The depth of water was only about four feet. He stood up, mortified and angry, gripped her under the arms and heaved her on to the steps where the others pulled her up. As he followed her, trying foolishly to squeeze the water from his cuffs and turn-ups, he noticed Captain Kilbride enjoying the scene with a serene detachment of an onlooker at a play.

" Turn her upside down," he said, watching their efforts to get the apparently unconscious woman on to her feet, and still making silly attempts to flap water from his own clothes. " Get the water out of her lungs."

Mrs. Forsyth resisted this idea by wriggling out of their arms and collapsing on the ground, moaning. The moans rose to wails, and became a succession of screams, regular and mechanical, horribly like the cackling of a triumphant hen. The boat returned while she lay kicking and crowing and John Forsyth hurried up the steps and stood over her trying to draw her to her feet, but her arms flailed his hands out of the way, her screams drowned his low appeals, she refused to open her eyes or acknowledge his presence. There was something obscene in the exhibition ; something that made the spectators want to retch or else, horribly, to laugh.

Alec knew he ought to take command ; he was a doctor. But he felt himself shaking, he shared the agonised shame of the young minister who stood over his mother, helpless. Indeed, they all shared it, except, perhaps, old Captain Kilbride, who smoked placidly. It was Father Kelly who pushed forward at last, coarse and pugnacious.

" Get back ! " he ordered. " Get back, all of ye ! Think shame staring round like a pack of goggling goldfish at a doited old woman showing off her skinny shanks ! "

The screams stopped instantly ; the crowd drew back.

" Come on, Mrs. Forsyth, I'll give ye a hand up."

Father Kelly stooped to help the silent woman, but John Forsyth turned on him a face white with hate.

" I'll thank you," he said in a quivering voice, " to keep your filthy, lecherous hands off my mother ! "

In the silence the ship's siren gave a blast. As if he seized the excuse it gave him Father Kelly turned and ran down to the boat. Torquil set off again.

Mr. Forsyth helped his mother to her feet. He leant over her protectively, his arm round her waist, his other hand holding both of hers as he led her back up the path towards the manse.

" He might have spared you a word of thanks, I'm thinking." Captain Kilbride looked with interest at Alec's dripping clothes.

" Not at all," said Alec idiotically.

" You better come and change, maybe ? " Danny suggested.

They returned together to the castle.

## Chapter Nine

HE HAD changed into dry clothes and had shaved, and now he sat in the parlour downstairs with breakfast before him and a fire crackling fussily and sending out more smoke than heat ; but Maura's pot of hearty Indian tea and Danny's fish, hot from the frying pan, supplied any warmth that was lacking in the fire.

He poured out a third cup and lit a cigarette, looking round vaguely before he realised that what he missed was the morning papers. He was not sure whether papers were available on Fionn at that hour. The clock on the mantelpiece ticked, for Danny had taken time to set that and the landing clock going before he left for school. Alec was still unsure what to make of Danny's calculating subtlety about the clocks. It was an absurd ruse ; anyone with a stronger sense of humour would certainly have laughed at it, but Alec thought of the boy with a mixture of tentative liking and tentative irritation. All his feelings about the island and its inhabitants were misty and unsure. He was there now, and reality was vaster, more puzzling, more complex, less crystalline than imagination.

This irritation he felt towards Danny might be a protective sheath for the affection he sensed under it. Affection was, surely, premature. Besides, a boy of fifteen was capable of exploiting an affection that was insufficiently guarded.

Fact is, Alec mused, I'm not much good at human relationships, and I've got to start a new set of relationships over here. Back home I had plenty of acquaintances, and Bertie Newnham for a friend. But Bertie was a school friend, and not my best friend at school by any means, but I seemed to lose touch with the others. Bertie and I are friends more from habit than from real understanding. And I've made no real friends since school, well, except Sir Hector, he's a friend. But that's a poor record. . . .

He threw his cigarette butt into the fire and pushed back his chair. He must write to Sir Hector and tell him about his arrival and his eventful morning. Tell him, too, about Kirpu. But where was Kirpu?

He went through to the kitchen to inquire, but when he got there he stood idly enjoying the sight of Maura's bronze hair, her generous figure in its faded cotton wrapper, her fingers slicing chunks off the potatoes and dropping them when peeled into a black pot. He remembered his mother's perpetual warfare against Betty's wastefulness in peeling vegetables just as Maura was doing. You couldn't teach ' them ' economy.

" Did you make a good breakfast ? " she inquired without turning from the muddy sink.

" Yes, thanks. I suppose I can get daily papers somewhere ? "

" Twice a week from Oban, if you order them."

" Oh. They come when the steamer calls, of course." He digested this evidence of his isolation, then asked, " Where's Kirpu got to ? "

" Och, he's not himself at all," said Maura. " He's just hanging. He's not well," she translated, seeing Alec's expression of alarm. " I took him in a cup of tea, the soul, and there he was holding on to his head. It's the flu, likely, folks from the mainland often bring flu and such things, but the air here cures them. It's clean air, Father Kelly says, not breathed to death like the air in Glasgow."

" I'd better see him," Alec murmured. " By the way, what do you do about mailing letters, here ? "

" Letters, is it. Torquil MacVean's the postman. He'll take a letter to Oban any day if it's in a hurry. If it's not in a hurry you post it at the Post Office at Mrs. Leatham's shop." She dropped the last potato into the pot and turned to explain the technique. " There's a sort of a hole in the wall, you see, and you stick them in there. You'll know it by it being painted red. We call it the letter box."

" Is that so," said Alec.

" And it's cleared twice a week regular."

" That's an advantage."

" It is," Maura agreed. " And then you only have to pay the stamp. If you get Torquil to go to Oban there's the fare there and back extra."

" Cheaper to send a wire or a cable, I should think."

" But ye'd have to go to Oban for that."

" Can't you telephone it from here ? "

" You could if there was a telephone."

" Isn't there a telephone on Fionn ? "

" There is not," said Maura firmly. " Sir Hector can't abide telephones. He says they lead to nothing but a lot of talk."

" He's quite right," said Alec. All the same he was amused that the old sybarite who so delighted in luxurious plumbing should be intolerant of the pleasures of others whose delight was in talking.

He went to the small room off the kitchen corridor where Kirpu was, in Maura's phrase, hanging. Kirpu was asleep on his back, head on one side, lips parted, frowning a little. His breathing was quick and a pulse throbbed visibly in his neck ; Alec counted the pulse without touching him, a hundred and twelve beats to the minute. He was pitifully thin. Life had not gone well with him, Alec surmised, since the days when Smith Bahadur had been the presiding genius in it. He had had the air and instincts of refinement and life on board ship as a member of the crew could not have been a pleasant experience for him.

Alec opened the window without waking him and returned to the parlour.

The morning that had dawned so charmingly had grown dull ; specks of moisture floated against the windows. He looked up at the sky with a townsman's mistrust. He wanted to explore his island but he had already had one drenching that morning, and the memory of cold, trickling clothes, of feet clopping in watery shoes, wrists chafed by wet cuffs, disinclined him for further essays in discomfort. It had, besides, been a humiliating introduction to the inhabitants of Fionn, and Alec, however much he believed himself indifferent to his fellow men, hated to look ridiculous and shrank from the humorous inquiries he might meet in the village.

He fidgeted at the parlour window, wandered to the fire, stared at a conversation piece cut in black paper. It held his interest for a minute. There were a father and mother, six children, a parrot in a cage, a dog, a cat and kittens and an urn full of flowers, and the artist had fixed them in decorous, silhouetted stillness; but they could never have remained like that for even one second. Father's didactic, upraised hand, mother's vigorous profile and ribboned and feathered mob-cap, children, toys, animals, suggested constant motion, vivacity and noise. Now the descendants of this clamorous family were reduced to one old man and his nephew. Their house was occupied by a stranger, a bachelor.

Alec turned from the silhouette. The silence was hushed by the waves outside. He decided again that he must write to Sir Hector, but instead of going upstairs for his writing materials he wandered into the library, an autumnal room full of old calf and vellum and crimson morocco, its walls, like every other wall in the castle, dangling with watercolours, daguerreotypes, intaglios and prints wherever bookcases left a free space. Alec stood in the middle of the floor with his hands in his pockets, too restless to examine either books or pictures. Time stretched before him like a yawn.

It was a relief to hear a man's voice in the hall, and Maura's replying welcome. He could not hear their words, only their voices, and he listened to the sound with the simplicity of a child at a loose end. The voices faded suddenly, as if the talkers had left the hall and closed a door. Then Maura's footsteps approached the library. The door opened.

"I looked for you upstairs," Maura said. "I'll give you a fire here if you want—— That's Mr. Dochy come to call on you and brought you a pair of pigeons." She held up the lovely feathery corpses with a smile of satisfaction. "I put him in the parlour," she ended.

Alec was already on his way to the parlour, eager to meet Dochy.

He hardly knew what he had expected. Not this giant with broad shoulders and small head whose eyes, as they shook hands, looked at him over half-moon lenses with an expression of calm curiosity. They stared at each other, each taking an inventory of the other's appearance. Alec's impression was of physical bigness

73

that was matched by psychic vigour; Dochy MacArdal would be noticeable anywhere. He was handsome, but not in any glossy magazine style. His brown curls were receding from his brow and thinning on his crown, his head was too small for his body and so were his hands and feet, yet his proportions had a rightness of their own; he might have personified some energetic drawing of Chesterton's.

"Welcome to Fionn," he said at last.

"Thanks," said Alec. "And welcome to Fionn Castle——"

He had a qualm as he said it, remembering Sir Hector's odd antipathy to his nephew, and a second wave of doubt struck him as he realised that the castle would one day belong to Dochy; his welcome might sound impertinent, for, after all, it was he who was the interloper.

"Thank you," said Dochy without irony. "I hope you're going to enjoy your stay here. You'll find it quiet, too quiet perhaps."

"I like quiet," said Alec.

"Well, you're in the right place." Dochy's voice was restless, as if underlying thoughts were struggling for expression. "And just wait till winter sets in. Nothing happens here. The place is cut off from life and activity. Though," he grinned suddenly and glanced again over his half-moon eyes, "your baptism this morning was hardly a good omen for quietness, eh? You may be the fore-runner of some tremendous emotional upheaval on Fionn."

"It was an unpleasant scene." Alec felt awkward and covered his awkwardness by producing cigarettes. Dochy accepted one and sat down near the window. Alec gave him a light and sat nearer the fire.

"I've never witnessed it," said Dochy. "I'm told Mrs. Forsyth throws a scene every time the minister tries to escape. So when he trysts to meet Torquil at the harbour, word goes round and the Fionnachs get ready for the show."

Alec flushed. "I don't share their notion of fun," he said angrily.

"I don't say they would call it fun. But it is an event. Have you any idea—no, you won't have, you romantic American—what wastes of boredom these islanders live in? No cinema, no politics, no strikes or lock-outs, no Salvation Army band, no football matches or razor-gangs or Girl Guides, nothing but an occasional winter ceilidh and an occasional hysterical scene from the minister's

74

mother. Apart from that, one day follows another. If anyone shows initiative it's pretty soon squashed by a snowstorm of forms from some Government office, or by——"

He did not complete the alternative, but puffed an angry breath through his nose and stared at the sea.

"The son looks pretty young to be a minister," said Alec presently.

"Yes. Younger than his age—and older, too. Well, what could you expect—only son, apron-strings, vampire-mother. I don't suppose he'll ever have the guts to escape."

"It's not so easy as you think."

"Dare say not. I know nothing about it, except from the outside. Do you?"

Dochy gave him a grave regard over the semi-circular lenses. Alec's feelings tangled him, but to his relief the other did not wait long for the answer that failed to crystallise.

"You know more than I do, anyway ; you saw the episode, and it jangled your nerves. Don't take other men's griefs too much to heart, you can't live their lives for them—nobody can break John Forsyth's prison for him but himself. But I want you to meet him to-morrow. He's a nice lad, and perhaps a bit of outside company will help him. Will you come to lunch to-morrow, at the Hotel?"

"Why, thanks, I'll be delighted," said Alec.

"Good. I'll see you, then, about twelve-thirty." Dochy stood up and Alec accompanied him to the door.

"But—aren't you an only son yourself?" Alec asked, having pondered this question before putting it.

"Only survivor of two brothers and a sister."

"Oh, I'm sorry. I didn't know—only about your parents."

"Well, I was the lucky one. My father was a planter in Malaya, and I was sent to school in Edinburgh, so I was out of it when a servant ran amok and murdered the whole family. My young brother, Ivor, was due to start school just three months later, but, well, they were all killed."

"How horrible."

"Yes. Uncle Hector wanted to adopt me, but I wouldn't have it. I was given the choice of living with him or with another uncle, my mother's brother ; and I chose him. And flourished exceedingly, went into his line of business and so on." Dochy's voice was dry, but Alec asked no more questions.

They lingered still in the doorway, Dochy adjusting the set of his battered hat.

"Sir Hector thought you were in the States a few weeks ago."

"I was."

"You—didn't look in on him."

"I'm not *persona grata* with the old boy."

"Perhaps because he doesn't know you."

"Doesn't give himself a chance." Dochy smiled satirically at Alec and strode off. The tide of his energy ebbed more slowly than his physical presence had done.

Alec shut the door against the cold, salty air, went briskly upstairs for writing paper and settled down in the parlour to write to Sir Hector at last. Once he had started his pen ran smoothly; he forgot the restlessness that fretted his mind, the suspicion that sidled persistently up to the edge of consciousness—the recognition that he had changed an overcrowded life for an empty one. He described his landing, his impressions of Glasgow, his meeting with Kirpu. He made an amusing picture of the teasing porter at Oban fobbing him off gravely while Torquil waited, a lanky figure looped over the railings by one arm. He quoted Maura's description of a letter box and was about to launch on Dochy's visit when Maura came in to lay the table.

"Maura," he asked idly as he cleared his scribbled sheets from the table, "Is there really no doctor on Fionn?"

"There is not," she replied, dashing his hopes of company. "We never need a doctor because there's Father Kelly. Before Father Kelly came there was old Mrs. MacPherson, but she died. But you're not ill, are ye?"

"No, no."

"Because if you are, get Father Kelly to physic you. He makes no difference for Protestants, and they say he's cleverer than most doctors. It was him that prognosed it when Tommy Cromarty took the Alec Passion."

"The—Alec Passion, did you say?"

"Likely you don't come across it in America, but we have it here, and if it's bad they open you up and cut it out of you. They had to open up Tommy Cromarty."

"Father Kelly did?"

"No, no, he sent him to Oban to the Cottage hospital. Mind you, I believe Father Kelly could have done it right enough, only his eyesight's wearing thin. They said themselves, in Oban, they couldn't have prognosed it a bit better than he did. He's a wonderful man, is Father Kelly, up to all the dodges."

She went out. Alec remembered his glimpse of Father Kelly that morning, hurrying towards the harbour with little tottering steps, fat, gross and hearty. He remembered his confident brutality in treating the hysterical woman, and how the confidence collapsed like a punctured tyre at John Forsyth's invective, "Keep your filthy, lecherous hands off my mother!"

He hardly knew, now, whether he looked forward to his meeting with the young minister at lunch to-morrow. It might prove an agony of embarrassment. Of course, Father Kelly would not be there. Perhaps it was as well that they should meet each other quickly, in the presence of a third person who had not witnessed the scene. Dochy would help them over the hurdle of awkwardness.

Musing over the ugly affair, he found himself fitting words and epithets to it more skilfully than he had done in his letter to Sir Hector. He thought of rewriting it, but rejected the idea. It was trivial after all, that he should find the exact verb for Father Kelly's mincing, toddling walk. All the same it kept nosing its way into his attention. For his interests here were doomed to triviality and he must make the most of them. After all he had always been conscious of the fascination of trivialities, the superstitions of a coloured girl, the small enigmas of Dog's usually predictable behaviour, the originality of a man who could kick a tin can all down the street, swearing . . . He had thrust the interest aside in deference to his mother's nobler scale of values. Here he could be as childish as he liked, for there would be nothing but trivialities to occupy him. A dangerous thought! But he had chosen to make this experiment and he must go on with it.

As Maura entered with a steaming dish of pigeons an idea struck him with cheerful clarity. He would start a diary!

"You must be starving," said Maura, dumping down the tray. "I am," said Alec.

# Chapter Ten

It WAS half-past twelve and three figures were converging on the Hotel.

An invitation to lunch was something altogether out of the normal pattern of life on Fionn, and John Forsyth was in a state of pleasant anticipation. He shut the manse gate carefully, turned and gave an almost imperceptible nod in response to his mother's wave from the doorway. She looked humble and pathetic waving him off, and he knew that her own meal would be a cup of tea and a scone ; she said she only cooked a good meal for his sake. Nevertheless he was not mollified. Every victory won by her hysterical love made him more shamefully her slave, but drove him each time a degree nearer to some unknown breaking-point or revelation. He was ignorant of what nature it would take. He only dimly sensed that under the surface his enslaved self was burrowing like an entombed creature towards light, or towards some dénouement that might be more horrifying than darkness.

But he could do nothing either to speed or slacken the activity of the tunneller ; he was only aware of it in disturbing flashes and then, in confusion and bewilderment, he prayed for singleness of heart, for patience and submission to God's will.

Often he felt that if he could get away for a while, away from the electrical, stifling atmosphere of the manse, he might breathe in a draught of clean, healing air and see his way more clearly, either to escape altogether or to return to take up the burden again, this time deliberately and surely with more courage and grace. But escape was always barred, even escape for one day.

Just now he welcomed the distraction of Dochy MacArdal's invitation. He liked Dochy. He was all there to see, all of him above board, no thoughts hidden under. He blethered a lot, but it was good, wholesome blethers, and he was even less of a snob than Sir Hector, who sometimes gave you a queer look.

78

He reached the Hotel first, but waited outside the white-washed house with its black-framed door and windows, for he saw Dr. Alec MacArdal thirty yards or so down the road.

John Forsyth felt no need to express any gratitude to Alec for his rescue of his mother, nor remorse for his wetting. It was natural that he should be grateful and he assumed that his feeling was known. Had there been the least swagger of authority in Alec's manner he would have hated him; he was compelled to endure his mother's tyranny but no one else's; but Alec, both yesterday when he dripped on the harbour, and to-day as he approached the Hotel, showed only a slight diffidence.

Alec, who had anticipated awkwardness at his meeting with the minister, found his expression one of untroubled friendliness.

"Good-morning, Doctor," said John.

They shook hands and went in together.

The hall inside was dark. Mrs. MacLennan's taste in indoor decoration was Calvinistic. Chocolate and dark olive green were good colours from every viewpoint. Nothing frivolous about them; rich and satisfying; and, guests being what they were, you had to choose colours that wouldn't show the dirt where their shoulders rubbed on the stairs or their hands pushed the doors or their pens spattered the carpets.

It took Alec's eyes a few minutes to adjust to the gloom, and what they first saw was a white-haired, spectacled face and a pair of fluttering hands apparently dissociated from any body; these, however, were attached to an old lady in black who was engaged, it seemed, in an eccentric dance. Three running steps to one side, clap hands; three running steps to the other side, clap hands; pirouette twice, clap hand above the head.

"This is Mistress MacLennan," said Mr. Forsyth. "Mrs. MacLennan, here's Doctor MacArdal."

Mrs. MacLennan brushed her hands together and advanced.

"How do ye do, Doctor," she said composedly. "You'll excuse me chasing the moths. I just can't pass them and that's the first one this year, terrible early for them, isn't it? Are you bothered with moths in America?"

"Why, yes, I believe so," said Alec. "I've heard my mother talk about them."

"Aren't they fair outrageous! Hang up your coat, Doctor, on the hook beside the minister. They keep me on the hop ever

79

since I had my best bedroom carpet eaten alive—literally eaten alive!"

"Too bad. I want to thank you for the scones you sent by Maura, Mrs. MacLennan, they were wonderful scones."

"I'm glad you enjoyed them. And had you a nice crossing?"

"Yes, thanks."

"Well, that's nice now, and I hope you have a nice rest on Fionn. Here's Mr. Dochy to welcome you both."

Dochy was still in the tweeds he had worn yesterday. Alec wondered if his gaberdine suit was too fine for Fionn, but was comforted by the sober respectability of Mr. Forsyth's black.

"Come into the snug," said Dochy. "We'll have a sherry, and Mrs. MacLennan will send Father Kelly in when he arrives."

Alec glanced at the minister, but saw no marked change in his expression at the news that the priest was to be a fourth. His own heart sank a little; he felt the occasion could hardly pass smoothly after the insults of yesterday.

They wandered into the small, rexined and linoleumed room that Dochy called the snug and Mrs. MacLennan, when she remembered, the lounge. Now Alec thought he could feel constraint creeping up. Mr. Forsyth cleared his throat; the other two looked at him but he said nothing. The drinks arrived, John cleared his throat again and this time he spoke.

"It's turned out a fair morning," he said.

"Just that," Dochy agreed. "Well, Doctor—to a good holiday on Fionn."

They tasted their drinks.

"What kind of weather do you get in your part of the world?" asked the minister helpfully.

"Well, we get it cold in winter and hot in summer. We get it more extreme than you do."

"I've heard of them getting it so hot you could fry an egg on the pavement," John suggested.

"That's what they say," Alec smiled, "though I've never seen it done."

"Not on the pavement," Dochy interrupted, half-absently. "On the sidewalk."

Willing to be amused, they all laughed, and Dochy began to sing. Alec, hearing the tune with a surprised feeling of emotion, joined in.

> " East side, West side,
>     All around the town,
> Boys and girls together,
>     Brooklyn Bridge is falling down !
> Boys and girls together,
>     Me and Mary O'Rorke,
> We trip the light fantastic on
>     The sidewalks of New York ! "

Father Kelly hurried in with an expression of eagerness.

" I'm late, I'm late ! " he exclaimed. " Good-day to ye all. And here you are all singing and hilarious, and me out of it all. How are ye, Doctor ; it takes an American to set the minister singing in Fionn."

" I didn't know the song," Mr. Forsyth said, the film of gravity returning to his pink face.

" You made a good shape at it, then."

" I was not singing."

" Now, Father, what are you going to have ? " Dochy asked.

" What are the rest of you having. Sherry. It'll be a good dry sherry I expect and I'll have the same. Pink fizz for the minister, ts, ts, think shame, Mr. Forsyth, the water at Cana was never turned to pink fizz."

" It's a nice Tio Pepe," said Dochy, " Mrs. MacLennan can always produce a good wine."

" For anybody that knows its worth," Father Kelly agreed.

Alec feared at first that the teasing Father Kelly was inflicting on John Forsyth might cause an unpleasant flare. It was, after all, a slender revenge for the minister's insulting phrase of yesterday ; but the insult itself might have been based on good reason ; he had no idea of that. He was glad of the easy, seemingly absent-minded control that Dochy kept of the talk and hoped that it would be adequate. The good sherry induced a dreaminess in him that, after the faint nostalgia of the street-song, tended towards melancholy ; and he rose to the surface suddenly to discover that Father Kelly had chosen him as a new victim.

" Mistress MacLennan is busy," Mr. Forsyth had said, " for the time of year."

" She is so," Father Kelly agreed, " and Maura Rafferty stolen from her an all. But she thrives on work, she thrives on it. The older she gets in years the bigger a zest she brings to her work. More than I do."

" I feel rather ashamed of having Maura," said Alec.

" Not a bit of you, you feel no shame at all, I can see with a flick of the eye at you—no shame at all, depriving a hard-working woman of her help. Besides, it's a change for Maura."

" It was an understood thing," Dochy rescued Alec, " Maura was only lent to Mrs. MacLennan while the castle was empty. Mrs. MacLennan told me so herself, so don't worry," he grinned. " But if you want an occasional taste of good plain cooking come over to the Hotel. I'd guess Maura's cooking to be a bit unpredictable."

" Take my advice, Doctor." Father Kelly reinforced Dochy's advice with a plump white forefinger. " Get the butcher to send your meat direct to Mrs. MacLennan and come over here for your dinner every day. Maura's all right for breakfast or high tea, she's a good, fine girl, but she cooks everything in the frying pan."

" I believe it's what Sir Hector did," said Mr. Forsyth. " It's very reasonable, considering the times. Three and six for a three-course dinner and sixpence extra for coffee. A scandalous price in one way, still she has to make a profit and it's less than you'd pay on the mainland—I'm told."

Dochy's eyes twinkled but he said nothing.

" Of course, that's the price if you make a steady arrangement," said the minister hurriedly. " It'll be more for just a casual once in a whiler."

" And that's food alone," said Father Kelly with a wink. " Pink fizz is extra."

" Well, come along and taste Mrs. MacLennan's cooking," said Dochy, standing. " And choose for yourself between Maura's cooking and Mrs. MacLennan's." The look he gave Alec was equivalent to Father Kelly's wink.

" Maura certainly cooked those pigeons perfectly," said Alec.

" That's good. I told her exactly what to do and dared her to frizzle them."

" I hear your Indian's out of sorts," said John as they made their way to the dining-room. " Sounds like a chill on the liver. I could let you have some calomel or salts. Not that I'd interfere—but you might not have the stuff handy."

82

Alec, amused and appreciative, accepted the offer of calomel. It might lift or jolt Kirpu out of his depression.

They bowed or nodded to two ladies at a table in the window, and to two youths in corduroys and nailed boots at another, and sat down.

"Do you play bridge, Doctor?" Father Kelly asked. "That's good, that's good, eh, now we've got a four all but one. We'll need to teach the minister, eh?"

John Forsyth raised a solemn hand, refusing the offer.

"Do your flock good," said the priest. "All the good in the world, to see the minister playing with the deevil's pictur' books. Knock some of the mimness and holiness out of them, turn them into decent human beings!"

"Pay no heed to him," said Mrs. MacLennan, appearing with their plates of soup. "Think shame," she said severely, "putting ideas into folk's heads!"

"And where else would you put them?" Father Kelly swivelled round truculently to face her.

"Some heads can stand them, others can't." She removed the coffee cups and cutlery from the table that the boys had vacated and whisked out.

"There's a lot in what she says," said Dochy seriously. "Some heads can stand an unlimited amount of ideas. You could say, in some cases, they cancel each other out, or they produce an immunity. Like bacilli. I've heard it said that if an infant is protected against every disease germ it dies of the first one it meets. That so?"

Alec hesitated, unable to summarise his views in a plain yes or no.

"To a certain extent," he said. "It's rather a dangerous hypothesis to build into a principle—medically at least."

"Well, I don't know. It's always the people who have kept their brains tight shut against anything in the nature of an idea who, when an idea does get inserted, turn into crazy fanatics. The Christian Scientists, the British Israelites, the Rosicrucians and so on."

"All Protestant fads, you'll notice. They miss the solid doctrine they'd find in the Catholic faith and they go haring off after some invention of their own—and it's got hold of a bit of truth every time, mark you, but without proportion, without discipline."

"I don't accept your explanation," said John Forsyth flatly.

" No ecclesiastical authority is a substitute for individual conscience and responsibility."

" If you act on your principle," said Alec, " you would go on giving filthy, infected milk to children on the plea that the menagerie of bacilli would cancel each other out, or produce a natural immunity."

" Or, if not, it would at least ensure the survival only of the fittest."

" I'm afraid not," said Alec. " It would ensure the survival of a large percentage of half-fit, half-alive children who would reach a listless maturity and breed—they always breed—a second generation of weaklings, and so on it would go."

" In my opinion," said Father Kelly, " there would be none of these fads and cults and craziness, no and no need for the lunatic asylums either, if everybody returned to the Holy Catholic Faith."

" Of course, it simplifies things if you can burn the folks that disagree with you," said Mr. Forsyth.

" As that harridan Elizabeth did to the Catholics." Father Kelly's face grew a shade redder.

" Oh, Elizabeth, I'm not saying any good about her," said the minister hastily, " but what about Bloody Mary, what about the *auto da fe*, what about the Inquisition—the *Holy* Inquisition ? That's the fold you'd ask us all to return to ? "

" Well," Dochy broke in easily, " the best thing we can say about all parties in those days is that they each had their own point of view and could see no other. Whereas nowadays, we can sit round a table, Father Kelly and Mr. Forsyth and the doctor and myself, and discuss microbes and see each other's viewpoint with the greatest geniality." He glanced at Alec. " By the way, the cows on this island were tested some months ago by a Government vet, and I understand the result was hair-raising."

" But the children are healthy enough," put in Mr. Forsyth.

" Healthy enough but few in number," said Father Kelly. " I was calling on Nell Patrick the other day. Nell's twenty-eight and she has two children. Her mother had thirteen. Nell won't catch up on that record. And old Mrs. Kilbride, she and the captain had seven children. They've only got four grandchildren. Four ! "

" And none of the children or grandchildren on the island," said Dochy.

" The island's dying," said John Forsyth.

84

" And for no reason," Dochy exclaimed with a gesture of his whole body. " It's just this . . . this fatal . . . lassitude. The lassitude of the West Highlands. They're dying of sheer lassitude, it's too much of a bother to go on struggling to live."

" Inbreeding ? " Alec suggested.

" M-m—perhaps there is some, but hardly enough to account for it. And partly the evil legacy of the Clearances, of absentee landlords, of semi-anglicised chieftains who lost their own roots in the clan and became useless parasites . . . That doesn't apply on Fionn, of course. Though in a way——"

He stopped doubtfully.

" I'd like to see Fionn revive," he began again. " And why shouldn't she ? We've got the natural resources, we only need initiative to revive what we've lost and use modern methods where they're applicable. That won't happen in Uncle Hector's time, of course."

Alec heard a chafing frustration in his voice, and wondered.

The two ladies at the table in the window rose. The fat, pretty, middle-aged one fluttered her eyelashes as she bowed. The younger one did not look towards them. Mrs. MacLennan brought their coffee and cleared the debris from the other tables.

" I'm surprised," said Alec tentatively, " to hear that Sir Hector —stands in the way of progress here. He rather championed it in the United States. Plumbing—he thought it was our great cultural achievement." He smiled at the memory.

" Don't ask me to explain Uncle Hector," said Dochy without bitterness. " I sometimes think he's just a born arguer. If I say black he says white, and so on. Have you noticed the plumbing in the castle. Aeneas's plumbing ! "

" He sounded rather hopeless about the chance of getting Fionn modernised. Permits, and labour costs, and storms——"

" In other words, stop before you start. The defeatism of the West Highlands."

" Ah, Sir Hector's not a fool," said Father Kelly, leaning forward with the frown of a man who mistrusts his power to explain something he only half understands. " He's maybe wrong in his ideas, but if so he's not wrong because of defeatism or indifference."

" Explain him," Dochy invited genially.

" I'm trying to mind the long argument he let off at me when he said good-bye, before he set off for the States. He took a wide

85

sweep in his talk. He had a notion that men had taken a wrong turning somewhere. Not just in our parts here. All Europe. Back about the eighteen hundreds. He had a great spite at machinery, you see. Machinery, he said, was fair damnation to the soul of man. It began by destroying natural skills. Spinning and weaving, sailing, agriculture—men and animals, too, were becoming more and more superfluous, he said. Men were turning into servants of machines instead of sons of God and of nature. Engineers and mechanics instead of sailors and fishermen and farmers and craftsmen. We've lost creativeness, and creatureliness too, except in a few rare cases, poets and the like. We're not all poets."

He rubbed his nose and pulled at the springy hairs that flourished on it. Nobody interrupted.

"Ye see, he had the idea that men and beasts lived in the same rhythm as nature, they took their natural subsistence from the sun and the soil and the sea. But machinery has no idea of the seasons. Machinery never sleeps, day or night, it's always horribly ready for action. Machinery tears up the soil and the sea and puts nothing back in. And the apotheosis of the machine is War, bigger and better War."

They had all listened intently.

"But you can't put back the clock," said Dochy restlessly. "It's idealistic dreaming to talk like that. And—muddle-headedness. Machinery has brought release from slavery to millions. It's not machinery that's evil, it's wrong use of it! Don't tell me it would be evil to give Mrs. MacLennan electricity instead of oil lamps!"

"Maybe," suggested Mr. Forsyth, clearing his throat, "there might be more to it than that. Granted, machinery has given mankind leisure. Is leisure a good thing? There was far less gambling and betting and football pools in the days before there was all this leisure. I've seen the pool coupons in the very hearths and homes of this island!"

"Ach, where's the harm," muttered the priest.

John did not deign to answer.

"Though I'll admit it's a symptom," Father Kelly conceded. "There's an emptiness in men's minds that turns to an itch for something they haven't got, and they think it's money. As if money would satisfy the hunger. But there's no good in treating the symptom for the disease. Get to the roots."

86

" And what do you diagnose wrong with the roots ? " Alec asked demurely.

Father Kelly gave him a shrewd look.

" You can pull my leg for using your medical jargon," he said, " and maybe getting it mixed. But I'll tell ye what's wrong. Lack of discipline. All this business of my conscience being as good as the next man's. Pack of damned nonsense. It's precious few," he stuck his head forward belligerently, " I say it's precious few that have the least idea what's in their consciences at all, without some help from them that's experienced in digging the truth out of consciences. And I'm not talking about your fancy psyche-artists."

Alec flushed. The priest's little pig-eyes saw too much for his comfort.

" I'm sorry you think I stake any claim to—to exclusive use of medical jargon by medical men," he said, and added placatingly : " Besides, I understand you are an expert diagnostician, and I hear you spotted a rare disease called," he hesitated, " the Alec Passion."

Father Kelly's aggressive stare turned to amusement, and he began to heave gently with laughter that seemed to have its source in his stomach.

" Alec Passion. That would likely be Maura Rafferty." He chuckled a little more, then wiped a hand down his purple face, restoring gravity as if by a conjuring trick. " The Iliac Passion, Doctor," he said, " is the old name for what's now called Appendicitis."

" Well, is that so ! " Alec was entertained. " Still, quite a bit of diagnosis, I'd say."

" You see," said the priest, " when there's no doctor in the place, like on a mission outpost or an island the like of this, it's the clergy that take his place. Mr. Forsyth here doctors the Protestants, God help them. I dose the Catholics. Luckily, there's one of my brothers a doctor; I got him to send me some of his old text books. Oh, I've a talent for it, I tell you ! "

" I'll know where to come if I'm ill."

" And where will you come ? " Father Kelly asked demurely.

" Why—I don't know ! " Alec glanced at the rivals helplessly. " I'll have to toss a penny after all."

Father Kelly was delighted to have got his own back, and the others laughed too.

" Let's go back to the snug," Dochy suggested.

"But I'll have to be getting back," said Mr. Forsyth. "My mother's alone in the house, and it's getting on for three o'clock."

"D'ye tell me that!" the priest exclaimed, astonished.

"No, don't break it up yet," Dochy urged, "we've only got begun."

"I've got an idea," said Alec. "Let's all go over to the castle and carry on the discussion there. And perhaps," he suggested, "I could persuade Mr. MacArdal to tell me a few things about some of its treasures."

This idea pleased everyone; even Mr. Forsyth felt that his mother might support solitude for a little longer, and with hats pressed down on their heads and coats buttoned up against the wind the four men took the road to the castle.

As they climbed the green cliff that screened the castle from the village for all the world like a great pig lying between them, they returned to the wrangle about the inherent evil of machinery.

"I believe there's something in it," said Alec.

"Before the days of the machine," said Dochy, "there was almost universal squalor, witchcraft, trial by torture, a life of misery for the masses and of merely tolerable comfort for a very few."

"But you can't show that machinery had anything to do with enlightenment."

"Yes, I think it had," said Dochy slowly. "You know they say you can only get rid of one idea by another idea. Well, it was a machine, after all, that made the spread of enlightenment possible— Caxton's printing press. And I believe Fionn could return to life under an intelligent use of the machines of civilisation."

"Ah, but," Father Kelly put in, "your uncle would argue with you still about that—not just the machinery bit. His view was that you can't revive a dying race by any help and advice and energy from the outside. The energy has to come from within. And it won't, it won't rise spontaneously as long as the dying remnant are prodded and poked at, and interfered with by thick-headed governments or thick-headed private individuals. It might flame into new life left to itself. Not otherwise."

After that they said no more but trudged over the crest and descended to the little castle standing proudly out on its spoon of rock.

"Well," said Dochy, "I see you've settled down in Aunt Jane's parlour!"

# Chapter Eleven

"THE WIND'S getting up," said Maura.

Kirpu looked out of the window and shivered. The sea was dark grey and the wind was flicking spray from the white curls of foam.

"Lucky for you you crossed when it was calm. We often get rumpled seas at this time of year. We've had it fine and quiet this year, though."

"I am glad it was quiet when we came. It was already too motionful for me, and if it had been worse I should probably have died."

"Och, folks don't die of seasickness. You're better now, aren't ye? You'll need to eat more and get some fat on you. Have a hot pancake."

Maura swung her girdle in an arc to give the heat to a new segment, and tossed a golden pancake over to him. The others she laid in an overlapping row on a cloth she had ready for them, covering them with the free end of the cloth and giving the empty girdle a rub with a knob of suet before spooning more dollops of batter on it.

Kirpu ate his pancake and watched the heat bring up great thick bubbles in the yellow batter.

"We make pancakes something like that in India," he said. "But they are thinner and dark in colour, and they are very good——"

Maura listened to his description of Indian cooking with a kindly air, pleased that the poor heathen was so much improved in health and spirits.

"Have another," she suggested presently. "Try a bit of butter with it, you'll find it an improvement. Danny's a great one for pancakes to his tea."

"When will Danny return?"

" The school comes out at a quarter to four but that's not to say he'll be in then. He goes off on the stravaig and comes in when he feels like it. The doctor didn't tell you when he would be in himself, did he ? "

Kirpu tilted his head, listening.

" I hear him now," he said, disappearing rapidly to open the door for Alec and his three guests.

They blew in on a gust of wind and found Kirpu waiting to receive their coats and hats, bowing with a grace that gave distinction to Alec's hospitality.

" And how are you feeling now, son ? " Father Kelly asked, clapping Kirpu on the shoulder.

" Better, thank you," said Kirpu.

" Let's have a look at you. H'm. It's nothing but a bad cold you've had, that's all. That's a cold herpes breaking out on your lip. You'll be fine now, the worst's over by the time the herpes breaks out, eh, Doctor ? I might get Danny to run along for some ointment I've got, the very thing for a herpes, stops it spreading. Is Danny in from school yet ? "

" He is not back yet, sir."

" I'll see him when he comes in. Tell him I want to see him and don't let him be sneaking off."

Kirpu bowed again and departed.

" I thought all these Indians said Sahib," Father Kelly remarked as he joined the others. " He's a nice quiet soul, a decent lad."

" I noticed that," said Alec. " It's rather a relief—I could never live up to Sahib. I believe he was with a rather original Englishman for a while, called Smith. He has a great admiration for him. Perhaps he stopped the Sahib, or perhaps he copied his brilliant brother who was at Oxford."

" Smith—I've heard the name before," said Dochy. " I'm not being funny," he added as they laughed, but smiling himself. " He was an original all right—— Well, this is Aunt Jane's parlour we're in."

" Yes, do tell us about the lady."

But Dochy was looking round the walls with a puzzled air.

" Where's the portrait ? " he murmured.

" Why—I believe I remember hearing Sir Hector say something —was it by Allan somebody ? Ramsay, that's it. Why, I think he said it was sold—but maybe I'm wrong," he added hastily.

Dochy MacArdal said nothing and his face showed no change of expression; but Alec sensed a sudden rigidity in him, the stillness of someone who refuses to show his pain. He had seen and admired a similar self-control in a patient.

"It's a charming room," he said, "cosier than the lovely drawing-room upstairs. Why is it called Aunt Jane's parlour?"

Dochy relaxed and went forward to the cut-paper conversation piece.

"Aunt Jane," he said, "was the sister of this old character here." He pointed to Papa. "She was quite a celebrity on a small scale, a little creature with a hunchback, but a wit, a lively, clever little person, quite a figure in Edinburgh society. She was Uncle Hector's great-aunt," he explained to Alec. "This youngster here was his father."

Alec looked at the silhouette again.

"She isn't in it herself," he said. "Is there a portrait of her?"

"There was," said Dochy dryly, "but I understand it's sold. No, she's not in the silhouette—she was the artist who cut this, you see. Oh, yes, she was clever. The collectors of this sort of thing know her work, she had quite a vogue in Edinburgh and Paris. These paintings on rice paper were sent home by my father. Pretty, aren't they? This old work-table was Aunt Jane's own, her embroidery silks are still there, look, in perfect order. She was at work on this fan when she died, a heart seizure I believe."

He went on to tell them about various articles of general interest, the bone snuff-box carved by a French prisoner who had escaped during Napoleon's campaigns, the dirk that had stabbed a Campbell to the heart, a lace-edged handkerchief given to Aeneas by the Prince, a knotted silk purse containing two small teeth said to be milk teeth of Aeneas's eldest son, Charles or Tearlach.

Then he led them through the castle describing scenes of family or clan history that had taken place in various rooms or with which the rooms had associations.

At four o'clock Mr. Forsyth departed, and at five Maura and Kirpu served tea and boiled eggs, with scones, pancakes, black-currant jam and cheese.

"Isn't Danny in yet?" demanded Father Kelly.

"He is not, Father," said Maura. "I'll send him to you the minute he comes."

"She's a good girl is Maura, let them say what they like."

Father Kelly launched into a hearty tea without slackening the activity of his tongue. " Better than some of the unco guid in this and other places." He chewed bitterly.

" I suppose," said Alec, " in a place like Fionn an unmarried mother is rather conspicuous."

" I don't think the Fionnachs are too uncharitable," said Dochy.

" Bad enough. Bad enough. You wouldn't have any experience of it——"

The priest pushed a large piece of scone into his mouth, munched it to manageable size and spoke through it.

" I fell out with Mistress Kilbride over the head of it," he said. " When she refused to give the poor girl a bed. The way of it was this." He turned to Alec, the stranger. " She was in service in Glasgow, you see, and she was taken advantage of by some sailor that was there just now and then, when his ship docked, like, and then off again. When she found she was to have a child, she waited till he was back, and then she told him. Oh, says he, but we'll get married all right. Go you to the Island of Fionn, he says, and go to my mother and she'll take you in, says he, because I'll write a letter to her and tell her you're coming so she'll know to welcome you. Well, what does the poor girl do but swallow his story and come to Fionn, and finds there's not a soul on Fionn by the name of Brown, which was the name he'd given himself, the dirty black-guard." He gulped a mouthful of tea to chase down the scone. " Well, naturally they came to me, the girl being a Catholic, and there she was in a state of grief and bamboozlement, the creature. And thinks I, I'll get her a bed, anyway, for there won't be a steamer calling again till next week, so off I went to Mrs. Kilbride and that's when the rumpus blew up. Of course, jealousy was at the bottom of it, she's not naturally a wicked woman, but jealous of that man of hers, and he old enough to be the girl's grandfather ! "

He paused to refuel rapidly.

" What happened ? " asked Alec.

" I lost my temper. I told her even if she changed her mind I wouldn't leave the girl with her to suffer her sour looks. And before I would ask old Rose to give her room in a barn, I thought I'll try Mrs. MacLennan, for there's room in the Hotel, and if need be I'll pay. But it was Mistress MacLennan that took the girl in, and waved payment back in my face. Yes, she's a good, fine woman is Mrs. MacLennan and her a Protestant and all, and I put Mrs.

Kilbride to shame with her. And Sir Hector, decent man, said he'd have her in the castle to help old Molly that was getting past work, and when Molly died she got the cottage and there she lives to this day with her boy. And a better brought up boy than many that's got a father as well."

"I think you give Maura a bit of help with him," Dochy suggested.

"Och, he's a good-natured boy, he just needs a word in season."

Alec chuckled. "He has a touch of his father's cunning," he said, "though I'm sure there's no meanness in him." He told them about the run-down clocks and they laughed.

"He keeps the clocks wound and oiled in exchange for the use of the boat and an occasional book from the library," he explained.

"It sounds just like one of Uncle Hector's arrangements," said Dochy. "But one or two of the books are rather nice," he added uneasily. "Nothing specially valuable, but—family name on the flyleaf, or a dedication, or that sort of thing. It would be a pity——"

"Perhaps I had better stop the book side of it till Sir Hector comes back. I'll be rather relieved to do it. I'd hate anything to be damaged while he's away."

"But is he coming back?" Father Kelly asked.

"Why, yes, he spoke of being back in six months, probably."

"He said that to you?"

"Yes." Alec wondered at the earnestness in the priest's heavy face.

"Because when he said good-bye to me he meant it as good-bye. He didn't expect to be back. He meant to finish his days in America, or even on the liner."

Alec listened incredulously.

"But," he said, "when he spoke to me he rather doubted how long he'd bear to be away from Fionn. He said six months—and that if he came back then there was no need for me to hurry away, which I thought was pretty nice of him."

"But," Dochy broke in to speak to Father Kelly, "what did he actually say that gave you the impression he was gone for good?"

"That he had the same kind of heart as his great-aunt Jane, and that sooner than lead a bath-chair life he meant to keep going and drop when his time came. Only he meant to have the comforts and luxuries that they can do so well in the States, for a while anyway, before he died."

Father Kelly looked from one to the other, nodded and drained his cup.

Dochy rubbed a hand over his head.

"I had no idea of this," he said.

"Well, I think," said Alec, "that he must have got a more reassuring verdict in the States, because he spoke as if he had years ahead of him."

Dochy was quiet, visibly perturbed.

It was in this restless silence that Danny opened the door and stood there, his hair rumpled with wind, his eyes bright and alert and with that slightly fey look that is the very expression of boyhood. He listened to Father Kelly's injunctions as to where to find the ointment and set off. His appearance had checked the uneasiness that troubled them all.

Later that night Kirpu, daubed with zinc ointment by Father Kelly, dosed by Alec with the calomel that John Forsyth had handed in, comforted with a final cup of tea from Maura, lay in bed staring at nothing. The lamp on the chair beside him sent a wavering line of smoke towards the ceiling. Kirpu was tired out but happy, too happy to turn out the smoking lamp, for then sleep might come too quickly and he would lose the wonderful feeling. The doctor had said little, but his eyes had been full of approval. He had been sympathetic, too, also without many words, and had given him a pill to cure him. He was a good man, as good as Smith Bahadur, very skilful in medicine, highly appreciative though silent.

"I am in my East West Home," Kirpu murmured. "My East West Home is best."

But a few days later he was still unwell.

"It's these pimples," said Maura. "You've got run down, poor soul. Likely it's the change of food that does it. Food does some queer things. I mind when I was in Glasgow the mistress was the very same, couldn't let so much as one strawberry pass her lips, and tinned salmon was poison—fair poison to her! Tomatoes, too, sometimes—och, you'd never believe the number of times I've seen her face break out through her stomach! Now what have you eaten that you wouldn't get at home?"

Kirpu groaned.

"It's the kippers, maybe. They're salty a bit for them that isn't used with them. That's what it'll be—the kippers. Would you take some MacLean's powder, would you?"

Kirpu shook his head. Just as well, Maura reflected, for it was Mr. Forsyth that dosed folks with MacLean's. Father Kelly preferred the Black Draught, and the Black Draught was too hearty for a poor wisp of a creature like Kirpu, but on the other hand Maura, as a good Catholic, had a shyness about using Protestant medicines.

" What d'you feel like, tell me? " she asked.

" My head is not well," said Kirpu. " It is full of wind."

" D'you think you're going off in a faint, likely? Is it a kind of a swimminess? Put your head between your ears, that cures a faint. Go on, put your head between your ears."

This was too metaphysical even for Kirpu. He glanced mentally at the idea, found it dizzily abstruse and clung to his own formula.

" I feel a good deal better than I think," he repeated. Or was it, I am a good deal better than I feel? He groped after a meaning, that kept slipping through his fingers like a serpent. The vanishing serpent of meaning, the clattering rain, the mutter and roar of the sea all swelled inside his head. I feel better than I think. that was not quite it. I think . . . I am better than . . . I think I am . . . Something like that.

" I think better than . . ." he said aloud. Something in Maura's expression made him doubt the success of his formula. Put your head between your ears . . . No, no, that made him dizzy. He groaned again.

Maura lifted the singing kettle off the range and filled a stone hot-water bottle.

" Here you are," she said. " Off to bed with you."

" But," Kirpu protested as he accepted the gift, " but the serving of the food—the—the secretarial duties—the——"

Maura's determination blew him before her like a fragment of chaff.

It was luxury to tumble into bed and give up struggling with formulas. But the formulas persisted of their own accord. I think better than I feel I am. Than. Better than I think. Something like that.

The serpent still flicked its tail out of his grasp and he was still wearily pursuing it when Maura ushered in Dr. MacArdal.

" We'd better have a lamp," said Alec in the twilight. " Out of sorts again, Kirpu? What do you feel like?"

Kirpu bowed, not an easy feat in bed.

"I feel better," he said, "better than "—he struggled with the slippery concept "—better than——"

"Better than you were this morning?"

Perhaps that would do.

"Better than I felt this morning," he repeated doubtfully.

Maura brought in the lamp and Alec sat on Kirpu's bed with a light hold on his wrist.

"Better open the window," he said at last, removing the thermometer from the Indian's mouth.

"Bring me a glass to put this in, Maura," he said. "We must get some kind of disinfectant, too. Let me see your throat . . . Bring me a spoon, Maura. . . ."

Kirpu retched a little as Alec, with the help of a spoon and the wavering lamp, tried to examine his mouth; then he leaned back on his pillow and watched the doctor's preoccupied face. All this was really, he assured himself, most gratifying. These two people were deeply concerned about him. Dr. MacArdal, that notable Communist agitator, was considering him with deep compassion. His words were few, but his face spoke his thoughts.

"Kirpu, my poor fellow," said Dr. MacArdal's expression, "I am profoundly worried about you. You are seriously ill. Your bones ache, you are hot, you are cold, you are clammy, you are parched, your respirations are thirty-two to the minute. Your eyeballs ache and evil essences swell and putrefy inside your head. Have no fear, my dear fellow, only trust in me and I will pull you through!"

"I am happy to be in your hands," Kirpu assured him. "My sufferings are nothing at all. Even if I die, I die with the assurance of your care and affection, and what could be more jolly!"

From that point it seemed that they held many delightful conversations, interrupted too often by the hordes of strangers who filled the room and melted through its walls, cloudy figures that would suddenly assume a hard clarity of outline, far solider, far more actual than the bed on which he lay. Most of them were enemies; senators hunting witches, Indian police, whiskered holy men with eyes like corkscrews. Sepu was there, waving his hands in gracious gestures, smiling a foolish, friendly smile that was worse than a threat. And behind the moving crowds was the recurrent crash! crash! crash! of the sea.

It was an ugly idea that had entered Alec's mind. He rummaged in his memory, trying to visualise the page in the textbook, trying to remember the symptoms.

Only three vesicles ; and Father Kelly's treatment had not been the best possible one for impetigo—if it was only impetigo. But there was the temperature, the headache, the obvious misery . . . Still it would be far worse if it were the disease he feared.

And he knew the power of his own imagination. He had nothing to worry him here on this remote island ; so he proceeded to manufacture a worry out of his own fantasy.

He would wait and see what the patient was like to-morrow. But in the meantime he could not settle to read in Aunt Jane's parlour ; he would take a brisk walk, look for a bit of human society to liven him up.

Father Kelly lived in a shabby stucco bungalow built some thirty years ago by a wealthy Glasgow merchant. It had been neat then, garish in white and red, a fragment of a Clyde coast resort stuck down in Fionn and named, romantically, "Faraway." One room in it had been consecrated and was the temporary chapel for Fionn's Roman Catholics, and the house was, at least officially, known as the Presbytery, but its appearance remained stubbornly that of a derelict holiday bungalow.

There was no light in any of the windows. Alec knocked at the door without much hope. He knocked a second time, and then turned to go away, when vague noises within suggested that the priest was after all somewhere inside. He waited.

When Father Kelly, lamp in hand, at last opened the door, he gave the impression of having been asleep in his clothes and having hurriedly added a collar and jacket when he heard the knock. It took him a minute to recognise his caller, then he opened the door wider and stood aside.

" Come in, come in," he said with a flat imitation of hospitality.

" I won't keep you," said Alec. " I've come to see if you can let me have any kind of mouthwash from your pharmacy here."

" Mouthwash." Father Kelly led the way into a chilly den, pushed a chair forward and lit a gas fire which began to plop and whine and emit a disagreeable smell.

" What did ye say you wanted, was it ? " he asked, trying to pull himself together.

"A mouthwash, an antiseptic gargle."

"Oh, I see what you mean. Wait now till I look. I might have something."

"Or better still, some penicillin lozenges or sulfadiazine tablets," said Alec, without much hope.

"I'll see, I'll see. But I don't think I've got any of those sort of tricks."

He lifted the lamp from the table, changed his mind and took the matches instead. Alec watched him hobble off in his bedroom slippers, old, shabby, unshaved and rather dirty.

Left alone, he looked round the room, at the floor covered with broken linoleum, the dusty table, cheap chairs with hair pushing through holes in their imitation leather seats, heavy sideboard and shelf of greasy books. It was a room where melancholy seeped into you slowly. Melancholy hung in the air, dank, like the spores of some unclean spiritual fungus. Father Kelly had not been sitting here, and no wonder. It was a room that repelled life, not even a mouse would frolic there.

Father Kelly returned after some time with a grimy bottle that proved to contain a thymol mouthwash, a packet of permanganate of potash crystals and a crumpled bag of cough lozenges.

"It's not for yourself, is it?" he asked as Alec accepted them.

"No, it's Kirpu. His temperature is up again and his mouth and throat are rather dirty."

Father Kelly scratched his cheek.

"He needs a good clean out," he suggested. "I could give you Croton oil, it's a good thing. I'm thinking of having it myself to-night."

"Why, are you out of sorts?"

"Bilious, bilious, that's all, just bilious."

"Croton oil is pretty drastic treatment."

"Not a bit of it. No use being namby-pamby. It's my experience, Doctor, that most things are cured by a good clean-out. However, I won't presume to advise you."

"Yes, the theory is quite sound," Alec agreed patiently, "but——"

"Well," the priest interrupted, "I'll give ye a blue pill if you'd rather. Wait now till I fetch it."

This time he took the lamp with him, leaving Alec in the glow of the gas fire which threw a scorching beam on his legs, but seemed to have no effect on the damp chill of the room. Alec moved his chair to escape from the scorching ; the fire gobbled like a resentful turkey, then subsided again to its sibilant whine.

The old man returned with the lamp and the pills.

" Och, I left you in the dark," he apologised. " Still, you had the fire. I'm out of the way of entertaining folks. I could offer ye a cup of tea ? "

" No, thanks," said Alec, touched by the variations from his usual aggressiveness of manner to diffidence, almost feebleness. " To tell the truth I drink more tea than I'm accustomed to ; Maura serves tea with every meal. But you know, you don't look too good yourself. I've got some brandy along at the castle ; I'll bring it along and leave it with you."

" I couldn't think of it," said Father Kelly wistfully.

" Medical orders," said Alec. " And you can call it an exchange for all this. I'll be right back."

He stood up, but at the same time steps approached outside, someone walked into the hall, rapped at the door of the den and opened it. It was Danny, carrying a quart milk can.

" I didn't know ye had company, Father," he apologised.

" Come in, Danny, the very fella we want." Father Kelly's manner attempted confidence again. " You'll carry a parcel to the castle and bring something back for me, in a bottle. But what's this, hey ? "

He lifted the lid of the can.

" It's some sheep's head broth from Mistress MacLennan."

" And that's the best broth in God's creation. Tell her I don't know how to thank her. She'll get her reward, so she will. Now, come you here with me, Danny."

Again Alec was left in the glow of the malevolent fire. He heard a good deal of rummaging and crinkling of paper, and a protesting outburst from Danny followed by reassurances from the priest ; then they reappeared, Father Kelly with the lamp and Danny with a large parcel insecurely wrapped in newspaper.

" Now what would you say to my idea, Doctor," Father Kelly asked, replacing the lamp on the table. " I'm saying Danny can just sleep at the castle, maybe in the kitchen, and he'll hear if the poor sick soul calls out for anything, and I'm sending along the necessary. He's a willing, good-tempered boy, just the one we could trust, hey, Danny ? "

Danny puffed through his nostrils, indignant but dumb.

"He's delighted to do it," said the old man.

"It'll be a nice thing," Danny burst out, "if I'm seen carrying this through the village!"

"It'll be a clip on the ear," said Father Kelly, "if I hear one word out of you. You're only too pleased to help the doctor and the poor Hindoo, d'ye hear?"

Danny snorted again but said nothing.

Alec concealed a smile, put the mouthwash in his pocket and led the way out, followed by Danny with the bedpan.

Maura arranged the cushions on the hearthrug in the kitchen, piled blankets cunningly on top, and invited Danny to crawl into the cocoon she had prepared for him. He was about to obey when she seized his face between her hands and scrutinised it angrily.

"What's that on your lip?"

"A scratch I got from Nell Patrick's baby—days ago."

"It's a pimple!"

"It is not a pimple, it's a scratch I'm telling you."

Danny wore his victimised expression as Maura reached for the ointment from the mantelpiece and anointed his upper lip. His brows were drawn together, his eyelids drooped disdainfully, his brown cheeks and short straight nose and ruffled hair looked childish still; and now a white moustache clothed him with absurd senility. Maura yielded to an impulse.

"Och, Mam," Danny chuckled, "what did ye kiss me for—you got ointment all over your mouth!"

"What d'you think you've got yourself?" Maura asked. "I've made up a bed for myself in the wee room upstairs, so you'll not feel lonely." She administered an affectionate smack.

Danny stiffened into dignity and inserted himself into the cocoon. She might remember he was fifteen. She was awful.

# Chapter Twelve

DOCHY MACARDAL was aware of the interest the two ladies showed in him. He was aware of it but felt no inclination to preen. After all they had no choice; since the two hikers had only stayed one night he was the only other guest in the Hotel and they were both, he guessed, women who found their own sex dull.

"How long does a wind like this usually last?" Lydia asked.

"Oh, it's seasonal just now; may last quite a while."

The lassitude of Mrs. MacLennan's midday dinner lay on them both; Mrs. Transom had gone to lie down, leaving her daughter in sole possession of Dochy in the upstairs parlour.

"How long do you mean to stay here?" Lydia asked.

"I have to be back in London by next Friday."

She began poking a match among the cigarette butts in a lettered ash-tray, pushing them into a pile, scattering them, pushing them together again.

"I'm afraid you're getting bored with Fionn," said Dochy.

Lydia was in a trance, it seemed. She raised her eyes and looked sleepily over his shoulder.

"Last week," she said, "I thought I could live here forever. This week it's too rough to get on the steamer, and we're like prisoners. I'm mad to escape." She sighed and leaned her cheek on her left palm, still prodding and disembowelling a cigarette end.

She was a girl you would not look at twice until, perhaps, the third time you encountered her. Her mother was quite obviously appealing; soft and pretty, billowing into fat like a Rubens model. Beside her Lydia looked colourless and hard, and queer. Her skin was all one colour, the colour of a peeled willow wand; her hair was the colour of its bark. At first you ignored her. Then her silence beside her mother's chatter became irritating. Then you began, half in annoyance, to notice her, and found that she was exquisite.

Exquisite, but not my type, Dochy reflected, offering her his cigarette-case and standing up.

" Oh, you're not going, are you ? "

She raised her queer eyes and he smiled frankly down at her.

" Yes. Invited out to bridge."

" Oh, you lucky beast. Where ? "

" At the castle."

" Don't go just yet. I'm almost suicidal with boredom. Stay and talk for another five minutes."

" Right," said Dochy, sitting on the arm of a chair. " Five minutes' talk. What about ? "

" Tell me your life-story. Where do you live ? "

" London. In Wycherly Terrace, that's near Queen's Gate."

" Oh, how odd. We live in one of these ugly old houses in South Kensington, near St. Dorcas's Church. Walk from your flat—it is a flat ?—towards Sydney Street and you pass us, the house with the wistaria."

" I know the house. Like a bit broken off the top of St. Pancras Station."

" Oh, how unkind you are." Lydia's laugh was flattering. " I never thought of that. And you—a service flat ? Or a devoted old housekeeper ? "

" No housekeeper. A service flat more or less. It suits me to be able to come and go, be away for a few months at a time, perhaps, with no fuss."

" Do you do a lot of—appearing and disappearing ? "

" Quite a bit. In the way of business."

" It sounds a heavenly life. Plenty of variety."

Dochy looked amused ; he enjoyed life almost anywhere.

" Tell me," Lydia asked, picking up the match and resuming operations in the ash-tray, " what is it that your cranky old uncle has against you ? "

She lifted her hypnotic eyes to his with disarming candour. This was a gambit she had used with success on previous victims. To ask a question that presupposed intimacy, in a relationship that was still in the cool and formal stages, could fluster or flatter a man into an assumption of intimacy which, when she chose, she could repudiate.

Dochy's face did not lose its pleasant social expression.

" I think," he said, " you must have misunderstood something

you've heard. My uncle is—no crankier than I am myself——
Now I must go off to my bridge."

He raised his hand casually and went out, leaving Lydia to
digest a snub.

There was no reply to his knock at the door, so he entered the
castle and went to Aunt Jane's parlour, where he heard the voices.

Alec MacArdal, Danny, Kirpu and Maura were all seated at the
card table. Each held a fan of cards except Maura, who wore the
detached, unenthusiastic air of Dummy. Alec was watching Danny
play the hand.

" Danny's fingers hovered over Dummy's hearts—four to the
Ace-Queen. He drew the Queen.

Kirpu threw a small heart ; so did Danny, and gathered up
the trick with joy.

" Now how did you know he hadn't the King ? " Alec asked.

" I just hoped," said Danny.

" Not at all. You knew I had it ! "

" Did I ? "

" Of course. Go back over the bidding."

Maura stood up while they went back over the bidding, saw
Dochy and beamed with relief.

" Mister Dochy ! " she breathed, " and you fair dying for a
game ! Sit down and enjoy yourself—it's fair beyond me and I've
got towels to wash."

" Come along," Alec welcomed him. " Danny's quite a lively
pupil ; he'll do when Father Kelly comes, for Kirpu isn't fit for a
whole day up yet."

" Glad to see you better, Kirpu," said Dochy. " Sit still—
convalescents have shaky legs."

Kirpu bowed again and sat. Danny sighed and sweated and
ruffled his hair into still worse confusion. They played on.

" There's the old King now," he exclaimed. " I'll put that
Ace on his nose—— Och ! "

" What's wrong ? "

" He's trumped it ! "

" But you have still to play. Aren't you going to over-trump
it ? "

Danny rejoiced. This was a great game and there was a lot of
sly jinks about it. Better than snap.

"Another ten minutes before the old priest comes," he said.
"I'll be fair perfect by then!"

"Optimist," said Alec, dealing the cards. "Two diamonds."

"Jings!" Danny exclaimed. "I've got——"

A sleek expression stole over his face. He must not let the others know that he held seven spades to the Ace-King-Jack. Two diamonds. He held three small diamonds and no clubs at all. This wanted careful thought.

Father Kelly's cottage lay at the far end of the village. It was a good walk to the castle. Father Kelly was huddled over the gas fire, staring resentfully at his watch.

"I won't be there by three, that's sure," he muttered.

The face of the watch stared back at him, flat and censorious, its second hand jerking round in a sort of fussy fury.

"Fifteen minutes of three, so it is, I can see that well enough. The longer I put it off the more I'll have to hurry. And me with my back the way it is. Still it'll warm me to hurry."

He put the watch back in his pocket. It was terrible, this inertia. Too much trouble to get up out of his chair. He was done.

I'm seventy-nine, he reflected, and I never felt my age before, not like this. Maybe I showed it. Send him to a wee snip of an island with no work to do. That was how the Bishop had put it, more or less. A sinecure, a small handful of souls and the Church just a room in the wee house, that was all. The Protestants had a proper building with a spire and all—but no cross on the spire, of course; a veering brass cock on the top of their heretical temple, a symbol of Peter's faithlessness in his unregenerate days.

Supposing a young man had been sent here, a young priest full of fire, he might have done great things in Fionn. He might have gathered his flock together, scooped in great armfuls of the poor doited heretics with their silly wee arrogant individual consciences, gathered them under the outspread wings of the True Church.

But they hadn't sent a young priest. They'd sent an old man, an old, done man, ridiculed and discredited in the eyes of everyone who had known him; sent him to a remote wee isle like putting a bad boy in the corner, or worse, like shutting him in a dark cupboard.

But he knew it was unfair to think like that, unfair to Fionn. Even on Fionn the souls were precious. The Patricks and Danny and Maura and the Kilbrides, yes, and poor Candy Andy the dafty. Bad luck on them all to be in the care of an old ape of a fellow like himself, rotting away in the damp mists of accidie.

Eight minutes to three.

The precious minutes were dripping through his fingers, as they had done these past sixteen years and more. Every single one of these minutes was golden with possibilities as it came, irrecoverable when it had gone. Even this very present minute that was on him now could be exploded in a great act of faith or love that would shatter it out of the mechanical chain of time and into the blaze of eternity. But there, it was past, and his soul still lay inert like a puddock. And when at last he levered himself out of the chair his body felt like a puddock's body. Wrong-jointed, splayed, waddling.

He groaned. He was out of sorts altogether. He diagnosed biliousness and lumbago and inflammation of the kidneys and probably a neoplasm of the brain judging by the feel of his head, and blood pressure and short sight. He would certainly take that blue pill to-night, whatever the doctor said.

He pulled on his outdoor boots, wincing as the corns jagged into the nerves, chose a stick out of the drainpipe in the lobby and stepped tenderly out on the road to the castle, pushing against the wind.

" A good day to you all ! " he greeted them half an hour later with his hoarse aggressiveness. " I'm late, I'm late, you'll just have to excuse me. Och, you've got a four without me ! "

" Kirpu will stop now," said Alec. " He's not quite right yet and he'd better get off to bed after tea. But Danny's coming on— and it's only his second lesson."

Danny looked tired and glum. The farther you went in this game the more there was to it. Pretty queer when you held seven spades to the Ace-King-Jack and your opponents went and bid— and made—a grand slam in diamonds !

" A rare game, hey, Danny ? "

" Yes, Father," said Danny meekly.

His brain was dizzy. He would have liked to escape from the card table now—and rush up the hill or along to the Craignashee where Candy Andy would be dottering along the rocks eating raw whelks. He would even like to go up to the school and swagger round a bit, show off to Miss Bradshaw about all the heathen gods

Kirpu had told him about. Fancy wanting to go to the school on a Saturday ! But his body was getting fair stiff with sitting.

"Will I—will I see does my mother want anything done in the kitchen before I start ? " he suggested.

"Yes, do," Alec agreed.

Danny escaped to the kitchen and found his mother sittin beside the fire with a small pile of mending beside her. She was relaxed in her chair, staring into the fire.

"What are you doing, Mam ? " he asked.

She looked round dreamily as if she hardly saw him. Her lovely vague eyes had an odd effect on Danny, opened a little shutter in his breast and let light in on feelings of tenderness and devotion that had no place in ordinary everyday life.

"You know yon two women at the Hotel, Mammy ? "

Maura nodded. "Mrs. Transom and Lydia."

"There's neither of them as pretty as you, Mam. Not near ! "

Maura moved her head, smiling but waving away such nonsense with a tilt of her chin.

"You're beautiful, so you are," said Danny, knowing she did not believe him ; she was awful obstinate and set in her ways and had no respect for his superior powers of observation. Mrs. Transom was a nice-looking body and Miss Transom carried herself with style ; but they didn't either of them have a creamy round chin and warm neck like his mother, or gentle eyes. That Lydia had a smooth, clear skin, probably cold to touch. She had a bad nature besides.

"Don't they want you there in the parlour ? "

"Och—them old cards ! "

"I couldn't understand yon," said Maura. "I like a quiet game of whist, but yon—just a lot of contraptious nonsense."

"It's a better game then whist," said Danny thoughtfully.

Maura picked up a sock. "I'm sure," she said, "I don't know what's come over you, wearing socks all the time. Look at what I've got to start to ! " She displayed a gaping hole. "Is your bare feet not good enough, or what ? "

"Och, Mam, I'm fifteen now—besides I can't go about in my bare feet now we're living in the castle ! "

"Maybe not inside the castle," Maura conceded, "but there's nothing against your wearing bare feet outside, with your old sandshoes if you like, and save your poor old mother's eyesight."

"My poor old mother ! " Danny jeered, tottering about like

Mrs. Kilbride and leaping out of reach of the blow Maura aimed at him.

"If you've nothing better to do you can clean his shoes that he was out in this morning," she suggested, drawing a thread through the dreadful hole.

"But I have to go back to the parlour," he said hurriedly. "I'll do them to-night."

They were playing three-handed when he went in, concentrated on the table as if affairs of State depended on the fall of the cards. Dr. Alec, aloof and neat, Dochy MacArdal big and good-looking, if it wasn't for his silly wee slivers of glasses with thin gold stems. Old Father Kelly with his black-rimmed ones was more like the thing. But Father Kelly had forgotten to shave; his chin was bristled like a cut cornfield. His old collar too, was nothing near white, grimed and greasy and disreputable. When he drew a card from his hand his fingers fumbled and shook.

"I thought you had no trump left," said Dochy, examining the trick.

"I had three," said the priest.

"But surely you . . ."

They were turning back old tricks, and Father Kelly was blinking and fingering his underlip. He was stubborn and irritable; the others could not convince him of his revoke.

"Look," said Alec, "when he played the last round of trump you threw a diamond, remember?"

"No, I don't remember any such thing," said the pugnacious old man. "Why would I throw a diamond when I had a trump in my hand? You must have miscounted."

The other two exchanged a helpless glance. Father Kelly saw it and flew into a rage, throwing his cards on the table.

"Are ye calling me a cheat?" he shouted, "go on, go on, say it to my face—ye'd believe anything of a man that came here with the reputation they gave me—is that it?" He stood up fumbling for a handkerchief to wipe the saliva that hung on his underlip, but his hands shook so violently he could not find the way into his pocket. "If that's what ye think why don't ye say it to my face. . . ." The rage was wearing itself out in futile search for a handkerchief.

"Because we don't think that," said Alec.

"Easiest thing in the world to make a mistake," said Dochy. "I've done it a hundred times."

Father Kelly, having found his handkerchief, relapsed into his chair but twisted round with his back to them. His face was hidden by the hand that clutched the handkerchief; the other hand lay on his knee making fidgeting, purposeless movements.

Danny stared in astonishment that changed to horror. That snuffling sound could mean only one thing: the old priest was crying.

"Go and ask your mother to make us all a cup of tea," said Alec.

"I will," said Danny.

"But, Mammy," he said, after giving his news and his message, "did ye ever hear tell of a grown man crying, let alone a priest?"

"Fancy the old priest!" Maura marvelled. "Were they on at him about it? About his wrong card?"

"They were not, they just said it was a revoke."

"Is that a cheat?"

"I don't think it. Mr. Dochy said he'd done the same thing a hundred times, so it couldn't be a cheat. They weren't on at him at all—it was him, he fair flew up. What's his reputation that he talks about, Mam?"

"God knows," said Maura. "A lot of wicked Protestant gossip likely. Never listen to a word of it, Danny."

"I wouldn't listen to a word of it," Danny assured her, "but I'd like to know what it's all about, would you not?"

"I wish I had made a girdle scone for their tea. Yesterday's are tough. Danny, run you to Mrs. MacLennan's and ask her would she have a soda scone or the like for their tea. Maybe she'll take thought to send a bit shortbread as well, for she knows fine I'm no baker. And be quick now!"

Danny went willingly, for he had a high respect for Mrs. MacLennan's shortbread and for her canister of toffee too. A pity he had to hurry; likely Mrs. MacLennan would know about the old priest's reputation.

But likely enough she wouldn't split, anyway. She was a deep one, was Mrs. MacLennan. He'd just ask for the scones and nothing else.

When Danny returned panting to the castle with a basket of scones and pancakes he found that the thought of tea had been pushed into the background. Sheets and blankets were draped round the fireplace, his mother was emptying the floor-bucket and had an air of emergency on her.

" I brought the scones," he said, wondering what had come over her to be washing some floor or other when the last he heard of was tea.

" Put them down, then. Fill you that hot-water bottle if that's the kettle boiling. And put it in my bed and be careful not to smash it against the one that's in already."

" You're not going to your bed ! " he shouted in a panic.

" No," his mother said, gathering an armful of blankets and linen, " but Father Kelly is."

# Chapter Thirteen

IT WAS almost seven o'clock when they had a belated tea of scones and ham and cheese, Alec and Dochy in the parlour, Kirpu, Danny and Maura in the kitchen.

" As well for the poor old soul to be here," Maura mused aloud. " No comfort for him in the Presbytery with nothing but Nell Patrick coming in twice a week to clean up, and she has enough to do now with her baby, and her man back and all."

" Was he sick right into the fire, Mam ? "

" He did his best to catch it in his hanky but it was all over. All over the hearth and the rug and the card table, and more on his way to the lavatory, the soul. And his suit ! Not that it was up to much before."

" What did he say ? "

" How would I know what he said ? "

" But when you went through, what did he say ? "

" Never a word, just sat and shivered."

" What did the doctor say ? "

" Poured him out a tot of whisky and gave it to him. Held it to his mouth for him to drink ; his hands were shaking so he could never have held the glass for himself. He was awful nice to him, the doctor was."

Kirpu listened to them, his eyes turning from one to the other as they spoke.

" You'll have to go back to the Presbytery, Danny," Maura

was saying, " and fetch his nightshirts and his breviary and all he wants. He'll tell you what to bring."

" I will."

" And look in and tell the Kilbrides and Nell Patrick he won't be fit to take services to-morrow."

" Will he not ? "

" The doctor says he won't, anyway."

This assumption that Father Kelly would submit to the doctor's decree completed his collapse in Danny's mind. He had been a figure of authority and wisdom ; now he was a poor, pitiful old man.

Danny went off with a list of instructions from the priest and a suitcase of Alec's to bring the things back in. He enjoyed passing through the village with the suitcase, a conspicuous bearer of news.

" Are you off for the week-end, then ? " asked John Forsyth jokingly. He was mowing the grass in front of the manse.

" I am not," said Danny, pausing at the gate to chat with the minister. " It's the old priest taken bad at the castle and I'm to fetch his nightshirt and his dressing-gown and all that."

" Is that so, now ? "

The minister left his machine and came to the gate for details. Tiny blades of grass speckled his black suit and his hair and even his eyebrows ; Danny reflected that to cut the grass in a wind like this was the sort of daft-like cantrip you might expect from a Protestant minister. Still, maybe he was glad to get a job outdoors and be away from Mrs. Forsyth and her harangues.

" He was playing cards," he explained, " and he came over sick and vomited up all over the hearth and all over the . . ." He gave the full catalogue.

" I could send over some MacLean's powder," the minister suggested. " That would settle his stomach better than whisky. If he would take it," he added doubtfully. " I'm right sorry he's taken bad. Tell them at the castle if there's anything I can do or if they want the MacLean's to let me know."

" I will," said Danny, liking the minister for all he was so ignorant.

He called in at the Hotel. Mrs. MacLennan was in the bar, and the usual men were in for their drams. He had quite an audience.

" All over the hearth, and the rug, and the card table, and his black suit and his boots. . . ."

"Tuts!" said Mrs. MacLennan when he finished, "the poor old soul, now. It's living alone that does it, there's no comfort for a man living alone. Wait you, Danny, I'll send along a sup of brandy for him. Tell him to take a good tot of that in hot water. It's a chill he's got, that what is it, a chill on the liver, and brandy's the thing—not whisky, tell him—brandy for a chill on the liver."

"Where are you going?" asked Miss Transom as he passed her on her way back from a walk.

"To the Presbytery," he answered repressively.

"But why are you taking that case?"

Danny had a struggle with himself, for Lydia made him feel uncomfortable and for that reason he disliked her.

"To fetch some things he wants," he said. "He's spending the night at the castle."

Miss Transom offered him her cigarette-case. Nonchalantly Danny accepted a cigarette and a light, noticing her hands, pale like the milky tea that Nell Patrick gave to wee Pad.

"It's the old priest," he said. "He's sick."

"Oh. I knew you couldn't be going off the island, because we want to get away and we can't."

"Where d'you want to go?" Danny asked, puffing companionably.

"Oh—London. It's dull here, isn't it?"

"I wouldn't say that." Danny stared judicially at the tip of his cigarette. "I wouldn't call it dull, exactly."

"What would you call it?"

But Danny mistrusted her innocent expression.

"Just ordinary," he said. "I'll be getting along now."

He knew he had been rather severe with her, refusing her the picturesque details of Father Kelly's sickness that would have made her feel less dull. Still, he distrusted that young one for all her pretty looks. Walking about in long trousers!

"The old priest's sick!" he shouted in at Nell Patrick's.

"Wheesht, will you!" Nell hissed in annoyance. "I've just got her off to sleep." She listened apprehensively, but no wail of fury followed. "What d'ye say, Danny?"

"Father Kelly's sick," said Danny, lowering his voice and giving her a full version.

Nell's nondescript little face filled with awe when she learned that no services would be held.

"He must be right bad," she said. "You'll have to tell the Kilbrides, Danny."

"I'm on my way there now."

Visiting the Kilbrides demanded more ceremony. Their green wooden gate, trim garden and white doorstep demanded formality. Danny pulled the bell.

The dark velours behind the lace curtains moved, letting a sliver of lamplight shine on the step. Footsteps approached. The door opened.

"Mistress Kilbride," said Danny, "I've to tell you that Father Kelly's been taken bad at the castle and there won't be any services to-morrow."

"Taken bad?" Mrs. Kilbride peered from the shelter of the doorway into Danny's face. "What's wrong? . . . Wheesht, will you!" she called over her shoulder to the invisible voice within.

"He was playing cards at the castle, and——"

"I'm saying who is it? WHO IS IT?" demanded the voice, rising to a bawl.

Mrs. Kilbride made a gesture of exasperation.

"Ye'd better come in," she said. "I get no peace."

They went into a cosy living-room where a pot bubbled slowly beside a hob fire.

"It's you, Danny, is it," said Captain Kilbride.

"Can't you see it's him without asking," muttered his wife.

"I can see now he's inside," said the captain placidly. "And where are you off to on your holidays?"

Danny put down the suitcase and told his story.

"Sit down," said the captain as he listened.

"Mercy me, what a clearing up for your mother!" said Mrs. Kilbride crossly. "A man would never think of that, though, messing the whole place up!"

Danny had a suspicion that her sympathy with his mother did not go very deep.

"He didn't vomit on purpose, did he?" the captain rebuked her.

"Some would," she said malevolently. "He's old and past work," she added in a sad, pseudo-pitying voice. "It's to be hoped he doesn't linger. We've all got to go, Danny, though you little think it at your age. We've all got to go, and when my time comes I hope I don't linger and be a nuisance to folks."

112

She chewed over this sad thought and made little spasmodic clutching movements with her elbows. Danny watched her with interest, wondering what she was always annoyed about. Women were the queer ones right enough. Just to look at Mistress Kilbride chewing away at her two bottom teeth, all that was left to her, was an education in the queerness of them. He noticed that his stare was beginning to exasperate her and turned his eyes to the old captain, who favoured him with a wink and a scarcely visible jerk of the head in his wife's direction. It was the same wink he had given that time the minister's mother splashed into the harbour.

"Well," said Danny, "I'll be for off, then." He picked up the suitcase.

Captain Kilbride accompanied him to the door; his wife had lifted the pot lid and was giving the supper-time porridge a good stir, venting her irritation on it. She ignored Danny's departure.

"Is he bad?" the captain asked, lighting his pipe at the door.

"I don't think it," said Danny doubtfully; he had not liked all that talk of dying. "He says himself all he needs is a blue pill or the like."

"And no wonder. Lives on cheese. Lives on cheese and shares it with the mice."

"It's wonderful the way he has them tamed," said Danny defensively.

Captain Kilbride's pipe stuck up at an angle of sardonic contempt.

"Shut the door!" his wife called.

The captain ignored her.

"Mice," he mused. "A grown man playing with mice."

"Still, they're bonny wee beasts when you look at them."

"Mice," said the captain dreamily, as if, having sailed the seven seas and witnessed human folly under many suns, he had returned to Fionn to find there the most superlative silliness of all. "The priest with his mice, and Sir Hector with his penguin; though that's gone to its long home." His eyes crinkled derisively.

"Do you want to bring on my bronchitis?" demanded Mrs. Kilbride, appearing with a shawl clutched round her throat. "It would be a nice fix you'd be in if I went first," she threatened.

"I'm coming, woman, I'm coming."

Captain Kilbride gave Danny a leisurely wave off with his pipe and shut the door, leaving him to fumble for the latch of the gate in the gathering darkness and then plod on to Father Kelly's bungalow.

The door was never locked. He groped his way inside and felt around for the matches, disliking the darkness, the cold stuffiness of a house where windows are always tight shut and no coal or peat ever glows ; Father Kelly cooked and warmed himself with cylinders of evil-smelling gas. He kept swallowing down the smell that clotted the back of his nose, listening to the rustling and scampering of the mice. He found a candlestick at last, with matches in its saucery base, and lit it.

There was no carpet, no rug even. His feet clumped on the wooden floor of the bedroom-living-room where all Father Kelly's belongings were accumulated. Those unafraid scutterings were the feet of the old priest's mice ; he had been worried in case they thought he had deserted them.

This was the box he meant, this big tin on the table beside his breviary and his tobacco. Danny opened the box and the sound brought an increase of the patterings. He broke a crumb of cheese and dropped it on the floor. A tiny grey shape pounced on it and ran off. They became less afraid, knowing that this was not their friend but discovering him to be, after all, no enemy. Now there was one on the table beside him, the cheeky thing ; the candle shone through its rosy ears, haloed its whiskers, cast a minute, wavering shadow that mimicked every action of the mouse, quick and delicate like the movements of birds ; even their leaps across the space between the table and the chair had the prettiness of flight.

Danny chuckled softly, rejecting the derisive commonsense of old Captain Kilbride in favour of Father Kelly's silliness. They were comic wee characters those ones, right enough ! There was one sitting on the toe of his shoe, sitting up like a squirrel with a bit of cheese in its hands, its tail draped over the toecap while it turned the crumb in its fingers and nibbled rapidly. There were several right inside the tin itself, the impudent wee baggages !

He looked round at the dingy walls, wavering back and fore as the candle flame flickered. It was a queer place. He thought of the old man sitting there in the cold, night after night, keeping company with the mice. It was funny when you looked at the little creatures scarcely larger than insects ; but when you saw the dank walls and the sad, torn curtain that hid the window, there was a recoil of spirit. . . .

Poor old doited body! thought Danny with a gust of contempt.

But you could hardly call him doited, after all. He was queer, but he was in his sane senses.

Was this a penance, then, this cheerless barren ugliness? He remembered Father Kelly's reference to his reputation; a chill crept up his spine. It must have been something terrible the old priest had done back in that place near Glasgow.

Anyway he would never feel the same about Father Kelly, not the same confident respect he had always had for him; he had wept in public, and the image in Danny's heart had crumbled into mere vulnerable humanity.

He broke off more cheese for the mice, but their caperings did not lift the sadness from his heart as he thought of the priest. First he swallowed the minister's insults, then he went into a temper tantrum and burst out crying. And he had been great and wise once.

It was beyond Danny and if he stayed here much longer he would be crying himself, that was sure. He shut the tin box, routed out the things he had been sent for and put them in the case. Shirts, books, half the contents of the medicine drawer—he collected them with an increasing desperation to get away. At last he had everything. He looked round, drew a deep breath and blew out the candle.

He did not mind the wind that battered him and pushed sideways at the laden case; he filled his lungs with it over and over again, cleaning out that smell of dank, corrupting loneliness.

He rushed into the castle kitchen and saw his mother buttering bread in the lamplight, and stared at her as if his eyes were feeding on the sight.

"You got it then," she said absently as he dropped the suitcase.

He came round beside her and pinioned her arms to her sides, ignoring her annoyance.

"I'm bigger than you," he said in a bullying voice. "Look!"

He lifted her off her feet and held her for a minute before letting her down.

"Och, Mam," he said in a changed, defenceless voice, folding his arms round her and hiding his eyes in her neck, "I'm sorry for the old priest!"

## Chapter Fourteen

ALEC LOOKED from the thermometer down to the blotched face on the pillow.

" What is it at ? " Father Kelly asked.

" Higher than it should be."

" What is it at ? " The hoarse voice brushed aside the silly medical convention of ' Keeping it from the patient.'

" A hundred and two."

The priest made a respectful grimace. A hundred and two was high enough to justify giving up to-morrow's services. He was ill all right.

He submitted in silence when Alec brought his stethoscope and percussed his chest and listened to the sounds of it. He only drew the line at saying one-one-one.

" Ninety-nine was enough in my young days," he said. " What's the point of increasing it now, hey ? "

" The price of everything has gone up," said Alec, but conceded the point ; and Father Kelly docilely repeated ninety-nine as often as it was required.

" Found anything ? " he asked when he sank again on the pillow.

" Nothing out of the way for a man of your age," said Alec. " Tell me exactly how you feel."

" Rotten."

" Begin at the top. Head ? "

" Too big for my skull."

" Throat ? "

" You looked at it yourself, didn't you."

" I want to know how it feels."

" Dirty. And a tongue like a wad of blanket."

" You can drink as much as you like. I'll try to get some cool drink for you. How's your stomach ? "

"It's sore and upset. I'm wondering if I should take some of the minister's MacLean's Powder, only I wouldn't ask it."

He turned his head to the side; he had stopped shivering, and the purple-grey colour of his skin was patched with red. A wisp of hair tufted out at either side of his bald head.

"Och, I doubt it's the flu I've got," he said. "Like Kirpu."

Flu, like Kirpu. Alec heard the words repeated in his head: Flu like Kirpu.

He pictured Kirpu lying in Torquil MacVean's boat, vomiting and shivering. He had taken too little to do with Kirpu; first assuming that seasickness was responsible for his misery, then acquiescing in the island's diagnosis of flu; as for the famous pimples, Father Kelly had successfully concealed them under a daub of zinc ointment. Father Kelly and Maura and Danny had done everything for Kirpu; he had looked on uninterestedly.

"Father Kelly," he said, "tell me, what were Kirpu's pimples like?" He compelled his voice to casualness.

"Like?" the hoarse voice echoed. "Like pimples, Doctor. Well," he amended, "no, not so much like pimples, more like herpes, for that's what they were. Blisters."

He looked inquiringly at Alec.

Alec swallowed. He was holding himself rigid under a flood of apprehension—not even of apprehension, for he knew already with a horrible fore-knowledge that his fears would be confirmed.

"We'll see," he said soberly, "what you're like in a day or two's time."

They had put Father Kelly too in one of the small, cell-like rooms off the kitchen corridor, next to Kirpu. The latter was back in bed, being still at the easily-tired stage of convalescence. Alec looked in on him and found him asleep with both arms raised above his head and a line of white showing between his closed eyelids. In the light of the lamp that sat on a chair beside Kirpu's bed he examined the pimples. They had dried up to darkish scabs.

He panicked for a minute, trying to count days since he had encountered Kirpu in Glasgow, then realised that the incubation period was not of great importance. Danny and Father Kelly had been in frequent contact with Kirpu, and between them must have been in contact with almost every soul on Fionn. If this was the disease he feared then it had been given every opportunity to spread.

But he might be wrong—it was still just possible. If he could be sure that nobody else on the island was sickening. . . .

There was only one way to find out, and he had to find out quickly. He must go round the contacts, beginning with Torquil MacVean.

As he went through the kitchen he saw Danny clasp his arms round his mother. They stood together in an attitude of unstudied affection for a few seconds, then Maura's eyes turned towards him with a glow of tenderness in them that vanished as she saw him watching, yet vanished without haste or embarrassment. She pushed Danny from her.

"Go on, then," she said. "Take his case in to him and give him a word to cheer him. Did you feed the mice?"

"I did," said Danny, taking up the suitcase.

"Wait," Alec said. But he hesitated to ask the question he had to put; the sight of the easy affection between the mother and son had made him begin to realise the implications of the predicament of Fionn. He stood in the kitchen, motionless, and in a second of silence fear washed over him again like a cold wave.

"Danny," he said, "have you been vaccinated?"

"I have," said Danny. "We was all done in the school, one time."

"That's right," Maura agreed. "It was being done free, so there was a few got themselves done as well as the children; but if we'd known what we were in for we'd have thought twice before we let them scratch our arms."

"What year was this?"

"Danny was—how old were you?—six, was it? About eight years back, it would be."

"I see. Well, don't either of you go near Father Kelly till I give the word, please."

"Not even take in his case?" Danny protested.

"No."

Suddenly he could not bear the kitchen, the mild, protesting surprise on their two faces.

"I'll explain later," he said. "I must go out now."

He paused for a minute outside the castle, buttoning his coat up to his neck, listening to the sound of the sea and smelling the spray while his eyes focused to the darkness.

His heart was beating just a little too hard; just enough for him to be aware of its beats. He wanted to pull himself together; he was unintegrated, there was no central force in him and his heart made a continuous protest, This is not fair, I'm not the person for this emergency.

This was the sort of thing that would happen to his mother's ideal doctor, and he would stalk into the fray, confident and selfless, working hard to save lives, giving up sleep, meals. . . .

"But, Doctor, you can't go straight out—your dinner is on the table; you haven't had your clothes off for three days—half an hour won't make all that difference!"

"Half an hour may make all the difference between life and death."

And so with a jaunty wave at the anxious little woman the doctor would set off in his car to save another life; probably a cute little boy of six with long, silky eyelashes and an adorable voice.

But this was different; this was real, not a film, and this doctor was no hero, this was Alec MacArdal who preferred a quiet life. . . .

He had forgotten how the routine of his quiet life had cramped him; he was afraid, now, of the unknown responsibilities that loomed.

Now at the top of the cliff he paused to arrange his ideas, for he must prepare some sort of plan.

First, to find out if there was any other case; and if so to impress the need of isolation until the authorities had time to act. Then he must impress on everyone the need to stay put at home. Luckily they had come here in Torquil's boat, so the contacts were fewer than if they had got the steamer; and Father Kelly, the last person from Fionn who had gone on the steamer, had made his journey before his encounter with Kirpu. But there had been the train journey from Glasgow to Oban, and before that the cheap little restaurant where they had had coffee, and the crew on Kirpu's boat from India . . . Was there an epidemic raging on the mainland? He had no idea; he had ignored newspapers since his arrival on Fionn.

Still, the mainland was no concern of his; and indeed, once he had contacted the health authorities, Fionn would be no concern of his either, he told himself, ashamed at his own cowardly relief; the vision of the doctor in the heroic film faded.

He drew a relieved breath and descended the track into the village.

But it was very late. The village was dark and deserted. Neither the manse nor the Hotel showed even a chink of light, and he had no idea where Torquil MacVean's cottage was. Here, too, it was darker than it had been on the crest of the cliff, and the moon only appeared in blinks and seemed to have withdrawn for good. He paused again, waiting for a fresh break in the clouds that hid the moon.

It came, and in its light he peered at his watch. Two minutes past twelve ; this was Sunday. He looked down the irregular vista of the village street and saw it dismally empty, gashed with the angular, motionless shadows of the cottages and trembling with the blown, patterned shadows of trees. Alec felt himself alien in the sleeping village. Not even a cat streaked across the emptiness.

The moon dimmed again for a second, and when its light reappeared he saw something move at the far end of the street. It looked as if it might be human. He stared into the far shadows, trying to pierce the darkness where a heather thatch cut off the moonlight. Now the creature moved again, coming towards him with a lolloping gait ; then it stopped again under a wall. It came on again, in gusts, not walking steadily but drifting forward on some erratic tide, sometimes bobbing up and down on one spot, then plunging forward again.

It must be human, yet it did not look wholly so. It was like something from a half-world, some troll or goblin.

He had seen this figure before, and groped in his memory to locate it. He associated it with boyhood, or still farther back, with childhood. He had seen it long ago, and in the same sort of ambiguous setting, drained of colour, a country of half-light and half-life. . . .

Now he remembered, and fear swept over him for the second time that night, but this time as an elemental emotion from the uncivilised deeps of his being ; this was the figure of a recurrent dream that had haunted his sleeping life and that now met him in reality.

In the childish dream he was walking through a little empty street lined irregularly with low houses. There were no lights ; the windows were shuttered or blinded, the doors locked. He was not yet afraid ; he went along with a skipping step, on some errand for his mother, not yet aware of the shuttered look of the street and the sky, for all his ordinary senses were dulled in unconscious preparation for the thing that would concentrate and focus them. Then at the far end of the street he saw the misshapen figure, the troll. Fear entered the dream.

At that instant he had a choice of reaction, and the dream varied according to his choice. Sometimes he stole silently up a side turning or in at a gate; sometimes he simply turned and fled. Sometimes he would walk towards the figure pretending confidence and friendliness, and the creature was easily deceived, for it was stupid. It lacked even the intelligence to be malevolent; it was merely horrible.

With a false, appeasing smile on his face, Alec would begin some game like statues, or hide and seek. He could never recall the process by which they arrived at the game, for the dream was speechless; but now the creature would be standing with its face to the wall, counting a hundred, and this was his opportunity to escape; he only had to run madly home.

But the end of the dream was always the same; whatever his ruse, when the time for escape came he could not run. His legs weighed a ton each, he had to drag each foot from the earth and was only able to set his foot a few inches forward; the ground clung to his feet like an adhesive, clamping them. Now the creature began to pursue his clumsy, slow flight, its feet making no sound but its breath puffing and bubbling, its mouth uttering a recurrent meaningless word, always softly and always on an intake of breath; and it came nearer and nearer till the last moment of ecstatic horror when he felt its soft body touch his back. . . .

He knew now that he had never recalled this dream when he was awake, never till this moment; he had remembered its recurrence only in the dream itself, thinking in the midst of the shadowy terror, this has happened before, this is familiar.

Now it was there before him, the nightmare become reality. He was no longer a child, but this was a fear that no development of mind or body could outstrip; this was a challenge to the soul.

Alec began to walk forward.

The creature stopped, watching him, but it did not retreat. Alec's footsteps were audible even in the murmur of the sea and the wind, but the troll made no sound at all. Even now when it made a wavering plunge forward and stopped again, its feet made no sound.

Now the moon darkened again. Alec waited with beating heart

till light broke through again, and saw that the troll had approached him and stood not two yards away. It was dressed in a tatter of sacks and old clothes ; its feet were bound with rags. Its face was as round as a turnip, with deep hollows gouged out for its small eyes and a hanging, grinning mouth ; an idiot blinking at him with feeble expectancy.

Alec gathered his resources, watching the creature. It was not malignant, merely repulsive. So long as it did not touch him he had, he assured himself, nothing to fear.

" Hallo," he said.

" W-rrr-l ! " said the idiot.

" You're out late."

There was no reply, only a continuous stare.

" What's your name ? "

There was no answer ; the question seemed not to have been heard at all.

" Do you know where Torquil MacVean lives ? " Alec asked, and repeated the question, trying to push it through the idiot's absorption in his appearance.

The third time he asked the question a gobble of husky sounds emerged ; he caught a word that sounded like Candy.

" I'll give you sixpence to buy candy," he promised, showing the silver coin.

The idiot showed unmistakable contempt for the coin.

" O.K.," said Alec, " I'll give you the candy if you show me where Torquil MacVean lives. Show me which is his cottage."

Another babble of gibberish followed. Then the creature peered into Alec's face for a sign of comprehension, and, finding none, gestured to Alec to follow and lolloped off in the direction of the harbour.

Torquil MacVean's cottage was right on the harbour. The half-wit led him to the door, dancing in anticipation of the promised sweet.

" I'll give it to you to-morrow," Alec promised, ignoring the shouts of indignation the poor creature set up.

He was reassured to see a light in Torquil's window, and knocked confidently. The door was opened by a young woman whose face was a white mask of patience.

" I'd like to speak to Torquil MacVean," Alec asked.

" He's bad," said the woman. " He's been hanging this two

days back." Then her face brightened. "Will you be the doctor?" she asked. "Maybe you'd better come in, then, and see him."

He's bad, he's hanging, he's not himself; Alec was to come to know these synonyms for illness. He followed her into the candlelit room and saw the dark, gaunt fisherman in the curtained bed.

"Good-evening to you," said Torquil MacVean. "Excuse me being in my bed." He waited to hear the reason for this late visit.

Alec sat down on the edge of the bed, his fingers feeling the hot wrist. He looked closer, bringing the candle over to examine Torquil's face and body and hands.

"He got himself soaked a while back," the woman explained. "The time the minister's mother went into the water, you mind. And instead of coming back and changing after he had taken the priest out to the boat he hung about in his wet things——"

"That had nothing to do with this," said Torquil.

"I blame the minister's mother," said the woman with soft persistence. "A hen with one chick."

"But this is not the rheumatism," said Torquil patiently. "This is the food poisoning."

"I've eaten them myself and taken no harm," said Shona. "I don't think it was them at all."

"It was keeping them in the pail that did it. I never thought it would harm them, but they're creatures that should be eaten fresh straight away."

"What creatures?" Alec asked.

"Sea urchins. They're very wholesome, but I had kept them two days in a bucket of sea water. That was the mistake."

"He wanted me to go to the minister's for a stomach powder," said Shona, "but I would not go. If that woman came to the door I would say my mind to her. And come to the door she would, for she has to know all that goes on, and her eyes go burning in and burning in till your very bones are scalded! A nasty, bad, inquisitive woman."

"Wheesht now, Shona; it's the minister's mother you're speaking about."

"Look, Torquil," Alec changed the subject, "I need your motor-boat to go to the mainland to-morrow, and you can't come. This," he hesitated, but decided to be frank, "this is not food poisoning; it's something more serious. Is there someone who can take me?"

Torquil's deep, mild eyes looked up at him, tolerant of his ignorance.

"Not a soul," he said.

"This is really urgent," said Alec. "Is there no one else who can work the engine and who knows the passage? I understand Danny has been out with you a good deal——"

"It's not possible, Doctor," said Torquil.

"It's imperative," said Alec.

The islander sat up on his elbow. "Listen," he said. "You hear that wind? There isn't a boat would be safe in that, going out from Fionn. It's a bad, rocky passage and needs a careful steering at best. You couldn't control the boat in that—I wouldn't attempt it myself, far less let a laddie go out in it."

Alec digested this new fact.

"Would you take a cup of tea?" Shona suggested.

"Thanks," said Alec absently. Then he asked, "How long is this wind likely to last?"

"Oh," Torquil opened his eyes wide, "There's no saying as to that. We get the winds at this season, you see. Days, maybe. Maybe weeks."

"But this is a matter of life and death!" Alec spoke impatiently, as if his urgency could affect the elements.

"If anyone tries to take the boat out in this, it is not a matter of life or death it will be, but of death alone." Torquil spoke firmly.

Alec passed a hand over his face and stood up. This altered his plans and lengthened the vista of his responsibility.

"I'll come in to see you to-morrow," he said. "I'll have to organise this . . ." He looked down at the scooped-out face on the pillow. "Were you in the War?" he asked.

"In the Merchant Navy."

"Vaccinated?"

Torquil nodded.

"Nine years ago," he said.

Alec's finger palpated one of the spots on Torquil's arm. It felt round and hard, a pellet embedded under the skin.

He stood up.

"But your tea, Doctor—the kettle's just on the boil!" Shona protested. "Are you going?"

124

" Yes," he said. But he turned back to the bed in response to a gesture from the sick man.

" Is that what it is ? " Torquil whispered. " Smallpox ? "

Alex nodded.

" But," he said, " You've got every chance of coming through it. You've been vaccinated—though some time ago."

" But," Torquil clutched his wrist, " she hasn't ! "

" That's just it," said Alec. " That's why I want to get to the mainland. Everyone on the island ought to be vaccinated at once. You see ? As it is," he hesitated, " we'll just have to do the best we can." He sounded helpless, but he pulled himself together, ashamed at his own weakness. " Tell Shona," he said, " to stay in the house, not to let anyone in or stand at the door talking to anyone. Tell her to do exactly what I say. We must keep down the contacts as far as possible."

Torquil nodded agreement.

At the door, where Shona was waiting to let him out, he looked back at the bed. Torquil's eyes were still on him; he raised his hand from the bed in a kind of salute. Alec answered the salute and went out.

He was aware of the idiot following him, sometimes puffing and babbling angrily, but he shrugged his shoulders and hurried on, ignoring the horrible creature.

When he got back to the castle he again looked in on Father Kelly. The priest was muttering in a restless sleep, struggling suddenly with the bedclothes and suddenly relaxing again, only to recommence the muttering.

However ill-equipped, he was the only person who could deal with this. Even the pugnacious old man, who would have made such a vigorous ally, was ruled out straight away by falling under the disease himself.

He would have to speak to Dochy MacArdal ; and Mr. Forsyth. To-morrow he would call a council. To-night he could do no more. He opened the window wider, refilled the cup of water that stood beside Father Kelly's bed, and climbed wearily upstairs.

Outside Father Kelly's window the idiot watched with growing resentment. Perhaps the man had gone to fetch the candy at last. He waited. But the man did not return.

The idiot clambered up to the window and pushed his face into the room. For a long time he hung half in and half out, staring at the sleeping priest, watching his restless movements, exploring the room with his eyes. There was nothing that looked like a box of candy. He heaved a gusty sigh of discouragement and his feet groped for the ground.

Dawn was overcoming the fitful moonlight. It was the coldest hour of the night. Candy Andy clutched his sacks round him and began hobbling along the shore, away from the castle, away from the village, over the rocks to the cave that was his home.

## Chapter Fifteen

Mrs. MacLennan was up at half-past six every morning. She and the minister's mother and Danny Rafferty were the only habitual early risers on the island. Nell Patrick too was up early these days, but that was because the children wakened her.

The first thing Mrs. MacLennan did was to clean out and light the big black range in the kitchen and put the kettle and the porridge pot above the crackling flames. Then she washed the doorstep, swept and dusted the bar, the lounge, the hall and dining-room and the kitchen itself. By twenty-past seven she exchanged her sack apron for a floral overall and sat down to her breakfast in the kitchen.

This was her best meal of the day, for it was the only one when she was sure of peace and privacy. She used to repeat this phrase to herself sometimes, in gratitude for the small daily treasure. She would draw the table near the fire, take off her glasses that misted up with steam from the porridge.

" Now," she would say, " for a bit of peace and privacy."

This morning, as often happened, she had to pause in the middle of her porridge to let Thomas in; but this she hardly noticed as an interruption. Thomas was the Hotel cat, presented to her as a kitten eight years ago by the skipper of the steamer. Yes, yes, a tom kitten for sure. Look at his wide brow and intellectual eyes, certain signs of masculinity. Besides, if further proof were needed, his very name was Thomas, wasn't it !

Thomas fulfilled the promised role of destroyer of mice, but had two inconvenient habits ; one, a perpetual burning desire to be on the other side of the door, the other, a habit of producing kittens three times a year. For both of these traits Mrs. MacLennan held the skipper directly and malignly responsible, for you couldn't blame the poor creature herself.

"There's your milk to you, Thomas," said Mrs. MacLennan. "Take it and be at peace."

She finished her porridge, poured out a cup of tea and stirred it meditatively, staring into nothingness. The wind was still bellowing away ; some day she'd have to get the roof seen to, a provoking expense ; the shipment of tiles from Oban added a scandalous amount to the cost of repairs. Against that, it was the wind that kept the two ladies and Dochy MacArdal in the Hotel, fifteen good guineas a week between the three of them, and her savings when she died were going to be very handy for the bairns. (Her youngest bairn was forty.)

Thomas finished her milk and leapt up on Mrs. MacLennan's lap, where she did some preliminary washing and then settled down to purr. Mrs. MacLennan poured out a second cup of tea.

She would do a good big baking of scones this morning ; enough to provide Maura with what she would need for the castle to-day and to-morrow, and maybe she'd get her to come up to the Hotel for a couple of hours to-morrow morning to help with the washing. Maura was a grand washer with a good strong back on her ; the washing was the thing that did for Mrs. MacLennan. If Maura would wash it and get it hung out she didn't mind doing the ironing herself. She poured out her third cup of tea and stirred it.

That was when her second interruption came. Thomas stopped purring and jerked upright. Mrs. MacLennan followed the direction of Thomas's gaze and saw Candy Andy at the window, mouthing and shouting and beckoning with his whole body in uncouth gestures.

She shook her head crossly at Andy. This was no time of day to come begging for food ; it was in the afternoon that he got any scraps and left-overs she had. If she paid any attention to him now it would just be the beginning of more pestering. She continued to ignore his irritated dance outside until he started banging at the window ; then she went out to deal with him.

"Off you go with you!" she said. "I don't know what you mean, disturbing folks at this hour on the Sabbath. No, you'll get no candy from me, and you'll get no dinner either this day if you don't stop your pestering and——"

She paused, for someone else had decided to interrupt her peace and privacy and was ringing the front-door bell.

Andy gave a shout of triumph when he heard it. He had been telling her the man was coming! Now, at last, he would get the candy he had been promised.

Mrs. MacLennan shut the back door on Andy and went through to the hall to find Dr. Alec MacArdal stepping in.

"Good-morning," she answered wonderingly. "Were you out fishing? Nothing wrong at the castle, then, is there?"

"Yes," he said, "something quite serious is wrong, and I want your help, Mrs. MacLennan."

"Certainly," she said, still wondering.

"I want to see Mr. Dochy MacArdal, too, and I've asked Mr. Forsyth to come over here."

"But I haven't taken up Mr. Dochy's shaving water yet," she said. "It's early to wake him . . ."

But she led the way into the kitchen and filled a brass can with water from the kettle.

"I'll wake him," she said, and left him standing in the kitchen.

Alec had passed a restless night cogitating and planning, dozing fitfully, waking to fresh apprehensions. His restlessness had had one good result : his initial feeling of helplessness had gone and he had worked out a plan of campaign. For, since there was no way out, he must take charge.

All the same he was tired. He looked round the Hotel kitchen, a brisk, warm, useful-looking place that yet had a dignity about it with its white casement curtains, gleaming windows and polished range with a cat sitting before it. The cat was licking its tail. The tail had a tendency to twitch away from the busy tongue and the cat held it firm with one paw until it was all dealt with, even the sinuous tip.

Alec turned his eyes from the cat to the yellow flames in the grate. He was tired enough to be hypnotised by any rhythmic movement ; the cat's round head nodding as she licked her tail, the flames streaming up the chimney. He rubbed his eyes and turned as Mrs. MacLennan came back.

Under her appraising look he felt a twinge of shame, not because

128

there was contempt or criticism in her regard but because he sensed the contrast between himself andt his small, elderly woman. She had the integrity that comes from doing hard work with a good heart. Beside her he felt himself complex, equivocal, a compound of several personalities that lived together without harmony.

" He'll be down directly," she told him and began clearing the table, refilled the kettle and set it on the fire and washed the dishes she had used.

" Did you have your breakfast ? " she asked, turning from the sink.

" I—ate a scone."

" I'll give you a plate of porridge ; you'll feel better for something hot in your inside. When the kettle boils I'll make tea. There, now—help yourself to the milk, Doctor. Ts ! " she exclaimed, " there's that creature back again ! "

She buttered a scone quickly, took it out to Andy and shooed him out of the yard.

" And go right away off ! " Alec heard her say. " Don't you come back here at this time of the day, d'you hear me ? And if I have to speak to you again it's not speaking I'll be ! "

This mysterious threat sent Andy, wrathful and frustrated, away to his own haunts and she returned to the kitchen brushing her palms together.

" A poor, harmless creature," she said, " but he gets to be a nuisance if he gets out of hand."

" I saw him late last night, hopping about in the empty street. He looked horrible, just coming across him in the moonlight. When I was a child I used to have a dream about a figure something like that."

" I never was one for dreaming. I haven't got the imagination."

" You needn't regret that," Alec said, smiling. " I used to dream far too much. Worried dreams—nightmares."

" Still, it must be an entertainment all the same."

" Entertainment ? It's more than that, it's—another life. A different life altogether. As a rule you don't even carry the memory of your dreams into this life. One memory for day-time living, another for the life you lead in your dreams. It's self-contained, you see ; or almost. Two parallel lives with very little interchange."

This, too, he had been thinking out last night, but he had not finished thinking about his dreams. There was more to discover about dreams, he felt, than the already stereotyped theories of the psychoanalysts. They had stopped too soon, content with too mean a harvest; that was why their books left you with a sense of shrunkenness, of life as meagre as the pre-Copernican universe, life without the majestic terror of infinity.

But there was no time now to investigate the deeper meaning of dreams. He stood up as Dochy MacArdal entered, shaved and trim and with his usual air of well-being, but still in his dressing-gown. At the same time Mrs. MacLennan went to the front door and ushered in the minister.

"Come in, Mr. Forsyth. We're all in the kitchen," she said. In the kitchen they looked at each other attentively.

"I won't take long to tell you why we're here," he said, finding it, all the same, hard to come to the bleak fact he had to disclose. "It's pretty grave or I wouldn't have roused you at this hour." Now he would have to come to it. "The fact is, the illness Kirpu had when we arrived here turns out not to have been flu. It was a mild case of smallpox."

"Smallpox!" It was Mr. Forsyth who repeated the word. They were all staring at him.

"Yes." He swallowed. "Father Kelly has contracted it from him and there may be other cases—almost certainly. Torquil MacVean is another case. I must go round every house in the island and find out whether there are any more cases yet." He cleared his throat, not yet looking at their faces. "As we can't get in contact with the mainland," he said, "I'll have to tackle the emergency as well as can be done—with what resources we can find on Fionn. It means—well, first of all we need a team."

Now he looked at their intent faces.

"That's why I called this—committee meeting."

"I'm at your disposal," said Dochy, still genial.

Mrs. MacLennan folded her hands, waiting to know what was required of her. Mr. Forsyth fingered his chin.

"First, then, have you all been vaccinated?"

"Not me," said Mrs. MacLennan virtuously.

"Yes," said both the men.

Dochy's vaccination was nine years old, John Forsyth's was seven.

"Pity they're not more recent," said Alec. "I've got to tell you frankly that there's a big risk for you both. You, Mrs.

MacLennan, we'll have to keep you away from contact with it as far as possible, that's all."

" What did you want us to do ? " John Forsyth asked.

"I need two stretcher bearers right away," said Alec.

" There's stretchers in my wash-house," said Mrs. MacLennan. " Left there by the A.R.P. and never removed. There's respirators and stirrup pumps too, and a handcart and a ladder."

" God bless the A.R.P.," said Dochy.

" I was in the R.A.M.C. in the last year of the war," said John Forsyth. " I did quite a bit of stretcher work and had a spell in the wards, too."

" That's good to know. Well, my idea is to make the castle into an emergency isolation hospital. The first case for you to bring in is Torquil MacVean. And when you bring in a case, bring their bedding as well, blankets and linen—all the linen you can get, we'll need it. Don't go into any house except the one where the smallpox is, and don't talk to people."

" But they're bound to find out," said Dochy.

" It's not that. Once you've collected Torquil you may carry the infection round with you. People will have to stay as far as possible in their own homes. No tea-parties or gossips in the bar here, no gatherings of any kind. We don't know who may be developing it, you see."

" I see."

" Well," said John, " we'd better get off for Torquil, poor soul, straight away, in case there's any other case to fetch before it's time for the kirk."

" There won't be any church service," Alec reminded him.

" No church ? "

" No. No meetings of any kind."

" I don't know if I can agree to that," said John doubtfully. " I don't know . . . matter of conscience. . . ." He was thinking of what his mother would have to say. And the elders.

" When I go round the houses," said Alec patiently, " I'll tell them that they can't go to church. It's my order. As the only doctor on the island."

" But—I'm the minister," said John, genuinely puzzled as to his duty and quailing at the thought of the disapproval he would certainly call upon his head whatever he did now.

" This is a grave emergency, John," said Dochy. " As the

131

leading figure on the island it's up to you to back the doctor. For the sake of other people's lives."

John looked worried.

" I'll take a message from you round all the houses, if you like," Alec suggested. " Would that help ? "

John sketched a message in his mind, framing it in pulpit terms, trying out the sound of it. Time of tribulation. Duty of us all as Christians, members one of another. Daily Bible reading and prayers in the secrecy of our own chambers till the days of trial are overpast.

He nodded reluctantly.

" Good," said Alec. " And there's another thing ; you can't go back and forward to your own homes—or to the Hotel. It means coming to live at the castle, both of you——"

To his surprise he saw John's face clear.

" We'll do whatever you think best," said Dochy.

" You'll need me to help with looking after them, anyway," said John.

This easy victory where he had expected further argument so pleased Alec that, to his surprise, he found himself slapping them both on the shoulder—quite like Bertie at an Elks dinner.

" Fine," he said, still like Bertie. " You're swell guys . . ." Then shame overtook him and he returned to reticence.

" Well, then," he said, " the first thing to do is to get what you need packed in a suitcase and taken to the castle. Take everything you want, remember. No return journeys. Then come back for the stretchers and go for Torquil."

Mrs. MacLennan had listened to all this in silence, only moving to lift off the kettle when it boiled.

" I can't offer to help with the nursing," she said. " I've got the Hotel and the two ladies to look after."

" Besides," Alec pointed out, " you're not vaccinated."

" I don't hold with it," she explained.

" But what I will ask you to do," said Alec, " is to help us with food. Could you cook something for us every day, if you will ? Maura will have a lot to do helping with the sick, and I'm afraid she'll have a lot of extra washing to do."

" I could cook your dinner every day," said Mrs. MacLennan. But her heart sank a little. Not only would she have no help from

Maura with her washing to-morrow, but she was undertaking quite heavy additional work.

" Well, we must arrange for someone to call for it every day."

" The A.R.P. handcart," she suggested. " And I'd just send it in the pots it was cooked in."

" That's an idea. Perhaps Danny could undertake that."

" But he'll be at the school——"

" There'll be no school," Mr. Forsyth reminded her firmly. " Well, I'll go and pack my case." He was quite jaunty.

Alec washed his hands at the sink to remove the dust of the stretchers he had been examining. Dochy went upstairs to pack his case and finish dressing. Mrs. MacLennan began to prepare breakfast for the dining-room.

" How many of you will there be, then, Doctor ? " she asked. " To cook for, I mean."

" Well, Mr. MacArdal and Mr. Forsyth and myself," Alec counted, " and Maura and Danny, and Kirpu—he seems to be a sort of vegetarian, according to Maura. And Father Kelly and Torquil MacVean, they need liquids mostly—soup and jelly and custard, you know. And fruit drinks."

Mrs. MacLennan swallowed her dismay and set her shoulders. Once she got into the way of all this it wouldn't be so bad.

" And somebody will come along to fetch it," she reminded him. " Say I have it ready at a quarter to one, that would let me get it out of the way before I serve the ladies at one o'clock. Would that suit ? "

" Oh, yes."

" A quarter to one sharp, then. Is it—is it awful serious ? "

" Pretty serious." Alec met her courageous eyes and smiled, but the smile was a weak effort.

" Well, we'll just all have to do the best we can," she said matter-of-factly.

Alec was grateful for her brusque fatalism. He set off on his round of the inhabitants of Fionn.

Mrs. MacLennan carried through the breakfast to the dining-room, banged the gong severely and returned to the kitchen. She drew breath and stared at Thomas.

" All very well for you," she said, " sitting there with your paws curled under you. Folks have more to do than that."

She glanced at the idea that a cup of tea would nerve her for the busy day ahead. She had only had three cups at breakfast, and had missed the pleasant lingering over the last cup in solitude, or at least with wee Thomas keeping her unobtrusive company. But she rejected that comfort; a cup of tea was nothing but a put-off of time. She filled a bruised enamel basin with potatoes and began to peel them under the cold water tap, sniffing and pushing up her spectacles with the back of her wrist.

In the dining-room she heard a sound of feminine voices and a lifting of lids.

" Haddock ! " said Miss Transom's voice, clearly and dispassionately.

There was a silence following the information, perhaps filled by some expressive look or shrug. Mrs. MacLennan wondered if the ladies maybe didn't think much of haddock for breakfast. But eggs were scarce and bacon worse, and you had to feed folks on something. And now—jellies and vegetarians and fruit drinks. . . .

There was a tap at the kitchen door and Lydia Transom came in.

" Oh, Mrs. MacLennan," she said confidently, " do you think we could have eggs instead of haddock ? Somehow, haddock . . ."

She left haddock floating in the air, disparaged without words.

Mrs. MacLennan did not allow herself even to purse her lips. She dried her hands and put a pot on the fire to boil the eggs.

" Three and a half minutes, please ? " said Lydia charmingly.

Mrs. MacLennan agreed to the three and a half minutes ; and when Lydia had shut the door she turned again to the muddy pile of potatoes and was moved to song.

> " Ye fearful saints," she sang, " fresh courage take,
>     The clouds ye so much dread
>     Are big with mercy, and will break
>     In blessings on your head ! "

Thomas, unused to outbursts of song, mewed and came forward to rub against her ankles. Mrs. MacLennan was cheered.

# Chapter Sixteen

ALEC BEGAN methodically at the beginning, by retracing his steps past the Hotel to the first little cottage that huddled beyond the manse. By the time he reached its gate he had developed a technique.

The manse was a narrow, two-story house with a pillared portico that seemed to scrabble after dignity and to achieve only a dismal pretentiousness. Still, Alec rang the bell, a formality he had dispensed with in the cottages.

Mrs. Forsyth opened the door and stood back.

" Good-morning, Mrs. Forsyth. I expect your son has told you the unfortunate news. Have you been vaccinated ? "

She stood there with one hand on the door, the other at her breast, staring at him from a white, stricken face.

" Have you been vaccinated ? "

" No," she said, moistening her lips. " No."

" Well, that simply means that you will be wise to keep as much as possible inside the house. You're quite well, are you ? "

She still looked tranced and stupid.

" You feel all right ? . . . No pains ? No headache ? "

Her tongue flicked again over her lips.

" A dreadful headache," she murmured. " Dreadful."

" I'd better have a look at you."

He had to push her before him, into a grim sitting-room on the right of the door, a grey room presided over by photographs of sitters, all of whom, he knew instinctively, had earned the title ' the late ' so and so.

" Sit down and let me see you."

Her pulse was surprisingly slow.

" Let me see your tongue."

She protruded the quivering tip.

" All of it. Open your mouth. Thank you."

" I'm sure I don't know——"

She was feebly resentful, not at all like the woman who had staged an ugly drama on the harbour with herself in the leading role. She seemed quenched.

" Have you been taking aspirin ? "

" Nothing is explained to me."

" I want to know if you have taken something for your headache."

" I don't mean that. John . . ."

She swallowed and was silent.

" What have you been taking ? "

" I never touch aspirins. Drugs. I get headaches. I suffer them without the help of drugs."

With a good deal of patience he discovered that she had, in fact, taken twenty grains of a patent brand of aspirin.

" I'll come back and see you to-morrow," he said. " Don't take any more of the tablets till I see you. Understand ? "

" Where is—what is John—what—— But I don't understand all this," she said desperately, following him to the door.

" John is going to stay at the castle till the emergency is over," he said. " His R.A.M.C. experience is going to be invaluable. It won't be for long—only until we can get word to the mainland. In the meantime we have to stop church and school."

" He could sleep here."

" Not possibly. You haven't been vaccinated."

" I don't mind the risk when my own son——"

Her mouth trembled, her voice rose.

" But we can't run stupid risks," said Alec firmly. " We don't want even one extra case to nurse—we're going to have a heavy task, you know."

" I could come to the castle and help," she said.

" Can't have you—for the same reason. You're not vaccinated."

Alec smiled and stepped away from her, but looked back from the path. Her face crumpled as he watched. She wept, without any attempt to cover her face, still staring at him. He hesitated, but remembered the visits that lay ahead of him.

" I'll be back to-morrow," he said.

He did not look back again as he shut the gate, but was sure she was still there.

The next household was quickly dealt with. A taciturn old man opened the door, heard his formula and led him into a low-ceilinged kitchen where four or five grown-ups and children in various stages of deshabille were eating porridge.

"We're all fine, thanks," said his middle-aged daughter. "We're late to-day, being Sunday; you'll excuse us. All the children were vaccinated at the school, and I would have got done, too, only I was nursing Nancy at the time and a sore arm is an unhandy thing to have, with all the folks I have to look after."

"I got mine done," said the grandfather, displaying his arm; at which all the children showed off their vaccination scars and were admired and praised by Alec.

"I'll look in again to-morrow. No school this week. And, Mrs. Alyth, you must stay at home and let the vaccinated members of the family do the shopping. No school and no church."

The children's eyes shone; they looked on him as a benefactor, a bestower of holidays from school.

He would have passed the Hotel when he came to it but remembered the two ladies whom he had not interviewed. He went in.

Somewhere upstairs Mrs. MacLennan was making beds, still singing, but with pauses between lines to puff up pillows or throw up blankets. Alec made his way to the resident's parlour upstairs. Mrs. Transom was there.

"Oh, good-morning, Doctor," she said, lifting a magazine off the sofa to make room beside her and looking like a soft, pink pæony rose. "Mrs. MacLennan has just been telling us the frightening news. I'm so glad to see you."

"Does it frighten you? I don't think you need be in much danger, Mrs. Transom." His voice was reassuring and gentle, for her softness appealed to him. "Just keep away from crowds. By the way, have you been vaccinated?"

"Vaccinated?" she echoed. "Oh, yes, I had to be done, you know, before I went to join my first husband in Burma. A girl of nineteen, Doctor, and you know what life in Burma is, especially Army life! The wives get so hard and catty, you know—I suppose it was my childishness that prevented me from becoming like that too. My husband, you know, was exactly twice my age." She sighed. "But I mustn't chatter to you, I know; you are so terribly busy. Can I be of any use?"

"I'll let you know if you can," he smiled. "I ought to see your daughter, too——"

" I'm here."

Lydia was leaning against the door. She must have come in while her mother was talking. Now she came forward indifferently, accepted his place on the sofa and ignored her mother's protest that she had entered so softly that no one had heard her.

" Oh, yes, I was vaccinated," she said. " I have no idea what year it was ; everybody was having it done, and I was at school so there was no escape—— Thank you."

He did not know why he offered his cigarette-case to her and then to her mother ; he had no time to spend smoking with idle women. He lit Mrs. Transom's cigarette, then held the lighter to Lydia's. Her mouth was very pale pink ; she frowned faintly and squinted at the flame ; then she raised her eyes to his.

Even when he understood the faint shock that he experienced when he met her eyes, he did not speak. He did not respond at once to her smile.

" Light your own," she suggested, still smiling.

" Well," he said, hesitating, " I think perhaps I'd better not put off more time." And he snapped the flame out and returned the lighter to his pocket.

He spoke a few words of advice to the two women ; recovered his equanimity and left.

But Lydia called him when he was outside.

" Can I go out for walks if I don't go near people ? " she asked. " Up the hill, for example, to the lochan ? "

" Why, yes," he said, " if you're not afraid of the monster ? "

" Oh, what monster ? "

" Kelpie or something," he said lightly. " I don't know."

" But who told you ? "

" I believe it was Sir Hector MacArdal."

" I'll certainly go there if there's a monster. If I disappear you must drag for me."

" But there's no bottom in the lochan."

" Oh, isn't there ? . . . You know everything about this place. Nobody else told me that ! "

He laughed and went on, wondering if she still hung out of the parlour window looking down at him. She might have been a pretty girl but for her eyes. He remembered the little jar of meeting her upturned eyes, large, almond-shaped eyes with a rim of white showing under each iris; one blue iris and one—was it hazel? Light brown, anyway. An odd effect.

Well, hardly pretty, he decided, remembering that he had scarcely noticed her at all the first twice he had seen her. Too pale, too colourless. But with one blue eye and one—light brown, or dark gold perhaps.

Nell Patrick, when he opened her door, still wore an old, stained crimson dressing-gown fastened with a safety pin at the waist and a brooch at the neck. Her face, a smudgy little triangle, was strained.

"Oh, Doctor," she said before he spoke, "I'm glad to see you. The baby's bad; would you spare time to look at her? I don't know what's wrong, she's been hanging this past three or four days and now. . . ."

Alec looked at the mite in the cradle and his heart sank. The baby's eyes were shut, the lids blistered and swollen, the small face covered with vesicles.

"I thought I'd go mad with her crying at first, and now she's quiet, I don't like it," Nell pleaded. "Is the sleep doing her good, Doctor? Maybe it's the very thing she needs? I would have gone to Father Kelly for some ointment, but Danny Rafferty told me he was sick in the castle."

"Your baby is very ill, Mrs. Patrick."

"It's a skin trouble, Doctor, isn't it?"

Alec looked at her. This was the sort of thing that he had always recoiled from. It passed across his mind that, in the clinic, he was sheltered from this. Sometimes he would find, when he examined a patient, a grave condition, a cancer; but he left it to the general practitioner to break the news to the patient or to his relatives. But now . . . this baby had no chance. And there was no one else to speak to Nell.

"I think," he said, "the best thing will be for me to get her taken to the castle, then I can keep an eye on her and—do my best for her." He swallowed.

"But what is it?" Nell's voice was apprehensive.

"I'm afraid—smallpox."

"Smallpox!" It was a whispered scream.

"Well, perhaps not—perhaps—but I should like to have her at the castle, anyway——"

Perhaps not, perhaps not, he insisted angrily to his conscience. Perhaps pemphigus neonatorum, perhaps—anything——

"Have you any other children?" he asked.

Nell removed the towel she had clutched to her mouth. Her eyes had filled with tears; she looked at him with hostility.

"Yes," she said, not moving.

"And—are they all right?"

"Yes," she said.

"I think I should see them," he insisted gently.

She did not move. "There's only one," she said. "He had a bad night. He's asleep and I don't want him wakened." She was fighting to keep tears out of her voice, but its hardness did not disguise terror.

"And has he been vaccinated? Have you?"

She shook her head.

"Where is he?"

After a second she led the way to an inner room where wee Pad was lying in her bed, feverishly asleep. Faint red spots were already appearing on his face and hands.

Alec took Nell by the elbows and sat her in a chair.

"Now, Mrs. Patrick," he began, but she clutched his sleeve and hid her face against it.

"Oh, Doctor, oh, Doctor," she whispered, "they can cure it, can't they? Make them better, Doctor, won't you—will you, Doctor?"

He said, "I promise to do my best."

He disentangled his sleeve from her clutch at last and left her.

"We'll take them together," he said. "Look out blankets to wrap them warmly, please; and have the—the things they'll need, nightdresses and so on—have them ready."

"Yes, I will."

"Your husband is not in?"

"He's fishing," she said.

"I'd like to see him too."

"I'll tell him when he comes in."

She ran after him when he left her door.

"I could come and look after them," she begged. "Let me be there with them; they'll feel strange without me."

"But your husband?"

" He can look after himself. Let me come, Doctor, I'd help Maura, too ! "

" It might be a good idea," he said slowly.

The tension in her face relaxed. She went back to the two sick children.

Alec forced himself on. He would never be a good doctor ; his nerves had never coarsened ; and he had nothing within himself to give, no courage to buoy himself and others, nothing but insecurity and emptiness.

He opened the neat gate of Captain Kilbride's.

" Good-morning," he said. " I'm afraid we have a rather serious illness here on Fionn, and I'm making a round of all the houses. Have you been vaccinated, Mrs. Kilbride ? "

I sound, he thought, like an insurance agent. Only I have no policy to offer. No vaccine.

Lydia Transom was still gazing out on the irregular street of the village that was scattered with wind-ruffled hens. A soft, secret smile lingered on her face.

She watched Alec emerge from the Patricks' cottage and go on past a jutting corner that shut him from her sight.

" Lydia, this is terrible," said her mother.

" What ? "

" Smallpox ! "

" Oh——" Lydia's cigarette was finished. She dropped it on the pebbled path beneath the window. " I don't suppose we shall catch it."

" It's such a disfiguring disease ! I once saw a woman with her face—all pitted ! "

" Was that in Burma ? "

Mrs. Transom made a pettish gesture. But there was no one else to speak to except Lydia. She restrained her irritation.

" The thing is, with this going on they may not let us go even when the weather does improve ! I heard of people who were in Glasgow when it broke out, and they wouldn't allow them to go back—I forget for how long ! Oh," she groaned, " as soon as I can get away from here you won't be able to see me for dust ! "

Lydia drew her shoulders from the window and closed it, thinking over this possibility of further imprisonment.

"Why did we come here in the first place?" she asked. "Can you remember?"

"Well, Lydia, everybody ought to be able to say they've been to the West Highlands, and preferably to one of the Western Isles. And if you've seen one—I mean——"

"You can improvise on the theme."

Mrs. Transom was silent.

"At least," she said, "it's been even cheaper than Mallorca, though it has been rather dull. No society. But when we get back to London——"

"Yes. When. Still, it may not be so deadly after all."

"You don't realise, do you, that Dochy MacArdal isn't to be here? He's staying at the castle now."

But Dochy MacArdal's absence was no disadvantage to Lydia. He was apparently immune to her charms. Whereas the doctor would call every day, and perhaps he would prove less insensible.

"But it has been interesting, all the same. . . ."

Lydia knew that her mother meant, rather, it would become interesting in retrospect; suitably garnished and served up with all the accompaniments.

"Where are you going now, Lydia?"

"To my room. My nails are chipping."

"Bring your things in here; I'll do mine, too. After all, we're private—as if we had our own suite."

"Right."

"But what I'd like right now," said Mrs. Transom when her daughter returned with emery boards and orange sticks and an assortment of bottles, "is to be sitting under the drier at Fernand's. No, not under the drier, yet—just having my waves set."

She visualised the process. The last swish of the rinsing water over her nape, the enveloping towel, the swinging back to rest against the curved chair-back; a soft rub from the towel, then, seen in the mirror, the approach of Fernand himself, drawing a dark comb from his pocket, his eyes first on her hair, then glancing up to meet hers in the glass. Fernand knew the exact gradation of deference, flattery and flirtation to supply to each client, and the probable fact that he despised them all equally did not diminish his charm in Mrs. Transom's eyes. She sighed.

"I think I'll have a manicure after all."

Now a handmaiden brought a stool and a tray of materials and set to work, a humble little artist, on her fingers. . . . Another girl stood beside Monsieur Fernand holding lotion, offering pins and clips, like an acolyte at High Mass. Yes, like an acolyte. If ever I go in for religion, Mrs. Transom reflected, it will be the Roman Church, incense and genuflections and a row of penitents waiting to enter the confessional. . . . So much better staged than in the C. of E.

"Does this island sometimes make you feel religious?" she asked.

Lydia stroked enamel over her thumb-nail from the half-moon to the tip.

"No," she said, waggling her thumb, giving the enamel a minute to fix before going on to the index finger.

"Does it you?" she asked, dipping the brush again.

She did not notice her mother's reply. Her own thoughts were on another tack. Religion on Fionn, a dull choice between Father Kelly and John Forsyth. One glance was enough for John Forsyth; that sandy type was stodgy. Even in despair they were stodgy, like Selwyn Bowman who had been such a wet-blanket latterly, refusing to recognise a plain dismissal.

Her mother was rambling on about something, but Lydia was reviewing a series of men, mostly young but not all; beginning with the riding-master at school, so spare and handsome that every-one had a crush on him even though they knew that, when he took off his hat, there was that patch where you saw pink scalp shining through the black.

"Sweet on you, Lydia——" All the excited whisperings and twitterings that sounded so juvenile and trite compared to the kisses in the dark stable.

It was like a snapshot, a series of snapshots. That last one, his face looking stiff and disastrous at the idea of her leaving, of her own unconcern, for, of course, she had a new life to look forward to and had no intention of wasting time coming back for poky kisses in a stable—or in a tea-shop either. Then the other snapshots: Roy, looking at her, suddenly interested; Roy laughing, entertaining; Roy becoming tiresome, then no more Roy. Neville interested, Neville entertaining, Neville tiresome. Jacky interested, enter-taining, tiresome. George——

Alec was at the interested stage. She knew the signs; once she had got that much response, that expression of startled awareness, she knew that the rest would develop. She had been mistaken all the same over Dochy . . . Perhaps she had gone too fast . . . Anyway she let him go without regret. Those absurd little half lenses simply wouldn't do.

" Oh—there it is," she said, discovering that her mother was asking for the enamels.

Scarlet on those stubby little nails ; how silly. How silly indeed, to be soft and floppy and past forty. At that age you should modify to a more becoming style. Was her mother much more than forty ?

" How old were you when I was born ? " she asked.

" Not twenty yet."

It might be true. Lydia simply did not know, and there was no use cross-examining. Mrs. Transom merely became vague and bewildered : you could never pin her down, you could never extract accurate information from her—it was like trying to clasp a handful of mist. Besides, for all her indifference—and it was not merely a mask—Lydia had a delicacy about asking her mother too many questions. The web of fantasy and contradictions that emerged shamed Lydia.

But to Mrs. Transom it never seemed like lying. She was merely improving the colourless facts, giving them a beauty treatment.

Alec emerged from the Kilbrides' cottage heartened by a glass of whisky. The captain's hospitality had been bland and generous and flavoured with an undercurrent of amusement. Alec was not sure if he himself were the joke, or if humanity, or the disastrous news he brought, provoked the twinkle in the captain's austere eyes.

Mrs. Kilbride's hospitality was blunt and calm. She listened to the doctor's advice intelligently, and he hoped she would enforce it on her husband. She evidently hoped so too, for she threw occasional severe glances at him as if to underline Alec's words, pursing her lips and chewing with satisfaction at points that pleased her. Not a particularly lovable old person, Alec thought, but probably capable.

The captain saw him to the gate and waved away his repetition of the advice to avoid company.

" I heard ye, I heard ye," he said, taking his pipe out of his pocket. " I heard ye the first time."

He put the unfilled pipe in his mouth and looked up at the sky. The wind blew his white hair this way and that, a dry wind still; the specks of moisture in it were spray from the sea, not spots of rain.

" Will the wind drop soon ? " Alec asked.

" It will not," said Captain Kilbride, staring sardonically at Alec's departure.

" Smallpox," he mused. " Good business for the gravedigger."

He turned at last, having heard his wife arguing at him, as he put it, for some time. There she was in the doorway with a shawl clutched round her.

" It's not smallpox that'll have the chance on you," she scolded, " it's the pneumonia you're trying to get, you with no hat on your bare head and leaving the door open as if my chest wasn't the way it is. And who's to have the pleasure of nursing you ? "

" What did ye say ? " he asked mildly, sauntering up. " If the cold annoys you, woman, go inside. I'll not prevent you. He's away in to the schoolteacher's now. It'll be a free holiday for her, I'm thinking."

" And you'll mind what the doctor said about no gossiping on the harbour or drinking in the Hotel," his wife warned in a softer voice.

" I heard him as well as yourself: wasn't I there in the flesh, sitting opposite him all the time he spoke ? "

" There's a big difference between hearing and doing. See you and do what he told you."

" Give us peace in our time, O Lord," said the captain without animosity. " And," he added, addressing his wife again, " when my times comes to be packed in a box I'll go quietly ; but until then I'll be master of my own actions, I hope."

Mrs. Kilbride's response was a syllable that might be spelt " Pffchk ! " Her secret thought was that, though she wished her husband no harm, the house would be a lot less work without him in it.

Captain Kilbride, still musing on the lethal possibilities of smallpox, decided that if either of them was gathered to the Lord, he would marry again.

He stuffed some tobacco into his pipe, poked a strip of paper into the red of the fire, and when it caught, applied it to the tobacco. He was ready for her if she started flyting at him ; the doctor forbade foregathering at the harbour for smoking or any other purposes. But she said nothing about it.

He leaned back in his chair and relaxed.

## Chapter Seventeen

JOHN FORSYTH had spent no unnecessary time talking to his mother. He had packed pyjamas and shaving materials, a set of underwear, three pairs of black knitted socks, his Bible and his Daily Light; had announced, in a voice that sounded harsh in his own ears, that he was required to stay at the castle " for the duration of the smallpox," and had walked off with his packed bag—simply walked out of the house, not impeded in any way.

It gave him a sense of volcanic achievement. He looked back on it with awe.

On his way back from the castle as he went to the Hotel, he passed the manse again. He did not look up at the windows; he walked tensely past, prepared for her to rush out at him; but nothing happened. Indeed if he had looked at the windows he would have seen nothing but the familiar curtains, for Mrs. Forsyth was at that moment in the parlour with Alec, their interview presided over by photographs of John's father and grandparents and great-aunt Sara.

" Now, Mr. Forsyth," said Mrs. MacLennan, " fine I know you didn't have time for a proper breakfast before you got here, and you're to have it before you set out. Finnan haddocks it is." She paused, but saw only respect in the minister's face and concluded that he looked on haddock in a proper spirit. " You'll just take it in beside Mr. Dochy, he'll still be at his."

" It's an awful big helping, Mistress MacLennan."

" You've got a big day ahead of you, laddie. Away to the dining-room with it." She had disposed of the fish that the ladies rejected.

" A serious situation," John observed as he sat down beside Dochy.

" But the doctor seems to have taken a grip on it, don't you agree ? "

" Vigorously, I would say."

" More to him than meets the eye." Dochy lit a cigarette and watched the minister eat. He himself was ready to tackle whatever was required of him. Without being flippant he was looking forward to this new experience.

John eyed him thoughtfully as he packed away fish and scones and tea. He was thinking : By the end of the week we three will know each other pretty thoroughly. I wonder will we get on.

" Right ? " said Dochy.

" Right you are," John agreed. " We'll be on our way."

They collected the stretcher and set off.

" They're coming," said Shona, rushing into the house.

Torquil turned his head on the pillow and looked at her. She stood distractedly looking round, feeling she ought to be busy at some last-minute arrangements, tightening the string on the parcel of shirts and bed linen she had laid out, trembling and staring at everything but her husband's face.

They longed to comfort each other but there was nothing to do.

" Shona," he said, " Shona, don't be worrying now. I'll be thinking on you. I'll be back."

" So you will, my heart."

When Dochy and the minister came in they remembered to speak in English, they bade them good-morning with sober courtesy, and yes, they had everything ready packed.

Torquil's face was flushed. He watched the minister unfurl the stretcher and lay it on the floor and drape it with blanket.

" You'll manage, will you ? " John asked.

" I've still got the use of my legs, thank God," said Torquil, but it was a good thing he had not far to go ; he was light in the head as if the force of gravity had lost effect on him and he might at any minute float off his feet.

Shona looked on with a hand at her throat. She did not want them to think of her husband as weak and wavering.

" Six-foot two, he is," she burst out. " A great man on the whalers before he got a harpoon through his foot. He is a wonderful mechanic, there is nothing he doesn't know about any machine or engine——"

Torquil smiled and spoke to her again in Gaelic ; and then, muffled up from crown to toe, was raised from the ground,

147

manoeuvred round carefully so as to go head first, and carried out into the beating wind.

Shona stood in the door and watched him go, the tall man she had married, passing through the village horizontal on a stretcher with his face looking up at the sky, helpless for any to look on.

Behind her was a dreadful gaping emptiness.

She turned back to the cottage and shut the door. Smallpox was a disease men died of. What if the emptiness of her house should last forever. . . .

She had hardly slept for three nights, and the sight of the stripped and dishevelled bed was too much for her. Work had never been much of a solace to Shona MacVean. She sank on to the still warm mattress and wept.

Her tears had ceased, but she still lay inert and wretched half an hour later when Alec opened the door and came in.

" Oh—they've taken him away, Doctor ! " she said, getting slowly up.

" I know. I've come to see you yourself, Shona. How are you ? "

Tears choked her voice again as she tried to answer.

" No pain or sickness ? Tell me how you feel."

" All right," she said.

Alec looked round the drab room, pitying her.

" You're not long married, are you ? "

" Only five months. I'm thirteen years younger than Torquil," she said, looking up.

" I saw there was a difference in your ages."

" My mother and father were awful against it," said Shona, gaining control of her voice. " So was Mrs. MacLennan. She's Torquil's aunt, you know, and her family are all in good positions in Glasgow and those places. It's funny," she said offendedly, " you'd think it was our business getting married. Fancy my father and Torquil's aunt not speaking to each other over the head of it ! "

" But you get on all right together, so they'll come round. Does your father belong to Fionn too, Shona ? "

" He has the croft on the side of the Cailleach," said Shona.

" And his name ? "

" John Rose."

" Well, I'll see him this afternoon, Shona, and I'll tell him about your husband. Can I give him any message from you ? "

Shona hesitated.

" I don't think it," she said at last. " I'll wait first and see does he send any message to me."

If only she had been vaccinated herself, he reflected, he would have taken her to the castle to help with the nursing ; though, to judge by the state of the cottage, she might be no asset.

" Well," he said, " I'm sure you have a lot of work before you, Shona, to tidy up after all this. Don't forget to eat. If you let yourself get weak and dispirited you'll be in a good state to contract smallpox yourself, and that won't help Torquil. I'll come in and see you again to-morrow and give you the news about him."

He finished the last of his visits in the village ; now he only had to call at the two crofts which lay at the other end of the island, beyond the castle. He walked back, surprised at his tiredness. The village seemed very quiet. Sometimes a face appeared at a window, but the little houses seemed hushed. These were the houses he had seen last night, mysterious and secret under the stormy moonlight. Now, in the grey light of day, they still had the same brooding secrecy.

But the castle had changed. Even as he opened the door and looked into the paved hall he was aware of the difference, even before he heard Danny's call, " Doctor's back !" he felt the difference.

" Well ? " he queried as Dochy came out of Aunt Jane's parlour.

Dochy was holding a sheet of paper. He came forward and displayed his work.

" Well," he said, " I knew there must be graph paper in the house. I remembered that once when I was here as a boy, Uncle Hector had a craze for keeping a graph of the weather, a very complex affair with barometric readings and winds, tides, phases of the moon—a sort of astrologer's dream it looked. I found the stuff in the library."

" But that's admirable."

" I'm making this one out for Father Kelly, you see. You'll have to fill in the details of his last-night condition. I've got Torquil MacVean's complete and John took his temperature before he began sponging him."

This was all very professional. Alec studied the chart. Patient's name. Date of admission. Diagnosis. Then the days and nights divided four-hourly, 10, 2, 6 in black for day-time, 10, 2, 6 in red for the night.

"Admirable," said Alec. "Were you in the R.A.M.C., too?"

"No, I was one of their victims," said Dochy. "I fell off a tank and cracked my coccyx."

They turned as a snort of laughter greeted this disclosure and saw Danny carrying a bucket of peats to the parlour and struggling to swallow his amusement.

"And I don't suppose you know what a coccyx is," said Dochy genially, "or what agonies I endured."

"I do so know what a coccyx is," said Danny, stung by the accusation of ignorance. "It's a—" his laughter bubbled up anew —"it's a rudimentary tail!"

"And you've got one yourself, you young puppy, and take care I don't give it a tweak!"

Danny took this threat for what it was worth and transferred the peats to the coal scuttle.

Kirpu hastened silently into the hall and removed Alec's outdoor things. He would have appeared sooner, but he had been helping the minister with Torquil MacVean.

"Thanks," said Alec absently. "I'll see what the patients are like."

He found Torquil chastened but comfortable; the minister displayed a chart with a firm black blob announcing the temperature on admission. The pulse was indicated by an (o) of the same size as the blob, but not filled in.

"I put the respirations down in writing," said John. "I thought it was getting a bit too much to make a graph of them, too."

Alec nodded, a little awed by the efficiency of his lieutenants. "Comfortable?" he asked.

"I'm fine," said Torquil. "The minister's a great hand at it. You'd never have thought it to look at him."

John Forsyth's face was expressionless but it was evident that the rueful compliment pleased him. He stood on the other side of the bed while Alec made a careful examination of the patient; then helped to cover him.

"Can he get some soup, Doctor?" he asked.

"Yes, and he ought to have a drink beside him. Has Mrs. MacLennan sent anything to drink?"

"A bottle of orange squash and a bottle of lime juice. She sent word she just hadn't the time this morning to make any fresh lemon squash but she's going to have it for to-morrow."

"But this is all right; drink as much as you want, Torquil," said Alec.

Then he and John went to Father Kelly's room.

Father Kelly was lying with his eyes shut but he was not asleep. His eyelids twitched faintly now and then, and his right forefinger was tapping on the counterpane, a steady, soundless tap, tap, tap, the sort of mechanical action with which a sick man sometimes fills time that has turned into a waste of dreary discomfort. His face was thickly spattered with vesicles. These had no longer the appearance of being filled with clear serum; they were becoming opaque, a drab yellow, each one dimpled in the centre and with an angry red areola in the surrounding skin.

"Hallo," he croaked, opening his eyes at a movement from John and blinking as if his lids were stiff.

Alec was trying to visualise a page of his old text-book. Fragments of forgotten knowledge were returning to him, but he longed for the books themselves.

"John," he said, "permanganate of potash; that's the stuff. He should rinse out his mouth with it, and we want him sponged over with it. Torquil, too."

"Permanganate of potash in my medicine cupboard," said Father Kelly. "Or did ye get it already? I don't mind whether there's more in the bathroom. Look and see."

"And you want to watch his back and heels."

"I was thinking to get some spirit to rub them," John said.

"Surgical spirit in my cupboard," muttered Father Kelly. "I don't know, though, it might have evaporated."

"Oil and spirit, that's what we used."

"I leave it to you," said Alec. "How are you feeling?" he asked, turning all his attention on the priest. "How's the mouth?"

"Like the inside of a sepulchre."

"Well, we'll get your mouth washed out again, and you must drink as much as you can."

Father Kelly was watching him. He wanted something. Alec waited for him to ask some question, some favour, but he did not speak, and presently his eyes closed again.

Outside, in the corridor, Alec told John Forsyth about the two Patrick children and they decided that, though they could both be carried in an adult's arms, the stretcher should be used—partly to avoid infection from the children's breath and partly because the stretcher could accommodate their clothes and blankets as well.

They washed their hands thoroughly and were joined by Dochy, who heard the news about the Patrick children with dismay.

" But—two children," he said. " That's going to involve Maura in a lot of work, isn't it ? Children need a woman to look after them."

" I told their mother she could come with them."

They all agreed that it seemed the best thing ; but the idea of the ill babies brought home the reality of the situation. They began looking at the other little cells, but for a mother and two children they were too small.

" What about this ? " Dochy suggested.

The door he had opened gave on to a sort of lumber room. Old kitchen chairs, a broken sofa, a mangle, a table with three legs and a good deal of miscellaneous iron pots and kitchen utensils crammed it dismally, but it had a good window and a skylight as well.

" Could clear this," said Dochy.

There was a discouraged silence. It was obviously the solution, since Alec did not wish to use the upstairs rooms for patients.

" Look here, send Danny to me," said Dochy vigorously. " Go and give Torquil and Father Kelly their dinner and leave us to it."

" I want to keep notes on the cases," said Alec uncomfortably. " If you're sure you and Danny can manage this——"

" That's right, we've got to have a division of labour. Off you go, both of you."

Dochy was hauling a cobwebbed spinning-wheel off the table. Alec and John left him and Danny appeared.

" Come on," said Dochy. " All this goes outside—right outside: can't have it cluttering the corridor."

They got it cleared at last.

" But what about some dinner ? " Danny suggested when he saw Dochy start work on the walls with a brush.

" They'll call us when it's ready, but I want to get finished with this first. Just the thing to give us an appetite."

Danny had a very adequate appetite already, but he got a broom and began, with fading enthusiasm, on the floor.

" Now get a bucket of water and soap and give it a good scrub over."

Dochy's energy was irresistible, though trying to the soul. Danny obeyed, wondering a little if school were as bad as all this.

Meantime, Dochy was exploring the rooms upstairs, tempted at times to stop and examine photographs or heirlooms, but driving himself on until in a bleak room near the top of the old part of the castle, he found twin camp beds. He dismantled these and brought them downstairs, leaving them in the corridor until Danny's wet floor had dried off. But as this process promised to be slow, he explored again, and returned with an antique oil-stove which he put into working order, filled and lit. He left it rather reluctantly to get on with its job of drying the damp floor, and consented to join Alec and the minister in Aunt Jane's parlour.

"I've got a bed each for Nell and the two-year-old," he said. "What are we going to put the baby into?" He went on to answer that question himself. "I think a drawer out of the old chest of drawers I threw out would be about the size of thing. Danny can scrub it out and leave it to dry before the kitchen fire. A pillow inside it for a mattress, and we'll get linen from Nell."

He began to drink his soup with great rapidity.

"That would be the very thing," said Alec belatedly. He looked at Dochy with respect, envying his zest for organising.

"Did you get your notes written?" Dochy asked while Kirpu brought the next course in. "If you want papers or ledgers I can get some from the stock I found in the library. Lots of stuff there."

"Well, I have got a note-book," said Alec, "but if you have any foolscap paper it might be better; and we ought to have a report book; we must arrange hours of duty, I think. Someone will have to be on duty at night, you see." He looked at them apologetically. They were both watching him. "Father Kelly is going to need care at night."

"Is he going to get worse?" John asked.

"I'm afraid so. He's a bad case. The vesicles are thickly scattered, and running into each other; you can see that he finds it difficult to keep his eyes open already—his eyelids are swollen and stiff. He—is a bad case," he ended, not willing to put his misgivings into words.

"And we must expect other cases, I take it?" said Dochy. "You and I," he said to John, "must work this out between us. We must both be there together through the day, to bring in any fresh cases. I suppose we had better divide the night?"

"Suppose," John suggested, "we divide the night into two shifts. Say eight to two and two to eight. Something like that."

"Well, remember," Alec put in, "you won't have any stretcher work until after I've made my round of the village. I'll see the patients here first, then I'll go round the houses and when I get back I'll let you know if there is any fresh case to bring in. You must try to arrange to have a bit of free time as well."

"Look here," Dochy leaned his elbows on the table, "going round the village is all very well; but if you try to visit those two crofts every day you're taking on too much of a walking marathon, you know. Why not arrange for them to give a signal if they want you? You could climb to the shoulder of Ben Cailleach and look down on both the crofts; and tell them to hang out a flag or something—something you could see easily enough."

"Well," Alec conceded slowly, "I might arrange some kind of signal. I'll see them both this afternoon, anyway."

He felt that Dochy was taking over the role of organiser that belonged properly to himself; but this was no time to be jealous of his professional rights and status. Dochy seemed to have a talent for it. And I, Alec reflected, have not. It took me a whole sleepless night to get even as far as I did. Better pool all our talents; we'll need them.

Kirpu appeared again. This time he brought coffee on a silver tray, in a silver pot and with fine porcelain cups to drink from. Ceremoniously he poured out a cup of black coffee for each of them.

"This is good," said Alec, pleased at the change from Maura's eternal tea.

Kirpu bowed.

"You made it?"

"Yes, sir. And if I may suggest, I will look after the sick gentlemen now and give these gentlemen"—he bowed to John and Dochy—"a rest for the afternoon."

So it was arranged, and the trio settled more comfortably to their coffee and cigarettes, stretching out their legs while Kirpu lifted away the Pembroke table on which their meal had been laid, and substituted a walnut chess table at Alec's elbow with the coffee tray laid on it.

"Kirpu," said Dochy as the door closed behind him, "has no

intention of letting us fall below his standards of civilisation. He's admirable. How did you acquire him?"

Alec told the story of his meeting with Kirpu in Glasgow, while both the others listened with astonished interest.

"Well—good for you," said Dochy. "You're not afraid of taking a chance; and your gamble came off. Good stuff."

Alec looked at him evenly.

"Don't you realise," he pointed out, "that if I hadn't picked up Kirpu there would be no smallpox on Fionn."

Dochy and John spoke together.

"That," said Dochy, "was a result that nobody could have foreseen. The point is you've got a good servant and Kirpu is rescued from destitution."

"If you hadn't," said John Forsyth, "there would be another smallpox epidemic all over Glasgow. We're isolated here."

"Perhaps there is smallpox all over Glasgow," said Alec, smiling, hoping that John's consolation might prove valid. But he remembered suddenly his mother saying, when he had adopted a scrap of a puppy, "Alec, you never stop to think."

Before he set out to visit the crofts, Alec looked in again at Father Kelly.

"Give me some of my ointment," said the priest. "I can be rubbing it on myself when I've got nothing better to do."

"I'm afraid ointment isn't the treatment for this."

"It's better than no treatment at all! If I'd had a bit ointment rubbed on my face and hands at the very start I would never be as bad as this now! Impetigo is a thing that has to be caught at the outset to prevent it spreading, and here am I with it all over my body!"

"It's the worst case of impetigo I've ever seen," Alec agreed cheerfully, covering the patient up.

Father Kelly looked at him.

"Is that so now."

"And zinc ointment is not the treatment for either impetigo or this."

Father Kelly blinked his sore eyes and tried to keep them open, focusing the doctor.

"What is it?"

"Smallpox," said Alec after a second's pause.

Father Kelly digested that.

"Kirpu had it when he came here," Alec told him. "I should have spotted it and kept him isolated."

The sick man did not speak; he lay with closed eyes, relaxed and apparently drifting off to sleep. But when Alec moved towards the door he said, without opening his eyes, "Ye'll let me know if any of my folks get it. Catholics, I mean."

"Nell Patrick's two children have just come in," said Alec. "But you must stay where you are; you're ill, you know."

"That's right."

The hoarse voice sounded almost cheerful.

Alec glanced at Torquil, found him asleep, and set off.

## Chapter Eighteen

"WE'LL HAVE to get a wee mug for Pad," said Maura. "There might be still that one I've seen them use for flowers, a bonny red and blue one with gold on it, the very thing."

"Would you like that, Pad?" Nell's voice had the false sprightliness of a mother giving her child a prod towards enthusiasm.

"I want home," Pad girned. "I want my own bed."

"It's a bonny wee bed that you've got," Nell encouraged. "And I've got one the same beside you, look! I'll be in the wee bed next to you, my lamb."

"I need a big bed," Pad insisted. "I need my own bed." He cried spiritlessly as if he lacked the energy for his usual hearty roar.

"He's used to being in the same bed as his Mammy," Nell explained.

"See the bonny wee mug I've got for you, Pad, and nice orange squash in it—taste it, will you?"

Pad accepted a drink from the old Crown Derby mug, then continued crying.

"Will I see where Danny is?" Maura suggested. "Will I get Danny to come and keek at you through the window?"

"No," said Pad, "I want my Daddy."

"You'll just have to want then." Nell dropped her wheedling tone and spoke impatiently, and saw Pad's tears stop as wearily as they had begun. She glanced at Maura, ashamed at her lack of patience. "I've never seen Terence since he left the house this morning; he goes off and never says when he'll be back."

"Ts," said Maura.

"Treats the house like a hotel, I tell him. Hardly get a word out of him when he is there." Nell's voice rose with complaint. "I little thought it would be like this when we were married. I thought it would be heaven on earth once I had got Terence Patrick. I'd have thought twice if I'd known!"

"Ah, it's hard on you, too, Nell," Maura agreed.

"It's like what Father Kelly says," said Nell. "He gave them their desire and sent bitterness into their soul. It's not fair. It's a cheat altogether!"

Maura watched her with vague, gentle eyes.

"You're lucky, if you only knew it, without a man at all. I little knew it would come to this."

Maura saw that Pad had drifted into a doze. She stood up.

"It's a pity he wasn't back before you left, Nell," she said. "He'd be having a bit drink with the men at the Hotel, likely——"

"Fine you know he's not!" exclaimed Nell furiously. "Fine you know he's not drinking at the Hotel, Maura Rafferty, as if Mrs. MacLennan would have time to open the bar at that hour." (Both she and Maura knew that it was the exigencies of Mrs. MacLennan's routine and not the whims of any arbitrary licensing laws that dictated the drinking hours on Fionn.) "You know fine it's not any men at all he'll be with, and so does every other soul on this island."

There was nothing to say to this. Maura sat a while in silence, then rose.

"I'll see is the kettle near boiling yet," she murmured.

In the kitchen, as she prepared tea for herself and Nell, she was remembering a talk she had had from Father Kelly long ago when she first arrived on Fionn.

"You've been sent here, Maura," he had said, "by a mix-up of chance and cheating, following on your own sin. Now the sin was yours, though the cheating happened to you; and when a thing happens to you, never mind if it seems unjust or cruel, you can look for God's will in it. Never fancy yourself ill-used by life, my girl. Look for God's will and work with it and you'll find your penance turn to peace."

She sighed, for she had taken the advice and knew it to be good ; but she had no skill with words to comfort Nell in her bitterness, and Father Kelly was ill. All she could do was to offer her favourite panacea, a cup of strong tea.

" I could do with that," said Nell thirstily, accepting the comfort Maura brought.

" D'you hear that wind," said Maura, looking out at the blown spray spattering over the walls. " And the doctor, poor soul, out in it, going to visit the farms. He's not used with walking over the rough."

" It's all pavements in New York," said Nell. " I'd love to see it, Maura, wouldn't you ? Fifth Avenue and Broadway . . . I wish I could see New York before I die. I wish I could even be in Glasgow, I'd be content with that. D'you miss Glasgow ever, Maura ? "

Maura thought of Glasgow. She saw herself in Bearsden in the morning, shaking the doormat, polishing the bell and the name-plate, dreaming her way through house and kitchen-work ; and in the evening, her dream translated to reality, catching the bus to town, waiting in an ache of emptiness because Tom was not there to meet her, then swept into joy when at last he did appear and whisked her off to the nearest dance-hall. . . .

" I miss it whiles," she confessed with a smile trembling at the corners of her mouth. " Och, but I like it fine here now, Nell. My friends are here."

" And Long Island," said Nell, reverting to her own dreams. " It must be wonderful to bathe there ! "

" You could bathe here," Maura suggested.

" Och, it's not the same thing at all ! "

" It's the same Atlantic."

" It's nothing to do with the sea," said Nell with contempt. " Would you be likely to see Humphrey Bogart or Lana Turner or Dorothy Lamour bathing here, on Fionn ? Or Ray Milland ? "

" You would not," said Maura. " I'd be glad enough to see the doctor back from his walk, the soul. I hope he keeps clear of the bogs."

It was a good walk to the other side of the island.

Alec had skirted the lower slopes of Ben Cailleach and was picking his way through the third bog he had encountered when a voice hailed him. He looked round and saw a dark blue figure higher up the hill.

"Where do you want to go-o-o?" asked the figure in a carrying sing-song.

"To Glen Beg and Skua."

"Come up then—back and up!"

Alec retraced his steps and began to climb rather unwillingly, for he was no mountaineer, and felt that he was adding length to his journey.

"It is the best way," the young man told him, coming down to meet him and give him a hand over a grey rock.

"It seems roundabout," said Alec.

"So it is, but the long way is the short way. You would never get out of the bogs by the way you were going, and a bog can swallow a man. Up the Ben and over and down; or you can go by the shore all the way, but you have to climb the cliffs beyond the caves and you would need a good head on you." It was assumed that Alec did not have a good enough head for the cliffs.

"I didn't see you this morning," said Alec. "I was in all the houses in the village."

"Were you now?"

"You must belong to one of the crofts."

"I do not," said the young man. "I belong to the village. My name is Patrick."

Alec stopped abruptly, partly to recover breath, and saw how handsome the youth was; dark and stocky, with eyes like speedwells.

"Are you—Nell Patrick's husband?" he asked.

"She is my wife."

"Well, I'm sorry to say your children are ill." He moved on as Patrick was waiting for him.

"Is that so now? That's bad." Terence Patrick looked serious but not deeply worried.

"Yes—gravely ill. It's smallpox."

Every time he was forced to give this news Alec felt an interior jolt. He did it so badly, without grace or gentleness. He could not imagine how better to do it, yet knew his own inadequacy.

"Smallpox, is it." There was concern in Patrick's face now. "That's bad, Doctor. Is it—is there danger?"

"Well, yes, the baby is acutely ill. She's too small to put up much resistance, you know. They're both at the castle with their mother, where I can have them under observation all the time."

" Has wee Pad got it too ? "

" The rash is just appearing on him ; it's too soon to say yet
how badly he has it. I'm glad to have met you to give you the news,
I'm trying to get round everybody to make sure there are no other
cases developing. Stay at home till it's over."

" I have no choice but to stay on Fionn as long as the wind
blows like this," said Patrick irritably.

" Is there anybody else has taken it ? " he asked presently.

" Torquil MacVean ; and Father Kelly."

" Father Kelly ! D'you tell me that ! " He was shocked now ;
he climbed silently, frowning, rubbing his chin with his dark, clever
fingers.

" Oh, yes, vaccinated two years ago," he said, coming to the
surface of some preoccupation to answer Alec. " Look." He rolled
up the sleeve of his jersey to show the pale scars. " I can go anywhere
—I'm safe enough."

" Not altogether," said Alec. " Your vaccination only ensures
that the attack will be light if you do get it."

The handsome face darkened angrily.

" You mean," he said, " it's not a guarantee against the smallpox
after all ? "

" If you have been recently vaccinated," Alec repeated, " it
ensures that, if you do catch smallpox, you are unlikely to have it
badly."

" Have you ever known of a man who's been vaccinated and
then caught it ? " Patrick challenged him.

" It's a man who has been vaccinated who started this on Fionn.
Torquil MacVean has been vaccinated, too. If the first case had
not been vaccinated I think I should have spotted at once what was
wrong. It was the mildness of the attack that was misleading."

" I don't see so much point in getting done at all—— Is wee
Paddy bad with it ? "

Alec repeated his answer, wondering why this apparently
intelligent young man should require everything to be said twice.
Either shock made him stupid or his mind was elsewhere.

" If you would like to look at them," he suggested, " come to
the castle and you can look through the window. Nell can hold Pad
up to see you."

" No, no, no" said Terence hurriedly. " Look, here we are

at the lochan now. Go along that pass there between the two jaggy rocks, you see? When you get over the ridge you'll see the two crofts below you, Glen Beg just below and Skua to the East."

"Thanks. I'll be going round the village to-morrow morning and I'll give you news of the children, then."

"And if there's anything they need, Doctor, don't let them want for it."

The lochan was cradled in the jagged hill-top, in the crater of a dead volcano, steep-edged except at one part where reeds and irises softened the sheer drop of the rocky sides. It was miniature scenery, yet it had the same quality of silence as Coruisk of the Coolins, the same look of immemorial waiting. Alec skirted the water and climbed along the path between two rocks, feeling that his haste was irreverent, that the dark jewel of water demanded a response that he had not time to give. He pressed on almost in flight.

When he had climbed over the crater's edge and descended far enough to lose sight of the loch he stopped. He was sweating. He sat down on the heather, breathing heavily, and wiped his face and hands, feeling himself to be a flaccid creature like all city dwellers. It takes someone like old Sir Hector, he reflected, to keep hard in a city.

Sir Hector must often have looked at this view of the hillside falling away beneath him, brown heather giving way to green turf far below as the slopes softened to a plain that extended to a white scalloped edge where it met the sea. The smooth undulations of green were marred by two patches of rectangular patternwork, each huddled round grey stone buildings; Glen Beg and, to the right beneath it, Skua.

Alec was trying, even as he rested and gazed at the two crofts, to recover his clear mental image of Sir Hector. It had become blurred by the amount of talk by those others, Dochy, Father Kelly, even Danny and Mrs. MacLennan, whose pictures of the old man were so unlike his own. Father Kelly had a fantastic idea that Sir Hector had gone to the States to die. That was surely wrong; it did not chime with the talks they had had together. But their conversations together had always been light and imaginative rather than serious; almost fantastic. With Father Kelly he had, it seemed, discussed deeper things, life and death and the things he believed.

But to Mrs. MacLennan he was a likeable old autocrat with

some cranky ideas. To Dochy he was an uncle who disagreed with all his projects for reviving Fionn, who eluded all his arguments and refused to meet him if meeting could be avoided. To Danny he was a benevolent owner of a boat, a number of clocks and a library. Madge and Bertie Newnham probably saw him differently again; and no one could claim that his view was the right one, the real Sir Hector.

But there was no time to sit on the hillside dreaming and conjecturing. He got up hurriedly and made good speed down the heather, startling a pair of grouse that shot up from under his feet with a whirr of wings and startled cries. Then he was treading on the turf, on hair-fine grass mixed with a multitude of vetches and milkworts, rock roses, saxifrage and thyme, none of them in flower, but all combining in a delicious matted resilience.

This was Glen Beg he was approaching and the two men sowing broadcast along the brown field must be John Rose and his son.

They had seen him, and realising that he wanted to speak to them, were coming towards the dyke of grey stones. Alec waited till they were a few feet off, answered their greeting and delivered his formula.

"Smallpox, that's bad," said John Rose. "We're all fine. You're fine, Ronald, are you?"

"I am," said Ronald.

"And is your mother all right, and Katrina?"

Ronald pushed his hat to the back of his head. "I think they're fine too," he said, evidently astonished at the idea that they could possibly be otherwise.

"I'd better go to the house and see them," Alec decided; and the crofter accompanied him, leaving his son to continue the sowing.

It was hospitality that took John Rose from his field. He produced whisky and glasses and waved aside Alec's refusal and his wife's absurd suggestion that the doctor might prefer tea or a glass of fresh milk.

"It'll be an ill day," he said, "when John Rose can't offer Scotch whisky to the stranger within his gates. There, Doctor, taste that!"

He uttered a Gaelic health and drank, smacking his lips and looking at his guest for signs of appreciation.

"Excellent," said Alec politely.

"Ah, you're a man that knows a good whisky, Doctor, and that's to your credit. This is the real Mackay, none of your blends as they call them, and "—he leaned till his shoulder touched his guest's—" there's no duty on this."

"Think shame," said Mrs. Rose, obviously making a conventional protest.

"It'll be an ill day," said her husband sternly, " when John Rose puts money in the pockets of a thieving English Government for what's made on his own land, with his own barley, by his own labour."

"And who all is it that's ill with the smallpox, Doctor? " Mrs. Rose asked. " Torquil MacVean? Is Shona all right, then? "

"All right so far," said Alec.

"And Father Kelly, the poor soul? "

"Pretty ill."

"Ah, it's a terrible thing to have to face Almighty God with a pack of Popish superstition in your head," said Mr. Rose seriously. " And he's a good-tempered poor soul for all he's a priest to the Scarlet Woman. I mind I gave him a sup of good whisky in a bottle, one time he had the bronchitis, and he thanked me like a Christian. He did so."

"And poor Nell Patrick, she'll be in a state about the bairns, likely? "

"Yes, she's worried, naturally."

Perhaps he imagined that the glances between husband and wife and daughter held some meaning he could not understand. Alec took another sip of his whisky and spoke of his plan for signalling to save his climbing down Glen Cailleach every day and this was arranged; a pair of John Rose's old trousers hanging out of the upstairs window indicated all's well; a white towel at the same window was a call for help.

"But you'll need more milk, Doctor, and eggs likely," Mrs. Rose suggested. " And no meat coming from the mainland in this wind——"

"Aye, we'll have to increase the milk," said John. " You'll just have to give up churning, Mother."

"I'll not complain," said his wife satirically.

"How does the milk come from here to the village? " Alec asked. " Is there a road? "

"No, only the track you came down," the crofter told him,

"We use a pack horse, you see; a churn on either side, and we measure it out in the village when they all bring their jugs and cans."

"Oh." Alec did not see how this occasion of infection could be avoided. He could not make life too complicated for the village, after all. The milk churns and the general store must remain danger spots.

He finished his whisky, thanked them all for their hospitality and set off for the other farm, Skua.

Here his reception was very different. The man who looked up from laborious planting of potatoes was not hostile, but showed an inhuman lack of interest in Alec's news. He was a man not yet in middle-age, of an unhealthy yellowish skin in which his lichen-grey eyes looked dry and sore and lashless. All his features converged towards his nose; his face was like a dog's, all nose.

"There's nobody got smallpox in Skua," he said flatly.

"How many are there?"

"Myself and my wife."

"I'd better have a word with her."

"She'll be in the byre, likely," he said indifferently.

Alec spoke about the signalling system he had arranged with John Rose.

"Ah, he'll have time for that. I haven't. Better see Lilias."

Alec wasted no more time but went on to the croft.

There was no reply to his knock; he walked in, called and heard no reply, so he began to explore the byre where the cow was lowing, the cart-shed, the stone dairy and the dilapidated outhouses. It was a dreary place; wood rotted away from its hinges, fungus thrust out fleshy fans and litter strewed the ground instead of feeding the fields.

There was no one in any of the sad outbuildings.

He returned to the house and went through kitchen, sitting-room and back room, and climbed a wooden ladder to the bedrooms. There was nobody at home.

Presumably Mrs. MacPherson was well or she would not have left the house; but he had a feeling of discomfort that was not due to the annoyance of having failed to arrange a signalling system. He returned to the ground floor.

It was a dark, sour house, low-ceilinged and thick-walled, grudging and indifferent like its master. A coat of white-wash would have lightened its interior, but instead its walls were covered with old discoloured papers, marled with damp, peeling at the corners of the rooms and dark with peat smoke. A wireless set on the dresser seemed to have absorbed the atmosphere of scrimping meanness ; you could not imagine the fantastic nonsense of a good variety programme emerging from it, only the tawdriest and most lugubrious of Workers' Playtimes.

But when a young woman hurried breathlessly into the room the atmosphere of the house shrank back.

" Oh," she said, " it's you, Doctor, is it. I was outside and I thought I saw somebody go in. The kettle's just on the boil ; you'll take a cup of tea ? "

" No, thank you," Alec smiled. A smile was the involuntary response to the flood of vitality that had entered. " I only want to make sure that you are well—but you haven't heard the news——"

" I have," said Mrs. McPherson. " It's terrible, terrible. I can't get poor Nell Patrick out of my mind." She did indeed look distressed ; her eyebrows knotted, she clasped her hands and her face was full of pain.

" Is she a special friend of yours ? " Alec asked.

The girl looked at her clasped knuckles and did not reply at once. Then, without looking at the doctor, she shook her head.

" It's natural that you should feel sympathy with another woman. You have no children yourself, Mrs. McPherson."

She shook her head again, and this time Alec saw that she was fighting against tears. To give her time to recover he spoke of the signal he had arranged with the Roses and suggested a similar arrangement for Skua.

" I'll do the same, Doctor," she said. " Only I won't use my man's trousers, he might object ; I'll hang out an old skirt of my own. I'd come and help you at the castle, but there would be no end to the fuss he'd make . . . But if there's any odd job I can do. . . ." She ended uncertainly, looking round the ugly, poor room as if she had not noticed it before.

" If I think of anything I'll let you know."

" And next time," she said, " I'll make you take a cup of tea."

Alec received a nod from her husband when he passed him again on his way back. The wind was against him now. He kept his head down, not even yielding to the atmosphere of the dark lochan, plodding on doggedly till he reached home.

Kirpu received him, helped him off with his coat, brought his indoor slippers and removed the wet shoes that had black bog mud caked on them. Kirpu looked all right again. Better, in fact, than he had been when Alec first saw him staggering along Jamaica Street. Kirpu had got over his original nervous fussiness and had become a gentle, reassuring shadow. There was no need for Alec to express his appreciation; he felt that they understood each other, that their relationship had become tranquil and permanent.

"All well at the crofts?" Dochy asked, coming into the parlour.

"All well. How are things here?"

"Much the same. John Forsyth has been teaching me a bit of nursing technique. We'll make a team all right. He's going to take the early part of the night and I'll get up and do the morning watch. You stiff after your tramp?"

"Yes," said Alec, stretching his legs to the fire.

"You'll soon be as hard as nails."

"I hope so. It's quite a walk going round these houses and the two crofts."

He was thinking of his afternoon walk, of his meeting with young Terence Patrick, who had not asked for his wife; his meeting with John Rose and his wife, who had asked, but with no show of special interest, for their daughter Shona MacVean; and of young Mrs. MacPherson, a creature full of animal vitality, married to a miser.

"You arranged for the crofters to give you a signal?"

"Yes."

"A good chap, John Rose."

"Very nice; and his wife too. I had to drink a glass of whisky before I got away."

"The famous whisky; and it's excellent, too. He's been distilling whisky long enough to give it time to ripen before he drinks it."

"He didn't ask for his daughter, you know. Mrs. Rose did, when I told her Torquil was down with it; but they seemed to have no particular feelings about her."

"I believe they were discontented with the marriage."

Alec turned to the case-book he had prepared and noted the result of his day's round of the village. While he was busy at this Kirpu laid the table for high tea; John Forsyth came in, rubbing his newly-washed hands ; Danny brought in a bucket of driftwood and put a few pieces on the fire.

"Lighting-up time, I should say," Dochy suggested.

Danny went to the kitchen and returned with a lamp, and the three men drew in their chairs. John bent his head and said grace. As he looked up again he said suddenly :

"I wonder what my mother will be doing."

"Having tea by the fire, like us, I hope," said Dochy kindly.

"I hope so, too," said John. "When you see her to-morrow, Doctor, tell her we were thinking of her."

"Yes," said Alec, "I will."

Later, after he had written up his case-book, Alec leaned back in his chair, astonished to find what he was doing.

Here I am, he thought, on the island. I've got here—in time for the primroses ! And with a supply of artist's materials in case I want to sketch, and writing paper in case I want to write. But it doesn't matter much what I want. . . .

"Hallo," he said as Danny came into the parlour.

"Hallo," Danny responded. "I brought some driftwood."

"Fine. Let's have a blaze."

He watched Danny kneel and pile silvery knobs of driftwood on the glowing peats ; presently transparent blue flames began to lick and hiss round the wood with a salty sparkle.

"I got it out on the far sands," said Danny. "I was setting lines, and afterwards I went out across the rocks and on along by the haunted cave. It's not a place to be on your lone with the twilight falling ! " He gave Alec a comic sideways glance.

"Is it really haunted ? "

"I wouldn't be the one to say it is or it isn't," said Danny, adding another piece of wood. "They say the seal-woman haunts it, and some others besides. And there's the fairies at Craignashee. I'm not saying I believe a word of it, but I keep out of the way of seeing anything there might be to see."

"Does anybody go that way at night ? " Alec asked idly.

"What would they go there for ? The only one that might go that way would be Candy Andy and he's safe, being a dafty. It's not a place you'd feel at home in even by day, that cave."

"I'd like to explore it sometime."

"I'll take you," Danny offered.

When Danny had left him Alec took off his shoes and wiggled

his toes before the blaze and thought of Bertie's fallen arches. He picked up a piece of wood with his toes and dropped it on the fire. Bertie seemed very remote and unreal.

" I'm fond of old Bertie after all," Alec discovered.

He chuckled and put on his shoes again, and went to see his patients.

## Chapter Nineteen

MRS FORSYTH was, in fact, cleaning her stair rods in the kitchen. If John went off and left her desolate and alone she would just bear her cross and get on with the cleaning.

She had worked all day, in feverish gusts and with intervals of limp idleness when her hands would sink to her sides and she would wonder what good she did with all her zeal for cleanliness. She had taken up the stair carpet and beaten it on the back green, alone, unaided ; and had rolled it up again and carried it, unaided, to the wash-house, for she would not lay it again until all the upstairs cleaning was finished.

She had taken down the curtains upstairs and had washed all the ornaments. the glass of the pictures and the frames, except the plush ones which were merely wiped over with a damp cloth moistened with water and vinegar. Now she was finishing the last brass rod.

She tied the shining rods together with a tape and stacked them inside the roll of carpet, and put away the box with the Brasso and the greenish cleaning rags, and washed her hands under the tap. The house was horribly quiet——not that John made much noise, but he was always there to talk to. She always knew exactly what he was doing ; writing his sermons, or working in the garden ; reading his Bible, cleaning the shoes or helping her to turn the mangle, the only household tasks that she felt he might undertake without detracting from his dignity as a minister. Or if it was one of his days for visiting she would know exactly which families he proposed to visit, would advise him beforehand how to tackle any sins or backslidings she had observed, and on his return she would hear how he had conducted the visits and learn the latest news about each family.

"John and I," she would say to other mothers in the congregation, "have always plenty to say to each other. He never gets bored with his mother's company ! I sometimes wish he would take a fancy to some nice girl, but no, he always just says his old mother is enough for him."

"Ah, he's a good son," they would say.

Well, he was good enough as sons went, but of course all men were selfish. . . .

"I wish I knew what he was doing," she muttered aloud.

She went round the house with a lamp, drawing the curtains and locking both doors, though it was not much after eight. But of course she had taken down the curtains upstairs ; it had seemed a chance with John away. In her own room she stood irresolute, staring at the blank windows that reflected her own figure with the lamp in its hand. She had to sleep here to-night, hadn't she ? She ought not to have taken down the curtains. Something had gone wrong with her routine. She had put the curtains to soak in cold water and would wash them to-morrow, but what about to-night ?

"I'd better drape something across the window," she said to her reflection. How timid it looked with its hand on its mouth, staring back at her.

The counterpane off John's bed would do, and anyway she would give him a clean bed to come back to. She went to his room, took off the counterpane and hurried out again with a lump in her throat, and, standing on a chair, pinned the drapery over the curtain pole.

She set the chair back in its place against the wall, still with a misty doubt in her mind. There was something wrong with her routine.

She would wash to-morrow ; this wind would give the blankets a good strong blow. She only hoped it would not be too strong for the fabric of her sheets, and anyway she did not look forward to a blanket washing without John's help in turning the mangle. Selfish . . . Though it would be the first Monday since his childhood that he had failed to help mother with the heavy mangling. He used to do it always before he went off to school, for Mrs. Forsyth was not a woman who dawdled on a Monday morning.

On a Monday morning . . . The clammy mist that had hung

about her mind all day rose higher. She wished John was here, it was eerie in the house all alone.

She was tired out and she had missed her tea, that was all that was wrong. She had no relish for food taken alone; it was only for John's sake that she bothered cooking and baking. She drifted back to the kitchen and pushed the kettle on to the fire, but decided that she was too tired for a proper meal. She would fill her bottle and take a glass of hot milk up to her bed.

She lit the primus to heat her milk, poured a glassful into the pan and smoothed her brow doubtfully, wondering if she were starting one of her heads. If so she would be in no fit state for the washing to-morrow, an extra heavy one with the curtains and everything. That feeling of mist was still there and she could not shake it off. She filled her stone bottle and took it up to her bed, returned for the alarm clock and set it for four o'clock to be up early on Monday morning.

Monday morning . . . She held on to the edge of the table, shaking with horror. What had she done! She had scrubbed, polished, even beaten a stair carpet on the back green, all on the Lord's Day! She, the minister's mother . . . on the Lord's Day!

"It's your fault!" she babbled, weeping, "it's your fault, John Forsyth—leaving your mother—neglecting the Sabbath Day services—so that I forgot what day it was, me that kept the Lord's Day holy all my life!"

The milk hissed up and frothed over the sides of the pan, and she watched it, sobbing and wringing her hands. Nobody came to comfort her and receive her execrations. She was all alone, her milk had boiled over, the primus was extinguished and the kitchen stank of burnt milk and smoking oil.

She stopped crying and went groping upstairs to bed.

Nell Patrick stared vacantly at the baby's face on the pillow, swollen out of shape, the little mouth cracked and sore. The doctor had given her glycerine to put on it, but she stared and did nothing. It was not glycerine she wanted, it was her own healthy baby in place of this horrible, heart-rending little creature covered with suppurating blisters.

Nell liked the doctor. She liked his quietness. When he came in on his round of the patients she turned towards him as if she might drink in healing wisdom, drink it with her eyes and ears and her snub nose and her half-open lips, and return it with love to her children; but at the same time she knew there was nothing he could do for the baby.

He had told her of his meeting with her husband.

"Did he say anything?" she asked.

"Yes, he said that—that you and the children were to want for nothing."

She looked at the baby. How long did it take for a baby to die? She hardly liked to ask.

Later, when she was giving wee Pad a drink of orange squash, Danny came in.

"Hallo," he whispered.

Paddy pushed away the cup and looked at Danny, and his face broke into a smile.

"Was that you I heard crying?" Danny asked in a severe voice. "Was it you, Pad Patrick? For if it was I'll tell the teacher on you, so I will."

Pad shook his head.

"Was it not you? It was so!'

"Was not!" said Pad, with tears still sticking to his lashes.

Danny settled a chair beside the camp bed.

"Did ye ever hear tell," he began, "of how Mr. Dochy MacArdal was in the War, in a tank. . . . ?"

Pad listened without his usual rapt attention. His eyes glittered, his face was flushed and spotty and he moved his head restlessly; but whenever his face crumpled in preparation for tears he would catch sight of Danny, he would listen to a bit more talk of tanks and Germans. The story had a funny end, too, in Danny's tradition; and Pad managed a loyal chuckle at the right moment.

"Cracksis cocksis," he repeated.

"Cracked his coccyx! And it's a rudimentary tail!" Danny giggled in ecstasy. Then he caught sight of the fevered eyes and grew serious.

"Will I give you a wee drink, Pad?" he asked. "Orange, eh? Mistress MacLennan sent that along for ye. That's right . . . Lie down on your pillow, so. The doctor said I wasn't to come in, but I wanted to see for myself how you were. You'll not tell, eh?"

Pad shook his head.

171

"You'll be fine soon, so you will. Good-night, wee Pad. See you the morn!"

But the next night Nell was still waiting patiently for her baby to die. Wee Pad was worse, but the doctor said not so bad but that he had a good chance of pulling through. There were two more patients in the castle.

"Did you see Terence to-day?" Nell asked the doctor.

"No," he said. "The door was open and I went in, but there was nobody in. I'll see him to-morrow."

"Tell him—tell him not to worry," said Nell stupidly.

"Now, Mrs. Patrick, do what I tell you and go to bed. You can't do any good watching the baby, and you'll hear wee Pad if he wakes. I want you to keep up your strength."

"I will, Doctor," she said. "I can't do any good watching the baby."

She had repeated his exact words, and she did mean to obey him; but always, as soon as sleep began to drift over her hot eyes, she would waken with a jerk and feel compelled to look and see if there was any change.

How long did it take for a baby to die?

"Stop breathing," she would implore in a whisper. "Stop breathing, my lamb, my love. Sh-h! Just stop breathing, it's hard for you to go on and on——"

Father Kelly was not sure whether this were his second night in the castle or his fifth or his third. His mind felt flabby; he could not grasp anything for long enough to be sure he had thought it out.

He groped often for the rosary under his pillow in the hope of disciplining his wandering thoughts, but presently he would be surprised to find it in his hands, and would wonder where he had left off. He struggled against distraction, but in vain. Out of the corner of his eye—he lay with his eyes closed, but in his mind a panorama of visions passed before him—he would catch sight of a flick of movement, a dart, a quickness that flashed too rapidly for him to have caught any shape to interpret the sense that a small creature had moved. He knew all the same what it was; if he kept still, presently they would emerge from the outskirts of vision.

An immoderate love of creatures. It had always been his sin; that, and melancholy.

He had always had a special compassion for the brute creation; especially, since he came to Fionn, for his own wee fellas. He saw them in his mind's eye, sneaking out with their quick flicks of movement, cheeky and fearless of the corn-knobbled feet that could have crushed a dozen of them at once, squeaking at him, running up his sleeve to remind him of their hunger. He longed to know how they were getting on without him.

" Are ye there, Danny ? " he asked.

There was nobody in the room. He sighed. Holy Mary, Mother of God, pray for us sinners now, my mind's fair taken up with the mice.

Beasts had no immortal souls to be damned or saved. They only lived their little span of life and then were snuffed out. The only felicity they knew was in this life ; and it was a humble, natural felicity, no glory of the spirit ; then snuffed out. If their short life was one of misery and fear, its end was the same : snuffed out. It didn't matter. That was the common-sense view, anyway. They died, and it was as if they had never lived.

He sighed and shifted on the pillow and felt the hard beads between his fingers. He said a Hail Mary.

There was Susan, the wee rascal, peeping out of his slipper ! She had a white chest and always an air of bustling efficiency about her. Her black eyes darted in every direction. She put her forepaws, like little pink hands, on the edge of the old slipper and peeped over, spying out the land, her whiskers vibrating. All safe. She utttered little reassuring, grunting squeaks and out of the darkness of the toe of the slipper the babies emerged, small and furry, as inquisitive as their mother.

What dangers she had nursed them through ! Enemies surround them everywhere. Cats, owls, cannibal fathers, the priest himself with his stupid feet.

He remembered the first time she had chosen his slipper for her nest. He had been a couple of days in his bed, not sick, just couldn't be bothered getting up. Then, on the Thursday it was, he'd taken the notion to go and watch the boat come in, maybe take a jaunt to Oban, see the faces of his fellow-men ; and he had sat up in bed and groped with bare feet for his slippers. And just as he slid his right foot in he felt a nip on the big toe. Tried again, nipped again.

That wakened him up all right. He picked up the slipper,

fumbled in the toe and brought out Madame Susan and one of her pink, naked offspring, and she set her teeth in his thumb to teach him his manners before he let her back into the darkness of the slipper's toe.

That was the end of him using that slipper. It was dedicated to be a maternity ward, a nursery, a school for Susan's babies—Susan, with the indomitable spirit and the dainty white chest. Susan had a way, when she sat up on his finger and looked at him, of wrinkling her nose so that her whiskers bristled and pursing her fat wee cheeks in what was, unmistakably, a smile—the sort of smile that's as good as a wink.

" Susan, ye wee rogue ! " he chuckled.

The words came out in a thick jumble. His tongue was all wrong. There was no room in his mouth.

He sighed, and the sigh was a groan of discomfort.

" Let me see if I can give your mouth a clean."

" Is that you, Doctor."

" I'm going to wipe round the inside with gauze. Open——"

That was thorough now. The doctor's finger, was it, wrapped in gauze and dipped in the mouthwash, rubbing over his caked teeth. Now a bit of fresh gauze, wiping his palate and his tongue ; now the same again, over the floor of his mouth and round his gums. His whole being seemed to focus in the new experience that left his mouth fresh and clean.

" A great comfort," he said. " Wash your hands now before you do another thing, or you'll catch the smit. And come back and give me a crack."

He heard the doctor chuckle. Thought it was cheek, likely, giving him advice. Maybe he'd have washed his hands anyway. Still, there was no use taking risks, and he might never have thought of it.

He opened his eyes as the doctor came back, just long enough to get a quick glimpse of him before they shut again.

" Bring up your chair here and let me listen to the sound of a human voice. The minister's very good, he's kindness itself, but he's silent. What's the news ? "

" Well, we've got two more cases in. Captain Kilbride and his wife."

" Is that so, now. I'll have to get up to them. They're old, they'll die, both the two of them. I'll have to get up while they're

174

in their sane senses ; give me a tot of whisky or some drug or other to put jip into me to hear their confessions and——"

" Lie still just now. I'll let you know if they're in any danger of dying."

" While they're still sane and conscious ! "

" Yes, I understand."

Father Kelly relaxed. He knew well enough he was unfit to rise. In a day or two he'd be better, maybe. . . .

Alec was talking about Dog. It was better that he should do the talking, rather than the sick man, and he had somehow rambled on to his childhood and boyhood, and now he was going over his memories of a lively young animal, gawky and bouncing and clumsy.

" —and then he would put his paws on my shoulder and stare into my face. He would stare—intently, you know. It wasn't that he wanted anything, he just—was trying to fathom the difference between us—he knew there was more in me than he could under-stand. Then he would whine and flop down, maybe give my hand a lick."

" Ah, they're wonderful creatures," Father Kelly agreed.

" There's more to an animal than a set of reflexes."

" There is, there is."

" These laboratory observers—they're too detached to get an all-round view. It's true that there's a lot of nonsense talked—a lot of sentimental self-projection. But they go wrong in the opposite direction. They lose the response that the animal makes to a human being—if there's a real, alive relationship between them, I mean. To the average farmer, his beasts are just machines, machines for dragging carts, machines for milking, machines that fatten into so many hundred pounds of beef and mutton. I don't mean that. They haven't got a glimmering of what any animal is—in itself—apart from its utilitarian aspect, apart from its glands and reflexes, and so on."

" Quite right."

" The scientific observers see more, but they can't get past reflexes and glands and internal secretions ; another sort of machine."

" And would you say, now, was there any sort of a free-will in beasts ? "

This was taking Alec far out of his depth ; free-will was not a subject he had considered even in relation to men.

"Well—I don't know," he said. "Is there such a thing as free-will?"

"If there isn't," said Father Kelly impatiently, "then we're all just sets of reflexes, men and beasts too."

Alec began to flounder in deep waters.

"That's true," he agreed.

"And if you don't believe it about beasts you believe it still less about men. Never let the scientists get you misfoozled, son." He opened his eyes. "And a good thing for us," he said, "that the holy angels don't spend their time observing us with field glasses and studying our wee bit souls under microscopes; they're not above mucking in and giving us a hand with our lives when we need it."

He shut his eyes with a sense of satisfaction, for hadn't he just given himself the best argument in the world for bothering about his mice! His role to them was that of the heavenly ones towards himself. Sure he couldn't be blamed for that!

"If Danny's about," he said, "tell him to mind the scrap of cheese for the mice."

This was a terrible thing, a terrible thing. Mrs. Kilbride had been quite prepared for her husband to catch the smallpox (we all have to go sometime). But that she should be ill too! A terrible thing.

"I'll need that spencer under my nightgown," she said querulously. "I should have had it on from the very start when I came this morning, but you bustled me into my nightgown."

"I didn't want you to be catching a cold," said Maura.

Catching a cold! What was a cold more or less when she had the smallpox! The irony of Maura's silliness quite upset her; she chewed it over, her face reflecting the bitter taste of it.

"My bedsocks," she ordered. "No, I will not be too hot! And that bandanna handkerchief. Ts!" she snatched it irritably as Maura made to drape it round her shoulders. It went on her head as any sensible body might know!

"I'll bring a cup of tea," said Maura. "That'll cheer ye up."

If she had been at home she might have been supping her bedtime porridge; and with him taking the smallpox she might have been eating it in peace and quiet, only herself to look after, no tiresome old man with his deafness and his nasty tobacco to bother her nerves. And she had gone and caught it herself!

"You'd think I'd had enough work with a lifetime of him," she said bitterly, forgetting how she had complained when he was away from her for months at a time. "You'd think I might have been given a bit of peace and quiet in the end."

She was not addressing God directly, she knew better than to presume. But she was certainly talking at Him.

Captain Kilbride, sitting up in bed as if he sat in a deck-chair or a throne, sent for Danny.

"Here," he said, when Danny entered his room, "I need you to fetch me some necessaries from the house. Go and get the door-key first from Mrs. Kilbride and come back and let me tell you what I need."

"She'll not give me it," said Danny, returning in a flash.

"Tell her I want it!"

"I—she gave me a row for going into a lady's bedroom," said Danny. "I'm not going back."

"Send your mother in for it, then. Tell her I'll be obliged if she'll fetch me my door-key from Mrs. Kilbride."

Danny departed.

He returned. "I heard her asking my mother what you want it for," he said. "She'll not give it to her till she knows what you want it for."

"For purposes best known to myself!" said Captain Kilbride terribly.

Danny departed again.

This time it was Maura who came in, bringing him a cup of tea. The old man accepted it, looking at her, as he looked at everyone, with an air of watching the antics of monkeys.

"Mistress Kilbride," began Maura, "sends her compliments and——"

"Better stick to the truth, woman," said the captain.

"Well, she says it's late," said Maura. "It's too late to be poking about the house with a lamp and setting the place on fire, likely."

Captain Kilbride laid the cup of tea on a chair beside his bed, threw back the clothes and began to hitch himself out.

"Oh, mercy," said Maura, "don't go near her, don't be upsetting her any more, Captain, for God's sake: she's as cantankerous as the devil's ass——"

Captain Kilbride gravely returned himself to bed, picked up his cup of tea and tasted it, and motioned Maura to sit on the edge of his bed.

"Listen to me," he said, with an air of quiet wisdom. "I'll tell you what we'll do, Maura. This needs diplomatic handling. Now, hang you about till she's asleep, and you'll know that by her snoring; you'll think she's strangling herself, but never heed; it's the way she has. And when you hear that, you get the key!"

"But where'll it be?"

"That's for you to find out.—— In her skirt pocket likely," he added impatiently.

"Oh, mercy! She'll think I'm robbing her!"

"She'll never waken, woman."

"But what'll I do if it's not there?"

"Look for it! A great, black, iron key, you'll have no trouble seeing that! And bring it to me."

"I'll have a try, maybe," said Maura doubtfully.

"That's a good girl. And the minute you've got it send Danny to me."

"Och, Captain, Danny's not going out again this night. It's time he was in his bed."

"I'm beset with women on every side," said the captain. "Well, well, let it be till morning, then. But get you the key the minute you hear the snoring, mind."

"I will," said Maura wearily.

"Send Danny to me," said Mrs. Kilbride, sitting up in bed. It was the second time Maura had peeped into her room.

"He's away to his bed! It's past eleven o'clock at night!"

"Is he in his bed?"

"Well, I'm just after telling him to go for the fifth time and if he isn't——"

"See is he still up, Maura my dear," said Mrs. Kilbride in her most persuasive tones. "It's important for my peace of mind. I'll not get a wink of sleep this night if you don't."

"Give me patience," said Maura under her breath as she went to find Danny.

"You're a bad, ungrateful boy," she raged when she saw him,

178

" you never do a single thing I tell you. Go and see what Mrs. Kilbride wants."

" And me just about to start going to my bed ? "

" Go and see her, I said ! "

" I will not, Mammy, you heard what she had to say when I went in that time——"

" Danny, do you want to drive me demented ? "

" But you said yourself—oh, all right ! "

Bewildered at the changeableness of women, Danny knocked loudly on the old woman's door, waited until she had told him three times, in a rising scream, to come in, and opened the door a crack.

" Did you say to come in ? " he asked, still from outside.

Mrs. Kilbride addressed several remarks to the saints ; and finally said, yes, she had been telling him to come in for the last ten minutes.

" Now, look you here, Danny," she said when he had at last obeyed her, " come here and shut the door. That's right. I need you to go to the house and——"

" To-night ? " Danny interrupted, aghast.

" This minute," said Mrs. Kilbride sharply. " And——"

" My Mammy won't let me," said Danny.

" Give me patience," said Mrs. Kilbride. Danny understood this to be addressed to Saint Anthony. " This is important, Danny, and there'll be sixpence at the end of it if you bring me back my key."

" Key ? " Danny echoed stupidly.

" I've looked high and low, and I'm not fit to be out of my bed at all either, and it's not here. I thought I'd better put it under my pillow before I fell asleep, just in case—and it's not here. I thought I had it in my bag, but it's "—she was trembling with annoyance, almost weeping—" Go you and bring it back to me, Danny. It's been left sticking in the door, a big black key. Lock the door and bring it."

" I will," said Danny, seeing how he could oblige both the Kilbrides and put a stop to all this key tiresomeness.

" What was it you wanted me to bring ? " he asked the captain. " The key's been left in the door and I'm to go and fetch it."

The captain gave him a list of the things he wanted, with instructions where to find them.

The cardboard box in the mahogany chest under the wardrobe and the oilskin packet in the inside breast pocket of the navy blue suit and the wee tin of tobacco in the hole under the linoleum in the spare room beside the window and . . .

Danny came back, tired and impatient, at five minutes to twelve.

"The house is all locked up," he said to Mrs. Kilbride. "There's no key in the door at all. There is not."

He went to the captain's room.

"The house is all locked up," he said. "There's no key in the door at all. I'm away to my bed."

## Chapter Twenty

NELL PATRICK offered to look after Mrs. Kilbride if she needed attention through the night. That let Maura go to bed shortly after midnight. John Forsyth was on duty until two o'clock, when Dochy MacArdal would take over.

Captain Kilbride had fallen asleep at last, but his wife still lay awake fretting about her key. Someone, she said, must have it! Someone must have pocketed it and was biding his time—or her time—to make off with the lustre jugs and the big bowl with the schooner on it and the frog mug; and the six glasses for sherry wine that rang like bells when you tapped them with the ivory back-scratcher; and the new hem-stitched linen sheets, never used, wrapped in tissue paper along with a nightdress of fine lawn, all destined for her laying out when she died; and her walnut two-canister tea caddy with orange pekoe in one canister and a hundred and forty-six gold sovereigns and four pound notes and two five shilling pieces all in a calico bag in the other canister, concealed by a screwed-up crumple of yellow newspaper. And her best coat and skirt, and her skunk fur, far too good to wear but the thief would have no scruple about wearing it, or letting his wife wear it if it was a man who had the key.

"But there's no thief on Fionn," Nell Patrick reminded her. She had looked in to see if the old woman was all right.

"The key's gone, isn't it?"

"It has, but it'll be somewhere?"

"Of course it'll be somewhere! In the thief's pocket is where it'll be! I always said there ought to be a policeman on Fionn—and here we are, helpless!"

"Och, there's nobody on Fionn would steal, Mrs. Kilbride!"

"Then where's my key?" Mrs. Kilbride almost screamed. "What's he keeping it for if he's not a thief, tell me that! You never know what the human heart is capable of till temptation is put in its way."

This was true enough, of course, because Father Kelly had said it himself in one of his sermons. Nell was silenced for a moment, then another idea struck her.

"If it's in somebody's pocket, he's a thief all right," she admitted, "but what if it's not? Likely it just dropped out of your bag on the road, and it's lying there all the time, waiting for the daylight and the first to pass will see it and bring it here."

This possibility brought some comfort to Mrs. Kilbride. She pointed out that they had still to face the possibility that the person who saw it and picked it up might not be an honest man, and that it might lie hidden in a tussock of grass or nettles and never be found, and if the door had to be broken down that would be a nice expense; but her angry trembling diminished, she wept a little, retied the bandanna handkerchief round her head and at last lay back on the pillows and closed her eyes.

Nell crept out of her room and met the minister emerging from the kitchen with fresh water for the priest.

"He has a terrible thirst, surely!" she exclaimed.

"He doesn't take a whole glass," the minister explained. "A few mouthfuls at a time; then he wants it fresh again the next time."

"You're very patient," said Nell humbly. She felt awkward that the Protestant minister should do so much for their old priest.

John agreed with her but did not say so.

"How's the baby?" he asked.

"She never wakes," said Nell. "She just goes on breathing, with a rickle in her chest all the time. Wee Pad's asleep, too. I'm hoping Mrs. Kilbride has got herself settled at last. She's in a great take-on about her old key!"

"Her key?"

"Have ye missed it all, Mr. Forsyth? Have ye not heard all the stramash about her losing her door-key?"

"She has not lost her door-key," said John. "Her door-key is in my pocket. Does she want it?"

"Does she want it?" Nell echoed. "I'll say she wants it!" She began to giggle. The minister looked so stuffed and silly. "She said it would be in some thief's pocket," she added.

Mr. Forsyth listened, first with distaste for Nell's cheap slanginess, then with incredulity.

"You're not suspecting me of burglary, I hope," he said.

"Oh, it's not me," Nell giggled, "It's her; I'm sure I don't know what she'll say when she knows; she'll never believe you didn't know she was fair demented looking for it—all the noise and stramash there's been—she'll never believe you didn't hear what was going on."

She knew it was wrong to provoke him like this, yet she felt she was taking some obscure revenge against him on old Father Kelly's behalf. It was a shame to think of the poor old priest lying helpless and sick, dependent on the kindness of his rival.

John heard her with increasing horror. He knew no one would believe in their heart of hearts that he could steal, but this nest of papists might go on whispering and jeering just out of wicked spite . . . it might come to his mother's ears. . . .

"Is Mrs. Kilbride asleep?" he asked stiffly.

"She is!" Nell assured him.

"I'll see her in the morning, then. You'll be wanting to get back to your children, I expect." To your dying baby, he thought, and almost put the thoughts into words. Giggling with malice and her baby daughter sinking into the grave! It was horrible.

Father Kelly seemed to have dropped into a nap. John sank into his chair and put a hand over his eyes. Just when he was enjoying helping folks, this had to happen!

I shouldn't take it to heart, he told himself. I should rise above it.

But if his mother heard of it! There would be no end. . . .

And his mother had a headache; the doctor had told him so when he returned from his morning round. She would be lying awake at that very minute, moaning with the pain in her head. Those headaches! They were like a sudden black cloud blotting the light out, blotting out the sky from both their lives. He had so often, since childhood even, felt himself quenched and drained of life by the onset of one of mother's headaches. If he were at the manse he could have given her a glass of hot milk and a couple of tablets.

And yet he would not have chosen to alter his present position, which was giving him, at last, an opportunity to discover what were the thoughts that kept forming and pushing up somewhere deep inside him, thoughts that he dared not look at in her presence.

Father Kelly stirred and his tongue groped between his lips.

" A mouthful of water? Or orange? " he suggested.

" Water," said Father Kelly thickly. " Fresh water."

John rose, emptied the glass and filled it again at the kitchen sink, and poured a few spoonfuls over the sticky tongue.

" Thanks," said the priest.

" What's the time? " he asked presently.

" Five minutes to one," John replied.

Now the blistered fingers were fumbling about for the rosary. John pushed it towards them; they clutched it, John thought, as a baby might clutch a rattle or a teddy bear. It was pitiful in a grown man.

Now he was looking again, nervously and ready to recoil, at the depth in his own mind where his thoughts were pushing up towards the light. He was afraid to look quite frankly; it was like staring down the shaft of an old, evil well; vertigo or something worse might land you down there in the slime and darkness, to drown. They said Truth lay at the bottom of the well, but what if Truth were nothing but slime and stinking fungus!

I should never have missed the Sabbath-day services, he thought suddenly. I should have had a prayer meeting here. I ought to pray more myself, anyway.

Oh Almighty God, he prayed, using in his mind the pulpit intonation that was associated with his approach to his God, What is man that Thou art mindful of him. . . . ?

Man is made in God's image. The days of man are but as grass. The grass withereth, the flower fadeth, but I the Lord thy God am a jealous God, visiting the sins of the fathers upon the children, reaping where I did not sow, casting sinners into a burning fiery pit; depart from me, ye curst. The king of love my shepherd is, and him that doth me feed. Their worm dieth not.

What art Thou, that man is mindful of Thee?

John recoiled as he caught himself asking the question. It wakened him in a flurry of dread. He dared not ask that.

He rubbed his hand over his face, awake yet with a sense of wandering in the subterranean corridors of a dream. Father Kelly had lost his rosary again ; he gave him the popish bauble and poured another spoonful of water into the foul mouth and dabbed the lips with glycerine.

" You're very good," muttered the priest. " You'd have made a good doctor."

It was a back-handed sort of compliment. For a minister you make a good doctor. . . .

John's mother had once, reproaching him for the feebleness of his ministry, said, " You were called to the ministry, John, oh, yes, you were called and no mistake ; but remember, many are called but few are chosen ! "

Maybe that was what was happening to him now : rejection.

He rose to see what old Kilbride was thumping for ; thump, thump on the floor with his stick, and if you didn't come at once he'd start shouting.

" Shut the window," said the captain.

John shut it half-way. The captain believed he was obeyed and snuggled down, and John returned to his comfortable chair beside Father Kelly. Twenty past one ; not much longer and then he'd wake Dochy and soon be in bed himself.

He shut his eyes, not to sleep but to have another attempt at prayer. This time, before he began, he forced himself to awareness of the Deity whose presence he sought. The earth is thy footstool, thy pillow the skies. No, that made a too invalidish vision ; he tried again.

His chin sank into his collar. He was awake. He was there beside the old priest, in a small bleak room with the wind battering and the sea crashing outside ; and he was also out under the vast skies, trying to climb a mountain that was made of glass. That was a fairy-tale, surely ! But there was no fairy-tale feeling about the mountain or the dark skies ; only a feeling of doom. The climb was dizzy and impossible, and his own strength would never have succeeded ; it was the power of God that drew him up the mountain to the peak of Judgment, and if the verdict was against him he would lose the help of that power, he would go slithering dizzily down the glass hill to the abyss where their worm dieth not and their fire is not quenched. Head over heels to destruction.

Now he stood before the Judge. His eyes were shut and he

184

dared not open them. He could never bear the blaze of that righteous indignation so he clenched his eyes shut, screwed them right back into his skull. . . .

But they opened in spite of him, opened to anti-climax. The Being that sat on the throne was absurd in its assumption of majesty. Its face was a sallow, censorious oval, its hands were small and the right index finger strained as if with peeling potatoes, and beneath its wet skirts its feet kept up a perpetual kicking.

" You're dreaming, son, you're dreaming," said a voice. " Wake up, it's a dream ! "

He was sitting beside a bed, and Father Kelly was leaning out, shaking his knee with the hand that still clutched the black rosary.

" Oh—Father——" John gasped, " yes, I was dreaming—I was dreaming a terrible dream." It was more terrible now that he was awake ; that paltry figure on the throne was unspeakably repulsive.

" I was dreaming of the Day of Judgment," he said. " I'm ashamed of——"

This would not do. He tried to regain his ordinary voice, his air of composed righteousness.

" I've been a bit worried, I suppose, having to miss out the services. And me the minister." Righteousness evaporated. He was still too near the horrifying dream and his conscience was disturbed on a deeper level than the omission of the church services explained.

" I'm not," he whispered, " not even sure of my vocation."

Father Kelly was not the one he should have let that out to, the great crass priest of Rome, a minion of the Scarlet Woman of Babylon . . . But he was saying still more.

" I've fair lost my way," he whispered. " I don't know what's right and what's wrong, maybe I've done wrong all the time . . . I can't think. . . ."

He felt a sob rise to his throat and buried his face in his hands to conceal its grimace. He fought for self-control, half aware of Father Kelly's attempts to soothe his distress. He was appalled at his loss of dignity.

Part of him longed to accept the priest's comfort. It was the very words of the Bible he was using after all, and there could be no harm in listening, at least.

" I was sick, and ye visited me," said the old priest in his hoarse croak. " Inasmuch as ye did it unto the least of these my brethren, ye did it unto me."

Behind the words was a vision of that god on the top of the glass hill with its feet kicking under its skirts, and a loud voice saying, " It's only a doited old woman showing off her skinny shanks."

John straightened up and stared at the sick priest.

" I don't think," he said, " I'm likely to get any benefit in religious instruction from you, Father Kelly."

He sat erect and full of zeal. He had rebuked presumption.

Father Kelly was lying quiet, his eyes closed as usual, his head turned away. Likely he was asleep. John crossed one knee over the other, then after a little uncrossed them and sat with folded hands, repeating whole chapters of the Bible he knew by heart. He repeated the first chapter of Genesis ; and the first chapter of John's Gospel ; and now he was in the middle of First Corinthians, XIII. He mind wandered off the sense of it though ; he returned to the beginning. Though I speak with the tongues of men and of angels, and have not charity, I am become as sounding brass, or a tinkling cymbal. And though I have the gift of prophecy, and understand all mysteries, and all knowledge ; and though I have all faith, so that I could remove mountains, and have not charity, I am nothing. And though. . . .

That was a nasty slap in the face he had given the old sick priest. . . .

Charity suffereth long, and is kind ; charity envieth not ; charity vaunteth not itself, is not puffed up, doth not behave itself unseemly. . . .

But there was nothing he could do anyway ; it had been right surely to rebuke the minion of Rome ! The devil himself could quote scripture ! It would be a terrible thing for a minister to accept comfort from a popish priest.

For now we see through a glass, darkly. That was true, oh God, that was true ! And maybe what you saw in the glass was nothing but the reflection of your own thoughts. How were you to know ?

" Oh, God, I'm lost, oh, God, show me the way !

God looked back at John Forsyth out of a prim, self-righteous face. There was no help there.

It was five minutes to two. He went upstairs to waken Dochy

MacArdal ; and presently he was able to drag himself away into the dark seclusion of his own bedroom.

## Chapter Twenty-One

NEXT MORNING Nell wakened to wee Pad's wailing. She looked first at the baby, dreading the change she might see, disappointed to see no change at all. Still the small mouth gaped as before, as dry as a dead leaf, still the rapid breaths rustled ; perhaps the blisters were darker.

She attended to the little boy. She had less patience than usual ; she almost cried at the wet bed she found.

" A big boy like you ! " she complained. " What will Danny say ? "

But wee Pad was too limp and ill to care. He cried drearily, setting her nerves on edge.

How long will this go on ? she wondered, a tear dribbling over her nose as she changed his under-sheet and his nightgown.

She got no peace to sleep. She was done, she could scarcely drag herself about. Last night she had been planning a great joke, letting on to Mrs. Kilbride she had caught the thief red-handed with the key in his pocket, and him the minister ! To-day it was flat. When she went in to answer Mrs. Kilbride's repeated calls her face was sulky.

" I thought you'd never hear me, Nell ! "

" I heard you. I was changing wee Pad's bed : it was wet ; I couldn't just stop in the middle and leave him to catch cold."

" Does he still wet at his age ? "

" The bairn's ill ! " Nell protested.

" Some never get over it, no, not when they're full-grown. You're not going off before you hear what I want, are you ? "

" Tell me what it is, then."

" I feel bad," said Mrs. Kilbride, her head quivering. " I'm all over with spots."

" You had them yesterday."

" There's more to-day. I never slept a wink. Just when I could

187

have dropped over your Pad started roaring. I could take a drink, but I don't know what I fancy."

" There'll be tea on the way when Maura gets up," said Nell without sympathy. Then, remembering the minister's patience with the old priest, she said, " I'll fill you a glass of fresh water."

" There's no comfort or nourishment in water," said Mrs. Kilbride, chewing bitterly.

Nell swallowed and brought it just the same. Right enough the poor soul didn't look herself at all, but Nell had no patience this morning.

" I could do with a cup of tea myself," she said sadly, but hurried on before Mrs. Kilbride seized that advantage, " your key's safe enough. The minister took care of it. Well, I'm going back to my bed; I'll catch cold in my nightgown."

She shut the door on some scathing comment on her fear for colds when other folks had a lot worse to contend with. If she raked out the fire and lit it and put the kettle on it would hasten the arrival of tea, but at the very idea of the dusty kitchen grate her joints melted, she drooped back into her warm bed and closed her eyes. But the warmth had gone from her. She began to shiver violently.

Somewhere one of Danny's clocks struck five. Nell moaned and pulled the clothes tighter round her neck. It would be two hours before Maura rose, two hours anyway.

She was very miserable. She wondered if Terence slept comfortably, all alone in the house. Fine, probably; he would never miss her: he was well enough used to doing without her on the merchant ships. He'd never have come to Fionn at all if she hadn't got the cottage, and it was a wonder he came at all the way he ignored her. Nell read all the advice columns in the cheap women's papers she bought, all the articles on how to hold your husband, how to remain glamorous though married, how to deal with a straying husband, but the advice took no root. How could she make a point of looking dainty and relaxed at night when she had the baby to change and feed ? What good was a dab of perfume behind each ear when her bodice always smelt of the milk the baby vomited after each feed ? How could she save that little bit of mystery that spells allure when—when he didn't care, didn't care, didn't have the least interest left to notice whether she looked alluring or not ? And whose fault if she wasn't !

Oh, if only they had got a room in Oban instead of coming to Fionn, if only they had had the luck to live in Glasgow where glamour prevailed everywhere! If even they had come to one of the other islands where there would be no temptation like Lilias MacPherson of Skua to distract Terence from his duties! Oh, if only Maura would get up, if only someone would fill her a hot-water bottle! . . .

When Maura at last appeared with a cup of tea Nell was too hot.

"Mercy, Nell, you're not yourself at all," said Maura apprehensively. "Stay you in your bed: I'm going to tell the doctor."

And when Doctor came, he said, "Well, Nell, I'm afraid you must stay where you are. Yes, it looks as if you've got it, too."

He looked down at her with such awkward, aloof kindness that tears filled Nell's eyes, tears of weakness and relief. She need no longer hang over her baby and watch the creeping approach of death; the responsibility was all on his shoulders now, and she could spare pity for him.

She heard his voice outside the door, having a discussion with Maura; now Mr. Dochy's voice had joined in. She wondered idly what they were talking about. Now they came into the room, Maura and the doctor.

"Mrs. Patrick," said Alec, "I think it might be better for us to take the baby out of this room now." He spoke tentatively, as if he would yield if she objected to the idea.

"Where are ye putting her?" Nell asked.

"I think in Father Kelly's room——"

Nell said thankfully, "She's got more need of him than of me now." She watched Alec lift the drawer with her baby in it, followed by Maura with a pile of Harrington squares.

Dochy moved from the priest's side and looked down at the still-living baby.

"Take long?" he asked.

"Not long," said Alec. "It's incredible what a hold they have on life all the same."

"Could she still——"

"Not possibly. She'll die before night."

"Eh?" said Father Kelly, hearing their low voices.

Alec went over to him.

Father Kelly, though his eyes were shut, had an air of keen

attention. His fingers tapped impatiently on the coverlet or crumpled it into his fist, dragging it up and letting it go.

" How is the mouth ? " Alec asked.

" It was the first step that did it," Father Kelly muttered. " I should never have thought of the cinema. Should never have thought of it. Never."

" He's been talking like this since about five o'clock," said Dochy, " and pulling at the clothes. He doesn't seem to grasp where he is."

Alec went round the others ; Torquil, improving slowly, Mrs. Kilbride in a slough of self-pity, the captain in a light doze, flushed and withered-looking, but wearing, even in sleep, his air of slightly cynical detachment.

They washed their hands and went to the parlour to await the arrival of breakfast. Alec was silent and preoccupied. Dochy leaned back in his chair clasping his hands behind his head, watching the flames flicker round the driftwood with which Maura had set the fire. He was content. In some ways life in the castle at present reminded him of the War ; you did what had to be done, taking each job as it came along and accepting whatever relaxations and pleasures came your way ; your perspective of life shortened, the future was a matter of the next few hours. This was a good moment —after the chill and loneliness of the small hours—a seat in a comfortable chair, a fire flickering, the civilisation of Aunt Jane's parlour after the ugly spectacle of illness and decay.

After breakfast, unless John wanted help with one of the patients, he would have a couple of hours of freedom.

" I might take a gun out and look for a pheasant," he said. " Look for a pheasant and bring back a rabbit probably." He yawned and stretched.

" If you go anywhere near the crofts," Alec said, " you can read the signals for me."

" Trousers at Glen Beg, a skirt at Skua. Sounds symbolic."

" Or a white towel at either."

Kirpu came in and laid the table.

" You're not worried, are you ? " Dochy asked when Kirpu had gone.

Alec leaned forward and prodded the fire with the steel poker.

" A bit," he admitted.

" Take a day at a time," Dochy suggested.

Alec put down the poker and looked at the carpet.

"You see," he said, "I have to look ahead. We're going to have the problem, soon, of—disposal of bodies."

"What's wrong with the graveyard?"

"That's through the village, up past Oran's cross. That——" He stopped.

"You mean you haven't got forms for a death certificate?"

"Oh, that isn't what worries me; I'll keep records, of course. It's infection. I'm afraid—I'll have to do something unpopular——"

He stopped again as John and Kirpu came in together.

As soon as Kirpu had gone again he explained what was in his mind.

John Forsyth looked appalled; he was already white and strained round the eyes and looked as if he had not slept. But Dochy accepted it calmly.

"Very sensible," he said. "We'll both back you; the minister's authority will carry us through."

"I'll back you all I can," John agreed, but his face wore a look of bewilderment and dismay.

Alec set off on his round of the village. This time he not only had to make sure that no further case had developed, he must also find a volunteer nurse for night duty.

Mrs. Forsyth? Real work might save her from her habitual hysteria. But when he went into the manse he found her in the darkened kitchen with a wet cloth on her brow, flushed with pain. He could not expect her to work.

"No, it isn't smallpox," he assured her. "It's only a bad migraine. Don't you remember telling me you often had them?"

"Never as bad as this," she moaned.

Of course, she wanted to be at the castle near John; but Alec insisted that she had not contracted smallpox, and persuaded her with difficulty.

He went on to the Hotel. Mrs. MacLennan was busy and well. Mrs. Transom greeted him eagerly, obviously because she found life dreary in the Hotel now. All her wiles were turned on him.

"But I needn't ask how you are," Alec smiled. "You're sparkling with vitality."

"Am I?" she asked wistfully, opening her eyes till the painted lashes stood out like a stockade.

"Quite ravishing."

It pleased Alec to grant her the short, teasing flirtation that she had hoped for. It was all so easy, like a game of pat-ball tennis to please a child, and she sparkled so prettily at the harmless innuendoes. She must once have been what he assured her she still was—ravishing. But she did not look as if she would be of the least use in the castle. He went to look for Lydia.

Lydia's strange eyes smiled at him with an assumption of lazy intimacy. She gave him a cigarette, pressing his case back into his pocket when he would have drawn it out; she lit his cigarette and her own.

"Seriously," he said, "when were you vaccinated? Have you worked it out?"

"Seven years ago," she said. "Why?"

"Because I need a nurse, someone to look after the women during the night."

She dropped her eyes to the cigarette between her fingers and he watched her, admiring the luminous quality of her skin, the perfect finish of eyelid and nostril and mouth. Her beauty had been invisible to him until he had seen its one flaw, her eyes. Now his original blindness made the loveliness more rare each time he saw her. He put his hand over hers.

"What about the postman's wife?" she suggested.

"The postman? I don't think—oh, yes, of course, Torquil is the postman. Well, you mean Mrs. MacVean . . . I don't think she . . ." He was not thinking of anything but the way her fingers twined through his, satiny fingers with pale coral nails. Now she was looking up, waiting for him to finish the sentence; her eyes had begun to smile.

"I wondered if you would come," he said.

"Oh, no," Lydia smiled.

He saw that the idea had been absurd. He stood up, but she stood, too, coming close to him.

"Why not try the school-teacher?" she said, her voice as smooth as a caress.

"Miss Bradshaw?"

"She seems the obvious person. I'm so useless."

"I believe you are. You're as lovely as—as a primrose in the twilight, and as hard as a diamond."

Her upturned face was smiling with a sort of sad humility that he knew to be false; there was no humility in her. She used her loveliness as a weapon or a snare, and when he kissed her he disliked her even as he yielded to the enchantment. She was smiling at her own power.

Presently he moved away. " I must go and see Miss Bradshaw," he said. " I'll come back to-morrow. Good-bye."

" Good-bye."

He went downstairs and out, and took a deep, exhilarating gulp of the wind that pressed against him even on the doorstep. He wondered if she might be watching him from the window and looked up hopefully, rebuking himself at the same time for the childish hope. But she was there, looking down on him with a faint, soft smile. He waved his hat to her and, walking almost backwards, bumped into Danny.

" Sorry," he said.

" I was waiting for you," said Danny austerely. " Mr. Dochy and me went to the top of the Cailleach and he sent me back for to tell you there's a skirt at the one and trousers at the other." He spoke with his face turned down, frowning.

" That's good. Oh, Danny, there's a thing I want you to do for me—important."

" What is it ? " Danny looked up with provisional interest.

" I want you," said Alec, " to gather all the driftwood and—all the loose dry branches you can get—and put it on that flat table of rock beyond the castle."

" Is that all ? " Danny was shocked with disappointment. " I do that already, only I bring it right in for the fires."

" But what I want is much more than that. A huge pile."

" For a bonfire ? "

" Yes."

Still, even a bonfire hardly deserved the solemnity the doctor had shown, or justified the hopes he had raised. Danny felt cheated, and his reason for disapproval still rankled. Waving his hat at the likes of her !

" That Miss Transom," he said, " her you were waving at, she's—she's not what she seems. She's not even a Miss at all. She's a divorcy ! "

" Run along and don't be silly."

He did not wait to see Danny's face freeze with rage ; he turned and went on, past the Kilbride cottage and up to the schoolhouse.

As he walked away from Danny he received a sudden glimpse

into himself; a vision in which he saw himself living in several simultaneous layers of his being. On the surface layer was Dr. Alec MacArdal, walking in a salty wind towards Miss Bradshaw the schoolmistress. Beneath that another Alec listened still to Danny's impertinence : She's not even a Miss at all, she a divorcy ! And beneath that he still laid his hand over Lydia Transom's, watched her finger twine through his, felt her mouth and the warmth of her skin, lingering in a velvety, sensuous dream. Beneath that again lay his preoccupations with the hospital and the care of the sick, and his feelings for his friends—developing feelings ; for even as he opened towards John Forsyth and Dochy MacArdal, Kirpu, Torquil and even impudent young Danny, at the same time his feeling for Bertie Newnham warmed and revived and became less stilted ; and his feeling for Sir Hector MacArdal, formerly so clear and untroubled, had become less simple, less understandable.

But underneath these layers, which were less simply stratified than that, was something deeper still ; a darkness that he had never looked at, where, perhaps, if he dared to look, he might find his essential self, the hidden fountain.

It was only a glimpse, the vision of the concentric worlds within him, and of the dark fountain he only felt a vanishing presentiment ; questioning himself on what the flash of vision had actually been he only remembered that he was, after all, in flight, in flight from the mechanical frittering of his daily life in the clinic, in flight from the suffocation of success, from the final surrender offered by the hypodermic, from—he knew not from what else ; and he did not wonder towards what goal his flight bore him.

Yet as he pushed open Miss Bradshaw's gate he felt that he had returned to a difficult lesson he had forgotten ; he must make a fresh effort at concentration or the living impulse begun on a park bench would be dissipated and lost.

Miss Bradshaw had begun by feeling a guilty satisfaction in her compulsory holiday, though she regretted its cause. A holiday in which she was confined to the house meant time for all the things she never had time for. Time to re-read Browning and wash blankets and clear out the attics and improve her French and get that pile of mending out of the way. She began with zest.

By the end of three days she had done it all. Those enormous, herculean labours that had been put off for years, she had accomplished them in a twinkling.

"Let that be a lesson to me," said Miss Bradshaw. "Never put work off because you think you haven't time. It's the excuse of deceitful laziness. You've got all the time there is—twenty-four hours a day—and a shorter working week than most folks, not to speak of holidays. Shirker!"

Every now and then Lois Bradshaw would catch herself out in some fresh example of hypocrisy or ineptitude or self-indulgence and would give herself a sharp reprimand. The experience was always invigorating. She shook her head at this fresh evidence of her shiftless evasions and looked round for something else to do.

She had read the *Grammarian's Funeral* with a dip into *Porphyria's Lover* in the middle for relaxation. She had sandwiched *My Last Duchess* between slabs of *Sordello*, and had also cleaned the house and the school, had emptied, washed and refilled the two inkwells on her desk, the red and the blue. She had prepared a fresh instalment of Algebra for Danny when she could get hold of him again, and had revised some elementary Latin, also for his benefit. She was just keeping boredom at bay; just and no more.

Dr. MacArdal's daily visit was a pleasure she looked forward to, but it was only a glance and an inquiry, scarcely more. It brightened the morning, and after it the day stretched in a dull, dwindling perspective towards night and bed-time. He would soon be here; it was ten past ten; and then a whole day yawned ahead.

She stood in the middle of the floor, stocky and pleasant, frowning.

"Come on," she addressed herself. "You're thirty-four, too old for dreams and vapours. Idling won't get you anywhere. Plenty of other lonely women on this island at this minute. Think of Shona MacVean and Mrs. Forsyth at the manse and—how would you like to be in Mrs. MacLennan's shoes, all that work to do single-handed! I bet she'd be thankful if she only had herself to look after!"

That was the way to speak to herself, briskly, making it plain that she meant to stand no nonsense. But at the end of it she was still in the middle of the floor, invigorated, yes, but to what end? Could she perhaps suggest to the doctor that Mrs. MacLennan could do with some help? An able-bodied woman like herself would be better helping in the Hotel than idling in an empty school. But until the doctor came and gave his permission what would she do? Read some more *Sordello*? Dust the room again? Or improve her French still further? She must certainly go to Avignon this summer and use her extra vocabulary before it went to waste. Or to Bordeaux, the wine-country. But just now . . .

She opened the massive ugly volume of Browning's *Complete Works* and began turning pages towards *Sordello*. *Sordello* is not the clearest or most appealing of Browning's works; the eye is apt to linger on shorter poems by the way, putting off the plunge into that knobbly obscurity. Miss Bradshaw's eye fell on a line as the pages turned sluggishly:

*One who never turned his back but marched breast forward.* . . .

She had read that yesterday, but had missed its immediate message. One who marched breast forward—it was inspiring. He would never sit idling at ten in the morning!

" Come on—quick march! " said Miss Bradshaw in her bright, schoolmistress voice. " Scarf round your head. Jacket on. Now then—breast forward! "

But the only place to which she was permitted to march was the garden, and it was not pleasant out. Still, breast forward, no shirking! How dark and dank the earth was. Those snowdrops looked miserable. Perhaps she ought to hoe, loosen up the earth a bit.

Miss Bradshaw's garden was neither useful nor beautiful. The same perennials struggled from the earth year after year; veronica, phloxes, Nancy Pretty, golden rod, Michaelmas daisies, all flowers that thrive or at least survive on neglect. Vegetables had no place in the garden. Miss Bradshaw knew about vitamins and respected them deeply, but there was no use bothering what she ate or failed to eat; she kept her health by ignoring it.

She hoed with energy and without compassion for the plants she jolted along with the weeds. Seen from behind she presented a short, wiry figure in strong brogues and an old slaty Harris costume, a patterned scarf flying about her head, a few curls of black hair blowing with the scarf. When she turned at the sound of the gate her face was witch-white and alert. She smiled cheerfully on seeing Alec.

" Coming in? " she asked.

When he assented she dropped the hoe across a clump of purple crocuses and opened the door with alacrity.

"I'll put the kettle on," she said. "It's just the time of morning when a cup of tea saves your life, isn't it."

To her delight he made no protest. She set a tray for two, combed through her wiry black hair before a strategically-placed glass in the kitchen and dabbed her nose and chin with powder, and returned to the sitting-room to find Alec turning over the leaves of her book of poetry.

"Browning," he said without looking up. "Your favourite poet, Miss Bradshaw?"

"Yes," said Miss Bradshaw in the defiant voice of one who admits to having a favourite poet.

"I think I should have guessed so."

Her suspicions evaporated.

"Oh—why?" she asked.

Alec looked at her. She sat erect, facing him eagerly, white from the wind, her hair black and shining and piled up like a Spanish woman's hair, curling and springing from her head as if it grew out of her deep vitality. She did not know herself. She was a woman who would be ashamed of her own sensuousness, who recoiled from mysticism, who mistrusted her own reaction to beauty, but who could accept it and feed on it clothed in the abrupt and knobbly language of Browning. But Alec could not put that into words.

"It's difficult to say why," he said. "I suppose because I feel your temperament is like Browning's poetry."

"Ungraceful and gnarled," said Miss Bradshaw with more acuteness than he had expected.

"Forthright," said Alec. "No fripperies."

"Blunt and unadorned."

"But capable of subtleties."

Miss Bradshaw shook her head.

"Browning is, but I'm not," she said. "I can't see any way through a brick wall. Sometimes I don't even see that there's a brick wall there at all!" She chuckled.

"That may have its advantages, I should think. Some brick walls crumple up if you charge through them."

"Have you found that?"

"Yes."

Miss Bradshaw heard the kettle boil and went through to infuse the tea. She was tingling with enjoyment, with a feeling of rare liberation. She had chosen the isolated life of a schoolmistress on a small island and she was not dissatisfied with it, but her ideas, even her vocabulary had been cramped by the simplicity of her life here. Now she felt her spirit expand. But when she returned with the tray, Alec began to speak of smallpox. She poured out two cups of tea, listening steadily, nodding her understanding when he looked up.

"And," he said, " Maura is the only woman there."

"Could I help ? " she asked.

"That's why I've come," he said. "I'd be very glad of your help. I'd ask you to take night duty."

"Yes," she agreed.

"It may be ugly in bits," he warned. "No eau-de-Cologne and cool-hand-on-the-fevered-brow stuff." He smiled.

Miss Bradshaw looked down at her small, blunt hands and took a deep breath, thinking of all he had said. Bedsores, suppuration, delirium.

"I'm not squeamish," she said firmly, giving herself at the same time a mental clip on the ear. "Could I come back here through the day ? "

"Yes, you would really have to, unless you would like a tiny room right upstairs in the tower. But it would be quieter for you to come home. Can you come, then, about eight o'clock to-night ? "

He stood up as she agreed. "And," he added, "go to bed this afternoon and have a sleep if you can."

She went with him to the gate and the wind whirled her black hair.

"I'll tell you," he said, "a thing I can never get straight in my mind."

"What's that ? " she asked.

"Did they bring the good news to Aix from Ghent or from Aix to Ghent ? "

She laughed and told him.

When he had gone she picked up the hoe and looked regretfully at the bruised purple petals where it had fallen. She was a clumsy creature. She would never make a good nurse. But there's no point in being defeated before you start. She might turn out to be a shameful bungler, but . . .

"Breast forward," said Miss Bradshaw, uprooting a rosette

of Nancy Pretty and tramping it back into the soil with the toe of her shoe.

It felt good to be alive.

## Chapter Twenty-Two

DANNY WAS offended by Alec's flippant rejection of his warning. It was the last advice he would give him, anyway.

He lurched back towards the castle, looking at everything under his brows, angrily. They were all ignorant; those hens, all running in the same direction because one hen had found a beetle; did they think they would all find a beetle under the same small stone? Mrs. Alyth slapping a rug against the side of the house, as if that was an important thing to be doing. The doctor, waving his hat, a silly-like smirk on his face as he looked up at that Lydia Transom . . . you'd think there was no reason to any of them.

Likely if he went back to the castle he'd get some job or other to do. He had a job to do already that was as important as anything they'd find for him in the castle. (He rummaged in his brain for some job that could keep him occupied with a good conscience.) Yes, the snares he was always going to set for the rabbits. That's what he would do.

He struck inland past the castle. Under his feet silver buds of thrift gave way to fine grass that soon was decorated with curls of pale young bracken. Here he began to set his snares of twig and wire, talking to himself, to the snares, to the rabbits.

Stick in there, will you. Och it's pure rock under here, I'll try further on. There. See can you catch a rabbit for the minister. Come on, rabbits, any of yous that want a look at the minister's insides, walk this way.

In spite of the wind there was a mist on the ben; but he climbed upwards, his hands in his pockets and his shabby black gutties soundless on the brown heather. Peewits screamed round him, swooping and rocking in the air, but never a nest to be seen.

It was a queer feeling, too, the mist shouldering round you in swirls and birds calling that you couldn't see half the time, as if it might be the mist itself screaming to mock you. He kept on, hoping for a clutch of plovers' eggs. It was eerie! Better set his mind on something while he searched.

That Lydia Transom, for instance, with her shameless man's clothes. You couldn't tell what went on in that one's head, her face was like a stone mask on a wall. There was a picture in one of Sir Hector's books, a wee temple reflected in green water, and two faces growing out of the stone. One was a devil, Pan they called him, with a flat nose and horns. The other was a woman. Both of them had empty holes instead of eyes, but that didn't mean they were blind; they could be watching you all the time and you wouldn't know what way they were looking.

Danny stopped, shaking off the comfortless thoughts that were no better than the mist. Where was he? He might be near the lochan, he might get a trout if he guddled for it, but he'd have to be careful of the sloping sides in this mist. He hurried on again.

The thought of the lochan dhu excited him. It was dangerous for two reasons: one, that if you fell in you wouldn't touch bottom, you'd sink in an unending depth of blackness; the other, that a creature lived there that it was wiser not to see, for as long as you didn't see it you could disbelieve and not need to be afraid. A kelpie or monster or some such nonsense. But the lochan bred fine plump trout with pink flesh, a good meal hot or cold.

He hesitated, wondering if it was wise to risk the eerie water in this mist, but it was impossible to stand still with the air seeming to listen to his thoughts; and to turn back would be to admit fear, a dangerous step in itself. He went on climbing.

Now he must be scrambling up the last edge of the hollow cone, the extinct volcano that held the loch in its crater. Now he stood on its jagged edge. He wished for a clearer vision, for he could hardly tell how the ground beneath him was shaped. He might be at a good bit, or he might find himself slipping on a sheer drop that offered no foothold and would plunge him down into the cold, endless depths. Even if you stepped on to scree it was possible to find yourself glissading downwards with nothing to catch a grip on.

The crater held the mist as if in a cup. Danny drew a breath and began the descent.

He was all right. The ground sloped gently enough, and though a hare bounded up at his feet and gave him a start there was something good in seeing a natural living creature. He had a clear glimpse of its pop-eyes, its ears laid back, its legs outstretched for speed in the instant of its vanishing. He gave a breathless chuckle and went on down.

He must be near the water now, surely. It was a creepy thing, not seeing the water that lay down there in its round hole. He paused by a boulder with a hollow feeling inside his back, straining his eyes to pierce the whiteness, and went on again. Suddenly the water was there at his feet. It gave him almost as much of a start as the hare had done, lying there as still as a cat. This wasn't a good bit after all for guddling; he could just see a few pebbles at the edge, then the water darkened. The ground must slope away pretty sharply. He began to work round to the right, to where the slip of shore ought to be.

Lovely the colour was too, clear for a few inches then brown that turned to purple before the mist ate it up. But the edge was always like crystal, far more clear than the air. Not that the air was clear at all! It was thick, like, Danny pondered, like as if it was hoarse. You'd say the air was sick and any minute it might burst out into a great coughing.

He stopped those thoughts too, and walked on more easily now, for the shore was beginning, just a strip of narrow earth and shingle; a bit treacherous till you came to the big rock that jutted out with a good ledge on its other side and a narrow one on this. It was a place where you sometimes got a sleek trout lying, just under the overhang of the rock. Not maybe a very safe place, either, but Danny felt committed to it.

Usually you could hear plenty of sound here. On a sunny day or a still evening there was the cropping of sheep and larks singing and a whirring of grasshoppers. Often, too, there would be mallard and widgeon and sometimes geese. Nearly always there was some sound if it was nothing but the plup! of a fish. But to-day the silence was like a holding of breath, and Danny was careful not to break it with his footsteps. He was not altogether enjoying this; he would just see was there a trout to be seen, and if not he would make for back home.

He stepped into the water soundlessly, without taking off his gutties that were soaked already. His hand was on the rock, his fingers clinging to the cold stone like suckers as he waded slowly in. Yes, there was a big fellow there. He saw the long elegance, the dark back and gold belly; he saw even the coral specks, the quiver of fins, the round, watchful eyes.

"He's too far in," said Danny. "He's sulking. Besides——"

Besides, the silence was beginning to curdle and clot like the air. Sometimes you almost heard a sound that wasn't quite a rustle or a pant . . . Part of him tugged away from the place, but his body was alert and focused on the fish. All the front of his body, at least ; creeping forward, sliding a hand into the water with imperceptible slowness ; while his back shrank from what might be behind him till he seemed to have eyes and ears all over every inch of his skin.

The trout had a small, clever head, brownish-black ; and a long smooth back, a glint of gold on its gills, a lazy watchfulness that was ready to dart out of sight in a split second. Over two pounds it looked, a nice troutie.

Danny was crouching now, his fingers moving nearer the fish. He had forgotten the uncanniness of the place, he was all focused on a circle of olive-brown water, his eyes intent and his mouth parted and smiling but with the lower lip held by his teeth. Come on, trout, he was saying inside himself, come on, trout . . . There was nothing else in creation but himself and the trout. . . .

Then as if it had materialised from nowhere, a white feather drifted down to the water. It was as small as a flake of snow, but the trout, which had been merely intrigued by the slow tactics of the boy, felt unequal to watching two simultaneous moving things ; it was out of sight like the blink of an eye.

Danny straightened with a snort of disappointment, and began to splash to the shore ; but there was more sound now than his own movements.

He stopped, listening and staring. Something rose above him, something that reared up on the top of the rock—but even as his hair prickled he laughed ; it was Lilias MacPherson and she was as scared as he was !

"It's only me, Lilias," he said.

She was panting. There was a silly, glazed look in her eyes.

"Are ye all alone ? " he asked.

"I am," she said in a wee voice, straightening her clothes as if he was company. "I came up to the lochan for a breath of air."

"I came up to see was there a trout."

Mrs. MacPherson moistened her lips. "You shouldn't, Danny," she said. "It's a very dangerous place, this, you shouldn't come here."

" The same to you," said Danny, " and many of them."

They stared at each other.

" Will I walk home with you to Skua ? " he suggested, seeing that she was afraid.

" No, no, Danny, go you home to your mother, quick. She'll be worrying about you."

" I suppose your husband won't be worrying about you ? " he retorted.

" I told you I was alone," she flashed angrily.

" All the worse for you if you fall in."

" Go on back, Danny, there's a good lad," she pleaded with her voice returning to its softness.

He couldn't make her out. There was no understanding women at all, or men either for that matter ; the doctor must be daft not to see the sort that Miss Transom was. His resentment had melted now into sad disapproval ; he had walked it off and the thought of home and tea was suddenly delightful.

" Right," he said, " I'll be for off. So long, Lilias."

He slopped out of the water and bounded up the side, his feet scraping on the small scree, for the risk was less going up ; the pebbles dislodged by his feet went tittuping down to land with a liquid click in the water, and the crater's cup repeated every sound. He did not mind that, though it would have been eerie before he knew Lilias was there. But he wished now that he had chosen a better way up. He paused, and heard other pebbles rattling down a little way off, as if some creature was making an ascent parallel to his. He froze to alertness again, and now he heard a scraping and gasping cry that ended in a scream—every sound followed by its own mocking shadow, even the splash that shut off the cry. She must be in.

He hardly knew how he got down to the edge, so fast he pelted down. Suddenly he was near her, so suddenly that his rush brought him right against her. She had not fallen in. She was staring at moving great rings in the purple water.

" Oh, Danny," she said in a sick voice, " oh, Danny." They clung together.

" What did ye see ? " he whispered, trembling and staring at the circles in the water ; something white and dark was coming up among the circles, and for the life of him he could not tear his eyes from the apparition. This was it, coming. . . .

But it was a man whose face broke briefly through the surface.

" Lilias ! " Danny said, ashamed that his voice was still weak with the fear that had shrunk him, " Lilias, listen ! I'm going to see can we get him. Hold my hand—no, I'll take off my jacket, hold the sleeve——"

They each held a sleeve, Lilias standing at the brink and Danny wading in till a plunge took him waist-deep ; a nasty feeling as he realised that an invisible precipice lay under-water at his very feet.

Now Terence came to the surface again, slowly drifting up with arms and legs trying to struggle but seeming to move with the dreamy lethargy of a starfish's rays.

" Catch hold, Terence," Danny was shouting while Terence's face was still under water. " Up ye come, come on, I'll throw the sleeve——"

Terence plunged towards the outheld sleeve but missed and slipped under the surface again, but desperation gave his slow struggles fresh impetus and he came up again, his face staring as if he would suck the shore towards him as he gulped in air. When he did catch the sleeve of the jacket his pull on it drew Danny in too, but Lilias held firm and they both reached the ledge of shore.

Danny trudged back at Terence's side, half-understanding and half-mystified. They had left Lilias to find her own way back to Skua, and Terence's desire seemed all to be centred on a half-bottle of whisky he had in his own house.

" And I'll get a fire lit and get warmth into myself," he said. He was blue and shivering right enough, and seemed less than himself, small and deprived of vigour.

Danny was cold too, and he was inquisitive ; but there was a small, savage triumph in his heart, unexplained but good to feel.

" But what were you needing to meet her up there for ? " he persisted.

Terence went on in silence ; it seemed that he would give no answer to that. But later on, when they were both in the Patricks' cottage wearing an assortment of dry clothes of Terence's and thawing with the warmth of whisky, he began to speak.

" Danny," he said, " I believe you saved my life. Thanks for that. Hold your tongue now about what you've done, and about me and Lilias being together."

Danny stared at him, feeling that a more generous show of

gratitude would be seemly. That horror when his feet took a slip down, and again when Terence's weight on the jacket had pulled him under—those were experiences that he would carry not just in his mind but in the very cells of his body. And now—hold his tongue? No fear, when words alone could translate the horror into glory!

"I'll not mention Lilias," he said, seeing what Terence feared and despising him.

Terence was still chafing his hands and holding them out to the mean flames.

"Danny," he said, "if ye can't keep from speaking about it, swear you'll do that: keep Lilias out of it. I'll murder you if you split."

"You're a nice one to be talking," Danny burst out angrily, "you with your wife ill and—and all——" It did not seem right to remind the soul that his daughter was likely dying and his wee son ill as well as his wife while he was capering with Lilias Mac-Pherson, but the words were in the air between them and Terence answered them.

"I know fine what you mean," he said. "And it's hard on Nell right enough." He looked into Danny's face.

"And Lilias a Protestant," Danny reproached.

"Be thankful if you pass your life without falling in love with a Protestant the way I did. But if ye do, Danny, don't be put off—marry her!"

Danny, like everybody else on Fionn, knew the story of Terence Patrick and Lilias.

"But—she wouldn't change her religion," he protested. "If she hadn't been so obstinate—if she had even agreed to let the children be brought up Catholics—they're awful stubborn, the Protestants. You might have lost your faith, married to that one."

The laugh that Terence answered him with was a queer sound. Danny left soon after that.

As he went into the castle kitchen he heard a familiar banging and went to see what the old captain was wanting.

"What's the noise?" he demanded as he opened the door.

Captain Kilbride, flushed and furious, glared at him from the bed. He was sitting upright against the iron back of the bed, having thrown his pillows at the door; his face and the triangle of chest that showed through his buttonless nightshirt were red and scabby.

"You saucy impudence!" he shouted. "There's no discipline in this place! Here's me been shouting this past hour; where were you at all?"

"What is it you want?"

"Shut that window."

"Put down that stick, then."

"Shut the window!" Kilbride almost screamed.

"It's the doctor's orders to keep it open. Against the stink," Danny explained. "I couldn't go against orders."

"The orders you'll obey are my orders," said the captain terribly, spoiling the effect by scratching his chest.

"And you're not to scratch," said Danny. But fearing that the old man might explode he good-temperedly shut the window.

Captain Kilbride was appeased and allowed Danny to replace the pillows. "Look, now, Danny Rafferty," he said quietly, "I want my gas-mask box out of yon drawer. It's got my tobacco in it and a poke of pan drops, and you're a good, sensible lad, whatever. That's it. There's a pan drop for yourself to suck. And always remember, it's MY orders you obey. MY orders!"

"Is it so," said Danny indifferently, putting the sweet in his mouth and going to look for his mother.

"Is there a scrap of food to be had in the place, Mam?" he asked. "I could eat the devil himself!"

"Mercy, where have you been and whose clothes is that?" Maura demanded, reaching for the frying pan.

"I'll tell you when I'm fed," said Danny.

But even while Maura was getting a meal on the table for him he found the story tumbling out. There was an abrupt halt in it while he remembered, with annoyance, that he had to keep Lilias MacPherson out of it. It was a pity that; it held up the flow; and besides Lilias had been frightened and it was he, not Terence, who had reassured her. But he skipped Lilias and went on to the escape of the trout and his own start up the bank; then the sound of falling scree—the cry—and the muffled splash of a body swallowed by the hungry wee lochan.

Maura was staring, frozen.

"Ye didn't go in after him?" she demanded.

"I threw him the arm of my jacket and I held on to the other arm myself."

" How were ye wet, then ? "

" I got pulled in when he caught it—— Mam, I'm hungry and you aren't making that toast——"

Maura threw down the toasting fork and the scone on its end and went right up to him, staring into his face.

" Do you tell me," she said, " that you near drowned yourself saving that shameless bad good-for-nothing that has nothing better to do when his wife and bairns are ill than chase Lilias MacPherson ? A nice thing if you'd got drawn under, a nice thing for me——! Don't dare interrupt when I'm talking to you, you wicked impudence, you ! As if I hadn't enough to do here without you going——"

" Mam ! "

" Trying to kill——"

" But I'm here, Mammy, what you getting in a foam about ? "

" Serve you right if I kept you in like the minister's mother does with hers ! "

" Will you give over crying, Mam, when I tell you I'm here. I wasn't drowned at all—— And I never said he was chasing Lilias MacPherson, either . . ."

It was most disappointing, this reception of his story. He ate his half-toasted scone in bitterness of spirit.

## Chapter Twenty-Three

When Miss Bradshaw marched into the castle she found the whole team ready to welcome her. Some of her apprehension was dissipated at once ; she felt the support of communal responsibility.

Her manner in response to their greetings was at first pugnacious, but this symptom of uncertainty vanished, too, as they explained their scheme of duties. They seemed to her different people from what she had thought them. Mr. Forsyth, the minister, she had always found tiresomely pompous and stilted ; he was quite simple after all. Dochy MacArdal gave her a friendly greeting. Maura too had changed, and Miss Bradshaw, normally unperceptive, saw her humility, a natural, unselfconscious humilty that was without abjectness, as if it were bathed in the supernatural clarity of her favourite Vermeer reproduction.

"It's a good thing you're here, Miss Bradshaw," said Maura. "Danny's getting fair beyond me. He's that obstrepulous!"

"I'm not obstrepulous, Mam," said Danny, frowning down at his shoes and fidgeting.

"And contradictious."

"I'm not contradictious!" Anger flashed from his eyes.

"He's growing up, that's what it is," said Miss Bradshaw in her sensible voice. "Have you any idea yet what you want to be, Danny?"

"Well, I—I've been thinking it over——" Danny stopped.

"You have? We'll have a talk about it sometime. I hope it's something that'll use your talents this time."

Danny looked at her and nodded, then suddenly had gone.

"I set a tray for you for through the night," said Maura, "and I've made up the kitchen fire. They're all in at Father Kelly: will I take the chance to show you where the things are and give you a few tips?"

Miss Bradshaw felt apprehensive again as Maura showed her the back-tray with its basin and spirit and soap, the bed-pan, the lysol, the permanganate of potash and all the details she must remember during the night while she was caring for sick bodies; and she had not seen them yet. Then Alec came out of Father Kelly's room and suggested that she should go round all the patients with him.

"We'll go into Torquil MacVean first," he said. "You are not likely to have anything to do with him, but you'll see a patient who is putting up a good fight against smallpox and obviously coming out on top. You've seen Kirpu already; he has hardly had time for convalescence, but he's better of the disease. Well, Torquil, I've brought Miss Bradshaw to see you."

"Good-evening," said Torquil politely.

"I'm glad to hear you're getting better," said Miss Bradshaw.

"Thanks to the doctor and the rest."

"He's a model patient," said Alec. "He doesn't fret. You can see the crusts getting dry and scaly; they'll soon drop off now. We'll look in at Mrs. Patrick and Paddy now. Well, Mrs. Patrick, here is Miss Bradshaw who will look after you through the night."

Nell turned her flushed and spotted face towards Miss Bradshaw and moved her lips into a smile. She did not speak; her eyes seemed darker than usual and her silence gave her a dignity she had never had before. Miss Bradshaw had always thought of her as a trivial little creature, but she saw her now as a woman who had travelled through countries unknown to the schoolmistress, marriage, motherhood and terrible illness. She was tongue-tied before Nell.

Wee Pad was asleep. They glanced at him and went on to Mrs. Kilbride.

Mrs. Kilbride was half-uncovered. She stared at them suspiciously.

" Stay in bed," said Alec, replacing the leg that was groping for the floor. Miss Bradshaw helped him to smooth up the covers.

" Disgrace," muttered Mrs. Kilbride, eyeing him with disfavour. " Goings-on . . . time of the night . . . Respectable woman. . . ." Her mutterings rose and fell and then dwindled to silence.

" You'll have to keep an eye on her," Alec murmured. " Now the captain."

He lay next door to his wife, peering up brightly from a ravaged face. Against the blotches and eruptions of his skin his eyebrows and the small dab of beard immediately beneath his underlip looked exquisitely white.

" I'm very well, thank you," he replied to Miss Bradshaw's inquiry. " And how are you ? "

His eyes had never twinkled more devilishly. He found it all, even the misery of illness, another example of the twisted humour of the universe.

" Now, Father Kelly ; just in case you should be asked to help with him in the night. We won't speak, better not to disturb him."

As they opened the door the room flashed like a vision across her sight ; the bed in the centre, humped with the shape of the body in it ; the chair beside it in which the minister sat, his hair gilded by the lamp behind him, his eyes turned down to the book on his knee ; the wooden drawer standing on a stool under the window, with Nell's baby in it.

Miss Bradshaw quailed at the sight of the priest. His face was a mass of blackish suppuration, swollen and unrecognisable. The stubble of his growing beard was messy with pus. His eyelids were too swollen to open, his mouth and tongue too swollen to shut.

Alec motioned to John Forsyth not to get up. They stood for a few seconds, looking, then went out.

Miss Bradshaw had never seen or imagined anything like this. She washed her hands obediently, adding a few drops of lysol to the water as the doctor told her.

"A bit of a shock, I expect, plunging straight into it like this. The others have had time to adjust; they've seen it develop."

She kept her eyes on her hands as she washed them. She had never imagined anything like—like what Father Kelly had turned into. She drew a deep breath, struggling to keep her balance.

As she turned to dry her hands she glimpsed the doctor's face and had another shock. He, too, was defenceless and ravaged by the thought of suffering; and how much more terrible that was for him, who had chosen medicine as his profession. How many times in his life must he have shrunk from the burden of other people's pain!

Maura was busy with a kettle, filling hot-water bottles, and Kirpu was bearing them off to their destinations upstairs. Miss Bradshaw found comfort in Maura's calmness; there was no raw surface to her sensibilities, she was whole.

"He's useful, the poor creature," said Maura, catching her eye. "He's a terrible one for thinking things out, though." She wiped the last bottle and shook her head. "Thinks it was himself that brought all this smallpox on us and goes off in a gloom about it. I said to him, well, what about the one that gave it to you, whoever he was? Might as well blame him for bringing us the plague, whoever it was, I said."

"Yes, that's true," said Miss Bradshaw, listening more to Maura's quiet voice than to her words.

"He took no comfort from it, then. Got into a fair take-on——" She broke off as Kirpu came back and received the last hot jar from her. "And it's your own," she told him. "Get you away to your bed this minute and have a sleep to yourself."

Kirpu was going away without a word when he recollected himself, turned to the two women with his gracious little bow and then went off.

"It's my belief there's something on his mind, the soul," said Maura. "Here, Danny!" she called.

Danny appeared from the scullery with a large brogue in one hand and a brush in the other.

"What was yon you said to me, yon time?" Maura asked.

"What time?"

"About—the Hindoo," Maura dropped her voice discreetly. "About all those gods."

"Oh, my, they're a terrible lot right enough." Danny came closer to them and spoke confidentially. "There's no end to their on-goings, what with their elephant heads and six or eight arms and dear knows what."

"That destroyer, what was that."

She had asked for it. Danny put down his shoe, concealing his glee.

"Kali," he said, "she's the bad one. Her fellows go round on their bare feet." He dropped his voice to a whisper. "You wouldn't know they were creeping up . . . with their wee cord . . . like this——"

"That's enough, now."

"I'm only telling you," whispered Danny, opening his eyes till a ring of white showed horribly all round the iris, and circling round his mother who kept rotating to face him. "I'm only just showing you the way they'd——"

"Stop that, I said. You're nothing but a bad, ungrateful boy, trying to frighten folks. Will you give over making dabs at me, will you !"

Danny straightened with an expression of deep offence.

"You asked me," he said, martyred and disdainful.

"I asked you a question, I didn't tell you to go in for a fair pantomime of wickedness ! "

Miss Bradshaw laughed.

"What am I going to do for Shylock or Othello when you leave school, Danny ? " she said. "Wouldn't you like to be an actor, go on the real stage ? "

"I might like it fine," said Danny, "but I've a different notion I thought of trying first."

"And what is it ? "

"Doctoring."

"Mercy," said Maura patiently.

"That means going on to the secondary school." Miss Bradshaw was full of zest for that.

"But he's too late now," Maura protested.

"No, he isn't—I've kept him at it steadily; he'll be fit to step into the third year with the rest of his age group. The only thing he'll have to make up on is Science."

" Och, that's nothing," said Danny, " I'll soon learn that."

" Optimist ! " said Miss Bradshaw.

Danny swung round on her suddenly.

" Why d'you say that ? " he demanded suspiciously. " It can't be any worse than Bridge ! "

Alone in his room Alec remembered Miss Bradshaw's face as she left Father Kelly. He had recognised in her expression a reflection of his own past horror of the pain he had to witness. Was it even past, with him ? He had never come to terms with it, had only learned to crush his awareness of it.

He felt that, here on Fionn, he was groping towards some realisation that might bring him to wholeness of mind ; the same wholeness that belonged to Maura. Maura, whose calm was only ruffled by trivialities, by some nonsense of Danny's that merely rippled the surface of her quietness, was able to bless them all by simply being there.

As for Lydia, she was the bar across his path. So beautiful that she captured imagination, but apart from her physical charm, dwarfed or deformed—as dwarfed in her spirit as the idiot Candy Andy was in his mind.

He tore his thoughts away from them both, but it was useless. His brain began its old dervish-dance, repeating past phrases over and over. He groaned. There was so much pain and deformity ; what was the good of the universe !

# Chapter Twenty-Four

JOHN FORSYTH was thinking along the same lines, but with him the question was not an acknowledgment of defeat, it was the base from which he explored the surrounding darkness.

He had travelled far since his snub to the priest. Losing the enthroned idol with the censorious face and hysterically kicking feet he had not lost his belief that God must exist; he had only discovered his own idolatry. Since then he had been fumbling for the truth, terrified of what he might find yet pushing himself on. It was the only thing that mattered; the discovery of truth.

At first he had tried using his powers of reason, the argumentative interior dialogue that is a native habit with Scots. But that method failed. It was not reason, but some other faculty, that would find the truth he sought. Scarcely knowing whether he possessed it or not he sent the faculty that only functioned when reason failed, groping through the dark. It was an exhausting and desolate exercise. He could not keep it up for long, yet even while he worked or ate or talked, or merely sat, as now, silent beside the dying priest, his being was facing towards the darkness, the vast eternity of darkness from whence the answer might never be revealed.

The book on his knees was the Bible. It had never seemed so enigmatic, so full of contradictions.

Father Kelly moved his head. John poured spoonfuls of water over the swollen tongue; after a minute they were gulped down. Now his hand was moving. John put the black rosary into it. The hand held it and then dropped it, and was held up again, palm downwards, a few inches above the coverlet.

John pressed the rosary again into the palm. The hot, thick fingers fumbled at his and again dropped the rosary.

"What is it you want, Father?" John asked. "Can you try to speak?"

A croak was all that emerged from the priest's mouth.

"Are you wondering about your mice? Danny was along to feed them. They're fine."

What could he want? He was unsatisfied still. John felt himself inadequate before the man he had hated and who was now rotting visibly towards the grave, stinking with corruption and still alive amidst his own decay. He suggested some possible wants of the body, but Father Kelly's head gave a faint shake to each.

"I don't know what you want," he said despairingly, slipping his own hand into the hovering palm.

The fingers closed on his. That was what Father Kelly had sought, a human hand to touch.

"Father," said John presently, "I've been sorry every day of my life for the way I spoke. On the pier and here, too. I'm ignorant and conceited."

Perhaps the old man was asleep; he had had a period of restless delirium, but now he seemed, most of the time, asleep or unconscious. It was a minute at least after he had spoken that John felt a pressure on the hand he held.

He looked down at his own red, healthy fingers clasping the cracked and suppurating hand. A trickle of dark pus ran under the ball of the thumb.

He tried to draw his chair nearer so that he could lean his elbow on the bed, for he was cramped.

Father Kelly made several attempts to speak, but knew that no faintest sign of his efforts was visible to the young minister. His mind was clear, but there was no saying how long the clarity would last. He knew that he was outside the current of time, that while centuries passed over him the watchers counted only minutes, that while he relived old passages in his life or encountered new confusions and struggled on new journeys they saw his inert body lying in the bed and said, he is delirious, he is unconscious or asleep. At times he did sleep, and the sleep might have lasted ten minutes or ten years, he could not tell.

Here I am, he thought, dying at last. Dying at last and without sacraments to help me over. And Nell Patrick's baby going too, and old Mrs. Kilbride like enough and maybe the captain himself too, and me not able to do a thing about it. And after all it doesn't matter. It's all out of my hands, and what's inevitable must be right.

He could not open his eyes but there were ways of seeing

214

without opening your eyes. He could see the minister sitting there. He could see him from all sides at once, not from one side only as his eyes would see him; he could see him as a solid body, and that was funny. He could see the room differently too, a hollow cube, all the walls and the ceiling and the floor at once, with the bed and the chairs and the dressing-table, the baby in a drawer with its breaths getting shallower every minute, the lamp sending a thread of smoke up to the ceiling. He could see it all like that because for a few minutes he was loose; but that was never for long. Soon he would be off again on one of his journeys, or else he would be back inside again, back in bed, stuck inside that horrible rotting body where everything had gone wrong together, hopelessly wrong.

He pressed the hand he held and felt a pressure in return. That reassured him; he relaxed and waited for another welling-up of strength, for he wanted to speak.

John seemed to have sat for hours in the one cramped position, holding the priest's hand. Every now and then his left knee would have a spasm of trembling, and the discomfort along his left shoulder-blade and across his ribs was turning to pain. He endured it humbly; it was an offering to his insulted enemy. When Miss Bradshaw tapped softly and opened the door he turned his head without moving the rest of his body.

" It's two o'clock," she said. " I've made a cup of tea. Do you want a cup? "

He looked at Father Kelly and at their two hands clasped together. He could drink a cup without moving that hand.

" I would," he said.

Miss Bradshaw was looking down at the baby now, smoothing the little creature's lips with glycerine. Its breath became audible to him—had been audible all the time, but his attention had been so fixed on the priest and on his own thoughts that he had not heard it; it was like a tiny, rhythmic crackle as fast as a pulse.

" There's nothing you can do," he said gently. " The doctor says she's unconscious; she doesn't feel anything."

It was difficult to believe it all the same; he knew that the tightness in Miss Bradshaw's face was her effort to conceal her distress.

" If you could put a spoonful of water in Father Kelly's mouth," he suggested. " I can't very well move——"

Miss Bradshaw came over and poured a teaspoonful of water

215

over the cracked and swollen tongue, holding her breath against the sickly smell of pus. She glanced at the clasped hands on the coverlet, the priest's scaled with dark blisters and the minister's glued to it where blood and pus had trickled round his thumb and dried against it.

"Would you like me to waken Mr. Dochy?" she asked. "It's time he relieved you, isn't it?"

"Just let him sleep on," said John.

Miss Bradshaw went out to wash her hands and pour out the tea. She brought a cup to the minister and set it where he could reach it with his left hand, the hand that was free.

Father Kelly let the spoonful of water lap round his tongue and his teeth and palate before he swallowed it. Now was the time to speak, before the strength he had gathered slipped away again. It was not to vindicate himself but to remove the smear they had daubed on his church that he wanted to speak.

"John," he said, "I'm going to tell you . . . about pinching women's ankles. . . ."

The sounds ran together and emerged in a jumble. He heard the silence after them.

"Never heed," said the minister. "It's just bad gossip. Nobody believes it."

So he had understood the jumble.

"I want to tell you," said Father Kelly, "what really did happen."

He paused, arranging his words in his head so as to make the story as concise as possible. He had not much strength and he might soon slip back into a babble of dreams again. He must remember what had happened and tell it all in order.

It was Lent; he was an assistant priest at St. Aloysius, and he was visiting the sick.

St. Aloysius was the parish church of an ugly industrial city in the diocese of Glasgow, and Father Kelly's last visit had taken him far into the new housing scheme that had extinguished the last green hill in the district.

It was uncommonly hot for spring and his feet were stabbing, but he was hurrying, tottering back past raw new houses, past empty gardens where children and whippets played in the dust, hurrying to reach the bus stop before the works emptied and the buses were full.

There was a story he had read as a child about a little mermaid. Her punishment for becoming human was that every step she took sent stabs of pain through her feet.

Ah, her corns were no worse than mine, thought Father Kelly, reaching the bus stop at last. I'd change them for a fish's tail and the cool sea any day.

He must just have missed a bus. He sighed and leaned against the iron lamp standard, wishing that he had changed into his summer underwear; this wool was baking him alive. The big iron foundry was just across the street from him; you would think the heat came sizzling across its cindery yards, across the black tar-bubbles in the street to pound into his corns. Men worked there naked to the waist, sometimes with goggles to protect their eyes. Horrible work it was. All round the horizon were black cones of slag and tall chimneys puffing grit into the sky. The tar macadam in the street trickled down the camber towards the gutters.

You would think the buses would be better spaced than this! But this was always the way of it; two or three buses in a string, then none for about ten minutes. Somebody should be spoken to about it. Those inspectors should see to it that the services were better spaced than this.

Somewhere in the housing scheme behind him a baby was yelling drearily, a monotonous cry repeated incessantly.

If he had known there would be this long to wait he could have walked on two stops farther to the far stage. A good Lenten penance, and the halfpenny saved would have gone into the foreign mission box. But since he had waited so long he wouldn't risk having three buses fly past while he was hurrying between stops.

But five minutes later consternation filled him. This was not normal. This was worse than a breakdown of one bus. He stopped a passing youth with a question.

" That's right," said the youth, eyeing him with distaste. " Bus strike."

The pavements he had to traverse between here and the presbytery! This was penance with knobs on. If he had been an ordinary man he could have taken off his jacket and walked in his shirtsleeves. Of course, even under his shirtsleeves were the long woollen cuffs of his winter underwear. He ought to have changed it. But then you could never trust the weather in April, and at his age he had to be careful of chills.

By the time he had walked half a mile Father Kelly was in agony. The corn on the sole of his right foot was the worst. Every step he took sent a dagger of red-hot searing pain right up into his stomach. The little mermaid had nothing on Father Kelly ; and he had not gone a third of the way yet.

For a few seconds he stood on one foot like a stork, easing the anguish ; but somebody bumped into him and made him come down on the sore foot with a thump so that he cried out with the pain of it ; and didn't even turn round to apologise, the dirty Orangeman.

He limped on for another hundred yards, then temptation stood before him.

It was a small, cheap cinema. You could sit in the front stalls for ninepence. For a shilling you could get in at the back. Nobody would see him in the dark interior. He could rest his feet.

The struggle was dizzily short. It was unseemly for a priest to visit a cinema in Lent, but the pain in his feet would surely provide him with a dispensation. He did not even look to see what the film was. He paid his shilling and went in, and as soon as he was seated, stealthily and suppressing small gasps of pain, he eased off his shoes.

At first the pain seemed almost to increase. The wee toe on his left foot began now, great stounding stabs as if a devil from Hell was at it. Father Kelly curled his toes and screwed up his face with the pain of it. But by degrees the sledge-hammer blows eased off. He began to notice the picture. It was his favourite kind, a Western, and though he had come in in the middle it was easy to distinguish the hero by his flash of teeth gleaming like a neon light in a naughty world. Then the hero and his friends Jim and Dopey had another typical trait, they were musical and liable to sing at any moment. They rounded up cattle with three voices, two ukes and a Hawaiian guitar.

Other people came in. Father Kelly moved to let two girls sit together. Then he moved farther along to let wee Gladys sit beside her Auntie Nan. They were shooting it out now on the skyline. Would they be in time to save Clancy McKitterick, whose arms were bound, who sat on his horse with a noose round his neck and a gag concealing the flashing smile while the villain tied the other end of the noose to a branch above his head ? Yes, of course they would be in time. Lissa Henessy had leapt on the mayor's wagon and was galloping the four-in-hand to warn Jim and Dopey—the saloon was on fire—the treacherous stationmaster crumpled with a bullet in his stomach and . . .

Now the usual close-up. Lissa and Clancy kissing to an accompaniment of guitars and voices and a comical wink from Dopey.

The news was all bad, of course, except for Celtic winning their big match, and a roar from the crowd—in which Father Kelly joined—when the clever goalie frustrated what would have been an equaliser.

But after the news came the Big Picture, and Father Kelly disliked its tone. Sulky, sultry Helga Dorado was not his cup of tea at all. She had too little on, and knew it ; he would have liked to present her with his long-sleeved woollen underwear. And the things she said were vapid but the way she said them—they could mean anything ! He grew alarmed and angry. They shouldn't put things like that on a public screen for silly-like boys and girls to see. All this kissing and messing about, and the softy with the bow tie had a wife already. It was—here, this was just a bit thick, he couldn't sit and watch this, he was going to speak to the manager.

Cautiously, his feet groped for his shoes. Damn. They must have got pushed out of reach. He bent down and began to fumble about in the dark. He couldn't find them. He had to get right down on all fours, no easy matter. Now he was lost in a forest of feet. He thought he felt a shoe just then, but somehow . . .

" Oh, sorry," he muttered. Ah, here was one—no it wasn't, it was attached to a foot and he got his fingers stepped on.

" Sorry," he mumbled again, " lost my shoe. Sorry." Under the chair in front, perhaps. . . .

An attendant flashed her torch to see what the subdued disturbance was. Heads were beginning to turn, there were small gasps and rustles of annoyance, then a series of shrill screams.

The manager came hurrying down. Someone was sobbing hysterically, a man was shouting and Father Kelly was trying to smooth things down, but his hoarse voice only frightened the woman more than ever. It was when the manager heard the words " indecent assault " from the angry little man that he switched on the lights and sent for the police, hustling the three of them to his room so that darkness could return to the audience and they could give their attention once more to Helga Dorado, whose indecency had, after all, been passed by the censor.

Mercifully the woman, the victim of the supposed assault, took a violent dislike to her protector and deeply resented the manager's assumption that he was her husband; and when the busybody saw that his efforts to stir up trouble for a Roman priest were recoiling on his own head he began to accuse her of conniving at the assault; and the whole thing might have melted into nothing but for the arrival of a police constable with a note-book in which he insisted on entering the names and addresses of all concerned, so that, although the woman had refused to lodge a complaint, the gossip began to work in widening circles until at last the bishop heard it.

The bishop, an austere man, listened blankly to Father Kelly's explanations. He had only been in the cinema because his corns were hurting. Because there was a bus strike. And he had walked a long way, and had gone into the cinema to take the weight off his feet for a minute. He had lost his shoes, which he had taken off for a minute, and then he had moved farther along so that he was in one place and his shoes were left behind in another, and when he had started to look for them there was this woman who thought— but he was only looking for his shoes, so that he could escape from the scandalous film they were showing, and . . .

The bishop, all the same, had believed his story, which was more than one or two of his fellow clergy had done. But he could not, he said, leave him in the district where his name and reputation—and through him that of the Church—had been smirched. He sent him far away from temptation, away from pavements and bus strikes and cinemas. He sent him into exile on Fionn.

" But that was where the real shame of it came in," said Father Kelly, " and the sin that's on my soul. I've done nothing on Fionn, nothing to redeem my silliness. Nothing to help the poor souls that were in my charge. And there's no time left now. This is the last loup of the candle, John."

He had finished his recital. He waited for a word of comfort from the Protestant minister; not that the word of a man could comfort him now, but the friendship behind it was what he wanted. But there was nothing. Then it dawned on him that he had, after all, told nothing. All the long story had been in his mind; he had begun a sort of clotted mumble but had been too weak to continue.

He heard the door open. A voice said, " John, you should have wakened me. It's after three o'clock." That was Dochy.

Then John Forsyth said, " I wanted to wait with him to the end." And he did not move.

" Don't you think I should waken the doctor ? " Dochy suggested.

" Maybe you'd better."

Dochy went upstairs to waken Alec.

# Chapter Twenty-Five

ALEC PUT on his dressing-gown and came down at once. He could hear two voices, Miss Bradshaw's and Mrs. Kilbride's. The old lady was evidently giving trouble. He rubbed his hand across his eyes as they went into Father Kelly's room, trying to rub away the fog of sleep that made everything seem unreal.

John Forsyth still sat with the priest's hand clasped in his, and Alec's first impulse was to rebuke him ; their danger was already sufficiently great without increasing it by needlessly dabbling in smallpox pus ; then the meaning of the clasp of those two hands silenced him.

" Yes," he agreed, " he won't last till morning—or I don't expect he will ; but it won't happen just immediately. I'll go and see Mrs. Kilbride ; Miss Bradshaw seems to be having trouble with her."

" Anything I can do ? " Dochy asked.

" No, I don't think so."

Dochy went off to stoke up the kitchen fire. He had an idea that they would all need baths before daybreak.

Father Kelly listened to their lowered voices. It was odd, he seemed to be in two places at once. Part of him was there in the lamplit room where men talked with as few words as possible ; but most of him was here.

Yet even this scene had something strange about it. He was himself, but he could also see himself from outside, a small barefoot schoolboy among others, his trousers darned at the seat, his jersey showing bare skin beneath the holes. His hand was clasped in Shaun's, he could feel the handclasp, the flow of warmth between their two palms. They were paddling in the pond with the others when they ought all to be in school.

Wee Shaun, ankle deep in water, was squelching the black mud between his toes, staring to see it puff in clouds over his instep when he wriggled his toes. Shaun was an innocent wee fellow, simple almost. He hadn't much sense, the way he would shrink if you made a sudden bowf at him, the way he went on trusting you afresh.

While he watched Teddy and himself paddling in the mud, Con Kelly was taking everything in. The blue sky and small clouds, the willows, the two other boys poking at the bottom with a stick, releasing bubbles of silvery gas ; the moorhen under the willows at the far side, unreachable and safe because the water was deep there ; the huge worm, crimson shading to grey, making a solitary journey among the grass at the edge where the geese had cropped it short.

He watched the worm nosing its way between the close green blades. He wondered why the worm chose that side of the plantain instead of the other ; it had no eyes, it couldn't see, but it knew its own mind ; this side was better than that. Con became the worm in his imagination, pushing his swelling and contracting body through a stubble of grass, knowing the grass by its feel and the sun by its warmth, but blind, ignorant of greenness and of light. It was a cramping sort of a world, that ; Con emerged again and watched the worm from his own boy's viewpoint, fascinated. Then into the fascination crept the familiar itching touch of evil. He let go of Shaun's hand, picked up the worm and dropped it, cold and wriggling, down wee Shaun's shirt.

How they all laughed ! Dancing with delight, throwing themselves about in an intoxication of mirth. . . .

Because Shaun was still standing there, sick and paralysed among their laughter. That was the way he felt about a worm ; its touch was like the slimy touch of death. He couldn't move. He just stood there in the water with the worm against his skin, intolerably suffering.

It was Con Kelly himself who stopped it, still laughing to cover his compassion—but dry cackles now, mere camouflage in case the others should jeer at him for a softy. He pulled Shaun's shirt right off, roughly releasing the worm that was looped over his trousers, and led the shivering child to the bank.

Shaun was like a dummy, white and unalive. He submitted as Con pulled the shirt over his head again and tucked it into his trousers, talking vigorously. " There y'are, Shaun. Put your arm in. Other arm, go on. Steady ! That's the way, Shaun. Ha, ha, I fair frightened you, eh ? Eh, Shaun ? Tuck it in. That's the way. Are ye all right now, Shaun ? Are you ? Eh ? "

Father Kelly became both children at once now ; Shaun, ill with repulsion, Con, comforting his victim, his breast swelling with an agony of remorse that he dared not reveal lest he too should become a victim of cruel laughter.

How odd his attitude to Shaun McNeile had been, a mixture of reverence and contempt. He could not remember now when the McNeiles had left the village ; probably soon after the worm episode. He had no idea what had become of Shaun. All the same it was the emotions and the fumbling, half-finished thoughts that Shaun, a fore-doomed victim, had aroused, that dragged Con Kelly into the priesthood.

Con Kelly a priest ! It was the biggest joke of all. He was the laughing stock now all right, only they didn't laugh out loud. They were awkward with him, the boys who had been part of his childhood and adolescence. Once he had swaggered confidently, once long ago, in his ragged, barefoot days. It was all over now.

Another lightning change of scene returned him to the body on the bed. He could no longer feel his limbs as separate parts of him ; all his sensations were concentrated in his throat, his mouth. Every breath pained his throat, rustling the dry leaves that drifted round something filthy there, something long-decayed that prevented swallowing.

How the dry leaves and bracken rustled in the mouth of that old cave ! It was a frightsome place, knee-deep in old dusty leaves ; wee Shaun drew back, looking up at Con as he always did. Their hands were clasped tightly in each other's and Con drew him along into the dark cave.

Con was afraid and tired, terribly tired, with a weariness that dissolved his strength, but now it seemed that Shaun was driving him into the darkness, driving him in by the trust in his great, luminous eyes. He had to go on. But it wasn't the same cave now, not the cave that he had once explored with Shaun. There was terror in this cave, and something that stank. It was the sea that rustled back and fore across its mouth, not the wind in a forest of bracken, and the terror in the cave, the stench and the terror, came from a creature that still lived. . . .

He pushed into the darkness and stood beside the creature that was not yet dead. Now there was no torment in his compassion. He had passed through terror and stood on the other side, creative and free, while the cave in his throat rustled with dry rottenness. Once he had thought nothing of swallowing a great draught of cold water, gulp after gulp, feeling it pour over his tongue and touch his palate with exquisite cold, lap against his tonsils and over his throat. He would never swallow again, his tonsils were great dry boulders, his tongue a carpet of dust, the arch of his palate rustled with dry dead creatures whose wings rattled in the wind.

He raised the frightened creature in his arms and its head rested against his neck ; and together they left the cave and walked along the cool, beautiful edge of the sea.

They could not leave him. Dochy had made up the kitchen fire and had cleaned and relaid the fire in the parlour ; now he leaned against the wall in Father Kelly's room. Alec sat in a wooden chair, watching the gathering darkness in mouth and nostril, the lifting chin that tipped up with every breath. Dochy had tried pouring a spoonful of water into the black mouth, but there was no effort to swallow ; the tink of spoon against glass had broken the silence that rattled with the bellows of Father Kelly's breathing. What a hurried breathing it was ! Dry like the rattling of cinders in a riddle. Now he took a deeper breath, then the hurrying rattle went on again. The sound of it seemed to fill the universe.

John Forsyth cleared his throat and began to sing.

Alec watched the changing rhythm of the breathing. With a constitution like that he might go on Cheyne-Stokesing for long enough. He had a sense of lost opportunity. The old man had rather irritated him and he had never troubled to find out what he was really like, what his home and friends had been, what skeletons crouched in his cupboards. He had had his chance, his glimpse of a character that could spare pity for mice, the outcasts among beasts, but his reticence had kept him from exploring further. Reticence like his was a shameful negativism, a frost that blasted fellowship. Human beings could not grow in frigid isolation.

All the same it was a shock when John Forsyth began to sing. It seemed gross almost, that strong baritone scooping its way through a second-rate tune. Yet the second effect of the music was unbearably moving. Alec put his hand up to cover his eyes.

> " As pants the hart for cooling streams
> When heated in the chase. . . ."

The rapid rattling paused, then continued through the song. The pause had been involuntary ; no consciousness could remain in that body. He had an impulse to feel the last flickers of the pulse, but checked it, for John still held the scabby hand. He went over to look at Nell Patrick's baby.

He was still looking down into the makeshift cradle when silence fell, complete silence. They all stared at the body, unable at first to realise that the struggle was over. Their ears strained for another of those harsh breaths that had been such agony to listen to.

John Forsyth broke the silence again.

" I am the resurrection and the life, saith the Lord. He that believeth in me, though he were dead, yet shall he live."

Alec fitted his stethoscope into his ears, but it was a formality to listen to the silence in those collapsed lungs.

" Our first death," said Dochy.

" Our second," said Alec. " The baby has gone too." He coiled up his stethoscope.

" We ought to start," he said, " if we're to finish before daylight."


## Chapter Twenty-Six

MRS. FORSYTH had kept going from day to day, emptily. She had often in the past indulged in prophetic visions ; now they were being fulfilled : Fionn was smitten with plague, the vials of wrath were outpoured over her inhabitants. Yet something was wrong.

Although she did not admit it, it was boredom that was wrong with Mrs. Forsyth. John was away from her, she was forbidden, like everyone else, to make social calls. She knew that John passed the manse almost daily, for it was often he who came for the handcart of food from the Hotel, sometimes alone, sometimes with Mr. MacArdal or Danny; but from the first she had chosen to ignore this chance of waving or chatting to him. Now she regretted her huffiness but could not alter her behaviour, for that would have acknowledged that she was wrong. Her only outing was to buy necessities at the general store.

Not that she wanted social calls. John was everything to her and she to him. He paid his duty visits, and for the rest his mother was all in all to him. (She invariably forgot his periodic tuggings at the leash, blotting them out as the Lord blots out the transgressions of the faithful.) But this enforced separation was damming up a flood of resentment that would break over John's head as soon as he was allowed home.

Sleeplessness was always Mrs. Forsyth's particular cross, and it harassed her now. She used, when John was in the next room sleeping, to lie and sigh until the sighs turned to moans; and if that had no effect she would tiptoe through with a candle to look at her sleeping son. (He was a gross sleeper like his father.) Sooner or later her moaning would waken him, and then, with the utmost gentleness, he would lead her back to bed, go down and heat milk in a pan on the paraffin stove and bring it to her with a biscuit. She used to make him wrap her patchwork cover over his knees, for he always sat with her while she drank it, talking to her as if he wheedled a sleepless child. Then she would insist on his going back to his bed. Yes, he must go, she would be all right now; she was silly to let him know how she suffered during the night watches. . . . She would stroke his brow when he bent to kiss her and tuck her up. These intimate moments were more than dear to her, they were sacred.

But now she could moan her head off and it would affect nobody; therefore she did not moan. Instead, she put on a skirt and an apron and did a bit of cleaning. She had already cleaned and polished the manse from top to bottom, but no house stays clean without care. She took out the stair rods and began to improve on their gleaming perfection.

She wondered how they were all getting on at the castle. The only news she got was from the doctor, who called daily but whose visit had become dry in the extreme. She disliked the doctor. His politeness was a mere surface decoration; he had no real sympathy in him. After all he was an American, and Mrs. Forsyth had an idea what that meant : petting parties and bootleg liquor and sun-bathing and Hollywood. She brooded on the wickedness of America while she polished, fanning the flame of her indignation to keep at bay the chill that crept over her soul in the small hours. Now she fitted the rods back into their sockets and put her pan of milk on the primus to heat while she washed her hands and took off her apron. The candlelight was trying her eyes ; leaping about so that the shadows bounced and slithered round her. It was a dreich business to be up and about alone in the house at three in the morning. Mrs. Forsyth wept a little, quietly because there was no one to hear, then stopped without noticing that she did stop, and fitted a new candle into the socket where the old one was guttering to death. Now the only light came from the primus that cast a flower-shaped pattern on the ceiling. She found the matches and lit the clean new candle, pressing the winding sheet of the old one round its flanks. Her milk began to froth up, she poured it into the glass, chose a snap from the tin of biscuits and carefully, milk in one hand, candle in the other, mounted to her room.

She sighed as she sloughed her skirt and slippers and climbed into bed. She ought to feel appeased and comforted sipping her hot milk and crunching ginger biscuit, but a desolate sadness filled the room. Even as she raised the biscuit to her mouth her hand became nerveless and fell to the counterpane. What could John be doing that was more important than her need for comfort ! She was exhausted, exhausted in spirit, and her body was betrayed by the desolation that filled her.

What's wrong with me ? she wondered.

It was no new question, and this sadness was no new experience.

Of course she was saved, she was a good woman, one of the elect, she kept all the ten commandments and a good many more besides. Thou shalt not smoke, thou shalt not drink, thou shalt not play cards, thou shalt not indulge in any form of levity, thou shalt not bow down in the house of Rimmon which means thou shalt not visit cinema, theatre or art gallery. There was no end to the things she didn't do, and all to please her Lord. What was wrong, then ?

She was exhausted, that was all. And if she was too tired to drink her milk there was no need to be wasteful with the candle. Wearily, with limbs as limp as wet seaweed, she turned and nipped out the candle.

But still she lay awake, her head beginning to throb, the weakening desolation pressing on her heart. She knew, after all, that John wanted to escape from her; and she suspected that God, too, was slipping through her fingers. Her mind was as restless as the waves and the wind. Grievances against her dead husband rose in her mind, grievances against John and against her parents. They were all selfish. She had had a hard life and had always done her duty by them all.

"You know that," she whispered almost accusingly.

But Jehovah had ceased helping her. She could not even visualise Him clearly, seated among the seraphim with lightning flashing from the throne. She saw instead a large blue eye in a pink cloud, an eye as inhuman as an optician's sign, with an inscription round it, Thou God Seest Me.

"Oh, dear," she moaned.

There was no one to hear.

"There's nobody to hear," she wailed.

She had said it aloud, and her voice gave the thought a supernatural significance. She sat upright in bed clutching her throat. What if it were true, what if nothing but empty sky floated above her with no benign and terrible Being seated above the cherubim. What if the God she had placated all her life through in order to receive preferential treatment at His hands was nothing but a story to scare children . . .

But that would be too unfair. That would mean that there was no justice at all, neither in this world nor the next. . . .

Perhaps there isn't, said an ugly voice.

Now she was in real fear. Her eyes stared into the darkness, she grimaced in terror of this vision of emptiness where she had visualised—what? A powerful old gentleman, bearded and wearing a toga with a gold border, clutching a handful of lightning.

But God is—God is Love, she told herself hurriedly. "Jesus loves me, this I know, for the Bible tells me so." She used to sing that to John when he was a tiny boy; the memory calmed her beating heart but increased the intolerable weight of sadness that lay upon her, for she looked back over years of aridity to John's childhood and saw him struggling against her love, struggling to escape, still a prisoner in his body but fleeing in his thoughts, fleeing successfully, for there were blank doors in his mind beyond which she could not pry. And it was, after all, John who really

228

mattered to her; she could support the loss of everything on earth so long as she still had John.

Loneliness had given Mrs. Forsyth time to think, and even the most formless thinking must be either creative or destructive. A cold wind was blowing through the cosy cosmogony that had enclosed her for so long. She was alone, alone not merely in the dark manse but in the enormous reaches of interstellar space, alone and without foothold.

" Oh, John," she moaned, " come and give me back the faith I taught you ! "

John was not there; he was in the castle nursing the sick, who needed him far less than his own mother. She tried to whip up resentment against him but resentment would not come, only a conviction of her own microscopic smallness and unimportance, a certainty that she had lost him, not only while this plague lasted, but forever.

She lay down again. A tawny dawn was creeping round the edge of the curtains. She watched it for a little, wondering at its unsteadiness, then she got out of bed and drew back the curtains.

Her first fear was that the castle was on fire. She threw up the window and leaned out to see better. Surely it was the castle !

There were footsteps running down the road now, a boy—no, a woman in trousers was coming along the road with a coat flying from her shoulders.

" Is it the castle ? " Mrs. Forsyth called.

" No," Miss Transom answered, " it's something blazing on the point. I'm going to see what it is." She hurried on.

Mrs. Forsyth lit her candle again and this time got dressed in earnest. It was all like a dream, flat and unreal; there was a dimension missing in her life. The sky had fallen but she went on living.

When she had done her hair and screwed up the combings she laid a cashmere shawl round her shoulders and sat at the window. The fire flamed up again; you could see now the velvet shape of the castle on its tongue of rock, and the greenish gleam of foam edging the blackness of the waves, sometimes with a reflection of rosy fire as it frothed over the rocks. The sky was leaden but stained with rust, and as she watched the horizon grew pallid. Now you could see the smoke, black eddies of it whipped into tatters by the wind.

If this had happened a fortnight ago how uplifted she would

have been ! She would have seen it as a symbol of damnation for the wicked, and all the gorgeous Biblical language of denunciation and destruction would have blossomed in her breast like those flames. But now she watched with aloof apathy. Her Lord, mighty in battle, had fallen like a gaudy cardboard figure. He could not survive the corrosive action of solitude.

Suddenly she remembered the girl who had passed on her way to the castle ; she might be back soon with news, and nobody up at the Hotel. Mrs. Forsyth hurried downstairs and began the work of the day.

Daylight was seeping into the sky when Lydia Transom knocked at the manse door. Mrs. Forsyth opened it at once.

" What's wrong, lassie ? " she exclaimed, shocked into familiarity. " Come into the kitchen and sit down. You're shaking—come close to the fire ; let me give your hands a rub, poor soul—what is it you saw ? "

Lydia did not speak at once. She saw with gratitude that the minister's mother was making tea and putting eggs into a pan to boil. She swallowed, recovering self-control.

" I thought I was hard-boiled," she said, " but that was too horrible." She laughed and checked herself sharply. " It was like a Bosco painting, the castle and the sea and the huge bonfire, and the men throwing on more fuel ; the Indian was there, too, and——"

" But what were they burning ? " asked Mrs. Forsyth.

" Bodies," said Lydia.


When Lydia had gone Mrs. Forsyth sat for a while longer before the fire, musing. Miss Transom had given a vivid description of the scene on the castle rock, and then, as they ate their breakfast, had answered Mrs. Forsyth's questions about the Hotel and its running.

There had been a coolness between Mrs. Forsyth and Mrs. MacLennan. She had seen it as John's duty to wrestle with Mrs. MacLennan on the subject of selling alcohol to the islanders ; and suspecting that John's wrestling had lacked the zeal that alone can overthrow wickedness she had tried wrestling with Mrs. MacLennan herself. Both combatants had retired badly bruised.

Mrs. Forsyth still felt nothing but horror for the demon alcohol, but now . . . it seemed that Mrs. MacLennan was cooking for them all at the castle now. That must be heavy on her, running the Hotel and cooking dinner for the castle as well, and no help at all.

On the other hand, she must do nothing that might damage the dignity of John's position. Or seem to condone evil, or look as if she admitted herself to be in the wrong. Though her hatred of the demon alcohol came from a conviction for which she might have found difficulty in providing chapter and verse, a conviction that the Lord Jehovah was a teetotaller, and though her support of Jehovah had been withdrawn, she must not seem to climb down or to eat humble pie. It was a problem.

Finally, still with trembling misgivings, she made up her mind. When Mrs. MacLennan opened the door in response to her ring she looked anything but pleased to see the minister's mother. Her silence made Mrs. Forsyth plunge into speech.

" Good-morning, Mrs. MacLennan," she said. " I've just been hearing that you're cooking the dinners for the castle, and I was wondering, well, it seems a lot to do, and Maura not there to help you. Could I give you a hand ? "

" Come in," said Mrs. MacLennan. " I'm keeping you on the doorstep ! Come into the kitchen."

She led the way through the dark hall, debating Mrs. Forsyth's proposition in her mind. She had not committed herself to anything yet, but by asking her into the kitchen instead of the dining-room or parlour she had, in a way, acknowledged the possibility of treating her as a fellow-woman instead of an adversary. She was running over the minister's mother's words, analysing the inflections in her voice. Good-morning, Mrs. MacLennan, rather condescending would you say ? I've just been hearing you're cooking the dinners, like a teacher giving you a good mark. Impossible up to that point. But . . . I was wondering, well, it seems a lot to do . . . Could I give you a hand ? No side about that after all, and she laid herself open to a slap in the face if I said No thank you. But then there was all that outrageousness over the men drinking decently in the bar : what if she started that impudence again ?

It was a thorny problem and Mrs. MacLennan's brain worked at lightning speed for the few seconds it took them to step from the hall into the kitchen ; but the outcome had not really been in doubt, for Mrs. MacLennan, who could give hard blows when she was attacked, was too chivalrous to trample on this overture from an enemy.

"Well, I don't know," she said, turning round a chair for Mrs. Forsyth to sit on. "It's true my hands are awful full, but it doesn't seem the thing for the minister's mother——"

Mrs. Forsyth made a sound like a genteel "Hoots!" waving aside the suggestion that the minister's mother was too refined to peel potatoes.

"I've brought my apron," she said.

"Well," Mrs. MacLennan yielded completely, "I'll be very thankful for a bit of help, to tell the truth, Mrs. Forsyth. I have to keep things up to the mark for the ladies, you know, and then this cooking for invalids and the rest of them as well."

"It's too much," said Mrs. Forsyth. "And," she added critically, "you're not looking so well—not so spry as usual."

"Oh, I've got my health all right. I'm maybe beginning to feel my age, I'm not so quick on my feet as I once was. You can't expect to be that, I suppose, at . . ."

She hesitated, gravely considering whether she might regret a confidence; but the minister's mother might attack you to your face, she was discreet behind your back, and her offer was real kind.

" . . . at seventy-seven," she concluded.

Mrs. Forsyth was astonished to learn Mrs. MacLennan's age.

"I'd never have put you at that!" she said. "I'm only fifty-eight myself, and to look at us there's not much to choose between us."

"Fifty-eight, do you tell me that, now?"

"Fifty-eight on the nineteenth of last month."

"Now, I'd have put you at . . . fifty-two, maybe. But of course," Mrs. MacLennan gave a sudden roguish chuckle, "if you and me were to daub ourselves up like the English"—she jerked her head to indicate the two ladies in the drawing-room—"we could pass for sweet sixteen, eh?"

Mrs. Forsyth laughed in scandalised amusement at this rather Rabelaisian joke. Lipstick on their respectable faces! The idea!

But now the coast was clear; they had exchanged ages, had laughed together over a rather daring joke: now they could begin to treat each other as friends.

"I'll just hang up my things, then," said Mrs. Forsyth, "and put on my apron."

She went back into the hall, hung her hat and coat on the

hall-stand and looked round it now with a different air, an air of intimacy ; and the royal stag over the dining-room door squinted back at her through the gloom, accepting her presence. You could do with a dust, she decided, compressing her lips. All these antlers ! She returned to the kitchen and plunged into the sinkful of potatoes.

Her experiment had worked. The danger of a snub was over and Mrs. Forsyth forgot that it had ever been a possibility. She began her work with a feverish zest, then suddenly relaxed to a reasonable pace. She was no longer working merely to fill in time, merely to bolster up some shaky idea of her own importance and indispensability ; she was working to help Mrs. MacLennan and to help the sick. There was a dignity in that that had been lacking in her frenzied midnight cleaning of the manse.

There was a lot doing in the Hotel kitchen. Mrs. Transom wandered in, sweet and billowy and opening her china-blue eyes to find a stranger there.

" Mrs. MacLennan's upstairs doing the rooms, I think," said Mrs. Forsyth. " Did you want something ? I've just come in to give a little voluntary help." She was not going to have any mistake made about her status.

" How nice," said Mrs. Transom vaguely. " I always tell Mrs. McLennan she works too hard."

" Well, with all the folks at the castle to cook for——"

" Yes, it was angelic of her to take that on."

" She has a good heart," Mrs. Forsyth admitted generously.

" So have you, to come and help her. I'm no use, of course, at domestic work . . . It all depends, I suppose, what you're trained for."

" And what were you trained for ? " Mrs. Forsyth's voice was touched delicately with acid.

Mrs. Transom gave her a weighing look out of her baby eyes and drew a breath.

" I was a knife-thrower's assistant," she said.

" A what ? " Mrs. Forsyth turned from the sink to stare, pressing a half-peeled Golden Wonder potato to her breast.

Mrs. Transom perched herself on the table. " A knife-thrower's assistant," she repeated demurely. " It was very exacting work, in its way, standing there with knives flying all round you. Dangerous too, wearing nothing but tights and ostrich feathers on a draughty stage. . . ."

Mrs. Forsyth gasped.

"Tights!" she echoed. "I should think you'd catch your death of cold. . . ." She gave a delicious shiver, reflecting that her charity had expanded since her discovery of Jehovah's non-existence. Once she would have thought only of the shame, the immorality of wearing tights on the stage—or off it. Like exposing yourself to the public in nothing but your combinations.

"Oh, yes, the previous girl had gone down with pneumonia; that gave me my chance. But it was not only the draughts," Mrs. Transom insisted, feeling that the romantic side of the danger was being overlooked. "The knives, you know. It was all right when he was sober, but when he'd had one over the eight. . . ."

"But what exactly was he doing?"

"Have you never seen a knife-thrower's act?"

"I've never been inside a theatre in my life."

Now it was Mrs. Transom who gasped. Here was her ideal audience; this pasty-faced woman whose eyes goggled with horrified fascination. She came over to the sink so that Mrs. Forsyth should be spared a crick in the neck while she peeled her potatoes, and began with gusto.

"Think of that!" Mrs. Forsyth would ejaculate at intervals. "And flaming torches! Think of that! . . . What is a G-string? Oh, mercy! . . . Think of that!"

She had finished the potatoes and was at the second-last carrot when Mrs. MacLennan came in to put away her dustpan and make a cup of tea.

"My, you're the quick worker, Mrs. Forsyth," she admired. "I was able to give the rooms a good do out, knowing you were at the vegetables. It's a grand help."

"I've hardly known I was working," said Mrs. Forsyth. "The time passes quickly when there's someone interesting to talk to." Interesting? She should have called these revelations scandalous, Babylonian in their horror. "I'll just carry on with the leeks while the tea's infusing," she said calmly.

"I'm such a useless creature, I'm afraid," said the knife-thrower's assistant plaintively.

Both the other women assured her that usefulness was not to be expected from her, though Mrs. MacLennan said it with a certain dryness; she had to spend some time each morning in clearing the litter from the floor of her guests' bedrooms, and had discovered a fresh cigarette burn on the mantelpiece that morning.

At that moment the doctor walked in.

" Now, Doctor," said Mrs. MacLennan at once, " I hope you're not going to be at us for Mrs. Forsyth coming to give me a hand, for I don't know how I'd have got through the morning without her and that's the truth. A great help she's been."

Alec rubbed his chin, looking from the vigorous little woman to Mrs. Forsyth standing awkwardly by the sink, taking off her apron with nervous movements. Mrs. Transom was there too ; his eyes gave her a smile as he considered his attitude.

" Well," he said, " I think on the whole it's a very good thing. Only the rule still holds, no visiting. But if Mrs. Forsyth stays here instead of in the empty manse there's no reason why I should object."

" There now," said Mrs. MacLennan, " that's an idea for you— cooking your own meals when there's plenty going here, you could just bring your things and settle in."

" I don't think I could do that," said Mrs. Forsyth stiffly.

Alec left them to discuss it while he went upstairs in search of Lydia.

Mrs. Forsyth had lost her elasticity, remembering the scene Lydia had described so vividly. She accepted her cup of tea and took it to the fireside. Yes, she would come and sleep in the Hotel: she could not bear another night in her own bedroom where she might see again that tawny light flickering round the edge of her curtains. She would accept the back bedroom that Mrs. MacLennan offered.

" That's fine, then," said Mrs. MacLennan. " You'll be far better where you have a bit of company than all on your own, worrying about the minister."

" Such a lovely boy," said Mrs. Transom. " I know just how you must feel about him, risking his life in that dreadful place." She shuddered prettily and the shudder ran through all her soft curves.

" A son's place is at his mother's side," Mrs. Forsyth exclaimed out of the pain of her loneliness. " And a minister's place is in his pulpit." She found herself trembling.

" You'd get no warrant for that in the Bible," said Mrs. MacLennan. " The Lord Himself left His mother and called the disciples to leave theirs, too ; and not for any safe pulpit job, either.

No, no, the minister's one that puts his faith into practice, and that's the best sermon any man could preach. Your son'll find himself a power in the land when he comes back to his pulpit, Mrs. Forsyth. Well, I'll get on." She went briskly off to continue her work.

Mrs. Forsyth stared at the closed door, her chin quivering. They saw John's side of it and praised him, never thinking what it cost her to give him up, to be alone and deserted. She turned convulsively to Mrs. Transom and, meeting her eyes, felt tears sting her own. She was struggling to keep hold of her resentment against John; the thought of her injuries was her security; it was like a hard frost that kept the ground firm beneath her feet. Under the frost there was a sense of treacherous movement, of something weak and alive that threatened the iron frost with its greenness. What if they were right; what if she were the unjust, the blind?

"What do you think," she asked, her voice croaking with her effort at control, "about John?"

"Oh, I think he's just wonderful," Mrs. Transom tried to soothe her. "Just like St. George and the Dragon in a pageant I once saw. A real Christian hero!"

"It's too much, too much!" Mrs. Forsyth broke into sobbing. "To lose God is bad enough, and then your son, and if your very self-respect has to go, too——" She was incoherent; the ice of her self-approval was cracking and the anguish was more than she could bear.

"Poor darling, take my handkerchief," said Mrs. Transom. "I think you need a little gin——"

"Whisky," said Mrs. MacLennan, appearing at the sound of sobbing. "Neat whisky's the thing for hysterics; acts like a slap in the face, but more respectful to the minister's mother. Yes," she insisted, "take it, lassie, it's what you need."

They were giving her spirituous liquor and trying to persuade her to lie down upstairs, but for once Mrs. Forsyth refused the limelight.

"I'm all right now," she said, "it was just a turn." She pushed away the rest of the whisky and turned a stiff, ghastly face towards Mrs. Transom. "And I was so interested in what you were telling me about your second husband," she said more composedly. "The one who bought a—dust-track, was it?"

"A dirt-track, darling," said Mrs. Transom. "Don't you know

what a dirt-track is ? " She drew a happy breath and began, " A dirt-track is——"

Mrs. MacLennan put away the whisky and went back to her work. She was getting a bit muddled between Mrs. Transom's various husbands. Surely the second husband had been a High Court Judge. Was it the thing for a High Court Judge to buy a dirt-track ? Maybe Mrs. Transom herself got a bit mixed. She seemed to have had a good many husbands, and some folks had no head for numbers.

It's none of my business, anyway, she decided, and there's wee Thomas away upstairs looking for a place to have her kittens.

She watched Thomas, heavy with kittens, nosing open the door of Lydia's room, and shook her head. Tom cat indeed !

" Thomas ! " she called, " come you and see the bonny box I've got for you ! And," she muttered, " wait till I see that skipper."

## Chapter Twenty-Seven

MISS BRADSHAW's initiation had been effective. During that first night, when she had shrunk with terror from the sight of Father Kelly and of the baby, but had compelled herself to work on, she had, it seemed, grown up ; and yet the process had made her at the same time less cocksure, less glib.

You're shallow, she told herself as she hurried towards the castle. What has education done for you ? Given you a good opinion of yourself, that's about all. You've gone round with your eyes shut, missing everything unless you bumped into it. You thought Nell Patrick was an empty frippet. You thought the minister was a prig. You even thought yourself better than Maura Rafferty, oh yes you did ! And any one of them is worth six of you, Lois Bradshaw.

She entered the castle in a state of exhilarating self-contempt. Her eyes glowed and glittered, her hair was blown into black corkscrews and vitality flowed from her.

" Are you alone ? " she asked, finding Maura in the kitchen. " How's Nell ? "

"The same," said Maura. "She just lies there saying nothing. She's got no heart to live."

"I think Terence should be allowed in to see her."

"The doctor told him he could come," said Maura. "He wouldn't. That's men all over; at the time when you need comfort, that's when they make themselves scarce."

Miss Bradshaw was silent.

"Och what am I saying," Maura went on, "there's good and bad among them, just the way we are ourselves. Yes, I'm on my own till Mr. Dochy gets up. The doctor's out."

They were silent again, both knowing that that meant out with Lydia Transom.

"The old captain's taken a terrible fancy to you," said Maura.

"Old rascal."

"He was saying to-day his wife won't last much longer. And it's a terrible thing for him to be saying it but he's right. The doctor says her heart won't stand the temperature she's running, poor soul." She eyed Miss Bradshaw thoughtfully. Supposing Mrs. Kilbride was taken, she reflected, it wouldn't be a bad thing after all—the teacher and the old captain. "He'll be the better of someone to look after him, and he's a fine-looking old man," she said; then remembered that Miss Bradshaw, a Protestant, would never do for the captain, and when the teacher remarked that she thought him cynical, agreed warmly, "So he is indeed."

Miss Bradshaw was slightly annoyed at this acquiescence and went to tie on the overall she used in the castle.

"He said you were to go to him as soon as you came in," said Maura.

"I expect he's asleep," said Miss Bradshaw firmly. "And I want to go round all the women first I haven't seen the two who came in this morning."

"We put wee Pad in the same room as Torquil and Shona MacVean," said Maura. "Let me know if you need help, but I think they're all fine."

She sat down thankfully while Miss Bradshaw went round the patients.

Nell Patrick was lying with her eyes shut, very still.

"I brought you a cup of chicken tea, Nell," Miss Bradshaw coaxed. "You have to keep drinking, you know. Come on, try a spoonful."

" Leave me, leave me," Nell whispered.

" Try a spoonful. See if it's right for salt. Come on, Nell, you must get well for wee Pad, you know——"

" Will you leave me in peace ! "

There was such tired despair in the hoarse whisper that Miss Bradshaw obeyed, but as she retreated with the rejected drink, Nell added, " Maura promised she'd take him . . ."

It was not until much later in the night that she received an imperious summons from Captain Kilbride, and hurried in to stop the noise of his stick.

" I'm very comfortable, thanks," he said conversationally. " Every time I wake up I'm a bit better than I was the last time. And how are you yourself ? "

" Oh, quite well."

" Sit down then. Shut that window and sit down : you'll not feel the draught if it's shut.—— Now, don't be hurrying off without passing the time of day ! "

" Day ? This is the middle of the night, time you were asleep ! "

" I've been asleep, I tell you. Sit down."

" But, Captain Kilbride, I'm busy. I've got your wife to look after——"

" She'll be all right, woman. Sit down when I tell you. That's it." He looked at her consideringly, searching for some conversational gambit that would involve her. " Tell me, now. Have ye got a clock in that house of yours ? "

" Yes, I have two clocks. One in the kitchen and one in the living-room. I take the kitchen clock into the school when I'm working."

" And what sort of clocks would they be, now ? "

" The kitchen clock," said Miss Bradshaw, " is an ordinary alarm : you know the kind, shiny metal with a round face. The sitting-room clock is black marble with a gold face."

" A tin clock and a marble clock," Captain Kilbride repeated in a kindly voice. " And do they tell you the true time, now ? "

Miss Bradshaw visualised her two clocks. The kitchen alarm ticking away so zealously that it shook with its own energy ; the black marble timepiece on the sitting-room mantelpiece, sober, dignified and dumb.

" The kitchen clock," she said, smiling, " goes rather fast. Gains about fifteen minutes a day. The marble clock hasn't gone at

239

all for a long time, but it was a presentation to my father so I give it house-room."

"One clock that gains a quarter of an hour, and one that doesn't go at all." He nodded gravely. "And how do you ever tell the time? The bairns could be late for school every day in life and you'd be none the wiser!"

"Oh, but I get the time-signal from the wireless!"

"Oh, wireless." The captain was put out at this escape from horology just when he had her cornered. "A wireless is all right in its place. But you need a decent clock to tell the time by, my girl. Like," he suggested cunningly, "a good wall clock with weights and a big face with roses and forget-me-nots across it. That's the sort of clock that's worth having! . . . It'll be yours one day," he added, lowering his voice.

Miss Bradshaw laughed that off.

"Your wife would have something to say if she heard you."

"Och, never heed her, lassie, she won't last much longer. Are you going? But what's the hurry? Leave the lamp, then."

"You don't need the light: you'll be asleep in a minute——"

"Leave it till I am asleep, then. And shut the door!"

"Then how will I know if you're asleep?"

"I'll give you a shout."

Hector Kilbride was not a monster of callousness. He was old; the horizon of the present had shrunk to a tiny circle of his immediate needs and desires, and the circle held one vivid figure who cheered its cosy dimness; the black-haired schoolmistress with her clear, sensible, always audible voice. His wife had turned into an old mumbler. She was finished.

Miss Bradshaw, smiling at his promise to call her as soon as he was asleep, returned to Mrs. Kilbride's room.

The doctor was there, his stethoscope in his ears, listening to her heart. Mrs. Kilbride, propped up on pillows, watched him. Her mouth was open because there was never enough air nowadays. Everything was inferior in these degenerate times, even the air was thin stuff. She was longing for the bluff confidence that Father Kelly brought to all ailments—he never plagued folks with fancy gadgets in his ears, but he had more plain sense than any of them when it came to the bit.

Alec felt his helplessness. This was like practising in the dark

240

ages. No drugs to help his patients, no digitalis for this failing heart. He would not trust himself to recognise foxgloves without their flower. He had once read a seventeenth century book on medicine; one third sound materia medica, two thirds witchcraft. An Infallible Cure for a Galloping Consumption: take a live Spider . . . He could not recall an Infallible Cure for Smallpox. If he could he would have used it, witchcraft and all. It was heart-breaking to fight a virulent disease without drugs, without hospital conveniences, without nursing skill; always desperately short of linen, with the island's supply of cottonwool exhausted, no more spirit or oil to be had and this old woman's heart thudding away in his ears like a demented tom-tom without rhythm. Thump, thump, thump, tat-tat-trr. . . .

He coiled up the stethoscope and Mrs. Kilbride shut her eyes with relief. Even that much weight was more than she could endure. But no sooner had she closed them that she opened them again in fright.

" I'm falling——"

" No, you're not," Miss Bradshaw assured her. " You're well propped up on your pillows."

Mrs. Kilbride looked at her in despair. Every time she felt like sleep there came this terrible feeling of falling backwards. Her hand made a faint movement and Miss Bradshaw grasped it.

" Shut your eyes now and see if you can have a nice sleep," she said.

Mrs. Kilbride resented being told what to do by the school-teacher, but she was too weak to disobey. These old maids, they thought far too much of themselves.

" My married daughter—" she said in the whispering gasps her voice was reduced to—" everything up-to-the-minute . . . incandescent gas mantles. . . ."

She heard the doctor speaking to Miss Bradshaw, but she had drifted to her daughter's well-furnished house in the Garnethill district; not a fashionable district but handy for the Sauchiehall Street shops, and beautiful with looped lace curtains and a gas chandelier in the dining-room, and an incandescent mantle in the kitchen too; Mina said she wouldn't be bothered with the poor light you got from a fish-tail burner.

Mrs. Kilbride laughed. " We'd be glad," she gasped, " to have a fish-tail coming out of . . . of the wall . . . in Fionn."

Alec and Miss Bradshaw exchanged a glance. Mrs. Kilbride opened her eyes and focused the schoolteacher's face.

"And a husband," she said, "and . . . carpet sweeper." It was more than the teacher had got for all her managing ways. And three children, or was it four . . . five . . . She was a bit muddled, and the Kaiser had been a great source of bother and she was tangled into a perfect stutteration with them all standing round her sucking up every morsel of air that was to be had.

"But they had . . . the suffragette," she gasped, "dressed up in . . . Hector's clothes——" She laughed again, but clutched Miss Bradshaw's hand in terror, pushing her away yet clinging to her in case she should fall head over heels backward as she seemed always to be doing.

That had taken a lot out of her. She was starving for air, desperate for it. She must be old. It was hard to believe that— she whose hair had been as yellow as broom and her mouth like a red poppy. Hector had told her so. He had been handsome himself then, dark and tall and with a teasing glint in his eye. But then he had kept going off on his long voyages and leaving her alone in the house. It was no life for a woman, that ; and she had hated the sea, refused to sail with him even when he suggested it. He only gave her a real settled married life when he retired, and by then he was nothing but a nuisance about the house.

"He's getting old," she said. "Old and—he's done——"

She felt Miss Bradshaw's hand return the sudden frightened pressure of her own. Silly woman, silly conceited creature, thinking that a mere handclasp would stop the dying from slipping backwards down the slope. For she was dying. The enemy in her chest was spreading a suffocating darkness through her, and she got no help at all, no help from outside. They kept the air from her, they kept her in bed in a room that tilted dangerously like the deck of a ship so that her head was below the level of her feet, and she was slipping head downwards——

Why was there no help! They ought to get Father Kelly: he would be the one to cure her. Or if she was past cure, he would say the prayers for the dying, shepherd her out of her body with the proper rites. Not that rites made any difference to her at this stage, but his strong, coarse voice would comfort the darkness of this headlong fall into the grave. Holy Mary, Mother of God, pray for us sinners . . . at the hour of our death . . . Fancy having to do it all alone. . . .

She was under the deep waters now. Far up above, on the surface, she could see a tiny scene all lit up ; a room where a doctor (silly thing) and a schoolteacher watched the old woman on the bed, the woman who had so recently been a yellow-haired girl, struggling to swallow one more breath of air, just one more breath.

" Is she dead ? " Miss Bradshaw's voice trembled.

" Yes."

She felt for the chair behind her and sat down. It had been frightening to watch that last struggle. It was the first time she had seen death.

She breathed heavily, using her will to appear as unmoved as possible, watching Alec remove the pile of pillows and lower the husk of a body from its strained uprightness. He closed the eyelids and drew the sheet over the empty face.

" Go and make yourself a cup of tea," he ordered. " Perhaps Nell Patrick would enjoy a cup with you. Dochy and I will look after this."

Miss Bradshaw obeyed him. Nell Patrick was asleep and she herself had no desire for tea ; but it was an occasion for obedience. She sat in Nell's room shivering a little and wondering at the strangeness of death. One minute Mrs. Kilbride had been there, ill, imprisoned in the frightening struggle for breath ; the next moment she was gone. Nothing was left. Truly nothing. The husk that remained was no more important than the pale blue fragment that floats down from a robin's nest.

But you can see the transformation from egg to fledgling. What was there to see here ? Nothing but the fragment of shell, the discarded husk.

She tried to recall the words of *Prospice*, but it was hard to find poetry in the death she had witnessed. The struggle had been ugly, its sudden cessation, its sequel of silence and emptiness, too astonishing. She covered her eyes, unable to select and organise her memories ; she trembled as if she had undergone some violent physical effort. Then from the violent jumble a moment of beauty emerged ; she saw again the doctor's hands closing the eyelids, drawing the sheet over the dead face.

She rose and tiptoed out to the door, leaving her untouched

cup beside Nell. As soon as she opened the door the wind caught her; she stood braced, clasping her elbows and clenching her teeth against the cold. Out there in the darkness where the waves beat there was a small flicker of yellow. She stared at it, puzzled. The bud of flame burst into an opening marigold and swept round the pyre, lighting up two figures who added fuel with gestures that were serious and beautiful, like gardeners burning rubbish yet remembering that what they burnt had once been leaf and flower and stem.

Miss Bradshaw made no effort to cover her wet face or conceal her sobs. She had no awareness of herself. She saw before her the terrible essence of poetry and she was caught up in it.

## Chapter Twenty-Eight

KIRPU HAD wakened with Miss Bradshaw's footsteps passing his door. He did not open his eyes. While she stood in the wind, amazed and staring at the blown flames, he lay half-awake, trying dreamily to recognise the footsteps that had passed.

Firm and even, but not heavy enough for Smith Bahadur; not light enough for his mother, they lacked the urgency that made his brother's steps sound always as if he were bent on some delightfully important business—something that only Sepu himself could do, and that he hugged secretly to his heart while his face wore a smile that pretended to say, " It's nothing—a mere trifle."

But of course the footsteps could not be Sepu's. Sepu was—dead—wasn't he?

Kirpu had never allowed himself to wish his brother dead. They were an affectionate family, they had all delighted in Sepu's brilliance, his scholarships, his glorious career in the University of Oxford where, they knew, he had been loved by all, admired by learned dons, invited to exclusive parties that he described in his letters home. How they had all looked forward to Sepu's letters ! And when he came home at last, he was not in the least conceited, he was still charming, still affectionate and full of wit. Everybody loved Sepu, everybody foretold a still more brilliant future ahead of him. Only . . . there had been no future. Sepu was dead.

Kirpu had often seen his brother's death prophesied in his dreams. Sometimes the dream-death was only a symbol; Sepu would walk and talk and dance vivaciously through the dream with a face as rigid as marble, eyes glazed and sightless; or he would stand smiling and bowing to all his friends while funeral flames lapped round him; or he would move through the sunshine, casting no shadow. Sometimes the dream was more frankly horrible. Kirpu would see his brother stabbed or strangled while he stood by powerless to help.

Meanwhile Sepu's career was opening like a bud that would soon be a gorgeous flower. He was beginning to practise law, which necessitated frequent absences from home to meet clients or friends whose influence would help him. He appeared and vanished like a bird of paradise, a creature of air and colour yet too kind to despise the dingy nest from which he had sprung. If Kirpu sometimes wondered if all the absences were as innocent as his parents believed he crushed the thought out of sight, like other jealous and worthless thoughts that crawled in the sediment of his mind.

And after all Sepu had not died by violence. One day he had sent a message to Kirpu, asking him to come to an unsavoury quarter of the bazaar, but to say nothing to anyone. Kirpu, disapproving but inquisitive, went to the address given, and when his eyes became accustomed to the gloom of the hovel he scarcely recognised the marred and blistered face as his brother's.

"But you are ill—come home and let mother nurse you!"

Sepu's swollen face smiled.

"Why should I pass this on to those I love?" he asked. "I only sent for you to give you my ring and this money—all I have left. And to tell you to be a better son than I have been, and "—he rose on his elbow to speak more earnestly—" to avoid places like this quarter—— No, keep back from me," he insisted. "Take this and go. Nobody will touch you: they have all fled and left me to die —I had to bribe the man I sent with the message or there would have been more to give you. Don't wait. Go home and tell our parents they have only one son left."

"I'll come back with a litter——" Kirpu cried.

"You won't find me here then. I'll crawl out of sight before you return, my dear little brother. No, do what I tell you and go."

Kirpu left the hovel, driven out by his brother's determination;

245

but the task of telling his parents was impossible. He could never tell them he had left Sepu to die. He rushed hysterically to the docks and fled to the other side of the world.

But guilt had accompanied him, clinging closer than his own skin. Even here, even in his East West Home, guilt was like a scorpion stinging his living heart. Kirpu turned restlessly and opened his eyes.

The window was moving. At first he thought it was trembling in time with his heart, and blinked his eyes to clear the sleep out of them. No, it was a fire, a fire on the rocks !

He jumped out of bed and stared out, seeing Mr. Dochy and his beloved doctor moving in the rusty glow. It must be the old woman who had died, so soon after the deaths of Father Kelly and the small baby. Remembering the fat old man who had anointed his pimples, and torn already with remorse for his brother, deserted to die like a sewer rat in a filthy hole, Kirpu burst into tears.

" They are dead and I live ! " he wept. " Why am I left, worthless rubbish, fit for nothing at all——"

His moans dwindled as he pondered the frightening idea that dropped into his mind ; and not for the first time, for it kept returning, the same idea over and over, drifting down like a succession of snowflakes, soft and delicate and cold.

I am too weak, he protested. I am ill. My legs are already bending under my weight. Besides I am afraid. I would not mind death, not really, but that particular death is one I should dislike most emphatically. Besides I know nothing about boats ; I have only heard Torquil say that the passage is very dangerous ; I would die and nobody at all would benefit.

You will certainly fail if you do not even try, said Sepu. But if you try and fail, the act of sacrifice will wipe out the stain you carry.

It is easy for you to speak, you who are strong and admired and safely dead already ! Besides the doctor will see me and send me back to bed. Kirpu, my dear fellow, it is a noble idea but you shall not make such a foolish sacrifice : I need you alive, not dead, my dear chap ! Come, I forbid it—back to bed with you—I positively insist !

He was pulling on his clothes with fingers that trembled, babbling to himself, arguing, sobbing occasionally, refusing obedience even while he obeyed.

Miss Bradshaw is standing in the doorway. I cannot pass without saying Excuse me, and she will at once ask what I am doing!

She does not hear you.

Mr. Dochy looked straight into my eyes!

He does not see you, he is blinded by the flames of the pyre and sees nothing else.

Shivering with horror Kirpu found himself in the boat. There was no exaltation in the sacrifice. His teeth rattled. The sea was alive, snarling with malice, tossing him and his little stuttering engine out to the distant emptiness where a great green mouth would gape to swallow him.

In the green graveyard the rain fell with a ceaseless soft hiss. A mound of earth lay beside the waiting grave, and John Rose noted its richness even while he listened to the minister's voice. It was beautiful black soil. He glanced at MacPherson of Skua to see if he was taking in its quality, but MacPherson was fidgeting; thinking of Lilias left in the house and wondering where Terence Patrick might be. A black shame, Terence not turning up to his own daughter's funeral.

Dochy looked around him easily, taking in the service and its setting, all the more receptive because he felt he would soon be back in a world of pavements and tall buildings and board meetings. He saw the black-coated islanders grouped round the grave, standing among long grass with dark yews and ilexes and the grey sea behind them, and the rain falling in a vertical silver curtain that wavered but never parted. One day he would come here and it would be his own.

Danny was sad and ill-at-ease. He kept trying to quell the misgiving that wriggled like a maggot in his mind, for he felt that it was contemptible. The minister was a right good sort, the more you knew him the better he was; and all the folks gathered there meant it for the best, a last mark of respect. All the same they were a lot of Protestants, and these were good Catholic corpses. There was Father Kelly being prayed over by a Protestant minister and couldn't defend himself.

Likely there would be a proper burial service later, with a proper priest when they sent one. But there was no saying what occult harm this might do. You weren't supposed to pray with Protestants. Even at school, when they opened each morning with Our Father,

Danny had to stand outside the door till he heard Amen and a scraping of feet as they sat down. It was a fair puzzler. He would have to talk it over with Mr. Forsyth, for, Protestant or not, he was the only one likely to understand.

Alec stood in the drizzle, staring as the coffin was lowered into the black hole lined with spruce and yew. It was all unreal, the whole scene had a dreaminess about it as if he had already left the site of his defeat.

They had wakened that morning to a strange clarity of bird cries and songs. The gulls, the lovely curlew calls, the songs of wrens and thrushes and blackbirds, the chatter and squawks and loud, vainglorious crows of the domestic poultry had all been distinct like patterns against a white ground, because the grumbling roar and sough of the wind had been withdrawn. They had commented on it at breakfast, Maura bringing in the tea and kippers with a smile. " What a difference when the gale drops," she had said, and her gentle voice joined the pattern of the birdsong.

" Will this be the last breakfast together ? " John wondered.

" Expect so," Dochy had answered. " If I get the boat through." For of course he was going to take the motor-boat to Oban rather than wait for the steamer on Monday to report on their predicament to the authorities.

Then there had been renewed discussion as to who, if anyone, should accompany Dochy. Danny had been determined to go too, but Dochy was adamant. He might capsize on one of the under-water rocks, and he said he was an incompetent life-saver ; he would manage to rescue himself but not a passenger.

At that point Danny had burst in on them.

" I've just been to take a look at the boat and she's gone," he gasped, " gone, I'm telling yous ! He's taken the boat and gone off all on his lone—Kirpu, the Hindoo ! "

When the disaster was verified Dochy had exploded briefly. " The flaming fool, he's probably drowned by now ! "

But Alec had understood Kirpu's madness. He was a fool, he would almost certainly capsize on the rocks and if not he would drift out to the Atlantic and vanish in its immensity. But Kirpu had overcome his personal dragon, and Alec had again fled from his.

Even as he stepped forward to throw his handful of earth on Father Kelly's coffin he relived that morning.

He saw Lydia bent over the case she was packing.

"Oh, it's you," she said without turning. "I'm all right. I didn't think you'd still be doing this round the village business, now the wind's dropped. We're leaving, of course, thank Heaven."

It was so cold, so indifferent, so like a handful of pebbles flung in his face. The brush-off, he muttered.

Of course, he told himself, it had not been love; but there might have been some tenderness, some regret in their parting. There was not even courtesy. She had forgotten him while he still stood there watching her, foolishly pierced by her brutality.

He completed his round, telling the Fionnachs that the funeral would take place that afternoon at three.

When he returned to the castle he could not bear to go in. Dochy came out and found him leaning against the castle wall, facing the sea.

"He's dead beat," he heard Dochy say.

John approached him now, looking at him with cautious concern.

"Come on in and have a rest," John said, taking his arm.

"I don't want to go in," Alec said.

John watched him anxiously.

"Come for a dander along the shore then," he suggested, and Alec fell in with that.

They walked along the bay where Danny set his lines for flounders. The rippled sand was uneven to walk on, but its smooth fawn expanse soothed Alec's stinging eyes.

"The wind's blown itself out, right enough," said John, breaking their silence.

Alec tried to force himself to normality.

"Will you be glad," he asked, "to return to your ordinary duties?"

"My ordinary duties," John echoed in a meditative voice. "Well, I'll take the funerals this afternoon. And I'll go on taking the services till they find a substitute. But I doubt if they'll want to keep me on as the minister.

"Because I believe," he mused, "I believe both more and less than a congregation expects. And I can't conceal it. I could never have the patience to tangle up my feet with the . . . the trimmings . . . . I mean the watchfulness over other folks' shortcomings, the Sabbath-day clothes, the sale of work when folks grudge money to support their church—och and far more than that, it's the whole regulating and pinning down and trimming up of what's far and away above trimmings . . . They'll say I've gone daft, but I should have gone daft long ago." He lifted his face with a strange look at the horizon.

" Will you be glad," he asked, " to get back to your clinic again ? "

" Back ? " Alec looked at the idea. " I have no idea what I mean to do," he said. " I thought I'd find out that here, but——"

But he had missed his opportunity, had failed in the test. He knew that without yet knowing where the knowledge came from. Somewhere he had lost his way.

" What will you do in the meantime, John ? " he asked.

" Well," said John, " it's in my mind that I might put my savings into a trawler, with Torquil MacVean as a partner." He paused. They were clambering over rocks now. " There'll be talk, of course," he said, " but it'll die down. I'm not afraid now of what folks will think." He spoke calmly and without defiance.

" And your mother ? "

John's expression did not change. " She'll have the choice," he said, " of life in a fisher cottage, if we can get one, or going to keep house for my uncle in Inveraray. I don't know yet which she'll choose."

" That is if they don't want you as their minister any more."

" It is. But what about yourself, Doctor," John asked as they trod on sand again, pale, fine sand. " You'll be staying on here for a while, anyway ? "

" I don't know," said Alec in a low voice. " I'm at a loss."

" I can tell that."

" So were you, when I came here first. At a loss."

" I was."

" You've won your way through."

John did not answer.

" You reminded me," said Alec, " of myself. I had a mother who . . . possessed me, managed me . . . like you." He looked to see if John were offended, then went on reassured. " I was afraid you might make the same mistake. I was too weak to fight my way free. I thought—I'll be free when she dies. I couldn't bear the idea of hurting her. I used to argue with her endlessly, but only in my imagination. I couldn't bear the effect her pain would have on me, if I spoke."

Pain . . . as he said the word a pang of shadowy recollection struck at him, but vanished before he could identify it.

" I've always shrunk from hurting people," he said. " It's wrong. It defeats itself, it leads to isolation, even to hatred. I still argue with my mother—in imagination."

" I've done that for years," said John.

" A possessive mother isn't a solitary figure," said Alec. " She's one of a pair. She shares the blame with the son who submits to possession. The son injures his mother too—as much, almost, as she injures him. That's why death doesn't bring freedom, it's too late. It ought to have been worked out between them. But now the argument never ends. Death clamps manacles on you both, and it's forever. The time to have struck them off—off both her wrists and yours—was when she was alive."

As you are doing, John, he thought but did not say it aloud. They walked in silence while slow clouds darkened the sky.

" Other folks' suffering has a great effect on you," John said. " I've seen it. It's queer in a doctor."

" My mother chose my profession," said Alec dryly.

" So did mine," John smiled. " But are you sure, Doctor—are you sure, if you had the freedom of choice, you'd choose something else ? If you could get over your shrinking——" He left the sentence unfinished. Alec put it at the back of his mind for future thought.

" But, John," he said, " what was it that changed you ? What gave you the strength ? "

" I doubt if I can put it into words," said John slowly. " It was more than one single thing, likely. I got away where I could think, for one thing. I believe . . . I believe what swung me right round was when I stopped thinking of the old priest as my enemy and took him for a friend. That was the biggest thing in my life.

" Not," he said in sudden argumentativeness, " that I hold any truck with the Roman viewpoint. I don't consider that they have the exclusive use of the truth. There's a terrible amount of superstition, even of downright deception and corruption and lies, in the Roman church. But on the other hand, they may see more of the truth than we do. More truth and more falsehood. More spirituality and more . . . spiritual fascism . . . That's not the point, though. The thing that gave me strength was just that : begging the old man's pardon. It was like tearing my guts out to do it, but it was the only thing to do. Thank God I was in time."

Alec stood still. Again the pang of near-recollection stabbed him. The enemy who was the friend. . . .

"These are the haunted sands," said John, thinking that he looked round at the scenery. "We're nearly at the cave now."

"The cave?" Alec disliked the sound of that.

"Said to be a prehistoric dwelling."

"I used to have a dream," said Alec, walking on as if he walked now in a dream, "when I was a child. I used to see myself in a little street . . . it could have been anywhere, but I was reminded of it one night when I saw the street of Fionn in the moonlight. About a month ago. The houses in my dreams were all asleep and shuttered, and I was alone, but quite calm going along the little street. Then I saw . . . a horrible figure . . . Not that it had any evil intention towards me, at least no conscious, focused malice, you understand. It was simply, in itself, repulsive and terrifying."

"Like Father Kelly and what he stood for to me."

They walked on slowly.

"What happened?" John asked.

"I can hardly remember," said Alec. "I know there is more than I can remember. But anyway, I ran away. I ran and the fact of my running made it pursue me. And then I couldn't run, my feet weighed like lumps of lead and tied me to the ground."

"And how did it end?"

"I never reached the end," said Alec slowly. "There was no end. . . ."

"A nightmare."

"Yes. Horrible."

Something had reminded him again of the nightmare. Weariness, perhaps; at this moment his feet had the leaden heaviness that made him long to sink down where he was.

"Here's the cave," said John's voice as if from a distance.

Alec looked. The entrance to the cave surprised him. He had pictured an irregular, gaping mouth in the cliff, but this was a man-made entrance; man-made yet with an aura of age measured by geological time. It was low, not four feet in height; two stone slabs stood upright at either side and a third was laid across like an architrave supporting the roof. The russet fronds of last year's bracken swept down the cliffside to its mouth, and among the russet were green blades of hyacinth, an occasional primrose and a single disc of shrill pink, the first campion to open. Spring growth had been continuing right through the storm.

" You have to go in on all fours," said John.

Alec did not want to go down on all fours; or not at once. He wanted to rest outside, looking at the cave's mouth, half repelled, till either fascination overcame the repulsion or he decided that, after all, there was no need to explore the cave that particular morning.

" Is it Pictish ? " he asked.

But John, producing his pencil torch, was already crawling into the dark rectangle and did not hear him.

Alec watched the minister's rear recede a couple of feet; then it emerged again.

" Pfugh ! " John coughed. " What a stink. Something has died in there."

" What was it ? "

" No idea. I didn't go in far enough to see."

" Let me go," said Alec.

He took the torch and stooped down to the darkness.

The tunnel sloped slightly upwards. Its sides and ceiling were lined with flat slabs of stone; the torch lit only the sterile greyness of the stones and the darkness ahead swallowed the faint light. The air was rank with the odour of corruption. Alec paused to cover his nose and mouth with his handkerchief, then crawled again forward. Part of him knew what he would find, but the knowledge stopped short on the threshold of consciousness. Part of him struggled against the foreknowledge and at the same time prayed, hopelessly, Let me be in time !

Suddenly the tunnel opened into a chamber shaped like the inside of a beehive, round, lined with stones and with a table-like stone ledge at the back.

He was, of course, too late. On his rounds of all the inhabitants of Fionn he had forgotten, or had chosen to forget, this one, the one who represented the enigma, the enemy of his peace, Pain itself. Candy Andy lay on the floor as if he had fallen from the table which had been, perhaps, his bed. His upturned face bore the stigmata of smallpox.

He had met death alone in the dark.

Retching and weeping, Alec dragged the body out and they

253

burned it there on the haunted sands, collecting driftwood and tufts of bracken, watching the smoke drift up to a sky that was now grey and serene.

On the way back John tried to comfort the doctor; and Alec managed to pull himself together so that he was composed although haggard. But he understood himself now, knew his own guilt, the guilt of recoil, of the averted eyes, of the ghastly fastidiousness that says No in the face of life. Instead of pity that could have been creative he was left with remorse that corrodes.

They were trudging towards the gate of the graveyard now; under rain that was dwindling to a soft mist. John Rose, as senior elder, was holding them up with a sober speech of gratitude to Dochy, Alec and "their deeply respected minister," who had combined to organise and protect Fionn against the plague that had come upon them.

Alec heard phrases of the short speech and was moved by it; then he gathered that Mr. Rose was providing whisky and Mrs. MacLennan soda water in the hospitable Hotel, if the doctor would permit this gathering of men who were already gathered together for the funeral. Alec mumbled his consent to this request and was trying to frame some reply to the rest of the speech when a cry from Danny broke through his tentative gropings.

"Jings!" he shouted, "will yous look at what's coming!"

They all turned to stare at the sea where a white launch pierced a furrow towards Fionn, and without discussion they all, in their sober funeral blacks, hurried down through the village to the harbour.

There were three men in the launch; Kirpu, sick and feebly smiling, the boatman, staring with curiosity at the black clad company, and a stocky young man with an attaché case.

Alec clasped the hand of the stranger who climbed first out of the launch.

"How d'ye do, Doctor MacArdal," said the stranger, "I'm Doctor James Boydell of the County Health Department, and I've got a supply of vaccine here to begin with. I hear you've been doing great work here."

"Glad to meet you, Doctor Boydell," said Alec. "Come on up to the castle."

He waited to help Kirpu off the boat, and the three of them walked towards the door that Maura held open.

The funeral mourners hesitated, clumped together in discussion, and then moved together towards the Hotel.

"I'm going with them," said Danny, politely declining Mr. Rose's invitation. "Likely I'll be needed to help with the vaccinations."

He gave a spring on his toes, then soberly followed Dochy and John into the castle.

THE END